# Point of the Circle

*A Novel*

*Leona Gibbs*

iUniverse, Inc.
New York  Bloomington

# Point of the Circle

iUniverse books may be ordered through booksellers or by contacting:

iUniverse
1663 Liberty Drive
Bloomington, IN 47403
www.iuniverse.com
1-800-Authors (1-800-288-4677)

Because of the dynamic nature of the Internet, any Web addresses or links contained in this book may have changed since publication and may no longer be valid.

This is a work of fiction. All of the characters, names, incidents, organizations, and dialogue in this novel are either the products of the author's imagination or are used fictitiously.

ISBN: 978-0-595-50070-3 (pbk)
ISBN: 978-0-595-61364-9 (ebk)

Printed in the United States of America

*For Larry who makes everything possible*
*HLH*

# *Acknowledgements*

**About the Cover:**

A special thanks to Jerri Wallis for painting the coastal scene on the inside cover exactly as I envisioned. She has been painting since 1979 and continues to have her work displayed throughout the United States and Canada. The artist and her husband Bill have three children and make their home in Lenore, Idaho.

**Nautical Expertise:**

I offer my sincere appreciation to Sea Captain Alvin Gorgita for sharing his nautical expertise. He also provided stories about sea storms, myths and superstitions—the superstitions still persist.

**Special Recognition:**

I wish to thank my long time friend Mary Ann Snider for her support and encouragement. Her council was invaluable and very much appreciated.

# *Characters*

| | |
|---|---|
| Karin Johansson | Norwegian Wife of Erik |
| Erik Johansson | Lighthouse Keeper |
| Mrs. Esther Webb | Grandmother of Erik Johansson |
| Mr. Quinton Webb | Grandfather of Erik Johansson |
| Mr. Rudolph Nash | Rich Merchant |
| Mrs. Elsa Nash | Wife of Rudolph Nash |
| Mei Ling Lee | Friend of Karin |
| Joaquin Cutta | Spanish Sailor |
| Cole Ralston | Fisherman and Dock Worker |
| Flint Ralston | Brother of Cole |
| Leroy Grazer | Perceived Slow Wit |
| Rue Beaudroux | Prostitute |
| Ian Fisk | Fireman |
| Charity Fisk | Wife of Ian Fisk |
| Chief Johnson | Fire Chief and Magistrate |
| Mr. Gordon | Insurance and Fire Investigator |
| Dr. Grayson | Doctor—Valda Bay |
| Mr. Chang | Traditional Chinese Medical Man |
| Dr. Sung | Chinese Medical Doctor |
| Mr. Edwards | Jeweler |
| Mr. Dency | Solicitor |
| Mr. and Mrs. Ivy | Butler and Cook—Nash Home |
| James Foster | Friend of the Johansson's |

| | |
|---|---|
| Daniel Batley | Friend of the Johansson's |
| Mr. Christian Delois | Brother of Rue's First Employer |
| Mrs. Chezique | Friend of Young Rue and Lissett |
| Mr. LeBlanc | Solicitor |
| Lissett Beaudroux | Sister of Rue |
| Fireman Dolman | Friend of Ian Fisk |
| Fireman Woods | Friend of Ian Fisk |
| Master Ivy | Stable Boy |
| Constable Jones | Seattle Policeman |
| Priscilla | Ralston Ship |
| Sea Star | Foster and Batley Ship |
| North Star | Foster and Batley Ship |
| Mystic Quest | Spanish Ship |
| Sea Maiden | Ship Going to England and France |
| Salty | Karin's White Kitten |

# A Past Revealed

$\mathcal{H}$e would not apologize for his life even now when dying. The years of sea mist on his face and salt upon his tongue left some evidence of the life most men only dreamed of. He knew the pleasures of good food, fine wines, women and rapture of true love. Before slipping into the realm of death he reflected upon the events leading to this moment, and wondered if his secret would be discovered. The year was 1807.

Fifty years later.

Several well wishers gathered at the home of the most respected couple in town. It was a lovely day in the Pacific Northwest and the sun was shining as brightly as the celebrations that were taking place. The Webb's were celebrating fifty years of marriage. Erik and Karin Johansson chose to begin their married life on this day in honor of his grandparents—Mr. Quentin Webb and Mrs. Esther Jensen Webb.

"Karin, I'm so happy that you will be part of our family. My grandson is a lucky man and I pray that your life together will be blessed and happy." Esther was sincere in what she said and in hugging the young woman, her eyes became misty.

"Thank you Mrs. Webb. I do feel blessed already. Erik has been so good to me and I hope I can be a good wife. I'm so happy." The happiness in her was apparent. She truly loved the man she was about to marry.

"I was wondering if I may ask something of you that I debated about for some time actually." Taking a short little breath, and putting a tissue to her eye she pulled out a Bible and handed it to Karin. "Many years ago a young man I cared for very much gave it to me as a keepsake. I wondered if you and Erik would consider getting married to words read out of this

1

Bible and make it your own?" She brushed away a strand of hair and with a somewhat nervous little laugh she continued to speak. "Please don't feel I'll be offended if that's not possible. I don't want to impose my wish on you and I'll completely understand. Perhaps you already have a family Bible that you are going to use."

"I don't have one. It's lovely and we would be so honored to get married with this Bible." She was moved that such a special gift had been given to her and Erik. "I'll treasure it always because you gave it to us. Thank you for making me feel loved and wanted. I wish my family were here to see this day. I think they would have liked all of you very much." Tears ran down her cheeks, it wasn't because she was sad, but rather because on this day she would gain a family and start a new life.

"My goodness, we had better hurry! You don't want to be late for your own wedding. You look so lovely." She started to leave then stopped and turned around to look at her. "Karin, your family is here, we just can't see Angels."

The young couple had decided long before the wedding, that they would live in the coastal town of Valda Bay. Most men made a living by the sea or related business and Erik was no exception. When weather and time permitted, he went fishing to make extra money. He was also a master navigator having learned navigation skills from his grandfather. His early years were spent working on various ships. The work was sporadic at times and his grandmother who wanted him to give up the sea, suggested that he pursue and learn a new occupation. He did and became the lighthouse keeper. The job was labor intensive and required lifting heavy casts of oil that made the gears turn and the lights function. The oil had to be carried up several flights of stairs often. The work made his six foot three frame hard and muscled. When most people met him for the first time, they stood back and took notice. He didn't mind the work or the results of it. The pay was fair, and with careful planning he and his bride could build a future upon it.

Several months after the wedding, Karin was in her small garden praying. She loved having things grow around her and she marveled at the miracle of every living thing. They had not been blessed with a child but in time hoped they would be.

"Praying in the garden again I see." Erik has approached unheard and it gave her a slight startle. He was hoping she would be more accepted in town by now, but people were slow to change. Her thick Norwegian accent set her apart from the other women.

"Goodness, you startled me! You know how much I like it here. I can see the sea so clearly and I love the lighthouse especially at night. Don't you think it's pretty?"

"Yeah, it's nice. I'm glad to see my house at night when I'm coming home. It means I'm close to my own bed and you." He hugged her from behind and kissed the top of her head.

"Oh, you are so bad." Hugging his waist they began to walk toward the house. "I'll start dinner now. I'm sorry it's going to be a little late. I was looking at some passages in the Bible and I found myself looking at the circles again." She scrunched her face at the thought of anyone marking up a Bible and not even very neatly. Underlining was one thing, but this circling on pages, that was something she didn't understand. What was the point in doing that? "Why do you suppose your grandmother did that?"

"I don't know. Tell you what, next month when we see her we can just ask. She was the only one that had it so she'll know. I guess I never thought about it." He went to the sink to wash up.

"No, that's not really true. She told me that someone very special gave it to her a long time ago. Don't you remember she told us that on our wedding day?" Looking over at him, she sighed as he made a small mess by the sink. He never could keep all the water and soap in the pan. He dried his hands.

"My love, I don't remember anything anyone said on that day. I only saw you." Reaching for her he kissed her. Dinner would be late, or maybe not be served at all.

Two weeks later, Erik was at the ice house picking up his weekly block of ice. He was making polite small talk with Mr. Rudolph Nash. As the owner of the local mercantile and ice house he was a respected and wealthy businessman. Erik was about to leave when a young boy of about six years entered the store with a sense of urgency.

"Mr. Johansson, I have an important message for you. I saw you come into the mercantile so I ran here instead of going to your house." The boys face was sweaty from running fast. He deserved a small reward.

"Here you go. Take this penny and buy yourself something. I'm sure that the mercantile has something you would like." The little boy's face lit up.

"Thank you Mr. Johansson." In a split second he was running out the door.

"I appreciate you delivering the message so quickly." Erik called out after him but it was doubtful that he heard the complete sentence. He was running directly to Mrs. Steele's Sweet Shop. A scoop of ice cream would be a real treat.

"I can have that block of ice delivered if you have to go. There's no sense in you carrying it to the telegraph." Mr. Nash motioned to his delivery boys.

"Thanks, I would appreciate that." Erik smiled politely at Mr. Nash and with a half worried look on his face headed for the door. "Can you add it to my bill and we'll settle up as usual?"

"Sure, glad to do it."

He stepped outside and even before opening the envelope he suspected that the news could not be good.

**Dear Erik: Your grandmother is seriously ill. She is asking for you. Please come if possible. Love Grandfather.**

Erik felt his heart sink. He knew his grandmother was elderly but could not imagine her passing away. She had always been there for him, raising him after his own mother died giving him life. He knew at once he would go. If all went well they would be with his grandparents in only a day and a half. He was grateful the weather was good and the fact that Karin always had their home in a state of ready. There would not be much time wasted in preparing to leave and if the weather held the trip would not be difficult. He hoped he would reach his grandmother in time. He knew his grandfather was not one to be easily alarmed so this was indeed serious. When he arrived home and upon entering Karin noticed he had no ice with him.

"Erik was there no ice left to … what's wrong?" In seeing his face, she knew immediately that something more than the lack of ice was wrong.

"It's my grandmother." With one swift motion, he removed his coat and handed her the telegraph message. She looked up after reading it visibly upset.

"I'll pack our things. We can catch the transport in about one hour if we hurry. We are going aren't we?" She felt the question was not really necessary but out of respect for him, she asked.

"Yes, of course we are. Let's hurry." He was standing near her and in an effort to give him some kind of comfort she hugged him tight. He felt lucky to have a wife like her. Releasing her from their embrace each set about doing what was necessary. She quickly began packing and in only a few moments had what they needed for several days. She thought to pack a basket with home canned goods, hard cheese and a bottle of wine. He prepared the outside of the house in the event a storm blew in while they were gone. They met the transport as planned and Erik rushed to the telegraph office to send a message to his grandfather that they were on their way. He carried the heavy food basket and when the coach arrived they quickly boarded and made themselves as comfortable as possible. Each of them was lost in thought as they looked out the window. She remembered to bring the Bible and Erik remembered that the block of ice Mr. Nash would have delivered would be melted by the time they returned.

They arrived at the Webb home without incident. Erik knocked at the front door and a gray haired middle aged woman in the service of the Webb Family answered the door. She recognized him and quickly stepped aside so he might enter.

"Mr. Webb is in his library. I'll have your things taken upstairs to your room. If there is anything else you need, please call upon me."

"Thank you. We appreciate that very much." Erik and Karin turned and headed for the library.

It was amazing how much his grandfather had changed since he last saw him. In the place of a distinguished looking older gentleman sat a very tired looking, unshaven man. His clothes were not crisp and Karin took in a sharp breath at seeing his condition.

"Grandfather, we came as soon as we received your message," Erik spoke quietly. He did not want to startle the man who was so lost in thought he did not hear them enter.

"Thank you for coming. It means so much." He got up from his chair to embrace them. They all embraced and he found some comfort in it.

"Please, sit. Would you care for a glass of brandy or perhaps some tea?" He rang for service. "The doctor is with her now so we have to wait until he comes down before we can get any more news on her condition." He then sat back down in his chair and put his head in his hands.

"What happened to grandmother? Are you alright?" Erik thought perhaps they were exposed to something foul and his grandfather might also fall ill.

"I'm doing alright considering everything. It's just your grandmother. She fell down the stairs two weeks ago and broke her hip. Now the doctor says she has some type of an infection in her bone and pneumonia in both her lungs. There is nothing more to be done."

"Mr. Webb?" At the sound of his name all three turned to find the doctor entering the library. "If you'd like you may go upstairs now and talk with her. I've given her something for the pain and that will help for a while. I'm so very sorry. I wish I had better news." The doctor put his bag down on a nearby table.

"Doctor, this is my grandson Erik and his wife Karin. They live in Valda Bay but I thought they should be here."

"It's nice to meet you. I'm sorry it's under these unpleasant circumstances." The men shook hands and then Karin offered hers. "Good to meet you doctor," Erik answered.

"Doctor, I appreciate all you have done. Please, make yourselves comfortable. I'll go and sit with her for a while and let her know that you're both here. Erik, I know that will make her happy." He patted his grandson's shoulder with tender affection.

"Sir, you rang for me?" A butler politely asked.

"Yes, please have the cook prepare something for everyone. I'll be with Mrs. Webb."

"Yes sir, right away." He bowed politely then followed him out of the library.

"Doctor, will my grandmother be able to speak with me and understand what I'm saying?" It was important that she know he came as she requested. Karin offered some brandy to the men but only the doctor accepted a small glass gratefully.

"Yes she can. But her breathing is labored. Try to do most of the speaking so it will be easier for her." He settled into a large overstuffed chair wishing he could do more.

Karin remained quiet not certain what to do. She was hoping she would be able to see grandmother for what may be the last time. Walking over to the huge bay windows she pulled the drapes closed darkening the room considerably. It was getting late. The table lamps were lit and returning to her chair, reached for her handbag to retrieve the Bible. It was the one she had given to them on their wedding day. Turning the pages she looked at the circles again. She resisted the urge to remind Erik to ask about them. He didn't need her curiosity added to his apparent worry. If they were meant to know they would.

It was not to long before Erik and Karin were called to his grandmother's room. They entered and she greeted them with a weak smile. The high color in her cheeks only confirmed that she was feverish.

"Hello grandmother. I'm so glad to see you." Erik smiled at her and gently reached for her hand. This seemed to please her and she gently squeezed his hand.

"Hello Grandmother Webb." Karin smiled but her eyes looked sad.

"My dears, I'm so pleased you could both come. I'm sorry it's under these circumstances." She turned her head and coughed into her handkerchief.

"Gram, perhaps you should rest for now. We're going to be here a while and after you have gotten some rest we can talk."

"No, I want to visit now. I may not have tomorrow and I want you to know …" She gasped a little and continued. "Karin, we didn't have a lot to time to get to know each other better. I do know that you make Erik happy and that makes me happy. You are a good person and I know you will be of comfort to him when I'm gone as well as the years ahead. One of the happiest days of my life was the day you married my Erik. I know you will take good care of him. I know your home will always be a happy one." She stopped and tried to catch her breath.

"Thank you so much for your kind words. Please don't tire yourself. You need to save your strength. May I bring you anything?" She loved this woman like a mother.

"No. I'm fine. Please, do you think I might have a word alone with my grandson? I promise not to keep him long." She reached out to her and Karin leaned over to hug her. She could feel the heat radiating from under the blankets.

"Of course. I'll be downstairs if you need me." With a quick turn she walked away thinking that this might very well be the last time she saw this kind woman alive. The door blurred before her and by the time she closed it behind her she had to wipe her eyes.

"She's a wonderful girl."

"Yeah, she is. I'm a happy man. It hasn't been easy for her since her parents died. I know that she's lonely and probably misses her native Norway. She hasn't any friends. Sometimes the so called ladies of Valda Bay can be cruel. And then there's the baby business. She's worried because we don't have one yet. I think we will in time." He put more cheer in his voice than he felt.

"I'm sure you will have many children. I wanted many children, but we don't always get what we want. I need you to know that your mother wanted you very much and when she died trying to give you life, I was deeply saddened but also very happy because she left us you." She coughed again and pressed her hand to her chest.

"Thank you for saying that. I wish I could have known her."

"She was a lovely person with a strong spirit and quiet strength. I see a lot of her in you. Do you know how it was I named you Erik?"

"No, I don't think you ever told me." He smiled at her.

"When I was young, like Karin, I fell deeply in love with a sea captain." Erik's eyes widened slightly. "His name was Erik Haussmann and I named you after him." She paused and it almost seemed like a light came into her eyes at the mention of his name.

"When your mother died she left no word on what to name you. I was not bold enough to chance a life with him but I was bold enough to name you after him." She lightly sighed.

"What happened to him?" Erik hoped his question would not cause her more sadness.

"We were so different. I had been promised to your grandfather and in those days ... well, let's just say it wasn't like today. Understand I learned to love your grandfather in time." He could hear the rattle in her chest and noticed the effort it took to just draw a breath.

"I know what you mean." He wanted to talk a while to allow her to rest a moment and ease her breathing.

"Grandfather is a good and decent man ... he just wasn't the love of your life. It must have been hard to leave your sea captain behind. You know I did wonder who I was named after. In the family Bible there isn't one man named Erik. You know what? If I have a son, I'll name him Erik in his honor and mine. No one will ever know the truth, except for you and me naturally." He reached for a cool cloth and wiped her brow.

"That would be a nice secret. But, here's another one. As the captain and I were saying goodbye he handed me a keepsake. It was the Bible I gave to you and Karin. I thought it an unusual gift because my parents as missionaries had so many Bibles already. But, I accepted it with all the love I knew he felt for me. Later, I opened it and found that he had placed a little poem inside. He had also circled my name along with some verses. I never understood the point of the circles on those verses. I still believe he was telling me something. The words in the verses offered no clue. I held the paper written by his hand so often it finally fell apart." She coughed again and this time an ugly red stain appeared on her handkerchief. Erik handed her a glass of water and she took a small drink.

"Gram, please, let's stop for now." Erik reached for the cloth and put it in the basin of water. He wrung it out and when he placed it upon her forehead, she closed her eyes to enjoy the cooling effect.

"No, I'm alright. I can't share this with anyone but you. Write down the words to the poem as I speak. He wasn't the kind of man to do things without purpose. Try to discover what he was really telling me. Keep it safe. Don't share it with anyone but those you trust completely. Know that if you never unlock the secret of the poem, I'll smile down at you because at least I shared this part of my life with you. Don't tell your grandfather, it would only hurt him and I would never want that. I do love him very much. Are you ready to write?" She licked her lips and began to speak.

> *For most of my life I've sailed the great sea*
> *As your husband I'd happily share my life with thee*
> *Few things I need more than precious stars at night*
> *One is the cascade of your hair so golden and bright*
> *In stream end and standing straight*
> *There we can see where Eagles mate*
> *From love's lofty edge where they do fly*
> *Walk away and watch the sky*
> *When the sun is half way to the crashing sea*
> *Old shadows will fall for my love and me*

Erik had taken a pencil from her desk and wrote the words down as she spoke. He repeated them to her to make sure that he had written them down correctly. It seemed to make her happy and he made sure she saw him put the paper in his wallet where it would be safe.

"Good. Now I can die happy." She closed her eyes and she seemed to draw breath with less effort. "I'm so very tired."

"I think I should call the doctor. Would you care for anything before I go get him?"

"No, I think I'll just rest for a while. Please ask your grandfather to come sit with me for a while. And forget that old doctor, he can't help me anyway." He noticed that she seemed more peaceful now than when he first came in. For some unknown reason, he didn't like it. They both knew she was dying.

Shortly after midnight Erik's grandfather came downstairs. His shoulders were slumped and the look on his face spoke what his mouth did not. Everyone knew she had passed away.

"She's gone. Oh my Lord, my beautiful Esther is gone." He placed his hands over his face and silently wept.

Erik turned toward his wife and without a word being spoken they both went to the older man. She cried freely and Erik trying to be strong for his grandfather said nothing because he knew there was little he could say. The doctor offered his condolences and left the family alone.

Erik left them and stepped outside for a few much needed minutes alone. He leaned against the wall and allowed himself to feel her passing. He made no attempt to wipe his tears he simply let them come. He had not really cried since he was eleven when his grandfather told him to put his much loved dog out of his misery. The animal was seriously injured. The memory of that incident, even after several years, still hurt. After a few minutes, he collected himself and went inside and gave thought to her final arrangements. It was the hardest thing he could remember doing. She helped make him the man he was. She taught him how to dance and how to conduct himself around a lady. He remembered how she taught him proper table manners and the importance of keeping clean. He hated doing those things at the time when all he wanted to do was go sailing or fishing. Most importantly she forged in iron the values that guided his life. He would miss her. Several people attended her services and he learned what a truly special person she was. Many people spoke of the things she had done for them. Erik learned she had paid in full medical bills for those who could not afford to pay. There were also those she provided with food or paid the rent on their homes. And to her credit, she never spoke of the things she did for anyone. Each person was amazed to learn she had done so much for so many. The only person not amazed at her generous nature was Quinton Webb. Ten days after her passing, Erik and Karin prepared to return home. He left his grandfather in the company of a distant relative who agreed to stay with him for an extended period of time.

Riding the coach home seemed to take forever and they were grateful there were no other passengers traveling with them.

"Can you tell me what your grandmother said to you the night she asked me if she could speak with you alone? If it's something you don't want to share, I understand," she meant what she said.

"You mean that don't you?" He gave her hand a little squeeze. He would tell her. "She just told me about her younger days, why she named me Erik, stuff like that." He said nothing else for a time.

"And ..." She waited a moment and nothing happened. She let out an exasperating gasp of breath.

"Oh, you are so vague it's like trying to see in the dark! Don't tell me, I don't even want to know." Now she was lying.

He looked at her and chuckled slightly. "Alright, I get it. You want more details."

For the next several moments she listened as he told her what he and his grandmother has discussed in greater detail. Afterward she fell asleep leaning on Erik. He remained awake thinking about the poem, his namesake and a side of his grandmother he never knew existed.

The house was as they left it and things once again fell into a comfortable routine. Only one thing had changed and it concerned Karin. Her name was Mei Ling Lee. She spoke so little English one could say she did not speak at all. It had been a warm day and having finished most of her housework, Karin decided to sit outside by her garden and enjoy the scenery before her. She looked and saw a young woman of about eighteen years approaching with a small basket in her hands. She seemed friendly and when they saw each other, both smiled. It was only polite that as the lady being approached, she should wait to be spoken to first. That didn't happen and an odd moment passed between them.

"Hello. I'm Mrs. Johansson, can I help you?" No answer.

The girl just looked and smiled. It then occurred to Karin that perhaps she didn't speak English. There were several ways to communicate when one wanted to, so she tried using gestures. It worked. She motioned for her to sit, but the girl declined. She instead pointed to herself and said her name.

"Mei Ling Lee." She smiled.

"Karin Johansson." She smiled back at her.

After about ten minutes, it was clear what brought her to the house. She was hoping for permission to pick some flowers from the garden.

"I understand. Please wait." No reaction. Holding up her hands to indicate she wanted her to remain, she rushed inside and returned with a pair of scissors. Handing them over, she motioned for her to take what she wanted. The woman looked at each flower carefully before making a selection. This fascinated Karin because to her, all the flowers looked the same. After placing the flowers in her basket she returned the scissors. Karin then noticed that she had brought a pair with her, but was gracious enough to accept the pair offered. Smiling she placed her hand over her heart and bowed slightly. She was saying thank you.

"You're welcome." Karin smiled. Mei Ling Lee turned to leave.

"Come back soon." Turning around she shook her head in the negative. With all her gesturing they often found themselves laughing softy. After a few minutes the message was conveyed and understood. To answer Karin, the young woman gestured as if she were asleep and held up three of her fingers. They now understood each other. It was determined that in three days she would be able to visit again.

"Goodbye Karin Johansson." She had spoken two of only four words in English she knew.

"Goodbye Mei Ling Lee."

"Mei Ling." She pointed to herself. Karin realized that her last name was Lee.

"Karin." Pointed to herself she left off Johansson. She was rewarded with a smile that told her Mei Ling understood that her last name was Johansson.

Looking back on the exchange, Karin actually felt accomplished in her non verbal skills. She decided not to share the news of her new acquaintance with Erik. She would wait a while, see what developed and if all went well she would tell him. Over the next few months, things did go well and with each passing day, a wonderful friendship developed between two young women from vastly different cultures. Mei Ling was learning to speak English and Karin was learning Chinese. After several weeks had passed she told Erik about her friend and he was happy for her.

It was the custom of the local fishermen to gather at The Foggy Inn Tavern. It was a good place to get some hot food, drink ale or spend time with a woman for a reasonable price. It was also the place where all manner of deals, shady or otherwise took place. The conversation naturally turned to current events. One event being discussed was the passing of Mrs. Webb. She had been a prominent person in the community and her passing created a stir in most circles. It was rumored that when she died, she took valuable secret information with her. The information concerned a lost ship—the Rip Tide. While several rumors and various conclusions were being formed, one man offered yet another. Sitting at a table in the corner of the room, three friends were eating, drinking and talking about Mrs. Webb.

"I'm telling you, she knew Captain Haussmann real well. I was told that she almost married him." There was interest in what he was saying. He looked around before continuing his story.

"Bullshit. How do you know? You weren't even born." Cole Ralston knew that Joaquin Cutta had a lot of life experiences and could tell a good story. He sometimes wondered if they were true.

"A distant relative of mine sailed on the Red Coral. He signed on as a deck hand when she came to Spain to trade for wine. Anyway, a few people had reason to believe that this Haussmann found the treasure of the

Rip Tide. There was never any real hard proof except for what my great uncle said happened." He crossed himself at the reference to his dead relative. "God rest his soul. Anyway, everyone wanted to know for sure if Haussmann and his crew knew more than what they said about the Rip Tide. They got the chance when a crewman from Haussmann's ship spilled his guts about the Rip Tide. My great uncle said that some of the crew from the Red Coral gave him a little help so he would remember all he knew."

Flint Ralston, Cole's brother said, "You mean your relative beat up the poor bastard from Haussmann's ship."

"Well yeah, he and a few others helped I guess. I can't think of that ship's name. Well, anyway my great Uncle told me that before the nasty gypsy died, he confessed to knowing the truth about the Rip Tide. The captain of the....damn, what was that ships name?" The conversation was interesting to the Ralston men. The name of the ship didn't matter.

"Go on Joaquin, forget her name." Cole wanted him to continue. His brother gave him an approving look. They both wanted to hear more.

"Well, like I said, my dead relative told the captain of the Red Coral what he learned. They rewarded in those days for valuable information. The Catherine! That was the name of his ship." He laughed. "It came to me like a sneaker wave, out of nowhere."

The men acknowledged his reference of the wave. They had all felt the effects of one and they knew how quickly death could come. Sailing men more often than not never saw the wave coming—hence the name.

"Ok, so it was the Catherine. What happened next?" Cole was extremely interested.

"Yeah, well anyway, both ships set sail on the next high tide. The captain and crew of the Red Coral lived to love another day, but the crew of the Catherine; they're drinking ale with Davey Jones. No one as best I know found anything of value. Still haven't."

"So where does Mrs. Webb fit in?" Flint had not forgotten that all this talk began with a reference to her.

"That's the unknown part." Joaquin took a long drink of ale. "After the captain of the Red Coral was informed, he ordered Haussmann watched.

They did and found out that he stopped at a shop of some kind picked up something and headed out to his lady love."

"And the lady was Mrs. Webb?" Cole had concluded correctly.

"You got it." Joaquin was pleased with himself. It had been a long time since his conversation was this appreciated. He was not considered boring or dull in any way but this story was most certainly interesting.

"I don't know about all that," Cole said trying not to sound too interested. "I mean, she came from some squeaky clean family, beating their religious drum everywhere they went. Even the article in the paper said she was some kind of missionary." Cole turned his attention to his plate of food. He didn't want to let on that he really wanted to hear more details. His mind was beginning to turn in a million directions.

"Nah, I don't believe it. She was a missionary type. What would a lady like that be doing with the likes of a sea captain? It's not true, let's stop talking about the dead. It isn't right." Flint drained his glass of ale and motioned for another. He didn't like talking about the dead. Bad luck always seemed to follow. When the waitress brought him his drink, Flint Ralston gave her a very appreciative look.

"Easy my brother. Rue isn't your type. She may be a whore but she's a high priced particular one. Besides, she would be too much for you." The men laughed at his teasing comment. Flint gave him a look that would have melted iron.

"Really, I've heard that about her." He decided to stop teasing his younger brother.

"She's from New Orleans, the French Quarter. She got into some kind of trouble there, that's the rumor anyway." Cole Ralston and his brother Flint were as close as two brothers could be.

"Yeah, well we all know about rumors. Yesterday we heard there was fish for the taking at Short Reef. There wasn't a damn thing there. We wasted our time and the Priscilla came back empty. At this rate we may have to sell her." Flint was shaking his head.

"Yeah, well we aren't the only ones getting the barb from the sea." Cole knew his brother was right. Things were getting desperate for them as well as other fishermen in the area. The fishing was bad. They had borrowed money to make repairs to the Priscilla and the debt was coming due. They knew others had to borrow money as well.

"Something will turn up," Joaquin said.

"So Joaquin is that where the story ends?" He asked casually wanting to get the conversation back to Mrs. Webb.

"Yeah, pretty much. No one found the Catherine, the valuable cargo, or the men on board. The only thing left they say was what Haussmann gave Mrs. Webb." He looked around the room noticing the clock. "I have to go." He drained his mug of ale. I'll see you later. Good night to you both." He stood up and left.

"Night," they said it at the same time and as if reading each other's mind, they knew they would stay up late aboard the Priscilla talking about all Joaquin said.

Not far from where the men has been enjoying their conversation, sat Leroy Grazer. He had overheard everything but even if the men noticed him, he was not considered a threat. Almost everyone in the town considered him an idiot. He was slow of speech; his clothes were in bad repair but clean. He did the tasks in town that no one else would. Leroy, however, was not an idiot. He knew more than he revealed and he liked it that way.

"Leroy, can I get you anything else?" The sweet voice of Rue Beaudroux was pure music to his ears.

He shook his head no. *Yes, you can sit with me a while because I love you.*

"Alright, just let me know if you change your mind." She gave him a pleasant smile before turning to leave. She moved with natural grace and elegance.

He watched her move around the room and in the smoky light of the tavern, she looked like a vision. Her long auburn hair and light green eyes made her an unusual beauty. He also knew that he would never stand a chance with her and he cursed his stuttering tongue. It had made him appear stupid and as a result, he could never get a decent job. It was always downhill for him rather than up. It seemed like she was the only person who treated him like a person. No, more correctly, like a man. In the quiet sanctity of his mind, he pledged his support and loyalty to her. If ever she needed him, he would be there.

# Deception and Discovery

*H*e knocked softly at her bedroom door. "Elsa, may I come in?" The concern in the voice of Rudolph Nash for his wife was apparent.

"Yes, I'm awake." Elsa, his wife was in bed looking fresh and pretty after having had a warm bath and light dinner.

He entered the room and closed the door behind him. "Are you feeling any better dearest? I was concerned because it's so late and your light was still on. Do you need me to get you anything?"

"No, I think I feel a little better." *Why don't you just leave?*

"Alright, that's what I like to hear. I know all this has been so hard on you and I want you to know that it doesn't change how I feel about you." He approached her and sat down on the bed next to her. He reached for her hand and held it for only a brief moment before she slowly eased her hand out of his.

"We can always have another baby whenever you feel ready. We have lots of time." He leaned over and kissed her lightly. He felt her stiffen and pull away from him slightly.

"I didn't mean anything by that gesture … I know that you aren't ready for that sort of thing." His voice trailed off.

"Do you need me to bring back anything for you from town? I'm going into Rock Port and I won't return until tomorrow." Rock Port was only twelve miles away, but by the time he traveled there, conducted his business, had a bite to eat; it was going to be too dark to travel home safely.

"Perhaps some tea cookies would be nice." She really didn't want tea cookies but had to say something to appease him.

"Tea cookies it is. Don't stay up to much later. You need to get your strength back." He got to his feet and before closing the door behind him he stopped and turned. "I love you Elsa. Goodnight."

"Goodnight Rudolph." She smiled weakly at him. She quickly thought to say something a good wife would say. "Be careful and have a safe trip."

The last thing that Elsa wanted to do was sleep. After about an hour, the house was quiet. Rudolph had gone to sleep. She quickly got out of bed, got dressed in a dark blue dress and fixed her hair. Opening the window slowly she fled into the night. Earlier in the week, a note had been delivered to someone special. It informed him that she was now recovered and was well enough to see him. Having a key to enter their haven made it easier to be together and not be seen by others. With the key pressing into her palm, she could hardly wait to see him. She arrived to find him waiting. He pulled her into his arms when she approached kissing her long and deep with primal hunger. His hands and mouth seemed to be moving all over her at once. She came to her senses first.

"Stop, we have to get inside, someone may see." She offered him the key to unlock the door. With a quick turn of the bolt, they entered and he locked the door behind them. He immediately reached for her again. He pulled her close and kissed her again. With one hand he cupped one breast, and with the other started to lift up her dress.

"I've missed you so much." He was holding her so close she could hardly breathe. "I'm glad you're alright. I'm dying Elsa. I need to make love to you so badly; it's been such a long time." He sought her mouth again and finding her tongue allowed him the pleasure of feeling it against his. He gently thrust against it. Soon, he thought, he would do more than just thrust in her mouth.

"I am much better darling."

"Good, loosen my belt and pants, they're becoming uncomfortable."

"Please, listen to me. We can't do this yet. You don't know what I've been through." She could hardly get the words out.

"What are you saying?" He was hearing but not really listening because he was aroused and wanted her. She could feel the heat of his body and inhaled the light scent of soap that was on his skin.

"You sent word to me that you were alright … to meet you here." He continued to feel her body, nuzzle her neck.

"I did because I just needed to see you. I needed to hear your voice, see your face. I needed to have you just hold me." She hoped he would understand.

He didn't.

"What are you saying?" He looked at her with desire still in his eyes.

"It was just so difficult. I thought I was going to die. The pain went on and on for hours. You can't imagine how scared I was." She was almost crying.

With her words, his desire had cooled considerably, but was still present.

"You can't just turn me on and off like a lantern. You should have said so in your note. I would have prepared myself for pleasant conversation and perhaps a cup of hot tea." He was being sarcastic, but he couldn't help it.

"I'm sorry. I never meant for it to be like this." She was feeling terrible, because he was right. She had misled him.

"I'm sorry too." He softened his tone. "I didn't have any idea it would be so bad. I wish I could have been there with you." Not true … he would not have been, even if he could have.

"There are other ways, if you still need to be with me." She was looking at him with a look that said she really didn't want that. He read it correctly.

"No, that's alright. Let me just collect myself. Why don't you pour us a drink and I'll go upstairs and wash my face. The walk will do me good." He smiled at her and gave her a little peck on the check.

"Thank you. I do so love you."

"Alright then, I'll be right back."

She was so happy that she never realized that he did not say he loved her. Upstairs he tried to calm down and found a new emotion had taken the place of desire … anger. He was just so angry at her he wondered if all this was worth it. For now, he would control himself and be the perfect gentleman. He considered it a waste of time.

After they parted company, he needed to go to The Foggy Inn. There he would bed the woman he knew would satisfy him completely. She would not want what he could not give. She understood a man. He didn't have to make polite conversation or feel pressured to pleasure her first. He always did because his male vanity demanded it. This was also part of the reason that she never turned him away. Rue Beaudroux would always make room in her bed him. Sometimes he wondered about her past and where she had been before leaving New Orleans. Just about everyone wondered how she ended up in Valda Bay. Rue was not too young, perhaps thirty but still very beautiful. Like all beautiful women, she was full of mystery and gave little or no information about herself. In fact, all he knew for sure was that she had been a prostitute for several years. She was smart enough to take care of herself and was thick skinned enough not to care what the other women thought of her. She had made enough money to be particular about who she took to her bed, how much it would cost and how often. He was among the privileged few. In fact, he was the exception to her basic rule. She never charged him a penny for her services and he attributed this to the fact that they were not romantic lovers but more than friends. He never abused her and treated her like a lady. They trusted each other.

"Cherie, you seem a little distant. Were you not pleased with me tonight?" Rue asked the question sincerely. His lovemaking had the usual urgency in it and he had pleased her well. Still, he seemed preoccupied and it was not characteristic.

"No, it's not you. I have a lot on my mind." The statement was true.

"Can I help in any way? I'm very good at helping, and not always between the sheets." She looked at him carefully. She didn't want to overstep her boundary.

"You are so beautiful, you know that?" He had changed the subject and she took the cue.

"Thank you. You are very handsome yourself. Where did you get your tanned skin, thick dark hair and those deep blue eyes? No! Don't tell me, let me guess. Your mother was a beautiful virtuous Spanish maiden. Your father—he is very tall, rich and powerful. Am I close?"

"Yes, except the part about my father being rich and powerful." He laughed and reached for her again.

"Oh no, I have to get some sleep tonight. Turnover and I'll hug you. Sleep well my friend."

"You too." He was tired and her bed felt good to him.

"Do you want to get up early in the morning, or shall I let you sleep?"

"Early." He wet his fingers and rolling over reached out and snuffed the candle.

"Good night Rue."

"Good night Joaquin."

Across town, Elsa Nash had no idea Joaquin was sleeping so soundly in the bed of another woman. She was lying awake reliving the evening and wishing he was with her and fearful that she had made a mistake in not allowing him to make love to her. The memory of how all this business had come about filled her mind. For several months she and Joaquin had been very frequent lovers. It started out innocently enough. He would come in the ice house for supplies when she was behind the counter. One flirtation had led to another and before long, she found herself very attracted to him. He was young, in his late twenties, well built and extremely handsome. He was a far cry from her husband of one year. The marriage had been an arranged one, and at first she was outraged at her parent's choice for her. Mr. Rudolph Nash was considerably older than she was. He was short in stature, portly and balding. But, he had one very favorable quality. He owned two well established places of business and a nice house close to the ocean. She could live the life of a well respected lady with plenty of money for all the nice things she wanted. It seemed like she always wanted something and as if by magic, he managed to get it for her. She did not love him and regretted the marriage. Divorce seemed out of the question, but she wished it were not.

Mr. Nash was also a poor and clumsy lover. She hated the thought of him touching her and after being intimate with him she cried in silent misery. She didn't want children as she was scared of the pain and birthing process. Her sister had died in the agony of childbirth and she still remembered the screams that came from her room that day. As a result she decided not to give herself to her husband to often and kept close account of her personal days. The arrangement seemed perfect. Perfect that is until Joaquin entered into her life.

The first time Joaquin made love to her was magic. She had no idea that loving a man could be so pleasurable. He took her to heights unimaginable and she found herself wanting his lovemaking more often than not. It was a dangerous game, but she could not get enough of him. She was in love. Then about seven months into the relationship it all came crashing down on her. She sent word to him that she needed to see him immediately. He went to the appointed place and waited for her. Seeing her approach, he noticed that she looked a little pale and there were faint blue shadows under her eyes. He extended his arm but she refused it.

"What is so urgent that it can't wait?" He asked.

"Let's walk further down the beach. I don't want to be overheard."

"Why don't you just say that you don't want to be seen with me?" He tartly asked.

"Oh, stop it will you! There isn't much time. I have bad new and I don't know what to do." She turned her face away from him but there were tears in her eyes and when she blotted at them, her hands were shaking. He noticed but said nothing. They continued to walk toward the beach and were soon out of sight from prying eyes.

"Alright, calm down, tell me what it is." He wasn't sure he wanted to know.

"I'm pregnant." She said it so quietly, he almost didn't hear it.

"Well, congratulations. I'm sure you and your husband will be very pleased."

"What?" She looked up and him in disbelief. "You know that it's yours."

"How can you be certain Elsa? You are a married woman after all. Besides, a baby is a wonderful thing. I thought all women liked babies." He tried to sound happy.

"I'm certain it's yours. My husband and I haven't been together in a while. I'm too far gone for this child to be his." She was feeling so many different emotions she was having a hard time sorting them out.

"Have you been to the doctor yet? Maybe it's something else." Wishful thinking.

"Of course I've been to the doctor. I went two days ago, I just needed some time to try and think. I can't, so I came to you." *Why are you acting this way? Why don't you at least try and hold my hand. Do Something!*

"Forgive my next question. How far along are you?" He had a good reason for asking this vital detail.

"The doctor says about ten weeks. Why?" She asked thinking that maybe he could help. He knew people she didn't.

"I want you to think carefully about this next thing I tell you. Take your time in deciding what to do. It's not without some risk."

"What is it?" She felt a glimmer of hope coupled with dread.

"First, let me ask you three questions." He needed to be sure that there was no doubt the child was his. "Are you absolutely certain that the baby is mine?"

"Yes. I'm as certain as I'm standing here. I swear to you it is." She looked him straight in the eye and held his gaze.

"Alright. Now, if you could convince your husband that my child was his, do you want the baby?" He desperately wanted her to say yes. He didn't like the thought of what he was going to suggest to her.

"It would never work. Don't you think I've thought of that?" She raised her hands in desperation and then dropped them to her side.

"Babies come early or late sometimes. This one could too." Hoping … hoping.

"Yeah, they do. But when this one comes out with dark hair, tanned skinned and is screaming in health, then what?" She felt a little nausea come over her.

"I understand what you're saying." Now he was committed to helping her. He knew she didn't get into this situation alone. He didn't want to suggest she leave her husband because it would ruin everything he planned and worked for. There was only one thing left to do.

"What were you going to tell me that wasn't without risk?" *Run away with you—my love I'd do it in a minute.* She looked at him with renewed hope.

"I know a woman who can help us. She's a prostitute and I'm sure that this situation is not a new one for these types of women. I'll go see her and then I'll let you know what she says. I promise I won't be long in getting word to you." There, he'd said it, but hated it. No, he couldn't do it. Maybe there was another way. "Elsa ..." He started to speak, but she quickly broke in.

"You have no idea how relieved I am." She was looking at him and let out such a sigh of relief that she actually looked better. He was a little taken back by it.

"Oh, Joaquin, thank you. I love you so much but I don't want your baby. In fact, I never want to have one at all. If you couldn't have helped me I would have killed myself rather than have it. I really would." She was that afraid, but he didn't know that. She would prefer a quick death rather than endure hours of agonizing labor and possible death. The thought of losing her petite figure and suffering morning sickness didn't appeal to her either.

"It's late, you should be getting back." He just wanted to be alone to think about all she had said. He did not have the luxury of the two days that she had.

"I should be on my way myself. You will let me know as soon as you can?" She looked at him and when he looked back, for the first time she did not look even slightly pretty to him.

"I will." He watched her leave for a moment then turned around and began walking in the other direction. Then changing his mind he turned around. He started to call her name, but about that time, a lady approached her and the two began to walk together in the direction of her home.

He took his time walking to The Foggy Inn. He'd have to talk with Rue now and ask her for help. The walk allowed him time to reflect on his life. He had a few things he wished he could have lived over. Like most men he had broken a few hearts. He remembered a young woman by the name of Estella. She gave herself to him after a yearlong courtship and only after he promised to marry her. It happened on the night before he was to leave for Portugal. Instead of getting married he departed on the morning tide aboard the ship he was a crew member on. Two years later he learned that she was forced to marry an older man well beneath her station because she was discovered to have been ruined by a sailor. She never disclosed his identify because she loved him. He was eighteen at that time and she a little younger. He regretted his actions—but what he would do now topped even that low act. He wished that the woman had not approached Elsa. He was going to say goodbye to all he ever wanted and ask her to go away with him. He had hoped to reason with her. He would provide for her and his child. Then he remembered when she said she didn't want his baby. He knew then that he would never want her without it.

When he arrived at The Foggy Inn, he sat down at a corner table and as usual Rue came by and greeted him. It did not take her long to realize that something was occupying him. She sat down next to him and since the place wasn't busy, she had time to talk.

"What really brings you here this time of day Joaquin?" She was wondering because for as long as she had known him, this was the first time he came to the inn in the middle of the day.

"I need to talk to you. After I do, you'll call me an idiot."

"I doubt that. Look, why don't I get us both some ale. I'll be right back."

"Good idea. But make my ale a little rum instead."

She returned quickly, sat down next to him and in typical Rue style, just waited for him to begin.

"Rue, I need your help concerning a woman's business." He shifted in his seat.

"Oh, I see. This business, does it concern you directly?"

"It does." She was his friend, but it was still difficult for him to tell her.

"Well, there is something we might be able to do, provided it's not too late. I need more information and it's going to sound like I'm just poking my nose where I have no business. Believe me when I tell you I have a reason for asking. Do you still want to have me help you?" She believed in putting all the cards on the table. He would have to trust her and do the same.

"What do you need to know?" He took a swallow of rum and prepared for her questions.

"Does she know that you are asking me for help? There is some risk involved and I don't need trouble with the law." She looked directly into his eyes for the answer.

"No, she doesn't know where I went to get help for her. I did mention that I knew a lady who could help us." He shook his head. "No, that's not true … I'm sorry Rue. What I really said was I knew a woman who was a prostitute and might be able to help us." He hated using that word to describe her.

"Well, that's honest and I see no problem there."

"How far along is the lady?" Funny she had said lady and not woman.

"She said about ten weeks."

"Has she ever been pregnant before to your knowledge?" There was a reason for asking.

"No."

"Are you certain?"

"Yes, she told me she never wanted a baby. Not mine or anyone else's."

"That doesn't mean she never has." Rue didn't want to sound cruel.

"Look, let's just cut this out." He wanted this over quickly. "The lady in question is Elsa Nash."

"The pretty little blond whose husband owns the mercantile and ice house?" She asked with a bit of surprise in her voice.

"The same."

"Well, I understand a lot more now. Here is what you must do. In China Town there is a tea you purchase. I'll write down the name of it and you just hand it to an old gentleman by the name of Hong Lei Chang. He and I have done business in the past."

"Then what?" He couldn't believe he would have to go there of all places.

"He will give you what you need. Pay him in cash and leave." She smiled.

"Will it be obvious what to do with what he gives me?" He needed to know more.

"Yes, remember I told you it was a tea? Have Mrs. Nash brew it and drink it hot. It's important that she brew it strong and drink at least two large pots. It doesn't taste too good. If it's going to work, it will start to do a cleansing of her insides in about six hours. If it doesn't start her bleeding, it was too late." She was looking down at her drink.

"Thanks for helping me."

"Well, you're welcome. Elsa Nash, on the other hand, will probably curse the day she allowed herself to be pleasured by you. It hurts like hell and after it's done, she will feel terrible for a couple of days. But, it will pass and hopefully so will her problem." She looked at him for under-standing of her instructions.

"You think I'm an idiot don't you?" He felt so damn stupid.

"No Cherie, I think you're just a man." She patted his hand and offered a reassuring squeeze to his hand.

"Rue, could she die?"

"I never knew personally of any one dying. But I suppose it's possible, I mean there is some risk to this. Look, don't borrow trouble by thinking like that. It's not that bad." She sounded confident and that helped him.

"And you know that from personal experience?" He could have bitten off his tongue for asking that question without thinking first. He would never want to offend her by asking questions that were so personal and none his business.

"What do you think?" She raised her eyebrows at him and finished the rest of her drink.

He made his way to China Town, and did as instructed. He sent the tea to her in a pretty box that arrived masked as a gift from an imaginary woman friend. He also wrote what Rue had said in every detail and asked Elsa to send word to him as soon as possible. What he did not mention, was how small he felt handing the note from Rue to the Chinese man. He didn't really look like he judged him, but it was obvious that Joaquin was there to be rid of a situation he probably created. He didn't know why it should matter to him; after all, he was only Chinese. He hoped never to see him again.

Leroy Grazer sat among his Chinese friends enjoying an inexpensive, but tasty meal. He had observed Joaquin going into the Chinese pharmacy where Mr. Chang was. In China Town, Mr. Chang was the recognized expert for all kinds of women's issues good or bad. Leroy wondered why Joaquin would be seeing Mr. Chang rather than the doctor in Valda Bay. This fact sparked Leroy's interest. As he watched Joaquin leave, he decided that it might be worthwhile to find out where it would all lead. Leroy had survived many years in Valda Bay by gathering bits of valuable information.

After what seemed like a week instead of just a couple of days, Joaquin heard from Elsa. She was alright and wanted to see him again. She would need time to recover. After reading the note, he felt the tension leave his body and was thankful that Elsa had not died.

Karin was in the back room of her house sitting by a window that allowed the sun to shine in brightly. She had her sewing basket at her side because she thought to make small repairs to several of Erik's shirts. She found it impossible to begin. There were too many tears in her eyes to allow her to thread the needle. Another month had passed, and it proved to be another disappointment. She felt like a failure and worse than that, she felt like she let down her husband. Her mother had always told her that a man knew few joys in his life, but holding his own child was certainly one of them. She wondered if Erik would ever hold his own child. Today was also a special one for them. It marked their two year anniversary.

"Karin, where are you Sweetheart?" He called out to her from the front door.

"Coming. I'm in the back room." She quickly wiped her eyes, straightened out her dress and smoothed back her hair. She put a smile on her face and went to greet him.

"Surprise!" In his arms he held a little white kitten and a small box of chocolates. "Happy Anniversary!"

"Oh Erik, that is so wonderful of you. I love you so much." She went into his arms and while hugging him gave him a kiss.

"Where did you get the kitten? And these wonderful chocolates, they must have cost a fortune. Thank you. You know how much I love chocolate." About that time the little kitten made a little mewing sound.

"Here, let me see that baby." She took the kitten from his arms and cuddled it close to her. She loved it immediately.

"I found him curled up on the salt barrel. I think something happened to his mother because I saw him there alone yesterday too. He's probably hungry."

"You may be right. I'll get some milk and bread. Did you give him a name yet?" She handed the kitten back to him and started to fix it something to eat.

"No, he's yours if you want him. You name him." He was glad she liked her presents. He knew that she had yet another disappointment and it broke his heart to see her so sad. He wanted to convey to her how much he loved her and make her understand that she was all he really wanted. Children could add no more to his happiness with her. He placed the small box of chocolates inside the dish cabinet next to her coffee cup. Later he knew she would enjoy an after dinner cup of coffee with a piece of candy.

"Well, let me see. You are all white, and found on a salt barrel. I know what I'll call you.... Salty. Yes, that's a perfect name for you. What do you think?" She was smiling at him and the smile reached her eyes. She felt truly happy and lucky to have such a fine husband. In no time at all the little meal was ready.

"Good name." He put Salty down to see if he would eat. They both laughed when in his eagerness, he put both his little paws in the plate and made little smacking sounds as he enjoyed a much needed meal. He was now part of the family.

A few days later, Erik sat at the dining room table looking at nautical charts. For the past year or so he had been thinking and working on the poem his grandmother had given him. He also memorized the scripture references that were circled. It made no sense to him yet. He needed a new perspective. He decided to start over as if looking at the material for the very first time. He had done much of this without Karin even knowing what he was doing. He had studied the note so much he had memorized it completely. He looked at the Bible countless of time for any clue it might reveal. There was nothing magical about the book. He held it up to the light, looked to see if something would reveal itself in the dark and even closed his eyes to see if he could feel anything on the cover. Nothing. He put it to a mirror, shook it well and turned it at different angles. Nothing. He even smelled it. He turned each and every page one at a time; he turned the pages from back to front. Nothing. It was now time to ask for Karin's help. A woman's perspective and a different view might help. There was only one problem. He had never mentioned the poem to her. He prepared to defend himself.

"After all this time you are just now telling me?" She was a little angry.

"I just wanted some time to think about it. It didn't seem like all that important and I didn't even look at it right away. I mean, I do have to work and do other things."

"I guess it just surprised me. I know you work hard for us."

"So what's next? We fight some more or will you help me find whatever it was that my grandmother wanted me to find?" He was losing his patience with the situation.

"I'll help. Don't leave me out of things again or I'll tell Salty to attack you." She pointed at the little kitten asleep on the chair.

Erik looked at her and at the terrible thing she threatened him with. He burst out laughing because he knew that crazy statement meant she was not angry any more.

Erik explained all he had done to date and she was now looking at all the items in front of her. They discussed several things and dismissed them just as quickly.

"I just don't know, maybe grandmother was feverish and this is all for nothing. It makes no sense at all. Do you want a cup of coffee?" He asked as he poured himself one.

"No, it's too late for me to have coffee. When you looked at the numbers circled, did you add them up, divide, or subtract them or anything like that?"

"Yes. They don't mean anything." He took a sip of coffee. "I don't know what they could be about." He sat back down and looked at the things before him.

"Maybe they don't reference anything. I think I will go to bed. Will you be long?" Karin hoped he would say no, he always warmed her up when the bed was cold.

"I'll be a little while yet. Goodnight."

"Goodnight." She gave him a hug and left for the comfort of their bed.

Looking at the Bible, the notes from the past months and his maps, he almost wanted to toss them into the trash. He firmly decided that he would not spend any more effort trying to figure out whatever it was he was supposed to figure out. With a quick motion, he folded the maps, closed the Bible and began putting the ink and quill away. He had not even cleaned the quill when he remembered his grandmother. It was her final words that gave him pause. Perhaps it was the way she had told him he could figure out the meaning of the poem that made him look again rather than forget the whole thing. He examined everything again until his eyes needed a rest. He closed his eyes and when he opened them, they focused on the open Bible. He never quit on anything in his life. He tried to recall what he had done and the things discussed with Karin. Suddenly, something flashed in his mind like a bolt of lightning. Karin said something that shed new light on the subject.

"Maybe they don't reference anything," he said it aloud. But then, maybe they were reference to something else. He put his mind into high gear. He wrote the numbers down and looked at them. It might make sense, but he needed to get one more thing. Could it be that easy and yet that complicated? He could not contain his excitement when the thought materialized into something that he could work with. He continued to pursue his train of thought and then put his theory to the test with a pair of calipers. After a short time he was rewarded with a very valuable piece of information.

"Sweetheart, wake up, I think I got it." Erik was kneeling by the bed and was gently rubbing her back in an effort to awaken her gently.

"What did you get?" She said trying to come awake from a deep sleep.

"I know what some of it means. At least I think I do. It's the only thing that makes sense. Now, all I have to do is study the poem and the whole thing may just come together. This is so important. It's hard to imagine how long this has been hidden from everyone."

"What exactly was hidden?" She asked in a slightly husky voice.

"I'm not sure yet but I know I'm close to finding out."

"What will you do next?" She was fully awake now.

"We'll keep it to ourselves and try to figure out the second half."

"What second half?" Karin was rubbing her eyes and was now sitting up.

"The poem's last lines. They are vital to the secret he gave my grand-mother."

"How did you figure it out?"

"It was something you said." He smiled at her.

"I said something good?"

"You did. It made me think in a different way."

"You're so clever."

"I'll be coming to bed in a while. I have a little more work."

"Try not to stay up so late."

"I won't. I'll clean up everything and join you in a bit." He leaned over to pull the blankets over her and she snuggled down into the warmth of their bed to wait for him.

# Plans, Propositions and Proposals

*R*udolph Nash had concluded his business in Rock Port and was very concerned. He was in deep financial trouble. His accountant had requested his presence to inform him of the situation. Since his marriage to Elsa, he had overextended himself to keep her happy with outlandish living. First, she completely redecorated the home by purchasing expensive new furniture. She had insisted upon a maid to attend to her personally, followed by a housekeeper, cook and maid. She insisted these things were necessary because of their standing in the community. At the time, Rudolph had just wanted to keep her happy. He never realized that there would be no end to her demands. When the opportunity came along to invest in a spice business, he thought it would be profitable. He borrowed the money pledging the mercantile, ice house and his home as security. He waited for a cargo ship filled with spices from the West Indies to arrive as spices were not plentiful on the Pacific coast. All the while, Elsa continued to spend without a concern to finances. He tried to curb his wife's spending but she failed to understand the situation. When the ship failed to arrive and was several weeks overdue, Mr. Nash received official word that the ship had sunk during a violent sea storm. This was the news that his accountant had informed him of yesterday. He was as good as ruined and had no idea how he would recover. The thought of telling Elsa that they were almost impoverished was simply too hard. He thought about all he could do to ease his situation and only one thing came to mind. He would give notice to his patrons who had credit accounts that he required payment in full due upon receipt of the notice. This would buy him a little time. He would try to think of another solution in the coming days. He began by telling his accountant that his services could no longer be afforded. The accountant offered a sympathetic ear and wished him the best. Mr. Nash was given all the financial papers and records to his business.

The notices created quite a stir in the town. People speculated as to the motive for such abrupt action. Mr. Nash turned a deaf ear to the complaints and shocked reactions from the town people. A few debtors were able to pay, while others were forced to borrow money from family or a lender. A few of the residents asked for an extension to the deadline and others tried to explain why they simply could not pay. The Ralston brothers were among the few who could not pay.

Sitting on the deck of their ship, the Ralston brothers were deep in thought and conversation about the recent developments with Mr. Nash. The night was cool and they were drinking warm rum and looking out over the bay.

"What are we going to do Cole? Do you think we could borrow money from the bank?" Flint was thinking about the notice of collection from Mr. Nash in his brother's shirt pocket.

"I don't know. Even if we sell some of our things, we're still short." This entire business caught them completely blind-sided.

"What about the bank?"

"No, the bank is out of the question. We already borrowed once this year from them and we're still making payments. I think we have about as much chance as a fart in the wind being given any more money now." Cole wondered what they would do.

"What if we hired out to another boat? With both of us working, we could make twice the pay, one for the bank and the other for Nash." Flint thought this sounded like a good idea.

Cole looked at his brother considering the idea. "True, we know our way around a boat and I guess most do consider us good fishermen. There is just no market for the fish that are out there right now. But, it's something to think about anyway."

"What is there to think about? Maybe we could crab instead of fish. I mean, it's not like we could jump ship or be killed by pirates and they get stiffed out of their money. Right? Then we could pay off Nash and maybe have a little left over for us." He saw Cole stand up and drain his cup of rum.

"There's truth in what you say. I'm tired of talking about it. I'm hitting the rack. See you in the morning."

"You'll think on it won't you?"

"I'll think on it."

There was little else to do but think on it. He would not allow everything he had worked for these past years to fade before his eyes. It was not beyond him to do whatever was necessary for him and Flint. He remembered that before their mother died she asked that he take care of him. His father had died years earlier and Mrs. Ralston did the best she could raising them. In his heart, he knew that his mother would not be pleased with the men they had become. They had to grow up fast in various fishing towns and there was a somewhat crude appearance to them. They were known to be opportunistic in the unfortunate circumstances of others. It was rumored that if the price was right, the Ralston brothers were your men. The same reputation that helped them to survive in the coastal community of hard drinking, whore seeking sailors, now worked against them. They were not considered credible individuals and it was too late if not an impossibility to change the reputation they created. His sleep was restless. It was in the hour shortly before dawn that Cole awakened. Lying awake, he thought of his brother's suggestion of hiring themselves out. It might have merit and little sacrifice. The thought of Flint's statement about the pirates made him almost laugh out loud. Suddenly, he wasn't laughing but thinking about a new plan.

Joaquin had received a letter from his sister. It was full of news from his home in Valencia, Spain. She wrote of the latest port news, his friends, a little town gossip and what he really wanted to read about—the vineyard. He had sent money home to purchase a vineyard with a reputation for its excellent wine grapes. It was more expensive than anticipated and she wrote she had spent all the money in acquiring it. There was no money left for fertilizers or bottling equipment. The house on the property needed some repair. Writing that she planned to live in the house until his return she would try and make the necessary repairs out of her own money. As he read on he learned that his family was fine, they all missed him and hoped he would return soon. Another part of the letter that greatly interested him was anything written about Senorita Brisa Isabella Deleon. He learned that she had organized a fund raiser for the local orphanage. Flora was Joaquin's only sister and she worked as a cook at the orphanage. The two women had spoken with each other at length. These conversations were a rare occurrence because Senorita Deleon was a woman of social position and great wealth. Senorita Flora Cutta earned very little money and despite her great beauty, she was not the most sought after maiden in the town. The dowry her family could provide was very small. Her culture was one in which families hoped to improve their social standing by making good choices in arranged marriages. In her heart, she knew that she would probably not marry well and was glad when her brother left Spain for a chance at a better life. He faced the same discrimination. He was not considered a suitable marriage partner for the same reasons. There were many nights as children that they talked about their life and how they could change it. Joaquin decided when he turned sixteen that he would seek employment on a ship. For her there was no respectable alternative so she stayed at home, helped her family and found some relief from her existence by attending church. It was at the local church that she and Joaquin first met and later developed a friendship with Senorita Deleon. As the years passed, they continued to nurture the friendship and soon Joaquin joined them after services or whenever it was possible. Flora soon noticed how much her brother like Brisa Isabella. The feeling was mutual. She made little excuses to be slightly late in gathering her things so that her brother could have a few minutes of conversation in the church with her. These conversations did not meet with the approval of Brisa Isabella's governess. When she confronted the young woman she told the governess that all they were doing was praying aloud together. In reality, they were talking and holding hands that were hidden under the several folds of her expensive dresses. They were telling each other how much they loved each other. The governess did not feel any threat by this, so she did not prevent what she thought was the verbalizing of joint prayers. She did not inform her employer. Had the governess known that the relationship was getting serious, she would have intervened immediately. Joaquin was only weeks away from being sixteen. He hated the thought of leaving Spain and his love but he needed money to purchase lands and valuable possessions. It was not his heritage to have a high social standing but with enough money he could buy his social position and gain the respectability needed to marry a woman of high society. He had written letters to Flora and each one contained a note for Brisa. He told her of his love and asked that she continue to wait for him. One day he promised they would be married.

After he finished reading the letter, he was pleased to know that he now owned property. But the letter had informed him of a new problem. He was once again short of funds. He had kept back some money in the bank to pay for his passage home. It would not be enough to make repairs and to purchase what was needed to run a business. He did not want to return and seek employment as a laborer but rather present himself as a well to do gentleman. He needed to think about his options. He would not give up Spain or the hand of Senorita Deleon. He did not know how much longer Brisa Isabella could keep her family from forcing her to marry. He needed a plan that would make money quickly. He decided to go to The Foggy Inn and think about his options.

Mr. Nash was also thinking about his options. He sat at his desk wringing his hands. Despite all the collections he was still in a bad situation. He was considering a loan from his brother who lived in California when he looked down from his area upstairs and saw Erik entering the mercantile. He went downstairs to greet him.

"Hello Mr. Nash, how are you?" Erik seemed carefree and happy. Mr. Nash was filled with envy and a little resentment. He perceived Erik's marriage as a happy one.

"I'm well Mr. Johansson. How may I be of assistance?"

"I'd like to purchase some goods and of course, I'll pay in cash." This was good news and he quickly began to accommodate him.

"Are you planning on going fishing this late in the season?" He sincerely wondered.

"Well, I know it's late, but I think there may still be a few fish left. Besides, I love being out there. I hate to leave Karin alone for extended periods so I don't plan on being gone too long. We plan on being back in six or seven days at the most." He began to look around the store for the items he would need.

"Then there will be a few of you going?" He heard Erik say 'we' and of course he was curious as to who else would be going out on a trip of this nature.

"Yeah, that's right."

"Mind if I ask who? I only ask because I'd like to prepare the equipment in the event you have luck. Some fishermen are better than others." He tried to hide his concern over the fact that a late run with a good catch was the last thing he wanted. He didn't have the funds to pay the fishermen the price of their catch. He did not want the people in town to know of his financial situation.

"I'm going with my best friends James Foster and Daniel Batley, they own the Sea Star." Erik had now gathered several items and placed them on the counter.

"Yes, I know them well, and you are fortunate indeed. They are good fishermen."

"Alright, I have all I need. What do I owe you?"

"I'll get that for you right away." The total was quickly calculated and paid for.

"Thank you very much. I must be on my way. Good night sir." Erik departed and headed for home. He was expecting his friends at his home later that night to discuss something important that required complete privacy. He knew they would be there.

"Hello Leroy, how are you?" Erik didn't really expect an answer. It was just a casual greeting to the man who was standing by the door when he made his exist. Leroy didn't answer he simply acknowledged the greeting with a nod of his head. He liked Erik and Karin, they always said hello to him.

Mr. Nash was now in no mood to receive any customers. The news of a possible catch coming into the mercantile for credit or cash sale was enough to put him in a nervous state. He never dreamed his life would be in such an unsettled state of affairs. He had just about decided that he would go home and have a light snack. His stomach was bothering him again and he knew it was because he needed to speak at length with Elsa about the unpleasant situation he was in. She was now feeling much better and was pretty much her old self. He was sorry they had lost their child and hoped that they would soon have another. His thoughts were interrupted by the Ralston brothers coming into the mercantile.

"Hello Mr. Nash." They were both pleased that there was not a soul in the store. They had some serious business to discuss.

"Good day. Can I help you with something, or are you just here to square up your account?"

"Well, sir, that's what we've come about. Flint and I just can't scrape together enough to pay in full what we owe. So, we were wondering if you would consider taking the Priscilla in exchange for payment. When we get on our feet again we would want to buy her back, plus interest of course."

"I don't need any more expense boys and I don't need a fishing boat."

"I guess you can tell that we're pretty concerned about all this. Do you know of anyone hiring anywhere? We could do about anything. We're up for whatever would pay us a few bucks." Cole hated spilling his guts to this old man but their backs were against the wall.

"Right now I don't know of anything." A thought came to him but it warranted a little more consideration on his part.

"Come back about this time tomorrow and I'll see if we can work something out."

"Mr. Nash we sure would be grateful for any help you could give us. We'll be here tomorrow." They departed leaving Mr. Nash to his own thoughts.

Walking out of the mercantile, Cole thought he had a pretty good read on Mr. Nash. He had known the man for years and today he appeared different somehow. He couldn't put his finger on it but he knew something was upsetting the normally collected man.

"So how do you think that really went Cole?" Flint had not said a word in the exchange as instructed by his brother.

"I'm not sure about all this yet. But, there's got to be some reason that he has called in all his markers. My guess is the old boy is in some kind of trouble."

"Why? Because he called in all the markers?" Flint was a little surprised.

"Yeah. Why do you think he did it so suddenly? Money problems my brother. Maybe that young wife of his is just a little more than he can handle." It was the only thing that made sense to Cole.

"Let's get us cold ale and think on it later. Tomorrow will come soon enough."

"Sounds good to me." Cole knew he would think on it before tomorrow.


At The Foggy Inn they found the place was busy with the usual early lunch crowd. Already seated inside was Joaquin who motioned them over to join him. They made their way across the room and sat down at his table. Joaquin was celebrating the good news from home.

"What will you men have?" Rue had approached them with her usual smile.

"Two mugs of ale and some bread and cheese." Flint placed the order. Rue left the table to fill their order.

"What have you been up to? It's early to see you in the tavern." Cole looked at Joaquin hoping that maybe he had some news they could benefit from.

"I got a letter from home. My sister is getting married, so I'm celebrating her good luck." He lied. He didn't want them to know too much about him.

"Well, congratulations." Cole said. So much for any good news they could use.

"What about you two? Anything going on?" Joaquin asked.

"We've been talking to Mr. Nash. He might have some work for us tomorrow." Flint answered but received a sharp look from Cole. The look did not escape Joaquin.

"Mr. Nash? Now what could you boys do for someone important like him?" Joaquin enjoyed giving Cole a bit of a sting. It didn't happen often.

"We have assets but not enough cash. He's thinking about buying the Priscilla with the understanding we could buy her back later. He told us he needed time to think a few things through, so tomorrow we'll see him and see what he can propose to us." Cole also lied for the same reasons Joaquin did. Rue brought their order to the table and left quickly. The place was starting to get busy.

"Well, I hope it works out for everyone." Joaquin halfway grinned at his friends.

"Yeah." Flint reached out to get a piece of hot bread and Cole started to slice the cheese into three sections.

"Please, help yourself to some bread and cheese." Cole made the nice offer.

The three men enjoyed pleasant conversation and when it was time to go, each went happily to their destinations. The feeling of contentment was short lived for Flint.

"What in the hell were you thinking spouting off about our dealings with Nash to Joaquin?" He was visibly angry.

"Cole, I'm not the one that told him everything. You mentioned the boat and seeing him in the morning. Not me." Flint was defending himself from the attack.

"I wouldn't have had to cover for us if you would have kept your mouth shut."

"I don't think it's such a big deal. It was just talk and what does he care? It's our boat on the block not his." Flint didn't understand his brothers reaction to what transpired earlier. They had reached the boat and were getting on board but the conversation continued to be harsh between them.

"Well, it's too late now, and there is a chance that he won't mention it again. You better hope so little brother. I don't want him or anyone else in our business. Get it?"

"Yeah, I get it. I'm going to bed and hope your mood is better in the morning." With that last statement, Flint went below and got into his bunk.

Cole stayed awake a while longer. He listened to the waves lapping against the boat and on the beach. He was thinking about the day's events. He scanned his memory for any hint of what Mr. Nash was really up to. He didn't fail to notice something come over the man's face when he mentioned they should come back in the morning. It was an odd look for only the briefest of moments. If his eyes hadn't been so keen in reading faces, he might have missed it. He also hoped that Joaquin wouldn't be coming around asking how things went. He meant it when he told Flint to keep their business private. He was however, thinking that Joaquin was no one he really wanted to mess with. He would be careful and keep an eye peeled on that clever Spaniard.

When Rudolph Nash entered his home later that same evening, he decided he would speak with Elsa. He would tell her of the financial difficulties and together they would think of what to do. She was recovered now and although she had not permitted him in her bed, she went about the duties of running the house with expert efficiency.

"Where is Mrs. Nash?" He made the inquiry of her maid who came to greet him.

"Sir, she is in the sitting room. Do you require anything?" She asked politely.

"No. Thank you." He handed the maid his hat and umbrella and made his way to the sitting room. When he entered, she didn't move to greet him.

"Hello Rudolph. You're home at an odd hour. Did you stop and get something to eat?" She looked up at him only briefly and returned her eyes to the needlepoint she was working on.

"No, I didn't eat. I was at the office looking over the accounts." He looked at her and wished they did not have to have this discussion.

"You work too hard. We should consider a vacation, maybe go to Boston."

"Well, that would be nice. Like I was saying, I was going over the books and I think we have to change a few things." His voice was strained but she didn't notice.

"What things?" She continued working on her pattern.

"I think we could get by just fine without your maid. I'm here. I could be of some assistance to you. It would also give us more privacy; there seems to always be so many people in this house." He hoped she could be reasoned with. The shocked look on her face told him otherwise.

"No. I need her. There are things a woman might need help with from only another woman. You can't begin to understand what I mean." She looked at him with pleading eyes and almost looked frightened at the thought of losing her maid.

"Alright, I see your point. Let's take a look at the housekeeper or perhaps the cook. The house doesn't get very untidy with just the two of us and...."

"Rudolph! How can you even think it? Can you see me washing loads of nasty laundry and trying to hang heavy clothes outside on the line to dry? My hands and nails would be ruined in a week. Then there's the sweeping, mopping, and dusting everything. In no time at all my hair would be full of dust and lose its luster. I'd look old before my time." She was standing up now facing him. She forgot about the needlepoint that was now in a small heap at her feet.

"What about the cook?" Rudolph was prepared to give her a small severance and an excellent reference. He would give her a two week notice and then let her go.

"I don't know how to cook. She does all the shopping, ordering and preparing of food. She goes out in all kinds of weather. She's a big woman. You've seen her, I'm very dainty. I'm more susceptible to fatigue and deep chills. I could catch my death of cold." Elsa was visibly upset and was pacing up and down. Her face was slightly flushed and when she looked at him, she looked like a frightened child.

"Calm yourself Elsa. I'll think of something else." He went to her and stroked her face and hair. She allowed it because she did not want to upset him and risk losing her comfort ability in her own home. She did not allow him to touch her for long and eased away from him.

"Maybe you could cut down on your brandy, not purchase the two business suits you ordered and eliminate eating out with the businessmen in town. We don't really need the butler. He does things for you that maybe you could do for yourself. We could write a letter of reference for him. That will help out right?" She smiled at him as if she had made a truly commendable suggestion.

"Perhaps. Let me continue to think on the situation." He saw her truly selfish nature for the first time and realized he was a fool.

That night Rudolph sat in the same room that he and Elsa had been in earlier. He looked back on the short time they had been married and realized that there were few really happy times. The marriage had not been what he hoped and he blamed it on the large difference in their ages. On the day he and Elsa were properly introduced by a mutual friend, he was taken aback by her beauty and grace. At the time, he gave little or no thought to why such a young and pretty woman would not already have been spoken for by some young man from a prominent family. As the months went by, he learned that the Wellington's were a family shrouded in a questionable past. It was common knowledge that the family acquired the wealth they possessed by unscrupulous means. Andrew Wellington had been the Governor of Panama when it was discovered he was collaborating with pirates and granting safe harbor in exchange for precious jewels and valuable goods. It was a foregone conclusion that he acquired property dishonestly and placed his own family members in powerful positions despite the protests of the people. Now, decades later, that practice had terminated but the scandal remained fresh. As a result, rich and respected families did not wish to be connected to the Wellington Family by marriage. It was this situation that made the elderly Rudolph Nash acceptable to the Wellingtons. He hoped for a good match for his daughter and Mr. Nash was a good choice. He had never been married, was a respected businessman and most importantly, he lived on the opposite coast. Elsa Wellington Nash could live a life of complete respectability. After only seven months of courtship he was granted his request for Elsa's hand in marriage. After a short but nice honeymoon, the couple returned to Mr. Nash's coastal home. It did not take long to uncover her true nature. He did love her even when she acted like a child and her extravagance caused him grief. Looking back now, he remembered his brother telling him not to marry her but to consider a widow they both knew. The widow was a little younger than he was and had a grown son. She was not nearly as attractive as Elsa. The widow had a substantial income and also possessed a sweet personality. He should have considered his brothers words but his vanity would not allow him to marry a woman that had already been touched. Elsa had been a pure woman but sadly now proved to be a less than willing partner in her marital obligations. She often refused him the pleasures of her young body and he could now add being denied the ability to speak with her of important matters. He turned his thoughts to tomorrow morning when the Ralston brothers would be coming to see him. What he was going to purpose might work. It depended upon what they were willing to do and for how much. He stayed up very late into the night and when he went to work the next morning, he felt more tired and older than his years.

In the galley of the Priscilla, Flint was making a good breakfast of bacon, eggs and potatoes. Cole had gotten up a little later than normal, but was now dressed and approaching the galley. He noticed the coffee was ready.

"Sure smells good in here." He noticed that Flint did not have a cup poured so he reached up for two cups. Cole poured the hot coffee and handed one cup to his brother. He took a careful sip and enjoyed the good flavor.

"I sure hope that Nash comes through for us today." Cole looked at his brother who was just about ready to serve up the meal. He sat down and waited.

"Yeah." Flint put the plates on the table and sat down to eat. He was to quiet to be the Flint that Cole knew and loved.

"Thanks, this looks good." He moved his plate closer to him and took a bite of food. "Flint, you Ok?"

"Yeah, I'm fine." He speared his eggs and stuffed some in his mouth.

"Well, you don't act fine. What's going on?"

I'm just practicing keeping my mouth shut for when we get to Nash's place." He said it with uncustomary anger.

"Oh, I see." Cole almost wanted to laugh at him. He had already forgotten the rift between them last night. He would make up to his brother because Flint needed to hear the words.

"Well, there's no need to practice. Maybe I just let Joaquin get under my skin too much. It wasn't that big a deal. You were right. We both have a lot on our mind. Are we alright?" He placed his hand on his shoulder and gave it a few pats. He let it drop and was hoping that would be enough.

"Yeah, we're always alright. Let's eat before the eggs get cold." He started to eat again.

"Cole?"

"What?"

"I'm still going to practice keeping my mouth shut." He started to laugh and Cole joined him.

Rudolph Nash was waiting for the Ralston brothers to arrive. It was already eleven o'clock and he hoped they would arrive before he lost his nerve. Never in his life had he done or contemplated anything like this. His thoughts were interrupted by the appearance of the two men at the door. He went downstairs and when he opened the door to let them in, he turned around and locked the door behind them. He placed a sign on the door indicating he was at lunch.

"Good afternoon Mr. Nash. I hope we aren't too early." Cole looked at him for a favorable response.

"No. We have a lot to discuss, so the sooner, the better. I've got a small table set up where we can talk undisturbed." He led the way and soon all three were seated. The Ralston's waited for him to begin as he had called them there.

"I know that you boys have had some difficulties and I can certainly appreciate that." He cleared his throat. "But, perhaps there is something we can do for each other."

"What might that be?" Cole could sense he was a bit uncomfortable and he began to feel a little apprehension himself.

"I hope that I'm not misjudging you in saying that I believe you to be men of certain accomplishments and are discreet in your business dealings."

"You have not misjudged us. Our past employers have felt comfortable with our assignments and ultimate results." This was not a lie, but he would not elaborate further.

"Good, that's what I hoped to hear. I have a certain situation that I would like to see resolved with efficiency and professional discretion of course." He looked at the two men for any unfavorable reaction. He saw none.

"Professional discretion is what we do best, for the right consideration of course. It goes unsaid that we are always very efficient."

"Yes, of course; the consideration. I would not be assuming incorrectly if that consideration included the dismissal of your debts and perhaps a little left over for any additional expenses or pleasures you desire." The conversation was proceeding the way he had hoped.

"When would this situation need to be resolved?" Flint was glad that Cole had a good understanding of the conversation. He did not. It was all he could do to hold his tongue.

"In two days there will be no moon. Under the protection of the night, you would be less likely to be disturbed."

"That's true. The night has been known to be a friend to many a man. But, in the light of day he might realize he has not yet been shown appreciation." Cole needed to know how this man planned to pay him for whatever it was he wanted.

"Two gentlemen could have a personal transaction at a prearranged location."

"Am I to suppose that would be after completion of the task? Is it possible to be informed for what purpose our services are being requested?" This was it, the reason for all this polite chatter. Cole just wanted to know so he could get home and get on with the planning of whatever it was.

"Of course. I find myself being burdened by the labor intensive requirements of this place." He waved his arms about and pointed to the inside of the mercantile.

"I would be very grateful and most appreciative if I could somehow become unburdened of it." Thank goodness he had said it. The tension in his body was almost audible.

"There are many opinions on how best to relieve the burdens placed on a person. Some may suggest a long vacation, but one can never discount the acts of God, or even a terrible accident. The results are always the same, complete loss." He nodded in the negative so as to show empathy and understanding.

"Complete loss. It has a final sound to it, does it not?" He looked at them with a very satisfied look on his face.

"Indeed. But out of the ashes one could rebuild a new life. At least that's what I've always been told. I've always appreciated that expression."

"Indeed." Mr. Nash's voice had a tone of finality and he stood up from his chair. "Well, I believe we are concluded. I am confident that the necessary arrangements will be completely taking care of and compensation for the task will be forthcoming once done."

"Yes sir, everything is acceptable." Flint and Cole stood up and when Mr. Nash began to walk to the door, they followed.

"Good day to you both." Mr. Nash opened the door, stepped away allowing Cole to exit and Flint to take the doorknob and pull the door closed behind them.

Walking home Flint was not exactly sure what went on. He decided to ask.

"Cole, what was all that about? I didn't really understand too much of what he was saying, let alone what he wants us to do."

"Wait until we get to the boat. I don't want to risk being overheard." Cole could not believe their good luck.

On the Priscilla, they went into the cabin area and closed the door. When they were alone and seated at the table, Cole started to inform his brother of what transpired.

"So, what did he really say?" Flint was focused on Cole.

"Well, he says he wants to pay us pretty good for doing something he needs done. I'm a little bit surprised actually. Imagine, a man like him having us do that."

"You didn't say anything I can get. Do what?" Flint needed more clarity.

"Well, it's like this. Old man Nash is in fact in some sort of bad financial situation. Exactly what, I don't know but wants us to help him out of it." Cole was thinking over the conversation.

"And you said we would do it?"

"Yeah."

"It involves the mercantile right?"

"That's right."

"What about the mercantile? Just tell me, you're sounding like he was."

"Sorry, didn't mean to. What we are going to do is get paid enough money to settle up with the bank, eliminate what we owe Nash, and have a little left over for us. We have to do something at the mercantile that would result in a complete and total loss of the building and its contents." Cole was looking at his brother for his reaction.

"That's something alright. What will we do? Do you know yet?"

"Yeah, I've got a pretty good idea. Let me think on it a bit more and I'll let you know as soon as I've got it figured out. Not a word about this, Flint. I mean it."

"I know. I'll get busy on deck so you can think. Call if you need me."

Karin was looking at her husband with adoring eyes. She was so proud of him for all the effort he put into things he thought would be of benefit to them. His efforts were beginning to pay off. As they looked at all the items on the table, there were still some things that eluded Erik. One of them was the poem and what it might mean. He had a pretty good idea of what the circles were about.

"Karin, look at the poem again. Other than the obvious way it rhymes can you think of anything else about it?" Erik handed the piece of paper to her.

"I've already looked at it several times and I can only think that the captain wrote like a man in love that's for sure."

"Yes, he did. Let's look at it again one line at a time shall we?" Erik placed the poem at an angle so they could both see the words. She got another piece of paper so that they would be able to write down their thoughts as they tried to decipher the poem.

*For most of my life, I've sailed the great sea*

"For most of my life. To me, it would mean most of his adult life or a time when he was responsible for himself. Do you think that would be right?" Erik asked the question but didn't really think she could offer any different opinion.

"I agree. Let me write that thought down."

"I've sailed the great sea. I think he's talking about the Pacific Ocean. It's the greatest sea of all."

"A man who sailed the Pacific Ocean." Karin said this confident that she was right.

"Yes, I'd say that's correct. Let's go to the next line."

*As your husband, I'd happily share my life with thee*

"As your husband. Grandmother told me that this Captain Erik wanted to marry her but she wasn't that strong to just up and leave with him."

"I would have gone with you anywhere if you asked me." Karin looked at Erik and he knew without a doubt it was true.

"I'm a lucky man to have you." He smiled at her.

"I'm lucky too. Now, let's get back to the poem." They looked at the next line.

*I'd happily share my life with thee*

"I can tell you what that means. He was going to give her half of everything he owned or would own. Things like land, property, money and servants. He wanted to take care of her." Karin was certain she was right. Most men who loved their woman would do such a thing. When a man didn't care, he didn't provide well for her in the time he was alive much less in death.

"I think you're correct. Write down that he was willing to share all his worldly goods with her whatever they might be."

"Alright, I did. Do we go on or shall I fix us something to eat?"

"No, Karin lets finish this. We'll eat later."

"But you said that James and Daniel were going to come over later."

"They are, but we have time. Let's get back to the poem." Erik just wanted to continue. He was curious and wanted to finally put all the pieces together.

"Alright. What does the next line say?" Karin began to refocus on the task at hand.

*Few things I need more than precious stars at night*

For just a few moments, they didn't say anything. It was Karin that spoke first. "It's a pretty line. It says he needs few things. Other than her, what few things would he need? You're a man Erik, think."

"I'm thinking about the few things part. Let's see, he's a young man, on the Pacific Ocean with the woman he loves. Would you say that's what we have so far?"

"Yes. He says there are only a few things I need more. What does a man need more of? Oh, never mind that's a dumb statement for a sailor with a woman at every port." She was thinking of personal gratification.

"No, it's not dumb. For some sailors it's true. But I don't think he would write that to a lady like my grandmother. Let me think. A man or anyone for that matter has to have things like food, water, shelter. But the last half makes no reference to those things. He wrote of something he needs more than precious stars at night."

"I wonder if after he gets those things, he starts living his life and going where he pleases. Just like most people do." Karin saw nothing special in that line of poetry.

"Karin! That's it. You just said it. There's not a doubt he needs food, water and shelter. Now all he needs to know is where he's going. Without knowing where you are on that sea—you are lost. Let's look at the last part of that sentence." Erik was feeling a sense of excitement at the thought of breaking the real message in the poem.

"The stars are showing him the way. That's got to be it. He's navigating by the stars."

"Would the stars be that valuable and precious to him?" Karin really had no idea.

"Oh honey, to a sailing man who didn't have the equipment we have today, they would save his life."

"Oh, you are so smart. I was thinking that the stars were something valuable, not knowledgeable."

"Knowledge is valuable. But, let's take a slower look. He did say precious didn't he? Why would he have used that word? Why not say something like important, or necessary. What does the word mean to you?"

"You said a lot of words, which one?"

"Precious." Erik was trying to think of something else it could mean.

"Precious. Let me think. To me it means something beautiful, wonderful, rare and valuable or ...."

"Valuable. You said that twice. Maybe that's how I need to think. What's more valuable than the stars?"

"God is. He is in Heaven with the stars." Karin thought about the fact that he gave Mrs. Webb the Bible.

"That's true. God is above all things. But, keep in mind that he was a pirate of sorts and they usually didn't have too much religion in their lives. Let's turn it away from religion. Let's stick with earthly value and not heavenly value."

"Alright. Then let's look at the stars part again. What do stars do? They shine, they are small, they are too many to count, they sparkle, what else do they do? I don't know. Erik! They sparkle. It's like in the children's poem; something about shine and sparkle like little diamonds in the sky. Diamonds are precious stones are they not?"

"They are indeed. That's got to be it. Alright, write this down. Captain Erik navigated the Pacific Ocean by the stars which resemble precious diamonds."

"Erik, he was writing about a treasure wasn't he?" The excitement in Karin's voice was apparent and she allowed herself to get excited.

"Yeah, I think that's exactly what he's talking about. But, let's take a breath and continue with the rest of it."

About the time that they agreed to slow down their thoughts, Salty jumped up on the table and scattered all the papers to the floor.

"Salty, get off the table!" Erik was instantly angry with him but when he lifted his tail and rubbed against his shirt and began to meow, his feelings of anger left him. Salty gently kneaded him with his front paws in an effort let them know he was overdue a meal. Erik caught the hint and scratching his ears began to soothe the hungriest member of the family.

"Karin, I guess you better get a little milk and bread prepared. There's a little fish in the bag I brought home earlier. Add that to his meal. He's a good watch cat."

"I will fix you something my little kitty come here and let Erik gather up our things from the floor." Karin reached for the kitten and placed him on the floor. "You must not do things like that again. It's not polite." After she finished mixing up his meal, she placed it on the floor and he thanked her by eating it with great gusto. She was getting very attached to that kitten.

"Have you collected everything again? I'm sorry Erik. I'm trying to teach him not to jump on the table. He's doing much better really."

"It's alright. He's just reminding us that he's important and is taking care of his business. I'd like us to get back to ours if you aren't too tired."

"No, I'm not tried. But I'm going to fix us something to eat. You keep working and talking to me, I'll make us a sandwich. Do you want milk or some apple cider?"

"That's a good idea, thank you. I'd like a glass of milk with mine. And, a couple of the oatmeal cookies you made yesterday, you make the best ones I've ever eaten." He smiled at her.

"You just love me. Now, let's go on. Get back to reading something to me." She started to make the sandwiches.

"Let's see, we were talking about the stars like diamonds. I think you are right. He means that the stars are diamonds, not just like them." Erik was certain he was on the right line of thinking.

"So, if the stars are really diamonds that would make them something that the Captain would share. Right?"

"That's right. So, not only would he navigate by them, he may have also had something, maybe diamonds to share with my grandmother."

"What does the next line say?" She finished pouring out their beverages.

*One is the cascade of your hair so golden and bright*

"That to me is easier than the first three lines. It's talking about gold and diamonds, don't you think? It has to be. He was also talking about the color of my grandmother's hair, but it was just a way to say gold, without saying it outright. Now, let's think about the cascade part." Erik was handed his milk and he took a drink.

"I never thought about your grandmother having blond hair. When he wrote, one is the cascade of your hair. What is a cascade? I don't know the word." Karin hated the fact that she did not have a more expansive vocabulary in English. She was still learning.

"It can mean a lot of things. A cascade is something that falls or hangs down. Like a cascade of soft curls in a hair style, or like a waterfall. I'm sure there are more meanings but I can't think of any more right now."

"A cascade. Is there anything like that around here?" She asked.

"Not that I'm aware of. But, let me think. Let me get the nautical maps. I'm going to check something out." He went to retrieve his maps and she finished making the sandwiches.

When he returned, his thoughts went into another direction. He looked at the maps, remembering the coordinates he had already figured out. The coordinates took him further up the coast heading north.

"The sandwiches are ready. Come eat." Sitting down she waited for Erik.

"Thank you." He took a bite out of his sandwich but kept studying the maps.

"I think I know what he was saying!" Erik was excited. "It's the name of the mountains."

"The mountains, what mountains are you talking about?"

"The ones up north from here, that's what people call them. By the saints, I've figured it out. Listen to this. In a nutshell the good captain took some kind of treasure into the northern country, somewhere in or by the Cascade Mountains. The treasure was gold, diamonds, jewels or whatever else. He used the stars to get there, and marked where he put it in the Bible he gave grandmother. He circled her name because he wanted to share it with her. It was going to be their future. The numbers circled on certain verses are the longitude and latitude of its location. The rest of the poem has to be figured out when you actually get to the general location. The rest of the poem contains the exact location and you need to physically see where or what he was talking about. I know it can be figured out. I can almost feel those gold pieces of eight."

"Then am I to understand that the point of the circle on each of the verses was to identify longitude and latitude?" She had wondered for so long about that.

"Yes. In fact I'm so sure, that I'm going to set sail to go get it."

"Oh my goodness, I can hardly believe it. When will you go? How will you go and will I go with you?" She did not like the idea of going alone with him. She was not an accomplished sailor and the two of them alone would be a great mistake.

"I'd like to go as soon as possible, maybe even tomorrow morning. Tonight I'll speak with James and Daniel. I'll tell them enough to agree to the trip and later I'll tell them the real reason. We can share our good fortune with them if there is any to be shared. I've already purchased the required supplies. I know they keep the Sea Star ready for sudden trips. I would want you to stay home."

"Erik, what about your job, and when will you be back?"

"I'll give notice that I need two weeks off. I'll tell them it's personal and they will have no problem giving me time off. I don't think I'll need the entire two weeks, but I want plenty of time to get this right."

"What happens if James and Daniel can't go with you after they know about the treasure?" She was concerned as treasure did a lot of strange things to people.

"I'm filling them in on the trip in general. They have no details and because they are my best friends they won't ask a lot of questions, they just trust me. I would do the same for them. Don't worry, all will be well." Erik got up from his chair, and held his arms out to her. She left her chair to hug him.

"Let's get this all picked up and put it somewhere safe. We've got to be careful about this. If anyone should find out, we could be in danger." Erik didn't want to frighten her, but needed her to be aware of what they faced.

"What kind of danger?" She looked suddenly concerned.

"I don't know exactly. But I do know for a fact that there was and still is a lot of talk about my grandmother and her past. I was made aware of it when I heard some of the men talking about her the other day. There are still some who think she had some knowledge of the Rip Tide and quite possibly the very treasure you and I are talking about right now. But, let's not think the worst of things. No one knows that we have this information." He kissed her lightly on the mouth and was interrupted by a knocking on the door.

It was James and Daniel as expected.

"Good evening. How are you two doing?" James was always cheerful and his smile was contagious. Karin liked him the most of all her husband's friends.

"Good evening. Please, come in and be seated. Can I have your coats?" She stretched out her arms to accommodate their hats and coats.

"Thank you so much." Daniel was the quiet one of the bunch. He was quick to laugh and enjoyed being in the company of the other two men. He just didn't say much.

"I have to admit, you have my curiosity up. I've been thinking all day about tonight." James knew that if his friend asked him to come to his home so they could discuss something in private, it was probably very important. He had visited before several times but never invited to come over to discuss something in private because it was very important.

"I know that I sounded a bit mysterious, but some of what I tell you is based upon years of friendship and trust." Erik knew that his friends would understand once they knew more about what was going on.

"I guess the best place to begin is, as they say, from the beginning." He looked at both his friends and began.

"You both know that my grandmother died a short time ago. Well, before she died, she told me about something that I needed to figure out. She made me promise to try and I promised her I would. I believe that I figured out enough to justify a trip to try and bring it to a good conclusion. I've already prepared some things for the trip. I've purchased goods from the mercantile, arranged for a replacement for my job and most importantly I have Karin's blessing to pursue this request from my grandmother." Erik looked at them for some reaction. He saw positive indications on their faces.

"So where do we fit in?" James spoke up.

"You guys are my best friends and I can't think of anyone I'd rather do this thing with than the two of you. We could leave when the Sea Star is ready for the trip. I think we would only be gone for about ten days at the most."

"You can count on us Erik. I'm sure I speak for both of us." Daniel nodded his head in agreement to the words spoken by James.

"The Sea Star is ready to go anytime."

"I wish I could tell you a little more about what we are going to do once we get where we are going. I'm not too sure myself, but I think it will prove a good thing for all of us."

"When do we leave?" James inquired.

"I'd like to go tomorrow on the high tide. That will give me time to inform my boss and not leave him in a pinch for a replacement worker. I know that Mr. Smith is always looking for more hours. Also, today when I purchased our goods, Mr. Nash was curious about me going out so late in the season. I told him I was hoping to catch some fish. So, he knows that we three are going. It wouldn't be a secret anyway when everyone sees us leave port. The fish story sounded good to me."

"Let's do it then." Daniel had spoken and everyone turned to look at him.

"Thank you so much for going with Erik. I won't be so worried if all of you are together." Karin looked at all the men and was glad that her husband had such loyal and good friends.

"Well, now that we have business out of the way how about a little rum?" Erik was pleased with how well everything went. He chose his friends well. As predicted, they did not ask questions as to the nature of the trip, rather they trusted him to know what he was doing. He knew he would have done the same if things had been reversed.

Karin was a gracious hostess and placed the rum container on the table along with some glasses. She then excused herself to allow them some male conversation and after about forty five minutes, she heard the door open and close. They had departed.

"You should have told me they were ready to leave. I don't want them to think I am rude." She frowned at him.

"Honey, they know you aren't rude and they told me to say good night for them. Come on let's go to bed. I have to get up early as we are going to depart on the morning tide."

"I'll miss you so much when you are gone. It's not for such a long time and I do have another man to look out for me. Salty is getting to be such a big boy now." Karin looked over at Salty asleep in her chair.

"I'll miss you too. Come here and let me show you just how much I love you." He reached out to her but she pretended to be shocked and alarmed at his behavior.

"Erik, please not in front of the child." She pointed to the sleeping kitten.

"He won't mind, besides, we've already had our father to son talk and he's looking forward to getting his own girl." He kissed her sweetly.

"Erik....did you lock the front door and blow out all the lamps?"

"Yes."

"Good. Let's go to bed."

# Fire and Water

$K$arin decided she would say good bye to Erik from the dock. All preparations were now complete and with a final hug and kiss, Erik departed. She stood waving and smiling as they started to pull away from the dock. She finished a silent prayer for their safe return when a familiar voice interrupted her thoughts. It was Mei Ling.

"Karin, do not be sad. He will return soon." Her presence was much appreciated and her timing was excellent. She gave her friend a gentle pat on the shoulder. "Think of when he returns."

"Oh, Mei Ling, I'm so glad to see you. Your timing is excellent."

"I don't know, timing. What does that mean?"

"It means that you came along when I needed you. It's just an expression."

"Good. I am glad I could be of help to you."

On the ship, the men had seen the exchange between the two friends. Erik was pleased Karin had a friend to spend some time with. For so long she had been lonely and to this day, she was still not accepted by the women in town. He could not believe how small minded some people were.

"Come on, let's go to the mercantile. I want to buy a peppermint stick," Karin said. Mei Ling smiled at the fact that her friend had such a sweet tooth.

"Perhaps later, if you do not have too much to do could I have a reading lesson? I would really like that." Mei Ling was doing well with her lessons. She was a very determined and dedicated student.

"Yes, we can do that. I'm sure I won't have too much to do." They watched the Sea Star until it was almost out of sight and then went to the mercantile for Karin's candy.

The women managed to spend most of the day together and by mid afternoon Mei Ling made her way home. She had responsibilities to her family and was promised to a young man that she would soon meet. She was eighteen years old and considered the perfect age to marry. She remembered her parents with love and felt so badly that the trip to the United States had proven too much for them. The ship they bought passage on was over crowded, of poor quality and had little or no conveniences. It was not very long before serious illness claimed many lives; among the dead were her parents. She was only five years old at the time. On the ship she had no one to care for her. She would have died if not for a man who was traveling alone and took notice of her. He did not care for her out of the kindness of his heart. He had thought to sell her to a house of prostitution for a tidy sum. As expected when they arrived on the West Coast, he did as he planned. He sold her to an exclusive brothel. Her early years were hard as she was made to earn her keep by doing the cleaning and cooking duties. The woman did not want to sell her to a wealthy client until the child was more developed and would fetch a more commanding price. This way of life continued for young Mei Ling until one day she was seen by an older gentleman. He made inquiries and learned her name and circumstances. It was only this fortunate turn of fate that allowed her maternal grandfather to rescue her from the house. Now, as the years passed, she learned proper skills and had the protection of her grandfather. She was not allowed many liberties, but she always found a way to spend time with Karin. She knew he would not be pleased if he learned exactly how much time she spent with the only woman in town she considered a friend.

Across town, Cole and Flint were in the final stages of planning what they would do to the mercantile.

"Cole, are you sure we can do this without any one seeing us?"

"Well nothing is one hundred percent certain, except for the fact that we are going to die one day. But, all things considered, I can pretty much guarantee that we will do just fine. In a few hours, the building will be completely engulfed in flames."

"What are we going to use to start it up with?"

"Nash has two full barrels of whale oil in the storage room. We'll bust them open with an ax and let the oil run all over the place. Just remember, we have to be careful not to get any on us." Cole was looking at his brother.

"I know you said it might irritate our skin."

"That would be the least of it. If anyone smells the oil on us we could end up with our necks stretched. After we start the fire, we need to make our way to The Foggy Inn quick."

"Why are we going there?"

"We need an alibi. I don't want anyone to suspect that we may have had anything to do with the fire or the fuel used to start it. Remember to act as surprised as everyone else when someone yells the mercantile is on fire and they sound the alarm."

"Are we going to order something to drink?" Flint wanted a mug of warm rum.

"Yeah. We're just going to be ourselves." Cole was confident he had thought of everything.

"Good. I could use a cup of rum. Let's hope Nash pays us soon. I'd like to leave this place with some money in our pocket. Maybe we could go to Mexico or San Francisco. I hear tell they have some pretty women there."

"Yeah, that's true. But, we probably have one of the prettiest women right here. You know who I mean." Cole knew his brother well.

"Rue. Yeah, I like her alright, except that she never really looks at me. Besides, she's too mysterious about everything. I always feel like she's hiding something."

"Could be. Now, let's go over this one more time. Tonight Flint, we make us some money. Let's wait for it to get dark."

The time seemed to pass slowly as the two waited for the safety of the night. As predicated, there was no moon and a light fog was beginning to develop over the bay. This was a fortunate turn of events as it helped to conceal them on their way to the mercantile. They looked around and when they were sure no one was present, they entered the building through the unlocked back door. The building was dark, but as promised, Mr. Nash had cleared an aisle for them to walk inside without stumbling into things.

"Are the ax and matches where he said?" Flint asked.

"I don't know. I'm reaching for them now." Cole felt around the base of a huge barrel of apples and wrapped up in two towels was the ax. "Yeah, I've got them."

"Alright Flint, stay behind me and let me know if you get any oil on you. Do you have my gloves?"

"Yeah, I got them."

"Let's find the barrels." Cole started to lead the way.

"I wish we could light a lantern." Flint never did like the dark.

"I know but don't do it. If we can see in the building, someone could see us from the outside. Just be careful."

"Do you still have the towels with you?"

"I do."

"Cole, what do we need the towels for?"

"When I bust open the barrel, the oil will splash out. But if I place a towel on each barrel where I hit it, the oil won't get on me. Now, stop asking stupid questions. I want to get this done."

"Alright, alright."

"I see the barrels. Now, wait for me to smash the side in. I'll hit them on the same side. Watch your feet so that you don't step into the oil. I can't tell for sure how fast it will come out. Just be ready to move quickly. Now, keep an eye out for anyone. Head toward the door and be ready. Do you understand? Got any questions?" Cole knew it was now or never.

"I got it. I'm just waiting on you." Flint didn't want to admit it, but his stomach felt a bit tight and he was little nervous.

"Give me my gloves. I need them in case some oil splashes out through the towel. Remind me to leave my gloves here. Are you ready?"

"I'm ready."

Cole put himself into position. He placed the towel over the chosen spot and placing the ax on top of the towel he gave the first barrel a solid hit. It split wide open, spilling oil onto the towel and his gloves. He quickly moved over to the other barrel and did the same thing once more.

"Move!"

Flint quickly did as ordered and now waited outside by the back door. In only a second or two Cole was at his side.

"Did you take off your gloves?"

"I took them off before I lit the match. They'll burn up sure enough." Cole was feeling satisfied with the way things had gone. It was much easier than he thought.

"Did you see anyone?" Cole was looking around to see if there was anyone nearby. He didn't see a soul.

"No."

"Good. Let's walk away like normal and get something to eat at The Foggy Inn."

As they started to walk, Flint noticed that the building was not engulfed in flames like he thought it would be. Looking back to the building, he decided he would ask why.

"You sure that match did the job? Why isn't the building burning?"

"It is. I started it in the center of the building. Let's hurry to The Foggy Inn. I want us to be in place by the time the fire is discovered."

In a small rented room Joaquin was writing a letter home. He was sitting by an open window to allow a breeze to enter. He began his letter by thanking his sister for helping him purchase the vineyard, of his plans for the house, and how much he missed family and friends. He made sure to enclose a bit of money to make the necessary repairs to the home that was on the property. He did not want to burden her with financial difficulty since the place was really his. The letter was closed with a promise to write again soon. In the morning it would depart with the other correspondence that was mailed out on a weekly basis. The view from the window was enticing as the lighthouse was clearly visible despite the fog that had moved into the harbor. Turning down the lamp enhanced the view and made it more pleasant to contemplate the next steps necessary to reach the ultimate goal. Finances were tight especially since having to pay Mr. Nash in full. It was now evident that working in Valda Bay was no longer a choice. He had to stay and make up the money he was sending to his sister. Turning the small vineyard into a small but very choice winery would take careful planning. The sale of some of the grapes would be good income, but the wines would be where the real money was to be made. Working on ships allowed him to be familiar with various taverns around the world and he'd often engaged in conversations with the sailors. He knew what they liked to drink and what they wished they could afford to drink. He observed carefully the handling and processing of cargo and what it took to ensure the safe and profitable movement of freight. With a renewed sense of confidence he knew it would be more than possible to have his wines go around the known world. That would indeed make him wealthy and socially acceptable. Once he had gained wealth, Senorita Deleon could become his wife. He was pleased with his future plans concerning the winery. He needed to make more money and was thinking and writing down some notes. Feeling mentally exhausted he decided to depart for The Foggy Inn when he saw two figures crossing the street. He turned the lamp completely down and opened the window a little wider. As the figures approached he recognized them as Cole and Flint Ralston. He looked about a little more and concluded that they were coming from the direction of the mercantile. He thought he saw a small glow inside the store, but could not be certain because of the fog. He continued to watch and saw that they went into The Foggy Inn. It was at that point that he would go make conversation with them. He would also inquire if Mr. Nash had provided any work for them as discussed earlier.

By the time Joaquin reached The Foggy Inn, Cole and Flint were already enjoying a mug of ale. The place was busy and he made it a point to seek them out without being obvious. When he saw them, he acknowledged them with a nod of his head. As hoped for, they motioned for him to join them.

"How's it going?" Joaquin greeted them cheerfully.

"Not too bad. Have a seat, have you eaten yet? Flint and I ordered some bread and stew. Rue said it was the house special today and pretty good." Cole was looking around for the waitress.

"No, I haven't. But, it sounds like a good idea. I'll order some when yours gets here. I heard that the Sea Star headed out today." Joaquin realized that he really was hungry.

"Yeah, I was working on the boat when I saw her leave. I think that Johansson was with them." Flint thought that whole thing odd.

"Johansson? I wonder what a lighthouse keeper is doing on a fishing boat?" Cole was more thinking out loud than really asking the question.

"It's pretty late in the season to be going out for fish but they might get lucky. Remember a couple of years ago, that late season haul? Wish I had cashed in on that one." Joaquin's conversation was cut short by the arrival of the stew and bread.

"Here you are. Two orders of stew with hot bread. Will you have anything else?" The tavern girl was pleasant and that made up for her plain looks.

"That looks good. I'd like an order and some ale." The girl departed promising to return quickly.

"So, tell me about your Nash meeting." Joaquin tried to sound casual without appearing to inquisitive. "Did he come through for you or not?"

"Well, we went to see him, he had work for us but he didn't want to pay what it was worth. Could be that young wife he has is keeping him happy but broke. She's a looker so I guess I can't blame him." Cole cut off a big piece of bread and stuck it in his stew.

"Yeah, seems to me that pretty women are always hard on a man; in every sense of the word," he said with a little laughter in his voice and was joined by the other two. He knew all too well how demanding and spoiled Elsa Nash could be. There had been a few times he did not enjoy being intimate with her because she constantly needed to be soothed or constantly reassured of something. It wore him thin. These days a little bit of Elsa went a long way.

"I wonder what a woman like that sees in a man like him anyway." Flint's statement was answered almost immediately and at the same time by the other two men.

"Money." They looked at each other and laughed.

"This stew is really good, Rue was right." Flint was already half way through the serving, when the tavern maid arrived with Joaquin's order.

"Here's your order sir. The stew and bread are nice and hot." She made an attempt to flirt with the handsome man by placing her large breasts almost into his face. He politely smiled and with his body language let her know that he was not interested in her. Normally, he would not have cared if he appeared rude displaying his disinterest at such brazen attempts to gain his favor. But she worked at the tavern and that meant she could be a friend of Rue. It was that thought that kept him from dismissing the girl in a curt way. When she departed they enjoyed a laugh at the girl's expense.

The men continued to talk and enjoy the meal, when a man in a highly excited state entered the building and gave the alarm that Cole and Flint were waiting for.

"Fire! The mercantile is burning!" With his words the entire place emptied and people began scrambling for buckets, pitchers or anything else that would hold water. The building was completely engulfed in flames and it gave off an odd looking glow in the fog. One could almost say it was beautiful, if it had not been so tragic.

"Did anyone send word to Mr. Nash?" Someone had thought of the man who now stood to lose his business.

"Leroy went running to his home. This is just terrible." One of the tavern women piped up.

Flint and Cole were among those who stood standing in pretended shock and dismay. Fire in a community was always dangerous as firefighting equipment was limited as were the men who would fight it. Valda Bay only had five firefighters and one pumping machine that needed to be worked manually. It was old and in need of replacement. The only thing that most people were grateful for was the fact that the night was foggy and still. There was not a breath of wind and everyone knew that this fact alone was responsible for the fire being contained to only the mercantile. The firemen were already hard at work. Huge clouds of thick black smoke filled the air all around the harbor. Everyone was getting covered in a fine layer of moist soot. The fog aided the ash in making a greater mess than normal.

"Here comes Mr. and Mrs. Nash." Rue was the first to see him approach as all eyes were on the burning building.

"What happened here? Is anyone hurt?" Mr. Nash to his credit was a great actor. Standing by with horror on her face, was his wife. She could not believe her eyes.

"Sir, we don't know for sure. But the firemen are doing their best. It looks like you may lose the entire building and contents." Mr. Elliot Stiles was the owner of The Foggy Inn and could certainly relate to a loss of this magnitude. He had lost a business to fire ten years ago. It had been diffi-cult to start anew.

"Look, here comes one of the firemen now. It looks like Chief Johnson, the Fire Chief." Mr. Stiles was interested in what he had to say, so he stood close to Mr. Nash.

"Sir, I don't know what to tell you about how it started, but it looks like we've lost it. I'm sorry there isn't more we can do at this point. We are going to concentrate on not letting the fire spread to the other buildings and risk the harbor. Two of my men are on the pump and two are inside the...." Chief Johnson never had the opportunity to finish his sentence. A loud thundering sound made everyone turn to the direction of the noise. The roof had collapsed and windows had been blown out. Chief Johnson ran toward the building and left Mr. Nash looking shocked at the scene before him.

In only a few moments, something more terrible than a burning build-ing would be the talk of the residents. The collapse of the roof and the fly-ing pieces of glass had seriously injured two of the firemen. The doctor who was also in the crowd ran over to the two men and ordered they be taken to the hospital as they were severely burned and cut. Some men volunteered to carry the injured men.

"Doc, am I going to die?" These were the words spoken by the young man who had only seven months earlier married a local fisherman's daughter.

"Let's not talk about that now. Let's get you taken care of."

"Wait! What happened to Mr. Wheeler?" The doctor did not want to tell him that his fellow fireman had already died of his injuries and that upon examining him he had instructed the volunteers to take the body to the morgue.

"He's being taken care of. Now, save your strength and stop talking."

"My wife, has someone sent for her?" He wanted her with him.

"She's coming." The doctor hoped she would arrive soon.

It took several hours for the large building to burn down. The thick smell of oil would assault the nostrils of everyone. A layer of soot and ash covered almost everything and several fishermen went to their boats to watch for flying embers that could have set their boats on fire.

The burned man was examined by the doctor and the news was grave. About forty five minutes later his wife was crying. She had been told by the doctor that her husband would more than likely die as a result of infection in large burns that covered about thirty percent of his body. His legs sustained most of the injury, and the left arm and shoulder was also burned. He had scorch marks on his chest and lower abdomen. There were no major organs injured so he would probably live for a few days. It would not be an easy death. The doctor could offer little more than pain medication which after very little time would not give much relief.

"Do you want me to tell him the truth?" The doctor hated this part of his job.

"No, I'll tell him." She allowed the doctor to hug her and tried to pull herself together for her husband's sake. She could not.

"Charity, I can hear you out there. Come in here. I want to talk to you." He knew that he would die and had much he wanted to talk over with her.

When she entered the room, she felt herself want to die. He looked so badly and yet was thinking of her. He wanted her to hold his hand and to just talk to him. The sound of her voice brought him comfort. After a few minutes he began to speak and gave her instructions on what he thought would be best for her to do in the future. They both cried.

Chief Johnson, the Fire Chief and Constable came to visit later that night. He knew the horror that awaited this kind man. He looked over at his exhausted wife who was seated in a chair on the other side of the room.

"Chief, thanks for coming." The man was now in obvious pain.

"Of course I'd be here. Don't we always take care of one another?"

"Yeah, we do. I'm thanking you for it too. I know that I can count on you to take care of her. You will won't you sir?" His pain was increasing with the passing of time and his breathing labored. Because of his age and overall body conditioning, both knew that he had a lot more time to live and suffer.

"I swear to you, I will." The Fire Chief looked at him with pride and respect.

"Is she sleeping?"

"I don't think so. Do you want me to get her for you?"

"No. I just wanted to make sure she was alright. She's the only thing I ever really wanted in this world."

"You're a lucky man to have her. Now, I want you to close your eyes and try and get some rest." Chief Johnson put the lamp back on the table. "I'll be here for a while."

"I'm so tired but I know I won't sleep. I'm hurting now." The fireman closed his eyes, thought of his wife and relaxed as best he could. The injured man had a slim chance of surviving unless something else could be done. Chief Johnson decided to speak with the doctor once more. He left the room and when he was sure that he would not be overheard, he spoke what was on his mind to the doctor.

"Doctor, how long does he have?"

"I can't say for sure. Perhaps a few days but I'm fairly certain not much longer than that. I've done all I can and it's almost certain that infection and loss of body fluids will kill him. Perhaps you should help her with final arrangements. It's always so difficult. Have you helped her notify his family yet?"

"No, I haven't. I need to ask you about something and I hope that you take it in the spirit in which I intend it. You're a man of medicine and that makes you one up from most people. You have an open mind and right now I need you to be wide open. Doc, I want to bring in another physician to help you."

"Another physician? Are you speaking of Doctor Hess from Boyd's Landing?"

"No, he's too far away to do us any good. I'm thinking of someone much closer."

"Who are you referring to Chief Johnson?" The doctor was curious and cautious of any new physician he did not know.

"Mr. Hong Lei Chang. He's well known in the Chinese community and some of my men have gone to him in the past for various reasons. He treats with herbs and other stuff, I don't know, but it can't hurt. What do you think?"

"I won't allow it. The man is little more than a savage, with absolutely no professional training of any kind. He will hasten the death of that man for sure."

"But, it's worth a try. I think we should pursue it. He may not even come help us but in the event he does, what have we got to lose?"

"No. I think it's a bad idea."

Standing close to the door and unaware that they had in part been overheard, stood the person with the power to ultimately decide what would or would not happen to her husband. Ian Fisk was in no condition to make decisions. His pain was becoming almost unbearable.

"Are you speaking about something else that could help my husband?"

"Please, go back to your husband. Believe me when I say that all that can or could be done has been. There's nothing here for you to be concerned about."

"Yes, there is. Doctor Grayson and I were talking about something totally untried and I'm not sure it would work." Chief Johnson wanted her to be informed and now she was standing before him.

"What is it you are thinking about doing Chief Johnson?"

"Well, I know of a doctor of sorts, his name is Mr. Hong Lei Chang. He's here in Valda Bay in the Oriental part of town. He has medical training, but it's not like ours. We've done all we can, and I was telling the doctor that maybe he could help us."

"Doctor, is this true?" Her voice had a ring of hope in it.

"I don't agree. We are better off to try what we have in the past that may work." The doctor was trying to convince her that any other medical course would prove lethal almost immediately.

"That's not enough right now Doctor Grayson. You told me that he was going to die. The way I see things, we have nothing to lose." Chief Johnson did not want to speak so bluntly in front of Mrs. Fisk but time was of the essence.

"Doctor, I have to try anything at this point that might help." She turned to the Chief and spoke making her intentions clear.

Chief Johnson, you have my permission to ask Mr. Chang if he will help my husband. Please go quickly and relay to him my complete trust." Mrs. Fisk hoped she made the right decision.

"I can't be a party to this insanity. I'll be in my office if you come to your senses." With that note, the doctor departed leaving them alone to put the plan into action.

"I'll do my best to get the other doctor here. You wait here and when Ian makes inquiries tell him what we are up to. Try to sound positive and say a little prayer for us all. I'll be back as soon as I can."

"I will. Thank you so much for your help." She touched his arm with a worried but grateful look on her face. He turned to leave.

"Wait a moment! Let me get my purse to pay for whatever items may be needed." She turned quickly to get her purse but when she looked up again to face him, he was already going down the corridor. She sighed and fresh tears formed in her eyes.

At the home of Rudolph and Elsa Nash, things were not pleasant. All morning and into the early afternoon they had been discussing the events of the past night.

"I don't understand how this could have happened." Elsa was still stunned that the fire had taken such a profitable business.

"Elsa, who knows how these things happen? They just do. Let's be grateful that we weren't hurt and that the insurance company will pay for our loss."

"But that could take days or even weeks. What will we do for money in the meantime?" She sounded like a whiney child and it was starting to get very old with him.

"All will be well. Just be patient and try not to worry. That's my job alright?"

"Well, maybe if you had done your job better this may not have happened. If we lose all our money, I don't know what I'm going to do. Oh my heavens, we won't have money for a new dress for me to wear to the Commerce Ball next month. I might as well just die."

"Stop that right now. All you think about is you. Don't you care about what others are thinking and feeling? Do you realize that a man was killed in that fire and that another is fighting for his life even as you speak of your damn dress?"

"I can't help that. I'm sure that his people are taking care of him. But who is going to take care of us? What will happen if we have to let the cook and the housekeeper go? I cannot possibly do the work they do." She was getting very upset.

"Dearest, please be calm. I have a little saved for an emergency situation. I will give you all you need. Haven't I always provided for you and made sure you were comfortable and had lots of pretty dresses?" Rudolph hoped she would be calm and let him have some peace so that he could think.

"Oh Rudolph, you are so good to me. I should have known that you would have things under control. You always take care of everything. I think I'll get my dress catalog and pick out an especially pretty one for the

Commerce Ball." She felt much better now that she was assured that all would continue as it had.

"That would be fine."

"What color would you like to see me wear this year?" She waited for his response but heard none.

"Rudolph, I'm talking to you."

"I'm sorry dearest, what did you say?"

"I asked you what color of dress you wanted me to get this year."

"Oh, I think you would look nice in just about anything." He did not lie on that account.

"Alright then. I think I'll order a light blue dress in satin. I want it to match my eyes. I'll order some ribbons for my hair in the same color." She whisked up the catalog from the desk and blew him a kiss from the door.

After she departed and left him alone with his thoughts, he felt lower than he had ever felt in his life. He never intended for anyone to be hurt much less killed. He hoped that the unpleasant business would be over soon and that the community could return to normal activity. Several people in town had expressed their shock and sadness over the unfortunate incident. He just wanted the building cleared away, the insurance money to arrive, and for the Ralston brothers to depart and never be heard from again.

# Storms of Change

*K*arin was sitting in her garden watching the ocean and the gathering clouds that were forming to the North. The weather was changing and she began to wonder about Erik once more. A storm would be blowing in soon but knew she had time before it actually came ashore. There was time to prepare the house and ensure that Salty was safe inside with her. It had only been a couple of days since he departed but it seemed so much longer than that. Her mind took her back to how they first met and all the plans they had made. She closed her eyes and breathing deeply of the salt air, let herself recall those special early days. She thought of her family.

She grew up in Norway in a small village by the coast. Her father and two brothers worked a small fishing boat that was configured to the catching and cleaning of Cod. Her mother took care of the domestic chores and the two milk cows. Every morning Karin would clean the barn, feed the cows then milk them. Some of the milk was kept as fresh cream while another portion was churned into butter. The butter and milk not used by the family was sold to a merchant who purchased it for a very modest amount of money. Finances were always a concern more so when the fishing was bad. It was this constant state of uncertainty that prompted the move to the most desirable place in the world. They decided to move to America. They began to save money and after four years of saving, they were almost ready to leave. The only thing left to sell was their home and a few pieces of furniture. Once done, they said goodbye and each one left with only Karin's mother taking one long last look back. She knew she would not return and some part of her would miss the place that she had been brought to as a young bride. She put aside her sentimental feelings and turning toward her husband, she smiled. He took her hand in his and together began walking toward a new life. They bought passage on a ship that proved sea worthy but was extremely overcrowded and dirty. Rations were limited and water for cleaning was almost nonexistent. They did have a saving grace that most of the passengers did not. Not one member of the family got sick from the rough seas. When it was permitted to be on deck, they took turns getting fresh air and walked around briskly to stretch their limbs. One of the men always accompanied the ladies to prevent unwanted attention from any of the sailors or unaccompanied men who were also seeking passage to a better life. These times on deck proved a wonderful relief from the small and smelly quarters below. When the crew provided the inferior meals that were promised to them as part of their fare, the meal was supplemented by food items the family had brought with them. Proper planning ensured they had plenty of dried fruit, hard biscuits, two blocks of hard cheese and several jars of home canned meat. In order to bring them on the ship, the men carried luggage that contained the food items, not clothes. The women carried luggage with only a few clothes and other personal effects.

On the day the ship arrived in San Francisco it was raining and cool. The docks were busy and people were moving about with organized confusion. Some of the new immigrants had relatives who met them, while others already had plans made to continue to a place that Karin remembered as Minnesota. Her family however, had no relatives to meet them and still had many days of travel to reach their final destination. Her father had planned to go to the North Country where they could work in the lumber mills, do some fishing and get a piece of land. The plan seemed perfect except for one thing. Not one of them spoke enough English to make known their intentions or to even ask for directions.

It was not long before the cold reality of the new land slapped them in the face. They were not welcome in San Francisco and soon realized that the American people did not treat those they called immigrants fairly. Work was hard to come by and lodging was almost unheard of. The money was running low and there was precious little to eat. One day a man offered Karin's brother a job as a janitor in a hospital. The janitor's position included two small rooms in the basement where the family could live. With no choice left to any of them, he accepted the job. He did the job very well but the conditions were almost unbearable. About three weeks after he began working, Karin got a job as a baker's assistant in an upper end restaurant across town. The baker was a very accomplished pastry chef and was sought out by the finer restaurants in town. She liked Karin very much and taught her some valuable techniques in baking. She also began to teach her English and in no time at all, she knew many words and what they meant. It became their custom that at the end of the workday, the head baker allowed her to take home bread that had not been eaten within two days of being baked and also the pastries. Her wages were not good, but allowed her mother to purchase fresh vegetables, coffee and some fresh fish on a pretty regular basis. For the first time since leaving Norway, there was some hope that things were getting better and that they had not made a mistake leaving their home.

The hope was short lived. Only five months later the city was in a panic. A fever rumored to have been brought in by a ship from Malaysia was killing the residents of San Francisco. The sailors had unknowingly spread the disease in every establishment they ate or slept at. The first to become ill were the dock workers, then the prostitutes, followed by tavern patrons. All who were able sought medical assistance and doctors not realizing they carried the germs on their person; facilitated the spread of the illness. It was not long before the doctors and nurses were sick. Hospitals were filled with those trying to get whatever assistance they could. Every bed was filled with the sick, the dying or the recently dead awaiting removal. In the basement, Karin was the only one that did not have fever. Her father was gravely ill and she knew he could not survive much longer. Her mother had come down with the fever only two nights after her father did. Her brothers had also died and she remembered dragging them to a cart that would take them to a public area to be burned. Later she was told they would be buried in the same large hole they had been burned in. There would be no private service or even a head stone. This was not what she had wanted for them, but an order had been given that all the dead would be disposed of in this manner. To add to her distress and horror, those who had died while at the hospital were placed in the basement awaiting burial. The hospital administrator did not care that a family was living in the basement. His only concern was for a place to keep the dead until they were claimed by family. Some bodies were not claimed at all. The stench of rotting and diseased bodies filled the entire area with an unbelievable nauseating odor. Two days later, Karin was alone in the world. She had survived but now faced a hopeless situation. She had no money, relatives or a place to live. Packing what she could carry, she left the basement and went to the only place she knew to go. She went to the restaurant and sought out the kind lady who was the baker. That kind lady had saved her life. She arranged for her to leave San Francisco and gave her references to a position in Valda Bay on the Pacific Coast. There was a gentleman of means who had a restaurant by the name of The Foggy Inn. He was in need of a baker and would pay enough for her to live comfortably if she was careful. It was here that she met and fell in love with Erik.

Sitting in her chair, Karin realized that the sun was starting to set and the evening was getting cold. She looked again at the dark clouds.

"Salty, come here. We have to go in, a storm is coming and you know how much you hate to get wet." She smiled when he appeared, tail high in the air, and when she scooped him up in her arms, he allowed her to cuddle him.

"Let me prepare the house for the storm that is coming. Then we can eat. Are you hungry? I'll get you some warm milk. I'm going to fix a sandwich and then we can read our Bible. What do you say to that?" The kitten was beginning to understand words in Norwegian and he purred loudly in response. She laughed and went inside the house.

On the Priscilla, Cole and Flint were talking about what they had done.

"Cole, we killed somebody. What are we going to do if they know it's us that set the fire?" Flint was feeling a sense of panic.

"Don't be stupid. We didn't kill anyone. If anyone is to blame, it's Nash. He wanted the building burned. It's not our fault."

"Yeah, it's Nash's fault. He didn't say someone could die. I think we need to talk to Nash about paying us more not to say he did it." Flint realized that Cole was right.

"Flint, I'll speak to Nash. The deal didn't include anyone dying. I'll let him know he owes us a little extra because of everything that happened."

"When are you going to do it?" Flint hoped he would do it soon.

"Don't worry about that now. There's too much interest right now about that fire. We don't want to be seen around Nash to soon and risk losing everything."

"Cole, you're so smart. I feel better now. Do you want to get a mug of ale?"

"Sure do. Let's go and see what's happening at The Foggy Inn. It's getting late and talk will be loose. Don't forget your jacket, a storm is coming."

Elsa Nash was in her room sitting at her desk. She was looking at the dress catalog and thinking about how nice she would look with her new dress on. As an attractive woman she felt she deserved to have nice things, and was glad that at least on one account, Rudolph had proved he was a good provider. There was little or no chance that she would be as comfortable with the man of her dreams. Joaquin would not provide her lovely clothes, or the status she craved. She closed her eyes and thought of him. He was powerful, handsome and an expert lover. It had been a long time since she had been with him and decided that she would send him a note to meet her soon. Her thoughts were interrupted by the shutters banging against the house. She looked out the window and was amazed at how hard the wind was blowing. She could hear the crashing of the waves against the rocks and could see the boats being tossed with the force of the waves. The lighthouse was clearly visible from her window. That structure always left her amazed and feeling somewhat spiritual. It was the strength of land against the sea. It was an old battle that began with the creation of the earth. For only the briefest of moments, she thought of all the sailors who would have no choice but to endure the torment of a rough sea. But, it was only for a moment, then sitting back down in her comfortable chair, she carefully selected a pattern for her new gown.

Chief Johnson had left the hospital with many things on his mind. First and foremost was the concern for his injured man followed closely by how the fire had started in the first place. As he walked to China Town, he hoped that he would be able to make Mr. Chang understand how much he needed his help. The storm was moving in quickly. By the time he reached the pharmacy door the wind was blowing with greater force and it had gotten much colder. He knocked loudly but not insistently on the door and hoped someone would answer. When the door opened a beautiful young Chinese woman appeared.

"How may I help you sir?" She politely asked.

"Miss, my name is Johnson. I've come to speak with Mr. Hong Lei Chang, is he here? It's very important."

"Please wait. I shall return in a moment." She closed the door and left him standing outside. In only a moment, she returned and motioned him inside the building.

"Sir, please come inside. I shall be with you always unless you speak Chinese."

"Thank you Miss. I don't speak Chinese and appreciate anything you can do."

She departed and left him alone. In a few minutes an older distinguished gentleman entered the room. He was accompanied by the young woman.

"Please say why you are here."

"Yes, thank you." Johnson spoke carefully deciding to speak as if the girl were not serving as translator. He thought that more respectful and looking at the man he began to speak. "I'm sure you are aware of the terrible fire that occurred yesterday."

She translated.

"He is aware but knows nothing more than that."

"I'm here because a friend of mine, a fellow fireman was seriously burned. I'm told that you have great medical skills. Will you help my friend?" The Chief hoped that he could hear the sincerity in his voice.

She translated.

"He says that you have a doctor in town. You do not need him."

"That's true. He's a fine doctor, but not every skill can be learned by just one man." He hoped that he was not insulting anyone.

The two exchanged many words before she finally spoke again.

"He wishes to know if your doctor has given you little hope for his recovery and that is why you are here." He was most perceptive.

"He does not give me much hope. But I cannot believe that there is not something more that can be done. If nothing else, perhaps he could recommend something to help him sleep or ease his pain." Honesty was always the best approach.

The young woman listened and then a faint smile came to her face.

"He likes that you tell the truth. Do you want him to come with you or will you bring the hurt man here?"

"Then he will help?" Chief Johnson hoped he was hearing correctly.

"Yes, he will help." No delay in answering.

"That's wonderful. I will have to take you to the injured man. He is in the hospital and can't be moved. His wife is with him." The relief was apparent in his voice.

The young woman spoke with the older gentleman for several minutes and then he bowed politely and left. The Chief was not certain what had happened and the look on his face must have betrayed what he was thinking.

"He will return soon. He must gather his things, please wait here for us."

"Miss, please wait a moment. May I ask your name if that's permitted?"

"It is permitted to ask. My name is Mei Ling Lee. Mr. Chang is my grandfather."

"Thank you for your help Miss Lee. Will you be going with us?"

"I will go with you and you are most welcome sir."

She smiled faintly and bowed before leaving the room. As she turned to leave, the Chief noticed for the first time, a rather large man standing in the shadows. No doubt he was some kind of protector to both the man and the young woman. He didn't understand these people's customs, but he was certain that he had not done anything improper.

In less than half an hour they were on the way to the hospital. Chief Johnson carried several small cases filled with what he presumed was medical supplies. The storm had increased in strength, and it made walking difficult. When they arrived at the hospital, they were wet and slightly chilled. Hot tea was ordered and after changing into dry clothes, Mr. Chang was taken to see the injured man. He was provided all the personal information he needed. He learned the injured man was named Ian Fisk and his wife was Charity. Everyone it seemed held their breath as the examination continued. When Mr. Chang stepped out into the hallway, his face could not be read. Mei Ling Lee approached her grandfather and the two spoke for a short while. He returned to the room and continued his examination.

"Chief, my grandfather will do things for Mr. Fisk that your medicine will think ... I can't think of the words." Mei Ling looked as if she was searching for something.

"Unusual, odd, or seemingly cruel. Is that what you mean?" He offered what he thought would help.

"Yes. But it will help and he must finish the cure. Will he be able to do this with the other doctor here?" It was a fair question and probably overdue.

"Miss Lee, I assure you that he will." The voice was that of Mrs. Fisk. "I spoke with the doctor and asked if he could not help, to please not interfere with Mr. Chang. Do what you must, I appreciate all his efforts." She would probably have said more, but her voice cracked and she could no longer speak.

After more discussion, Mr. Chang was ready to begin. It would prove most unusual to say the least.

Mr. Chang ordered fresh sheets be brought in and when they arrived, he covered Mr. Fisk and removed him to another room. He ordered that Mr. Fisk's room be scrubbed clean, the old curtains taken down, and the blankets replaced. He also requested the windows be kept ajar to allow for fresh air to enter the room. The order was given that visitors were not allowed. The only exception was Mrs. Fisk and she was asked not to touch him. Perhaps the most bizarre thing he did to the untrained eye was when he ordered a tub be brought into the room and had it filled with warm water. From his medical supplies, he added a liquid to the water. He then called to his granddaughter. After a few moments, she had much to say.

"Chief, please help bring Mr. Fisk to this room and place him in the tub. This will help with pain and stop infection. He must have no clothes. You must also cover your clothes with a clean sheet, remove your shirt and wash your arms and hands." She looked at him waiting for an answer.

"You want me to undress him and put him in that tub?" He was a bit stunned.

"Chief, you can't allow that. That's ridiculous; he's too hurt for that. The shock of it all will be too much." Mrs. Fisk was getting hysterical.

"Mrs. Fisk. Please calm yourself. We agreed that Mr. Chang would do things we didn't understand. We have to trust him now. Let's do what he says. It's Ian's only chance."

"Please, we have to hurry. My Grandfather is waiting."

"Alright, I'll do it." He hurried down to the other room and spoke with Ian who was in obvious pain.

"Ian, I've got to talk with you and we don't have a lot of time. I know that you're miserable, but you have a chance of getting better sooner if we do what Mr. Chang says. We've already talked about this once, but now I need to take you down to the other room where he instructed me to place you in a tub of warm water." The Chief was looking at him to ensure he understood what was being said. He felt that he did.

"Chief, why is he doing that?"

"To wash the burns clean, and help stop infection. I'm sure it's going to hurt a lot, but he says he has some medicine that will help and after it's done, you'll be given something to help you rest. I'll be here the whole time."

"Where is my wife?"

"She's waiting for you in your room with Mr. Chang. Are you ready to go?"

"Yes. Let's just do it."


Prior to entering Ian's room the Chief was given a pair of scissors that were hot to the touch. They had been boiled and he was to use them to cut away the clothes the fireman wore. The removal of his clothes was agony. Instructed by Mr. Chang not to pull on any clothing that was stuck to Ian's person, the task had to be done with great care. Chief Johnson cut away as much as he could and covered him with a clean sheet. He rolled his bed into the clean room where Mr. Chang and the bath were waiting. Also in the room was Mei Ling who was sitting behind a curtain so as to allow Mr. Fisk some privacy. She could hear every word. Mr. Chang had prepared a pipe filled with something he called opium. When Mr. Fisk was lifted and placed into the warm water, he screamed to the top of his lungs.

"Chief, get me out! Get me out now! This is worse than the fire. I'd rather die than be in this tub. I don't care." His loud voice was filled with pain.

Mr. Chang noticed the indecision on the Chief's face and put his hand in the air to acknowledge his concern. He spoke quickly to his grand-daughter.

"Please do not take him from the water. The medicine will work in only a short time. Very soon he will have no more pain. You must believe and trust."

"Ian, listen to me. Listen to me! In a few minutes it will be better. The man knows what he's doing. I believe in him. Try and be calm, breathe deeply and hold my hand." The Chief was saying it, but he wasn't sure he really believed it. He prayed he had not made a mistake.

"Chief, what are you allowing that man to do to my husband? Make him stop now. This is too cruel, I won't stand for it. I can't." Charity was in the room adding to the confusion and noise in the room.

"What in blue thunder is going on in here?" Standing at the door was Dr. Grayson. He didn't like the idea of this Chinese medicine man doing anything with a person he considered his patient. He had never been dismissed as Mr. Fisk's primary physician.

"Doctor, we are attempting to help Ian." The Chief hoped he would not interfere to the point where Mr. Chang would want to leave.

"Charity, you can't possibly be a party to any of this insanity. They're going to kill that man for sure. I must insist that you stop immediately." He started to walk over toward Ian.

"Doc, wait. I feel a little better. I don't know for sure what happened, but the burns don't hurt so much for the first time since I got hurt." He looked over to Mr. Chang and smiled weakly in appreciation for the bit of relief he was now feeling.

"I see. Well, I don't think I'm needed here." Dr. Grayson left feeling a terrible mistake had been made. He did not expect to see him alive beyond tomorrow night.

That smile proved to be the universal sign of acceptance. It gave Mr. Chang the assurance that he was trusted. He was optimistic that his treatments would do some good. Time and continued care would determine if he recovered. The Chief felt that his decision to ask Mr. Chang for help was the correct one. He was truly Ian's only hope.

After the bath and washing, Ian did in fact feel better. He was dried with great care. Mr. Chang placed some salve on the burns with expert hands and wrapped them up in clean linen. He ordered some beef broth with a few finely chopped vegetables. He instructed him to drink a bitter tasting blue liquid that Ian began to look forward to taking every few hours. It not only took away the pain, it made him relaxed and allowed him to sleep. It was amazing what the treatment was doing for his moral. He felt that he would not die and no matter what trial came his way, he would trust Mr. Chang. It was not long before he did face another trial. In the morning, after a light breakfast, and the cleansing of the burns, he found himself staring at some very sharp needles. He wondered what they were for.

"Grandfather says he will place these on you. They help with pain and make your blood move easy in your body. They will not hurt, but you must be still." Mei Ling smiled at Ian and her gentle manner put him at ease.

"How long do I have to have the needles on me?"

"I am not sure. Grandfather will take them when it is time. Do you understand?"

"Yes. I'm ready."

Ian thought he was ready. When Mr. Chang began to place them into his skin, he had to resist yanking them out. He had no idea that the sticks would be gently placed by light insertion into his skin. He thought they would be placed on top of him. Sticking out of him was another thing entirely. He laid there for a while as instructed and as told they did not hurt. In fact, he felt nothing at all.

"Ian, my goodness! What are those things sticking out of you?" Charity could not believe what she was seeing when she entered his room.

"Please Mrs. Fisk. They are part his care. They help with pain and they do not hurt him. My grandfather will remove them in only a few minutes."

"I understand. I've just never seen anything like it before." She went to the basin and washed her hands but did not touch Ian. She wore a sheet over her street clothes and had removed her shoes prior to entering the room. She did notice that he looked much stronger and she was thankful that his pain was under control. She began to feel some hope for his recovery. He wasn't dead as predicated by Dr. Grayson and that was enough for now.

"Honey, is the Chief still here? I want to talk with him about the fire." He felt strong enough and wanted to tell him something important before he forgot the details, or took a turn for the worse and died.

"Yes, he's here. I can get him in a while. Do you mind terribly if we just talk for a little while? I miss you. Are you feeling better?"

"Yeah, I am. Maybe this Chinese doctor will pull me through after all. He sure does fuss, that's for sure. How are we going to pay him?"

"Don't worry about that. I'm sure we can make some kind of arrangements. Now, let me tell you a little bit about what's going on in town."

She stayed a few minutes longer and then not wanting to tire him too much, she left and got the Chief as he requested. While she was gone, Mr. Chang came in and began to remove the needles from his person.

"Miss Lee, please ask your grandfather why everyone is wearing sheets and all the stuff is gone from my room?" It gave Ian a feeling of dread and doom.

The young woman spoke to her grandfather and after some time she turned to Ian.

"It is hard to say all what he has talked to me about. He says it is most important to be very clean. Infection comes from things that are dirty. He is trying to keep you from getting a bad infection. Your burns will heal more quickly when clean."

"Thank him for me will you. Did he tell you if I was going to die?"

"Grandfather will not say something like that. He does not even know when he will die. You are strong and we are doing all we can."

I understand." He settled down again and waited for Mr. Chang to continue with his work. While he removed the needles, Ian began to think about what he would tell the Chief.


The storm Karin predicted arrived with a vengeance. It passed but was credited by the sailors as being one of the worst they had experienced. Several boats sustained damage while in the harbor and several large trees were uprooted by the driving wind. Portions of the pier were washed away. There were many homes with large exposed sections where a roof had once been. Shutters had been blow off and windows broken. Garbage was scattered everywhere and the smell of dead fish and seaweed that had been washed ashore filled the air. It would take the community a few days to clean up and make repairs. In Valda Bay, there was no life lost. A shaken community came together and for a few precious days they forgot their differences.

At sea it was a different story. Sailors who had the misfortune to be at the mercy of the sea did not fare as well. Several ships were lost, exactly how many would remain uncertain for several weeks. On the Sea Star the damage had been severe, but she was still sea worthy. James, Erik and Daniel had done all they could to prepare the boat when it became evident that they would be in the path of the storm. It was not long before they were being thrashed by high winds and a sea so rough that not one of them had ever experienced anything like it before. They took turns at the wheel to keep the boat taking the waves over the bow and not on the side. For a time they were able to keep things under control, but after twenty hours of battling the ocean, she dealt them a fatal blow. The mast had been severely damaged and was hanging dangerously loose above them. It could not stay that way. They decided they would try to secure it to keep it from doing more damage.

"James, you can handle her better than either of us. Erik and I will go out and try to secure the mast," Daniel was yelling to be heard over the crashing waves.

"Alright, go." He gripped the wheel tight.

The two men went out into the weather and tied themselves with heavy rope which they tied to the railing. This would keep them from being blown or washed off the deck. The waves were high and wind was stinging their faces. The coats they had on became heavy as the water saturated the fabric and soon offered little or no protection from the cold. As they attempted to reach the mast and secure it in place, a small piece of wood flew at Daniel and hitting him on the forehead, made a small but deep cut. The blood began to run down his face.

"Are you bad hurt?" Erik could only see the stream of blood and had no idea how badly Daniel was hurt. He was thinking the worst.

"No, just a bad cut. Let's get this thing tied down before one of us gets killed." He truly feared that they could in fact be killed.

The two men resumed trying to tie down the swaying mast. About the time that Daniel finished the temporary repair, the boat rocked wildly and the mast hit Erik knocking him down from where he was standing. Daniel ran to his aid, forgetting the mast for the moment, and saw a sight he did not want to see. Erik was knocked unconscious and was bleeding heavily from his temple. James saw what had happened and was powerless to help Daniel. He could not leave the ship's wheel for fear of being swamped and possibly sunk. Daniel was a good sized man and with the rush of adrenalin in his body, he managed to get Erik untied and inside the small shelter of the boat.

"Daniel, is Erik alive?" James yelled out.

"Yeah, but he's out cold. I don't think anything is broken but he's hurt bad."

"Put him on my bunk. Then come up here and help me." James needed his help in plotting a course to the closest town that he knew for certain had a doctor. In a few minutes, both men were at the wheel discussing what to do.

"We should head back to Valda Bay. I know for sure that Doctor Grayson is in town." Daniel thought that best.

"What about going to Boyd's Landing?" I know its closer."

"It is closer. But what if Doctor Hess isn't there? We would have wasted time that Erik may not have. I think we should go for the sure thing."

"Alright, but we can't make good time and there's no telling how long the mast repair will hold. It's damn near in two pieces now. Let's hope the wind quiets down a bit." James knew that probably would not happen.

"Yeah, let's hope. I'll go down and see to Erik. You call if you need me to take her for a while."

Down in the berth, Erik was unresponsive despite all of Daniel's efforts. They had been out to sea for several days and were trying to go around the storm when it hit. The storm proved too large and they could not avoid it. Now they were crippled in a raging sea. The repair to the mast failed to hold and broke completely into two pieces after about two hours. Under the best of circumstances they were four days from home; these were not the best circumstances. The only thing in their favor was the fact that these two men were well experienced and knew the waters well. They also had plenty of provisions.

In Valda Bay, Erik and Karin's home suffered only minor damage. Two of the shutters had blown off and one window was cracked. Her flower garden was a total loss, and the front yard and porch was filled with all manner of nasty debris. She looked around for her favorite chair and found it about twenty yards from its original location. She was surprised to find it so far from the porch; the chair was heavy. When she reached the spot where it lay, she despaired slightly. It was broken and beyond repair. She knew that Erik would make her another. Thinking of Erik, she looked out to the sea and prayed that he was alright. The worst of the storm had passed over land several hours before. She could tell by the sounds of the waves crashing against the shore that it was not over in the Pacific. The waves were still high and white capped. She bowed her head and clasped her hands together. She prayed for everyone in town, expressed gratitude for her safety and that of her home, but mostly she prayed for the men on the Sea Star.

At The Foggy Inn, Joaquin and Rue were going upstairs to her room. He had received a note from Elsa, but not wanting to really be with her he had gone to get a mug of rum instead. He would answer her note later and confirm a time to meet. Now, an hour later, he and Rue were in her bed relaxing and drinking wine.

"Are you getting hungry? I can have one of the girls bring us something from the kitchen." Rue asked as she ran her hand over his taunt stomach.

"Not really. I'm enjoying the wine and you. I don't need anything else."

"I have a little cheese and bread on the table. I'll be right back." With that, she got up and returned with her light snack. She took a bite of bread and realized that after such a wonderful love making session with him, she was hungry.

"Give me a little of that. You've tempted me now." He reached over and took some cheese into his mouth.

"We have a feast; cheap wine and good cheese. The bread isn't too good. What else could we want?" She smiled at him.

"I could think of a million things."

"Really? Like what?"

"Oh, let me see. I envision a prosperous vineyard with a nice home on it and the woman of your dreams holding your child in her arms." He looked at her, then thinking he may have said too much, he tried to laugh as if what he said was not serious.

"That would be wonderful. Is that what you want?" She had read him correctly. For a second, he hated that he had spilled his guts concerning his dreams. He also knew his dream was safe with her so he decided to answer.

"Yeah. It's what I want. I'm almost there Rue." He took another long drink of wine and picked up a piece of bread.

"What do you think I want?" She asked him in a serious tone, and for a moment, he was a little taken back. He had never given any thought to what she wanted.

"Tell me." He didn't often indulge women and what he considered to be their silly chatter. She was different.

"I want to start over in a new and faraway place that's beautiful. I'd like to own a place of business or at least be in charge. I'm tired of sailors and the smoke of the Inn."

"What are you doing to make it happen?" Joaquin knew she was a shrewd business woman and he was certain she had something already in the making. "I have a little plan I'm working on. Here, fill my glass with wine." She handed Joaquin the glass. He stretched his arm down to the side of the bed, took hold of the wine bottle and poured some into her glass. He replaced the bottle and turned toward her.

"I also have a plan." He looked at her and there was a new expression on her face. She was looking serious and interested in what he was saying.

"I'm glad for you. I've known you a long time and you deserve something good in your life. I hope your plans make your dreams come true." She raised her glass as if in salute and took a drink.

"Rue?" He turned to face her squarely.

"What? Are you alright?" She now was looking at the serious side of him and when that happened, she always gave him her complete attention.

"I'm fine. Were you serious when you said you wanted to leave Valda Bay for good? Go some place different?"

"Sure. I really do have plans and if all goes the way I hope, perhaps in as little as six months I'll be able to do just that."

"What's holding you back?" He had an idea.

"The same things that hold you back probably." She was looking at him seriously.

"I'll tell you what holds me back. Money, or should I say the lack of it."

"How much money?" Rue knew it was personal, but they had come this far.

"I need five hundred dollars. Right now, I only have about half that. So, I guess you could say that I'm like the bread here. Only half way done and not too good." He picked up the bread and gave the small piece a toss across the room.

"And, if you had the five hundred dollars, what would you do then?" It was a fair question and she felt he would answer her honestly.

"What is this woman; five hundred dollars, five hundred questions?" He was getting a little tired of this worthless conversation. He wanted to just relax for a while in peace and quiet.

"No. But if you could get the five hundred dollars…."

"Rue, let's stop this now. I don't have it so there's no need to discuss this any longer."

"Maybe there is. I have five hundred dollars."

"You have five hundred dollars? Why is it that you are still here?" Joaquin was a little shocked and surprised that she had not left long ago.

"I don't have enough to see me to a new place. I don't have family anywhere I want to go. I'd have to stay at an Inn or someplace until I have time to purchase a place of my own, who knows how long that would take, not to mention pay passage, and of course I have learned it's better to travel with a companion. I'd have to pay her passage. And, then I have this nasty habit … it's called eating regular meals. That's why." She looked at him as if he didn't have a real clue as to what it took to move.

"Together we could do it almost immediately if we wanted." He would share his idea with her and see if she would agree.

"What do you mean? Together?"

"If we both put up what we saved, we could do this. I have about two hundred fifty dollars now. I need another two hundred fifty for passage to Spain but mostly to make repairs to my home and vineyard. I can't show up empty handed. But, if you put in your five hundred we could go to Spain. Your five hundred would pay your fare and help with mine. There would be no more expense to you once we arrive in Spain because you could live with me in a house I share with my sister. You could stay there as long as you like. You could be my partner and help manage the winery once it gets going. You'll still have money left over for whatever you wanted. It would work because I get to go back home to Spain, you have a new place to start over and we both have a place to live. I know it's a lot to think about. Rue, please think on it." For the first time since coming to America, he allowed himself to feel excited about returning home.

"My goodness Joaquin! That's a lot to think about. You left out one important thing I think. What about the woman and the child in her arms? Does she already exist?"

"She does but there is no baby. I'm not married to her yet. She is a pure woman from a noble and powerful family. She's waiting for me causing her family great disappointment and embarrassment." He put his wine glass on the floor and moved the remaining cheese and bread to a small table by the bedside.

"I see." She did not love Joaquin, but she did not imagine him in love with anyone else either.

"Will you think on this and let me know as soon as you can? If you already know that you would rather not, I want you to know that I still think of you as my friend and hope this changes nothing in our relationship." He wondered if it would change. There had been a lot of soul bearing this night and it was not likely to leave either the same.

"We will always be friends. I promise I will think on it." She took his face in her hands and kissed him lightly on the lips.

"What time is it?" He asked.

"I don't know. It's late. Let's get some rest if we can. I have to help the baker in the morning. Her bread is the worst if I don't help her and that means getting up very early." She put her wine glass on the floor, pulled up the blankets and snuggled down into the bed.

"Come closer and turn your back to me so I can hug you." He allowed her time to turn over and he once again with practiced precision snuffed out the candle. He allowed himself a deep sigh and hoped that she would agree to his plan.

One hour or so had passed and they were both pretending to be asleep. They did not move or speak.

"Joaquin?" She said it softly.

"Yeah?" The reply was instantaneous.

"Let's go to Spain."

# Suspicion and Tragedy

*A* little boy with a telegram stood proudly at the door of Mr. Rudolph Nash. He felt proud to be entrusted with such an errand as he was the most respected and wealthy man in town. He rang the bell and waited.

"How may I help you?" A lady with a black dress and stiffly starched white apron answered the door.

"Miss, I've a telegram for personal delivery for Mr. Nash. Is he home?" He stood very straight so as to appear older.

"He is. Please come in and wait here. I'll get Mr. Nash." She turned around and left him alone.

He had never seen such a beautiful home. It smelled so nice and was bigger than he imagined. There were flowers and fresh fruit on several tables and lots of nice paintings on the wall. He noticed the fine carpets and pretty drapes. He knew that this must have cost more than he would ever earn in his life.

"Hello, young man. What is it you have for me?" Mr. Nash appeared from around a corner.

"Hello, sir. I have a telegram." He handed it to him.

Mr. Nash took the envelope and when opening it he noticed that the boy did not move. "Is there something else?"

"I was told to wait in the event you wanted to send a reply." He had rehearsed that line so he would not stammer or sound silly.

"I see. Let me read this and I'll let you know." Mr. Nash read the telegram.

**Reference: Mercantile fire. Claim received. Partial payment forwarded in form of credit notice. Notice wired directly to your bank account as specified in our policy.**
**Sincerely**
**Frederick & Lawrence Insurance Company**

Mr. Nash was relieved by the contents of the telegram. He had sent one earlier to his creditors at G.T.& K. Bankers informing them that he would soon pay off the loan used for the purchase of the spices. He did not understand exactly why he was receiving only a partial payment but he was glad to get any amount of money.

"Sir?" The boy was still waiting.

"Yes? Oh, of course, the reply. There will be none. Thank you for your outstanding service." He reached into his pocket and gave the boy two pennies.

"Thank you, sir." He quickly turned and thanked his lucky stars for the opportunity to have come to this fine house. He thought Mr. Nash a nice man.

Chief Johnson now stood by Ian's bed covered in a long clean sheet. He had removed his street clothing and shoes and a mask was placed over his mouth and nose. Mr. Chang said it was necessary to stop dirt from getting into the wounds. The Chief wasn't sure he understood all that dirt business, but Ian seemed much improved and so he did as instructed.

"Ian you wanted to see me?"

"Yes. I wanted to say thanks for everything and to tell you something about the night of the fire."

"No need to thank me. I'm just glad this Chinese medicine seems to be helping you. Now, what's all this about the night of the fire?" The Chief was looking at the man to make sure he was not too medicated and would in fact be speaking clearly. He seemed alright to him.

"Well, I know that there was a lot going on, but I saw something that seemed a little funny for lack of a better word. But, then again, maybe it's nothing and I'm looking for fish in a dead lake."

"Tell me anyway." The Chief was pleased that he was willing to talk about the fire.

"Well, I saw this ax head all scratched up. That in itself isn't too unusual, but I saw it where the old oil barrels used to be. It made me wonder if it had been used to bust open a container. The ax crate was across the way from the barrels about ten feet. The crate they were in was all burned up, and about twenty ax heads were in a pile. When I picked an ax head out of the pile they were clean and not one of them had a scratch on it. And then, right before the roof caved in, I noticed a piece of leather laying close to where the ax was, and it had some initials on it."

"Could you make out the initials and what that piece of leather may have been a part of at one time?" The Chief didn't want to exhaust him but he needed to know more.

"I could not say what the leather piece belonged to. But, I did make out the letters. The letters were an L and an E. They were close together, but there was a bit of a space between the other letters." Ian looked at the Chief to see if he was thinking as he was.

"Did you get a good look at the other letters?"

"I did. There was an R and then a bad burned up area. But I could make out an L and the letter N. I think the N was the last letter because there was a bit of unburned leather next to the N and nothing else was there." He felt better that he expressed his concern to the Chief. He felt certain that he would know what to do with such information.

"Have you told anyone else this, perhaps Charity?" The Chief would look into this. It was something that sparked his interest and would test his expertise.

"No I haven't. I didn't want to start rumors or make accusations about anyone. And, it is Mr. Nash we're talking about. I wouldn't want to get his dander up. I could be wrong."

"Wrong about what Ian?"

"Aw come on Chief. We both know what we're talking about."

"Arson." The men had said the word together and both hated the sound of it.

"I better go. You are about due to be tortured by your healer. He tells me you are doing well. He has high hope for your recovery. I heard something from Charity that surprised me." He had a light tone in his voice so Ian braced himself for something that would probably make him laugh or embarrass him.

"Yeah, what's that?"

"She tells me that you are taking the pipe now. You actually look forward to it."

"She's not lying to you. I get the pipe three times a day and for sure before I'm put into the tub. I also take a few puffs before bedtime. It helps with the pain and helps me to sleep. Mr. Chang is careful not to let me get to many puffs. He calls it Opium, and says if I do it too much, I'll develop a dependency on it. For now, I could care less if I get dependent. I'll fight that later. Right now, it helps control this pain. You know, I didn't even smoke before I got burned."

"Mr. Chang is right. Don't enjoy it too much. I don't need a drugged out fireman on the job." He grinned and turned to leave.

"Chief, are you saying that if I get better I still have a job?" He sounded surprised.

"Yeah, that's what I'm saying. I don't know if you could be on the hose anymore, but there is a new position coming our way I'd like you to consider. In fact, a good friend of mine is currently in that type of work right now. These men are trained to find things that normal folks miss."

"What does he do?"

"He's what they call an Investigator. In our case he will be a Fire Claims Investigator. They look at a burned building or whatever and can tell if it's arson, accidental or acts of nature. It's the way of the future. Insurance companies get robbed by thieves setting fires all the time and they got sick of paying out. Makes sense to me."

"Chief, I think I'd like something like that since I probably can't be on the hose. Do you think he would train me? How can I get in touch with him?" He really did like the idea.

"You won't have to contact him. I'm sending a telegram to him as soon as I leave here. But, I need to know where that leather is. He'll want to see it."

"It's in my coat pocket. I picked it up and put it in there."

"Good man." The Chief would make sure he collected it and kept it safe. It would be a valuable piece of information to this fire puzzle. "Ian, I need to go. I'll be in touch again. You try to rest and do what Mr. Chang says, if for no other reason than to piss off Doctor Grayson. He's a good doctor but he overcharges for everything." The Chief laughed and Ian joined him.

"See you soon. Thanks for coming." Ian turned to see Mr. Chang arrive.

The Chief left and went to see Charity Fisk. She had the clothes that contained the piece of leather. He hoped it would mean something. His gut feeling was that it would. He knew his friend Mr. Gordon would know exactly what it meant. He was an expert investigator and very little went by him. If there was an arsonist in Valda Bay, his days were numbered.

"I really appreciate you taking time to get me what I need from Ian's clothing. I know how hard this has been for the both of you."

"It has been hard, but I really believe that he's getting better. I know it's only been a couple of days, but that's certainly more time than Doctor Grayson gave him. He's strong and a fighter." She sounded tired and she needed to get some rest.

"I know that's true. Mr. Chang is working very hard to help him."

"It's the baths and scrubbing that just kills me. I know that's got to be the worst thing for him. He tries not to make any noise, but about half way through, it's too much for him and I can hear him moaning. So, when you wanted the leather, I guess I turned into a bit of a coward and was glad to get away. I didn't want to hear him suffer. I still can't believe this is happening."

"These days will be the hardest, but his attitude is good and he has you. Right now I'd say he has a more than a fighting chance." He wanted to sound hopeful for her, but he really was beginning to believe he had might recover.

"Well, here we are. Please come in. I'll hurry and get you the clothes he had on. I threw them out when they had to be cut off him at the hospital. I only brought them home because he told me to. Imagine that, in some kind of terrible pain and he wanted me to save them. I hope you find whatever it is you are looking for."

"Thank you Charity. I'm sure that I will."

"May I get you a cup of coffee?"

"No, thank you I won't be long."

"Alright. The clothes are in a bag on the back porch. I had to put them outside because they smell terrible." She considered the clothes ruined.

In a few minutes, the Chief found what he was looking for. It was as he had been informed. He put the piece of leather into a small bag and looking at it closely, he decided it warranted further investigation based upon what Ian Fisk had told him.

"I found what I was looking for. I have to make a stop at the telegraph office right away. May I walk you back to the hospital?" The Chief wanted to be about his business as soon as possible.

"No, you go ahead. I'm going to freshen up and I'll be along a little later. I'd like to look pretty for Ian." She smiled and slightly blushed at thinking she might be considered vain.

"I understand that completely and I think it's a good idea. A man likes to see his lady get pretty especially when it's for him. Please tell Ian that I'll see him a little later." The Chief smiled at her and went to the door to leave.

"Thank you for everything. I'll tell Ian you'll visit later. Goodbye." She stood by the door and watched him leave. She turned and went inside.

On the Sea Star, things were going as well as could be expected. Erik was still unconscious and even with the seas much calmer, the going was slow. The ship did not respond well to the wheel and the sheets were torn to pieces. It had been a while since the accident and James needed a break from the wheel. He decided to call out to Daniel for an update on Erik's condition.

"How do you think Erik is doing?" James was worried and didn't like the way he looked last time he saw him. He was very pale and his breathing was shallow.

"I'm no doctor, but this is bad. I don't know if we should keep him warm, cool him down or leave him alone. He hasn't made any type of sound or moved at all." Daniel was hoping that there was some sign of good news.

"Well, at least the blood flow from his head stopped. He just looks worse because the bruise is moving down his face. Who knows, it might even improve his looks when he wakes up." He tried to make light of the situation to help with the tension but they both knew it was a worthless gesture.

"Yeah, he would say something like that. But really, it's pretty dark and for all I know, he's busted inside too." Daniel felt helpless to help his friend.

"Let's not go down that path. We don't know for sure anything. I just wanted to know what was going on. Let me know if anything changes." James turned his attention back to the task at hand.

Several hours passed and two men now stood looking down at the body of their friend. He had passed away in his sleep. He never regained consciousness and their only comfort was the fact that he did not die alone and he was not in any pain. They wrapped him in a blanket and prepared for a burial at sea. The sea slapped the boat gently but the sky was no longer as gray as it had been. The sun was threatening to break out and a gentle breeze was coming in from the southwest. The two men made their way to the deck carrying Erik.

"Lord, we aren't especially religious men, but we do believe as Erik believed that there is a place for each of us in Heaven. You know he was a good man and treated everyone right. Please take him with you and help us find words to comfort his dear wife Karin when we have to tell her he's with you. We accept your will Lord, even if it is hard at times. Be with me and Daniel as we make our way home. Amen."

When James finished his prayer, both men gently lifted Erik up and let him go into the depth of the ocean he loved. In only seconds he disappeared from sight. Both men stood quiet for a moment and James wiped his eyes on his sleeve. Daniel turned away and with the back of his hand wiped his tears. They were no longer three best friends, but two.

"James, did Erik ever say to you why we were out here?" Daniel was wondering.

"No he didn't. He started to but the storm came up. I guess we'll never know."

"One thing I do know. We have to figure out how to get home. We need to repair that mast."

"Let's began by sitting down and discussing what we have to work with."

"Alright. Maybe it would be best if we kept busy. I'm going to miss that man."

"Me too."

With that said, the two began to discuss options, tools and the feasibility of doing the work that needed to be done. The weather looked good and if the sea remained calm, it was possible that in a few days they could be on their way. As it stood right now, the current was taking them further and further away from Valda Bay.

Chief Johnson was leaving the telegraph office when he encountered Mr. Rudolph Nash about to enter the telegraph office. It was not a comfortable encounter for Mr. Nash, as he did not want to discuss anything about the fire or anything else of that nature with him.

"Hello Mr. Nash. This is a fortunate encounter. I was just going to your home to discuss some important developments about the fire. But, don't let me keep you from your business in the telegraph office. I'll come to your home in about an hour if that's alright."

"Well, I'll only be a moment can you tell me a little more about it now?" Mr. Nash was concerned about what he may have discovered.

"I prefer not to discuss it here. Why don't I just come to your home in about thirty minutes? It shouldn't take too long, but it is important."

"If you think that's best. I have to send a wire now but I will see you then."

"Great. See you in about thirty." Chief Johnson nodded his head in agreement and headed in the direction of Mr. Nash's home. He would pass the mercantile on his way.

Inside the office, Mr. Nash was feeling anxious and tried not to show how nervous he was suddenly feeling. His mind was turning in a hundred ways and he wondered if there was any possibility that Chief Johnson had discovered something or been told something by the Ralston brothers. Maybe, they had been seen by someone. A thousand thoughts ran through his mind and he both looked forward to and dreaded the encounter that he was going to have with the Chief. He had received only a partial payment credit notice and based on that he was now wiring money to his creditors. The bank considered it as good as cash since the notice was from a very reputable insurance company. He still owed the creditors, but this bought him some time. He decided to send a wire asking why he received only partial payment on the mercantile. He had no money of his own and he had not yet been able to pay the Ralston's. Then there was the matter of Chief Johnson coming to his home. It appeared his torment would never end.

"When a reply is received Mr. Nash, shall I send the boy to your home with it, or will you check with us a little later?" The clerk was polite and waiting for an answer.

"Excuse me, please tell me again." Mr. Nash was obviously preoccupied.

"I was just asking when we get a reply, do you want me to send the boy to your home or will you check with us later?" She smiled at him.

"Send the boy. This is important and I may have to reply immediately." He reached in his pocket to pay for the wire. He needed to get home.

"Thank you very much." She took the money and offered him the change.

"No, I'd like the boy to have it. It's not that much and he earns it." Mr. Nash tipped his hat to her and headed out the door.

On the way home he told himself he would be calm and cooperative. He knew he had to be careful, but then he was well respected and at the moment, there was no reason to think he was a suspect in anything. He would listen carefully to the Chief, and then if necessary, make plans accordingly. For now, all he could do was wait.

As Chief Johnson was walking toward the Nash home, he did in fact stop by the burned rubble that was once the mercantile. He looked around touching nothing but taking in the scene with a new perspective. He was looking for anything that might help his friend, Mr. Gordon when he was interrupted by Leroy Grazer.

"Hello Chief. How are you doing?" Leroy had managed to say that without stuttering.

"Hi Leroy. I'm doing well despite looking at this small disaster. It was something wasn't it?" He wondered if Leroy might provide him with a little information.

"Yeah. How is the fireman that was hurt?"

"He's improving but still serious. There is hope that he'll recover and I'll be sure to tell him that you asked about him." A thought came to the Chief.

"Leroy, you've lived in Valda Bay a long time haven't you?"

"Sure have." Leroy was pleased that the Chief was making conversation with him. It made him feel like he mattered.

"Do you recall seeing any strangers around town lately?"

"Nope, can't say as I have. Just the usual crowd." Leroy had no idea what the Chief was doing or where all these questions were going.

"I suppose you know most of the folks around here then." The Chief made his tone easy and light. He didn't want to arouse undo interest in anyone at this time.

"That would be right."

"Didn't you work for Mr. Nash at the ice house for several years?" He knew he was treading on personal ground. Mr. Nash had dismissed Leroy over a claim that he had short delivered an order and kept the money for himself. This was untrue, but Leroy felt if he was not to be trusted, he would rather not work for the man. He quit on the same day that he was accused of dishonesty.

"Why do you want to know about that?" Leroy was looking a bit defensive.

"Well, let me tell you." The Chief needed to sooth him quickly. "I need your good memory with some names, if you don't mind that is. I don't want to impose on you, but everyone in the area needs ice so I thought you could help me." He saw that Leroy relaxed and knew he had appeased him.

"I'll help if I can."

"Alright. I'd like you to think about any businesses or people that had the letter R as the first letter and N as the last." He wanted to keep it simple.

"The letters R and N. You mean like the word … rain?" He needed to be sure he understood. It was better to give no information than have it be wrong.

"You got it."

"How soon do you need it?" Leroy was hoping he would have a little time.

"How about you and I going to Mrs. Steele's tomorrow? We can speak a little more freely there. I'll buy us both a nice breakfast so we can talk over a few things at the same time. Do you think that will give you enough time to come up with a few names?" The Chief hoped it would be.

"That would be real nice. What time do you want me there?" This was the first time he had an appointment with an important person like the Chief.

"Well, how about six o'clock. Is that going to work for you?"

"It will. I'll see you tomorrow morning." Leroy would not be late.

"Tomorrow then." The Chief nodded his head in approval as each went their separate ways. Maybe Leroy had information that would be of help. It was worth a try.

Rudolph Nash was a nervous wreck by the time he reached his home. Upon entering he went right to his library and poured himself a glass of brandy. He needed to compose himself quickly. He went into the kitchen, and was thankful that the cook was out shopping. He went to the pump and placing his hands into the cool water, thought to run his hands through his hair. He splashed his face, dried it quickly and reached for a piece of clove. He wanted his breath fresh and not smelling of liquor. It was too early in the morning to be having a drink. He thought to go and sit in his study, relax by the open window. He picked a book which he would pretend to read. He would make sure that the Chief thought him reading and unconcerned about his visit. After ten minutes had passed, the doorbell rang. He waited for the maid to answer. She came running from upstairs and politely answered the door.

"Good Morning. I'm Chief Johnson and I have an appointment with Mr. Nash."

"Yes sir. I'll inform Mr. Nash you are here." She motioned for him to enter, but did not offer him a chair. She went to the study where Mr. Nash was usually reading or working.

"Chief, please do come in." The voice came from the direction of the study.

"Please sir, this way." The maid led him into the study.

"Would you care for a cup of coffee or freshly squeezed juice?" Mr. Nash was forever the socially correct one.

"No, thank you. I'm fine." The Chief replied.

"That will be all. Thank you." Mr. Nash dismissed the maid with those words.

"Please, sit down and make yourself comfortable." He put down the book that he was pretending to read.

"Thank you. You have a very nice home and quite the library." The Chief always did appreciate a good book.

"Thank you. I admit I do enjoy it." It had taken him years to have such a nice collection. "So how can I help you?"

"Well, first let me tell you that I'm sorry for the loss of your mercantile. But, aside from the damage, I think there may be something more damaging going on right here in Valda Bay than anyone may suspect. As you may have already heard, Ian Fisk, my hose man in the fire department told me something that warrants another look into things." He kept his voice unemotional and even.

"I didn't realize that the man was still alive. Last I heard Dr. Grayson was saying he would not see more than a day or perhaps two at most." Things were going from bad to worse for him. What could possibly be next? What did the fireman know? He felt his stomach tighten.

"That's true. But he is continuing to improve every minute. He's not out of the woods yet I'd say, but he is lucid. I have high hope that he will recover. He's young, strong and has a tremendous will to survive. He found something that led him to believe that there may have been foul play at the mercantile. I did a little digging on my own and I agree with him."

"I see. So what will happen next? How may I be of assistance?"

"You can't at the moment. But as you already know I was at the telegraph office this morning and I sent word to an investigator who informed me he would be here in only a couple of days. He's an expert at these things. I'll show him the evidence and he can take things from there. I only ask your indulgence in not clearing up the damage. He will go through things and let you know when it can be cleared away." The Chief looked at him for reaction and thought he saw him a little strained. A small bead of moisture appeared on Mr. Nash's forehead.

"What evidence might that be?" If he learned what it was, he might be able to come up with some kind of a cover story.

"I'd rather not say now. It may be nothing and I would have created undo concern for everyone. But, rest assured. We will look into this matter completely and leave no stone unturned."

"Chief, we are talking about arson aren't we?" Now he really felt like vomiting.

"That's right. But, don't you worry yourself about this. I guarantee if we have an arsonist, we'll catch him. I'll see to it myself that the strong arm of the law gives them the maximum sentence allowed."

"Yes of course. I would expect no less." He wished the Chief would leave; he needed to be alone to think. He needed seltzer water for his stomach.

"Mr. Nash, we're actually quite fortunate to have Mr. Gordon personally investigate this fire. Not only is he a good friend, he's truly one of the best. He's been utilized by the insurance companies for some time now. So many unscrupulous persons burning down their own business or homes have caused thousands of dollars be paid out in fraudulent claims. The whole thing is out of control." The Chief did not want to overstay his welcome and thought to conclude his business.

"Will you let me know when Mr. Gordon arrives? I'd like to meet him."

"Of course. I'm sure he will have questions for you." The Chief stood up from his chair and reached for his hat.

"Thank you for your interest. I appreciate all you can do." He also stood up and began walking out of the study and toward the front door.

"Oh, one thing Chief."

"Yes?"

"Do you happen to know which insurance company Mr. Gordon works for now?" He hoped it was not the one he insured the mercantile with.

"I'm not certain. Why do you ask?" This sparked the Chief's interest.

"I was thinking I could collect the information for him and save a little time, that's all."

"Well, thank you for making time to talk to me. I'm sure we'll talk again soon. Good day and please give my best to Mrs. Nash." The Chief stepped out of the house and began walking down the long walkway. The question had been answered in his mind. Mr. Nash was hiding something. The questions he asked were all wrong and the ones he didn't ask were just as important. He would prove that there was in fact more to his story than met the eye. He found it odd how often big and powerful men fell to such ill temptations.

About the time that the Chief reached the end of the walkway, a little boy from the telegraph office ran passed him. He recognized him as one of the company's delivery boys. He watched as he ran up to the door and entered. The Chief resumed walking and in no time at all, he heard the sound of someone running behind him. It was the little boy running toward the telegraph office. Inside the house Mr. Nash lost the battle to settle his stomach and became physically ill. He received an answer to his inquiry about his insurance claim and any chance he had of settling his stomach was lost. He read that it would be perhaps as long as ten weeks to settle his claim. The company was certain they would be no problem with their investigation into the fire and would be pleased to wire the remainder of what was owed once the investigator on scene informed them of the finding. He was of course welcome to borrow money against the policy if he so desired for a very modest amount of interest. He felt like the walls were closing in on him. He had to have the money to pay the Ralston brothers and ensure that they would leave town prior to the arrival of Mr. Gordon and the start of the investigation. He would have to talk with Elsa. She would have to give up some of her comforts and perhaps sell off some of her expensive jewelry. He knew of a custom jeweler who had expressed great interest in some of her pieces. She would have to accept this or they would be utterly ruined and shamed. He began to think about how he would approach her. He wondered where she had gone this morning. She said something about a nature walk with her friend and not to expect her until late afternoon. He was glad she was gone. He needed time to prepare and show her on paper the situation they were in. He went into the study and began to lay out the papers. He filed away all the telegrams he had received in his special drawer. He pulled out a piece of paper and taking a deep breath he began to work. He made two columns to show what he could credit or debit.

Joaquin Cutta did not really want to see Elsa Nash. She had sent a note saying she wanted to see him. He debated on how to tell her their relationship was over. She looked beautiful when he saw her approach. Her dress was a soft peach color with a tight waist and a barely modest neckline. Her matching wide brimmed hat allowed him to only see several long curls that fell down the side of her neck. She saw him and quickened her pace. Her moves were graceful and seductive. At last she reached him.

"Joaquin, I've missed you so much. It's been a long time since we've been alone. Did you miss me?" She was very close to him and she smelled nice.

"It has been a long time. You look beautiful." No mention of how much he missed her or loved her.

"Thank you, I feel wonderful. Wonderful enough for anything you may like." Her meaning was clear.

"Why don't we just sit and talk for a little while? Tell me what you've been up to." He knew this sounded ridiculous. In their entire relationship, the last thing he wanted to do was hear her talk. Normally by now, he would have pulled up her skirt and begun to enjoy her womanly gifts. But, he was sated from loving Rue all night and even if he was a rogue, he didn't want to have his way with her and then tell her in the next breath that she was no longer wanted.

"You want to talk? Don't you want me? It's because of the baby isn't it? You're afraid to put me through something like that again aren't you?" She thought him so considerate of her.

"Yes, that's it. I don't want to get you pregnant again. That was terrible for both of us, but especially for you." He allowed her to believe that was the reason.

"Maybe it is best we don't do anything. My system hasn't completely settled down yet and that tea is the worst. I don't want to think of anything unpleasant now. Let's talk about us." She smiled up at him.

"What about us?" He asked quietly.

"When will we really be together?" She waited for his answer.

"We have lots of time. But, if for some reason we could not, you still have your life and it's a very nice one I should think." He was calm and hoped she would be also.

"I'm sick of Rudolph and I love you." She was back to sounding like a child.

"I can't give you the things he can. You know that I'm not a rich man and can offer you nothing like he does. If you really love me as you say, you would know that I only want the best for you. I don't want you to suffer." He was amazed at how easily the lies were coming to him. Part of what he said was true, but mostly it was not.

"I won't suffer."

"But you would. Think about it before you decide what you will do. Let's give ourselves a couple of weeks then we can meet and then plans can be made more final one way or the other." He was buying time. In less than one week he planned to be on a ship going to Spain with Rue. By the time she found out, he would be long gone. He felt no responsibility to her.

"That's reasonable. Two weeks it is." She smiled sweetly at him and put her arm in his as she chatted and enjoyed the beautiful sights and sounds of nature. His mind was in Spain.

Mei Ling was enjoying a cup of tea with Karin. The two were sitting in her garden and looking out to sea. Salty was as usual sitting near Karin demanding attention.

"Salty, stop rubbing on my skirt and go play with something. I don't know what to do with you. Mei Ling must think you have no manners at all." She reached down and scratched his ears lightly. He purred even more loudly.

"He is getting big now. He is so pretty and such a good friend. Look how he stays near you." She looked at the kitten with tenderness. She always had a love of animals and wished she would be allowed to have one.

"Yes, he is a good kitty. He keeps me company at night when the house gets so still and lonely. I wish Erik would come home soon. I miss him terribly." She sighed deeply and brushed at a strand of hair that came loose from her bun.

"When will he be back?"

"I don't know for certain. I think in about one week."

"The time will go fast and soon you will be together." She tried to sound supportive.

"I'm so worried for them especially since that storm a few days ago. I hope they are alright and the ship is not damaged."

"Erik and his friends are very good sailors. They will be not foolish and take chances."

"You are right. I'll stop thinking the worst and try and think the best." She straightened herself in her chair and took a deep cleansing breath of fresh salty air.

"For good news, the fireman my grandfather is helping has been very well. Better than grandfather thought he would do. He is a strong man and there is a good chance he will live." She felt so proud of her grandfather.

"That is good to hear. I know that his treatments must be making Doctor Grayson go through the roof! I wish I could see his face when your grandfather works his magic on that injured man. Oh, to be a fly on the wall." She actually laughed out loud.

As she began to laugh, she noticed that she was laughing alone. Mei Ling was looking at her in a very odd and somewhat disturbing manner. Slowly she halted her laughing and looked at her friend.

"What's wrong?" Karin asked suddenly worried that perhaps her friend was sick.

"My grandfather has good medicine and is not using magic to make Doctor Grayson be on the roof. He is doing his best to help. I thought you of all the people would understand this. He cannot turn you into a fly or anything else. How could you say such a thing?" She stood up and started to walk away slowly.

"Wait! Please let me explain. We are friends and I don't want there to be a misunderstanding between us. The words are not what they seem. Don't leave." Karin was walking after her.

"Your words seem so unkind. Now, you say that I did not understand what you said? Please tell me how I did not understand." Mei Ling hoped with all her heart that she had misunderstood. She loved Karin like a sister.

"You did misunderstand. Come back and I'll explain what these expressions mean. English is a funny language and you have a wonderful understanding of it, but there are still many more things to learn. There are still some things I am learning even after all these years. I would never offend you on purpose. I love you as the sister I never had."

After about thirty minutes, and an explanation of metaphors and idioms Mei Ling was still not laughing. She was feeling regret that she had judged her friend so harshly and quickly. This was practically unforgivable.

"Please forgive me. I don't know what happened to me. There is no good thing to say about how badly I behaved."

"There is nothing to forgive. And, I think I would have done the same if I thought someone had insulted one of the finest people I knew and loved. I'm just glad that you allowed me to explain. I'm the one that should apologize for saying something you did not understand. Let's promise not to get upset again. We'll ask each other instead for an explanation." Karin smiled sincerely at her one true friend.

"Thank you. You are a good friend. From now on, we ask for explaining please. Now, tell me more of these funny things." Mei Ling smiled.

After about another thirty minutes of idioms and explanations coupled with laugher, the two women said goodbye. Karin and Salty went inside and she decided to make Erik's favorite cookies. A feeling of doom had overcome her and she could not shake the feeling. She went to bed early but did not sleep well.

Doctor Grayson was walking the hallway of the hospital when he decided it was time to speak personally with Mr. Chang. He had noticed how much better Ian Fisk was doing and despite the severe burns, the man remained alive. He exceeded all expectations and this made him wonder how he was being treated. He knew he had to tread lightly as he had been so defiant when it came to accepting or recommending the unconventional treatment that was currently saving his life. He had been wrong and he wasn't so proud that he would put future injured people at death's door because he did not want to admit his mistake. Mei Ling and Mr. Chang were leaving Ian's room when they met in the hallway.

"Good evening. I was wondering if I might have a moment or two of your time. I'd like to speak with you about Mr. Fisk." He kept his tone even and looked directly at Mr. Chang. He did not know that Mei Ling was his translator. In fact, he did not know exactly what she did.

"Good evening Doctor. I am Mei Ling Lee and I am the translator for Mr. Chang. He is also my grandfather. I will tell him you wish to talk with him. One moment please." She turned her attention to her grandfather.

"Grandfather does not wish to create any problem. He asks that you please excuse him." She had no emotion in her voice and Doctor Grayson admired that.

"I understand why he would think that. I do not want to create any problems either. I realize that I was wrong in thinking he could not help Mr. Fisk. I just wanted him to know that I realize his contribution to this terrible situation." He was looking at Mr. Chang and hoped he could read the sincerity in his voice.

"Excuse me. I do not know the word *contribution*. May you use another word?" She hated feeling inadequate, but it was better to be honest.

"Of course. I want to tell him I know that his part in all this has been very good for Mr. Fisk and as a result, he is much improved. In fact, he's better than I ever expected." He did not want to sound condescending.

She turned and translated again and this time the older gentlemen nodded his head and looked directly at Doctor Grayson.

"Grandfather asks if you would like to sit down in the waiting room and talk for a while."

"Yes, I would. Thank you." The doctor accompanied them to a small room that had a nice view of the harbor and soon they were seated by the small window. It was raining lightly and gray outside.

"Mr. Chang, when I first became I doctor I promised myself that I would do the best I could for my patients." He waited for translation.

"Until recently I thought I was doing just that. I realized that I allowed blind prejudice to cloud my judgment. There are many forms of healing and one way may be different from another, but it's still good." More translation.

"I'd like to apologize for thinking that only my way was correct. You have given Mr. Fisk back his life. If it's not to improper, I'd like to discuss with you at length more about your medicines and observe you at work." He said it even if it was the hardest thing he'd done in a long time.

When Mei Ling finished speaking with her grandfather, Mr. Chang stood up and looking at the doctor began to speak.

Mei Ling clearly admired her grandfather. When she spoke she seemed to be speaking a little louder and stronger.

"Grandfather says there is nothing to offer apology for. He understands about prejudice and the extreme difference in cultures. You show great courage in accepting different medicines and would be very pleased to share all he knows about burns. He thinks that if two worlds could come together to share medicine ideas, then those who care for the hurt become two times better."

"Thank you. I'll look forward to tomorrow." Doctor Grayson smiled sincerely and departed the room leaving them alone.

"Grandfather, will you really teach him some of your medicine?"

"Of course I will. He has shown he is more wise than proud. He is truly a good and caring man. It was not easy for him to admit his error. You should admire him."

"Come. Let us go home and rest. I'll fix you a nice meal and then we can check on Mr. Fisk a little later." They walked out of the hospital and saw Doctor Grayson speaking with two men. They were ignored by the men, but Doctor Grayson acknowledged them with eye contact and a nod of his head.

# Rue

In the quiet safety of her room, Rue had just finished writing a letter. She carefully worded the letter to make sure that her decision to relocate to Spain was clearly explained. Ever since she was forced to leave New Orleans, she had faithfully written weekly inquiring about her family and friends. It was also her practice to send money on a monthly basis to help out with any expenses accrued in the day-to-day activities that come and go out of one's life. She held the letter in front of her and began to read it aloud.

*Dearest Lissett,*

*I am writing this letter with a hopeful heart and a dream for the future. A few days ago I made the decision to leave Valda Bay. I will sail in a couple of days with a man by the name of Joaquin Cutta with whom I have established a strong friendship. He will also be my partner in a vineyard that we hope to start in southern Spain. I will write and keep you informed of our progress so that we may be together as soon as possible once I arrive in Spain. Please ensure that on June 23rd, you go to the Bank of San Francisco where a bank draft will be awaiting your signature. It is a considerable amount of money as the trip to Spain will take several weeks and I don't want you to be concerned about finances. Take care and please tell my son how much I miss him. My love to you both.*

*Love Always,*
*Rue*

Rue was thankful for the love and support she received from her sister. She remembered the first time Lissett saw her pregnant. There had been

no outrageous words spoken in anger or disapproval, only an expressed
desire to help in any way she could. Prior to that time, the two women
were working as domestics in the same mansion for the Delois Family, an
old and prominent family in New Orleans. The sisters shared a rather large
bedroom with only one double bed. There were few furnishings and only a
small window that overlooked the gardens. At night, if there was a breeze,
the fragrant aroma of the Magnolia blooms filled the room with a sweet
scent. The only time they did not have to work was Sunday afternoon.
They usually took walks on the large grounds, or went to visit the only
friend they had, an educated widowed woman named Mrs. Chazique.
They especially enjoyed her company as she was full of wonderful stories
of her youth. She had been disowned by her family after falling in love
with a man beneath her station. Mrs. Chazique never regretted her decision and found comfort in her books and friends. She taught the girls to
read and write and enjoyed the times that they read aloud to her. For a
time, things were comfortable and predictable. After about two years in
service, there was an announcement made by the family that caused a bit
of excitement. It seemed that their employers were going to expand their
business interests to include some parts of Europe. They were informed
that a large home had been purchased and would need to be staffed in part
by some of those in service at the New Orleans home. The girls wondered
if either one of them would be chosen to go to Europe.

In order to legally solidify the expansion, the family met with various
experts and hired a well respected attorney to draw up legal documents. It
was not long before the much anticipated announcement of who would go
to Europe was revealed. When Lissett was chosen, both were torn between
feeling excited and unhappy at the thought of being apart. After one week
everyone was ready to travel and Rue waved goodbye to her wonderful sister. Only four house servants remained along with two men who took care
of the horses and stables. The grounds keeper and his family were also left
behind. The entire place seemed to quiet and often times she felt lonely.
There were some advantages to the situation; her workload was considerably less and she had the bed all to herself. One day after cleaning in the

library, she sat down in a big overstuffed chair and began to read a book. She was lost in her reading when a voice behind her gave her a small fright.

"What are you doing with that book?" The voice was that of a man and he didn't sound pleased.

"Oh sir, I was only taking a moment to rest. I meant no harm. If you will excuse me, I shall return to my duties immediately." Rue felt embarrassed and frightened at the same time. She recognized the man as Mr. Robert LeBlanc. He was the attorney for the family and was left in charge of the estate during their absence. She began to move toward the door.

"Wait a moment. What is your name?" He asked in a stern tone.

"Sir, my name is Rue," she answered politely and hoped he would dismiss her.

"How long have you been employed here?"

"Sir, I've been here two years." She wished she had never stopped working, if she had kept dusting, this conversation would not be taking place.

"I see. Well, I don't want to keep you from your duties." He moved away from her almost as if she did not exist.

"Thank you sir." Rue was relieved she had not been dismissed on the spot. In the future she would be much more careful.

What Rue did not realize was the impression she left upon Mr. LeBlanc. He found her quite beautiful. She was only a servant and he doubted that she mattered much to the family. Servant girls came and went with the seasons. He began to frequent the estate and made himself wise to her activities. He learned what days the cook went to town, and when the horses were being exercised. He made inquiry concerning the grounds keeper. He found that most of his duties took him some distance from the house and that his children went to the orchards daily to clean up dropped fruit and water trees. The rest of the servants were assigned to other wings of the mansion and were seldom seen. He knew his interest in her was foolish, perhaps even dangerous, but it didn't seem to matter. He would try and win her heart and the consequences be damned. Three months after that first encounter with Rue, he knew he loved her. She did not express any interest in him, and he found himself wondering why it was so. He was destined to never know the answer. In a letter he received from the family, he was instructed to prepare the mansion for the arrival of Mr. Christian Delois. The news did not please Mr. LeBlanc because he knew that the man was a scoundrel. If he had not been born into such a powerful and rich family, he would have been jailed many years before. As fate would have it, he was the younger brother of Mr. Phillip Delois. There was no doubt in the mind of the young attorney that he was leaving Europe to escape from some form of trouble. On the day he arrived, things changed almost immediately for the worse. He was rude, demanding and despite being very handsome, his mannerism made him unappealing.

"Why are you trying to get away from me Rue? You know it will do no good. Go ahead and scream, who will hear you?" Christian Delois had closed off the room and had her trapped alone with him.

"Please sir, I must be about my duties. I don't want to lose my position."

"You should worry about your duty to me. I could make your life more pleasant if you would be more pleasant to me. Show me how nice you can be." He had her pinned between the door and his body.

"No. Please leave me alone. I'll tell Mr. LeBlanc of this and he will inform Mr. Delois." The tone in her voice angered him and she realized it almost immediately upon finishing her sentence.

"You won't tell anyone anything. Do you really believe that my brother would believe you over me? And as for Mr. LeBlanc, I have the power to dismiss him. Do you really want to cost him his job?" He squeezed himself closer to her and she felt his hand slide down her leg.

"Don't touch me! I may be a servant, but Mr. Delois knows I'm a decent girl. I'll take my chances and inform him anyway." She struggled to free herself and managed to somehow slip from his grasp. She ran to the other side of the room and found momentary protection from him in the form of a large round table.

"Alright Rue, you win for now. I'll go, but this isn't over." He laughed as he made his way to the door.

She watched him leave and she knew that the time had come for her to give notice. She was no longer safe from his unwanted attentions. In the morning, she would speak with Mr. LeBlanc. She had to find a place to go and decided the best place to stay until a new position became available was with Mrs. Chazique. Later that night as she slept upstairs, Christian Delois was having sinister thoughts. He made his way to her room and entered quietly. He approached her bed and placed his hand over her mouth. He quickly overpowered her defensive attempts and forced himself upon her. If he took notice of her innocence, he made no visible acknowledgement of it. It did not take long and he departed her room leaving her mentally and physically hurt. In the quiet darkness of her room she cried for some time. She decided close to dawn that she would pull herself together and would inform Mr. LeBlanc of what happened. She prayed he would call the authorities.

"Mr. LeBlanc, may I have a moment?" Rue tried to be calm so as not to be considered a hysterical female, but rather a woman with a serious complaint.

"I would like to accommodate you Rue, but I'm very busy right now. Can it wait?" He was busy looking at his papers and had not really looked at her.

"Yes, I suppose it can. If you'll excuse me I have a busy day myself …" She didn't' finish the sentence before her voice betrayed her and he looked to see her eyes fill with tears. The shattered look on her face gave him instant alarm.

"Rue, my word! What has happened? No, don't tell me yet. I want to give you my complete attention. Please have a seat, and I'll call for tea. Just let me finish this one transaction for Mr. Delois." He rang for service and turned his attention to the task at hand.

"Yes, of course I understand. Thank you." She sat down in the chair next to his desk.

"It seems like everything is crazy this morning. Mr. Delois plans to leave very early tomorrow morning to parts unknown and needs me to do a few things prior to his departure." He tried to be quick but she was proving a distraction. He wondered what she could want with him.

"He's leaving tomorrow? Is that what you said?" Perhaps if he left, she could stay on and let the law do the rest.

"Yes, that's what I said. He seems to be in a great hurry. Now, if you'll excuse me I need just a moment of quiet to put pen to paper." He began to scribble something down. After a few moments, he concluded his business and turned his attention to her.

"Now, what is so important that it brought you here first thing this morning?" He smiled at her in a vain attempt to put her at ease. He noticed it didn't and for the first time, really looked at her.

"Sir, I've brought your breakfast tea." The servant placed the hot pot and cups on the desk and departed. Mr. LeBlanc turned his attention to Rue once again. She looked pale.

He felt angry and disgusted when she began to tell him all that transpired between her and Mr. Delois. He assured her the authorities would be informed. He would see to it himself. He suggested she leave the mansion for a time. He felt she would be safer if she was not so close to her assailant. Rue decided she would take a couple of days and spend time with Mrs. Chezique. She would wait for word from Mr. LeBlanc who promised to keep her informed. The authorities were informed but not how Rue had hoped. It was not Mr. LeBlanc that informed the authorities of a crime, but rather Mr. Delois. The crime was murder and the victim was Mr. LeBlanc. Rue learned that the two men had a heated argument over her and in an attempt to avoid scandal; Mr. Delois simply silenced the attorney. He would blame Rue for the crime. His plan was perfect. He would say that she was caught stealing valuables from the mansion by Mr. LeBlanc. He had informed Mr. Delois of his discovery and was instructed by Mr. Delois to dismiss the woman immediately. Upon hearing of her dismissal and potential arrest she panicked and then in anger, she murdered the only witness. She then fled into the countryside and despite the authorities searching for her, she was never found. Warrants were issued for her arrest.

It was not long before news of the murderous scandal reached the social circles of Europe. The Delois's were shocked and embarrassed that such a thing could have happened. They decided to leave Europe and offer support to Christian. They were certain that all the investigative procedures and interviews were causing him great distress. As was the custom when domestics created problems, they were dismissed from service with no money or references. Such was the case for Lissett. She was now the sister of a wanted murderer and could not be associated with the family. Only two days after being informed of her dismissal, she found herself on the streets looking at a bleak future. She was a pretty woman, and although not the beauty her sister was, she was forced to accept work at a brothel. She was hired as the laundress for only room and board. The house madam was a cruel and demanding woman and Lissett was certain that she made work for her in an attempt to have her join the group of woman who were paid well for their services to men. The more women the madam had, the more money she made. After only three weeks, she realized that there would be no way out of her torment if she did not have money. With great reluctance she joined the other women and in no time at all, became famous for her pleasing attitude and her quiet manner. She made it a point not to talk to men—they were not paying for conversation and this technique soon put her in the position of the most highly paid hostess. She saved as much money as she could and hired a man to find her sister. After five months, the investigator informed Lissett that the trail was cold and she was more than likely living in another country. This prompted her to leave Europe and look for her sister herself. There was one lead that she had not given the investigator. She never mentioned Mrs. Chazique because she learned early on from one of her clients, that he intended to collect on the warrants as well as collect from Lissett. The man did however serve a purpose. He confirmed that Rue was not dead, in an institution or in prison. She left Europe and went back to New Orleans to the home of Mrs. Chazique.

"Lissett, what a surprise! Please come in. It's so wonderful to see you." Mrs. Chazique gave her a warm smile and a hug.

"Thank you for receiving me. With all that's happened I wasn't certain that you would." Lissett was tired and the uncertainty of her reception added to her burden.

"Of course I would see you. You and Rue are my friends. Please, make yourself at home and I'll fix us a light lunch. Would you care for tea or a brandy?"

"I'd appreciate a little brandy. The trip was long and a brandy would taste really good." She wanted to ask about Rue first thing, but thought it rude.

"Good. I've been saving a bottle of brandy for a special occasion, and by my reasoning, this is one. I suppose you want to know about Rue?" She went about getting glasses and pouring out the brandy.

"I do. I'll get a room in town for a few days and then I will start looking for her." She accepted the glass of brandy then raised her glass to make a small toast.

"To special friends and wonderful memories." Lissett smiled at her friend.

"To special friends and wonderful memories." Mrs. Chazique lifted her glass and took a small sip of brandy. Placing the glass on the table she began to make lunch.

"I have some wonderful news for you. It's about Rue. I offered her protection from that mess with that devil of a man. Do you remember that I had a vacation home in San Francisco not far from China Town?"

"Yes. Why, is Rue there?"

"She is. I gave her money to travel quickly before to many people in the area learned of the murder of Mr. LeBlanc. She told me what happened and of course I offered her a chance to escape. The authorities came to me and I assured them that I did not know where she was. They don't know about the summer home because it's in my maiden name. Anyway, she's been there all this time. I've given her a little money to see her through the months ahead. I wish I could give more. I received a letter from her just last week. I wish I could show you, but I'm taking no chances and as soon as I read the letter I destroyed it. It's just too dangerous for her."

"I'll go to San Francisco tomorrow. How can we ever repay your kindness? You have been so good to us in so many ways." Tears of gratitude filled her eyes.

"You just take care of each other. I'll give you the address and all the information I have. I wish I could ask you to stay with me, but I know someone would inform the Inspector on the case. He's certain I know more than I'm saying, but can't prove it. Be careful and don't trust anyone."

"I will. I'll leave in a couple of days instead of tomorrow and even make a few pointless inquiries. Then, I'll go to San Francisco. We will continue to stay in touch." She reached out and gently touched the hand of her one true friend.

"That sounds just fine. Now, let's eat and plan on how to get you to San Francisco safely." The women spoke for hours and Lissett learned all about the incident that sent her sister into exile. She was glad she had saved money because she also learned Rue was pregnant with Mr. Christian Delois's child.

Lissett rejoined her sister and was of great comfort to her. The baby boy was born healthy and Rue recovered quickly. By the time the baby Jacque was two months old, their money was almost gone. With no references and a dubious past, Lissett felt they were short on options. One day she learned that the town of Valda Bay was accepting women to work in a red light house.

"I should be the one to go. I've already been ruined and I know what's involved." She said to Rue one night as they were deciding what to do.

"No. Jacque is my responsibility and I have to support him. It will be alright because everyone thinks I'm a widow and am getting remarried. We can say that my husband wishes to have time alone with me and you graciously offered to stay with him. After a short time has passed, you can tell them I fell ill and died." Rue had thought this idea best so her son could have respectability as he grew up.

"That's crazy. Someone will find us out."

"No they won't. I'll send money home often and then in a few years, we can move to some place where no one knows who we are or what we have done. We can start over."

"What about Jacque? Do I tell him you are alive or what?"

"We can think of that when the time comes. Please Lissett, this is the best way. I can't do this if you won't take care of him. I can't bear the thought of placing him in some orphanage for my own sake. I didn't plan on having a baby, but I did and I love him. Now, I have to find a way to make the best of it. Will you help me?"

"I will. I love you and I promise to take care of him as if he were my own. We will wait for as long as it takes." Lissett hated what her sister was forced to do—but she understood her reasons for leaving San Francisco for Valda Bay.

That had been ten years ago. She had sent money home on a regular basis and kept in touch with Lissett over the years. She missed her. Rue was brought back to the present by a loud crashing noise in the hallway. She knew it meant that the banister on the stairs had broken again, and she shook her head in slight annoyance. She folded the letter and sealed it inside an envelope.

# *Plans and Schemes*

*A*s Doctor Grayson watched Mr. Chang and Mei Ling depart, he felt good about the way things had gone and he was looking forward to learning more about Chinese customs and medical practices. He now turned his attention to the two men who had approached and were speaking to him. They were two friends of Mr. Fisk and were making inquiry about his condition.

"Doctor, when do you think we'll be able to see Ian?"

"Not for a while. He needs rest and a great deal of care. I assure you that everything is being done for him that can be done." He offered a reassuring look.

"I'm hearing that you and the Chinese medicine man are working together to help him. I can't believe that's true. It's not is it?"

"You heard correctly."

"That's something alright. We spoke with Charity and she told us that he's getting better faster than anyone thought he would. Has he said anything about the fire?"

"He is improving. I know that he has spoken with Chief Johnson at length and later told me that he would be glad when the fire investigator got here. He's supposed to be an expert at what starts these things. The whole thing is just so tragic."

"Yeah, it sure was." They were all thinking of the man that died.

"Well, if the investigator does come I'd be interested in what he discovers. I think we all will." The fireman looked at his companion who was nodding his head in agreement.

"I'm sure you aren't alone in your thoughts. I'll be sure to tell Mr. Fisk you inquired about him."

"Thanks Doc. If there is anything we can do, will you tell us?" The offer was a sincere one and since it had been made, he did in fact have something they could help with. Mrs. Fisk had no one to help her with heavy chores around the house.

"Mrs. Fisk could use your help with wood chopping and the like. It would help Mr. Fisk greatly knowing she was being watched over by his friends."

"We'll go see Mrs. Fisk. Please tell Ian that he can count on us for as long as necessary." They began to leave.

"I'll do that." Doctor Grayson also turned to be on his way but was glad that the conversation had not turned controversial at the start. It left him feeling that Mr. Fisk was indeed a lucky man. He had friends who wanted the best for him and it didn't matter where the best came from, as long as it came. The two men decided that they would go to The Foggy Inn for a meal and a mug of ale. They would celebrate Ian's improving health and their decision to help his wife until she no longer needed them.

At The Foggy Inn the usual crowd was there. When they entered, it took only a moment to hear a familiar voice that asked them to join him at a corner table. They immediately recognized the man and joined him at the table. They were not friends in the strictest sense of the word, but more like good acquaintances. They did not know the other two men who were also at the table, but since there was no other place to sit, they accepted the offer.

"Sit down and have a mug of ale. There's room for two sorry looking firemen." The voice was that of Joaquin. The men moved over to accommodate them.

"Thanks. Don't think we've met. I'm Woods and this is Dolman." He extended his hand to Cole and when the two shook hands, he extended it to Flint. The same happened with Dolman.

"Good to meet you." Cole looked at them and quickly decided that maybe they could be of help to him. He heard Joaquin say they were firemen and if he got lucky, he might find out some news about the man hurt in the fire.

"I'll get the serving girl. Everyone want ale?" Flint looked for approval from the group and when everyone nodded, he felt good. The ale arrived along with an order of bread and lamb which was thinly sliced. There was enough for everyone to have a little.

"So, what's been going on with you two?" Joaquin asked of the two firemen.

"Well, since that damned fire, Chief Johnson has us sharpening axes, checking our ropes, practicing our hand signals, stuff like that. I mean, it's good but I'll be glad to get back to the usual routine." Woods looked at Dolman and he agreed.

"We heard a rumor that Doc had asked that Chinese medicine man for help with the care of the hurt man. You know anything about that?" Joaquin was curious to learn if Doctor Grayson who was set in his ways would even permit such a thing.

"It's true. We just left him and asked about Ian. He said he's getting better everyday and it looks like he's going to make it." Of the two men Woods was the closer friend of Ian Fisk.

"He's got to be getting better because he's talking up a storm about some investigator coming to town. That's like Fisk alright, always thinking about the job making the rest of us look bad." Dolman half laughed and took a drink from his mug.

"That's good to hear." Joaquin reached over for a piece of lamb and bread.

"It sure is. I'm sure that investigator will find out what happened at the mercantile and maybe it can be prevented in the future." Woods was looking across the room at all the people there.

"So, how long have you been in the fire business?" Cole wanted to keep the conversation about the fire and what Fisk may have said, but he needed to be careful.

"Well, let me see. For me, it's been about eight years and how long has it been for you Dolman?" Woods never really thought about how long Dolman had been a fireman because he was there before he even arrived in Valda Bay.

"This October it will be ten years. It doesn't seem like that long." He let out a long sigh.

"And your friend Fisk?" Cole had accomplished what he had sent out to do.

"If I'm not mistaken it must be close to five years now. He's a good man and not one to panic in a pinch. We've both been side by side with him on more than one occasion." Woods looked like he was remembering the incidents.

"Sounds like a good man. He must have suspected something odd about the fire." Joaquin was reading Cole's mind without knowing it.

"I guess so. The investigator will be here in a bit and then we'll all know. Who knows, maybe it was some rat that knocked over a lamp that was left on. You never know about these things." Dolman motioned for the waitress to bring him ale.

"I'll tell you what. It had better been some rat or who knows what will happen." Woods said that with a great deal of conviction in his voice.

"What do you mean?" The question came from Flint.

"Well, let's face it. People do funny things sometimes. Buildings get burned for insurance purposes, revenge on someone, mischief of some sort, natural disasters that sort of thing. Happens all the time." Dolman was nodding his head at the comments made by his fellow fireman.

"What happens when it isn't an accident?" Flint asked to the horror of Cole. A little inquiry was fine; this might draw their attention as a little too much interest.

"Why, you boys set that fire?" Woods teased but looked keenly at Cole.

"Yeah, for all the money that old man Nash owns us for taking that pretty wife of his to bed when he couldn't." He threw his head back and laughed out loud. Flint taking the hint from his brother also laughed and in just a second, they were all enjoying the joke. The conversation continued and soon the men were talking about a variety of different things.

The evening ended as Cole hoped, no one indicated they suspected anything. Once Cole and Flint were on the Priscilla they could freely talk. They had learned quite a bit from the firemen and it opened up a new concern for them.

"We have to plan on what we are going to do prior to that investigator getting here." Cole was thankful that he had learned of this early on, to have been caught blind-sided could have proven disastrous.

"What do you mean?" Flint heard the same thing his brother did, but didn't process the information in the same manner.

"Flint, when the investigation starts, there is always a chance, no matter how small that he can connect us to setting that fire. From what Woods and Dolman said, he's supposed to be the best. We can't take a chance that he could discover it was us." He got up and poured himself a hot cup of coffee. He needed to be clear headed and think.

"Alright. So what do you think we should do? I think he said it would be a while before he got here. I would think that would be a day or two anyway. What do you think?"

"I think you're right." Cole wished they had more time.

"Why don't we just leave? We could go on the high tide tomorrow and who would be the wiser? In no time at all we could be in some other port far from here before anyone even knew for sure it was us." Flint thought that sounded like a good idea.

"We can't go just yet. We have enough money to buy a couple of mugs of rum or ale, but not enough to buy what we need for an extended trip. Then there is the matter of Nash paying us. He owes us and that's going to give us a new start someplace else. Then of course we haven't mentioned to anyone that we are thinking of leaving, so that makes it look odd especially after just learning that that investigator is coming."

"So if we stay, then what?" Flint was a little concerned for the first time.

"I'm not sure just yet. But, I think I'll speak with Nash tomorrow. He must have money someplace in that house. Rich folks always do. I'll press him hard tomorrow and see what comes of it." Cole would think on it later when he would not be interrupted by his brother.

"That sounds like a good idea. Maybe we can even turn respectable. I might even become a lighthouse keeper like the one here in the Bay."

"Are you talking about Johansson?" Cole asked.

"Yes." Flint yawned and gave an upward stretch of his arms.

"Didn't Joaquin tell us that his grandmother was some kind of rich society lady or something like that?" Cole had listened to the story but wanted to refresh his memory.

"That's what Joaquin said. Why?" Flint was wondering where this was going. His brother never failed to amaze him.

"He's been gone a little while hasn't he?"

"Yeah. I heard that they went fishing."

"Maybe we should call upon the lovely Mrs. Johansson." Cole was really thinking more out loud than anything else.

"What are we going to say to her?" Flint was feeling a little confused.

"We aren't going to say anything. It's what we are going to do."

"What's that? What are we going to do?" Flint never would have guessed in a million years what his brother was contemplating.

Leroy Grazer was watching the face of Chief Johnson closely. He could not form any conclusion as to what he might have been thinking. He had carefully put together the list he was asked to do and was now seated across from the Chief. He was thoroughly enjoying a cup of hot coffee and some breakfast scones. It was his first time in Mrs. Steele's Sweet Shop as he considered it a bit fancy for his taste.

"Is that a help to you Chief?"

"Yes Leroy it is. Thank you for getting this to me so quickly. I really appreciate your efforts." He was pleased that Leroy had not taken long. He wanted to provide this list to the investigator when he arrived. He also wanted some time to act upon it himself.

"There were only four names that matched the initials you gave me. One of the four is a lady that just moved away from here last spring. She had a fainting sickness or something like that and her son took her to Boston. I hear she passed but I can't be sure. The others are right here in Valda Bay."

"Leroy, does anyone know that you were doing this for me?"

"No sir. I kept it to myself. There is only one other person that could offer you a better list than me." Leroy thought he should mention it because he felt it was only right to say so.

"Who would that be?"

"Doctor Grayson. He sees everyone at one time or another. Maybe he can provide more names but he's very private about his patients. I don't know, but it's a thought."

"I'll see the doctor later today."

"Well, I guess I'll be going. I have a few errands to run." That wasn't true but he knew that the Chief was an important man and he could tell he wanted to begin working with that list.

"Yes, I understand. Thank you again for all the help and for taking time to join me for breakfast." He stretched out his hand toward Leroy.

"It was my pleasure to do it for you. Most folks don't even talk to me let alone ask me for something this important. You just call on me anytime. I'm your man." He smiled and gladly extended his hand for a firm handshake.

As Leroy departed the Chief was interrupted by the waitress who offered him another cup of coffee. He declined the offer and reached into his pocket to leave her a coin for the good service. The Chief looked at the names provided. Three of them were in question. He doubted that the elderly woman who left was involved in this business so he crossed her name off his list. He looked at the other three names but did not recognize any of them. Getting more information was vital and the doctor would be a good place to start. If he would not provide any useful information he felt certain the doctor would not compromise his investigation. He collected his materials and decided he would visit the doctor as soon as possible.

The Sea Star had been at the mercy of the sea since being damaged by one of the worst storms on record. The damage was great and the men had been working to make repairs as best they could. Tools were limited and the effort monumental. They had been working at a steady pace repairing the broken mast and sewing torn sheets together with rope. They took turns sawing the huge mast down to a more manageable size, but still allowing them the efficiency of having one. They had plenty of supplies and fresh water, but they had been drifting for some time and needed to get back on course. They did not want to fight a storm at sea again especially with a disabled ship. It was just daybreak and the day promised to be a nice one. The seas were calm and the weather good.

"James, the mast is ready to be seated. The broken ends are matched and using some rope we can secure the two pieces together." Daniel had been working on the mast since the storm broke it almost in two.

"Good. I'm finished with the sheets and even if we don't have all of them up, we'll still be able to catch the wind."

"That just leaves the mast. It isn't as heavy as it was but it's too much for us to lift and seat it. What do we have that could help us?"

"Not much. We have about forty feet of rope left and some grease to help slide it under the log. We need a way to make a hoist to move it into place."

"Do you think we could remove some iron from the wheel house and hammer it into the side of the boat so we could tie the log and swing it into place?"

"Yeah, that would work." Daniel began to think about where to place the iron so they would have the best leverage and control of the log.

"I could pound out some spikes of a sort if we heated the metal. There's the cast iron stove in the galley. It's small so we could carry it out of there and put it on deck. I'll put the iron in it for a time and then I could go to work." It was not going to be easy, but James felt he could do it.

"Let's get started. I'll get the metal we can use for spikes, and you see about unbolting the stove. Try and save the coals if you can, every one of them will be needed."

For several hours the stove was piping hot and long strips of metal that once served to reinforce the wood were pounded into spikes. The work was hard and they took turns reshaping the metal. When enough spikes were made, the hot stove allowed them a fresh pot of coffee and the last hot meal they would have for some time. They had used all the coal in making the spikes.

"So what do you think? Do we attempt this now or wait until tomorrow morning?" James was hoping that Daniel would want to make the attempt now. He was not one to put off things and there was still plenty of daylight.

"Let's wait for the real attempt until tomorrow morning. I'd like to give her a try without the log to work out any problems we may find we didn't think about." Daniel was looking carefully at the deck.

"You mean pretend we are attempting to seat it?"

"Yeah. It's just the two of us and we need to work out any things that we may find don't work or could go wrong."

"You are such an old lady, I swear." James looked at his friend squarely but there was humor in his eyes.

"Yeah, but I'm only your old lady." He chuckled and James just shook his head.

It was a good thing that they had taken the precaution. As it turned out, the rope reaching from the mast to the nearest spike was about eight inches to short. The log would never have been secured and seating it would have been impossible. After a few adjustments the problem was resolved.

"I take back every thought I had about you being an old lady."

I'm just glad we found the problem now. I don't think we could have moved it while it was suspended to make up those eight inches." Daniel was glad they decided to check it first.

"I don't see any reason why we can't proceed now. I'm ready to do it, are you?"

"Yeah. Let's take one last look around for anything that may move or get in the way. Any ideas on what else we can do?"

"I think we covered everything. Let's try and get a good night's rest."


In the morning they prepared themselves for the seating of the mast. The task was not easily accomplished. The log was extremely heavy and for a brief time, both of them had to pull on the rope to lift it. This resulted in it swinging freely for a few moments. It hit the side of the boat and cracked the railing. The crack only went about ten inches down the side, but it could be repaired when they reached port. It would not create a safety issue for them. After a few moments, the log stopped swinging and

James was able to reach out with a large fish hook and get control of it. Once it was under his control, they secured the spikes and were able to guide the log into place. At one point, James suffered a bloody nose when the log shifted position and hit him squarely in the face. Blood flowed from his nose. He had no choice but to turn his face into his shirt in an attempt to clean it away. He wondered immediately if he had suffered a broken nose. Daniel was immediately aware of the mishap, so James motioned to him that he was alright. After several attempts, the log was set into place. When the sheets were secured both men watched them puff out and catch the wind. The Sea Star now had a working mast. They were on their way home.

"Thank you, sir. We appreciate you selecting a ship from our fine fleet. I hope you and the lady will enjoy your trip to Spain." The man at the ticket office was polite and impressed that there had been no debate over the fare. Most people who came in expressed dismay at the cost. Joaquin had already done that some years earlier. He was now wiser and a little richer.

"I'm sure we will. Thank you for your help." He left the office with the two tickets and felt as if he were on top of the world. He had not felt this kind of excitement since leaving his home unsure of what awaited him. He decided to stop at The Foggy Inn to speak with Rue.

"Rue, may I come in?" He was knocking at the door to her room.

"What on earth are you doing here so early?" She answered the door and it was clear to him that she had just been awakened. Her hair was down and she looked warm and still a little sleepy to him.

"I'm sorry if I awakened you. I can come back later." He hoped she would say not to. She was beautiful in the morning and he felt the quiet stir of desire when he looked at her.

"No, please come in. I've been dozing for about ten minutes just being lazy this morning." She motioned for him to enter.

"I got our tickets and wanted to give you yours. I was excited about it and I forgot the hour." He tried to look sorry for the intrusion.

"Do you want me to ring for some coffee and sweet bread?"

"No thanks. I've already had my coffee."

"Well, let me see the ticket." She stretched out her hand.

"Here you go. We're as good as there." He placed it in her hand and she didn't even look at it. She went to her jewelry case and placed it inside.

"Rue are you alright with this? You aren't changing your mind are you?" He felt a twinge of alarm as he noticed her reaction to the ticket; almost like indifference.

"Of course not. It's just really happening that's all." She smiled.

"There are lots of things happening." His tone suggested something else.

"Oh yeah? Like what?" She looked at him and tossed her auburn hair.

"Like you making me want you without even trying."

"I do that to you?" She placed her hand to her throat pretending to be surprised.

"Yeah, pretty much."

"Do you have any place else you have to be right now?"

"No."

"Then why don't you stay and enjoy a second cup of coffee. You might want it after getting out of bed again."

"Are you inviting me to stay?" He knew that she was.

"Certainly. My feet are cold from standing here talking with you. I need you to warm them up for me. You didn't think it would be anything else did you?" She gently teased.

"Never my lady. I know you keep me around only to warm your feet." He undressed and they slipped into her bed. He warmed much more than just her feet.


"Cole you stayed up so late last night. What were you doing?" Flint had gone to bed and when he stirred from his bunk to use the chamber pot, he noticed that his brother was not in his bunk.

"I was thinking about a lot of things." He got up and went to the basin to splash water on his face and wet down his hair.

"What things?"

"Well for one thing, it's like I told you. We need to push Nash a little bit for our money. So, today I'm going over to his house and talk with him in person."

"He won't like that. What if he refuses to talk with you?"

"That's right, he won't like it and it's because of that very fact that he'll talk. He doesn't want trouble Flint; he wants us to go away."

"Yeah, that's true alright. So what are you going to say to him?"

"I'm going to tell him I want to be paid in full by tonight. No excuses, no waiting. Keep in mind that basically he's a little man who doesn't have enough backbone to do his own dirty work. If he did, he wouldn't have hired us." Cole reached for a towel and brush.

"I sure hope he pays us. I go to thinking about that investigator that's coming. Do you want me to get the boat ready below so we can leave in the morning?"

"Yeah, but don't get busy on top. We can both do that when it gets dark. Wash out the water barrels and put fresh water in them. Check the ropes and our dry goods like coffee and sugar."

"You want me to do all I can in secret."

"That's right. Just take it easy and continue to work until I get back. With a little luck, we might be rich men by tonight."

"Cole, what are we going to do if he says no?"

"Do something different."

"Like what? Does it have something to do with Mrs. Johansson?"

"It does." Cole looked at his brother as if he dared to challenge him on the matter.

"What does that nice lady have to do with us?" Flint did not like the idea of hurting her or better yet, having her husband on their back.

"He had a rich grandmother that recently died. The old lady may have left them something valuable that we could use."

"You want us to rob them?" Flint could not believe what he was hearing.

"Yeah. She's alone and we could be in and out before she even knows what hit her."

"I don't know."

"Flint, you little coward! I always have to think of everything for us. I come up with a second plan and it isn't good or safe enough for you. I'm sick of it and you can go it alone if you want. I'm going to have money one way or another." Cole was angry and even if he had never thought to say those things to his brother before, he had said them now and was glad he did.

"Shut up! Don't I always back your play even when it means I put myself on the line too?" Cole had stepped on his pride by indicating that he was scared and therefore worthless to him.

"You do. Look we have a lot on our mind. Let's just go with the original plan and see what happens from there."

"Don't worry. I'll do my stupid part as always."

"Hey, you know I wouldn't want anyone else for my brother. I'm just tired. I swear, when we get that money, I'm going to sleep a week in a real bed with clean sheets. I'm not going to stay up all night worrying about this kind of stuff again."

"We're both tired. Look, I'll do as much as I can and when its high tide, we can be on our way."

"Hey, I know you always have my back." Cole looked at his younger brother and knew that he would never betray him. He felt the same about him. Good times or bad, they were brothers to the end and nothing would ever change that.

"Want me fix us some breakfast before you go?" Flint was back to being Flint.

"Yeah. That would be great. I'll get the plates out."

"Before you do that, maybe you should comb your hair. You wet it but never combed it and it's sticking straight up." Flint started to laugh at seeing his brother's hair look like a cat with its hair on end. He turned into the glass and seeing his reflection, he laughed also.

After breakfast, Flint cleaned the galley and Cole departed for Mr. Nash's home. Only time would tell which plan would prove profitable.

Chief Johnson had just about reached the steps to the hospital when he saw Charity Fisk. She smiled when she saw him and he noticed that she had taken care to look especially nice. Her dress was fresh and ironed crisp and she had pulled her hair into a high loose bun that was accessorized with a nice hairpin. She was carrying a basket covered with a lace cloth and he could see some flowers poking out from beneath the cloth. It was certain she was feeling better about her husband's condition and felt renewed hope for his recovery.

"Good day Chief."

"Well hello there Mrs. Fisk. Ian will be happy to see you looking so nice."

"I hope so. I hadn't realized how tired looking I was and that didn't do anything for him. He was worried about me. I'm just grateful that he's feeling better. Have you seen him yet?" She had no idea if the Chief was coming or going.

"No I haven't. I hope to see Ian after I speak with Doctor Grayson on some other business."

"Ian is alright isn't he?" She looked alarmed and didn't realize that she had grabbed him by the sleeve of his coat.

"Yes, Ian's fine. This is firehouse business. I'm sorry I didn't mean to upset you." He should have realized that she might think the worst. He felt her drop her hand.

"Forgive me. I should have known that you would have told me from the start."

"I understand. Well, I must be going if I plan on talking with the doctor before he gets too busy this morning." He tipped his hat and started for the doctor's office.

"Chief, wait. I realize it's a late invitation, but I hope that you can join Ian and me for lunch today, if your schedule will permit you to join us. Ian can only have chicken soup, but the men at the firehouse told me you like roast beef sandwiches on freshly baked French bread and chocolate pie." She lifted up the lace cloth to reveal the tasty contents of the basket.

"Thank you. I'd like that very much. Those firemen know me well; I'll be sure to thank them. What time shall I join you?" He really did appreciate the offer.

"Let's plan on twelve thirty." She began to recover the basket.

"Twelve thirty it is."

"I'll tell Ian," she said that as she was turning away to be with her husband.

Chief Johnson watched her go and remembered his wife. She was about
the same age as Charity Fisk when she died. They were married only ten
months when the house they were renting caught fire. He never learned
exactly what happened but it was thought that the kitchen stove exploded
knocking her unconscious. That tragedy prompted him to become a fireman. He never remarried but sometimes late at night when he found it
hard to sleep, he wondered how his life would have been different if he
had. He still missed her.

When he reached Doctor Grayson's he found the door slightly ajar and
saw the doctor was writing something. The doctor was concentrating so
intently he never heard the knocking. He debated if he should interrupt or
not, but never had the chance to decide. The doctor put down his pen,
looked up and saw him standing at the door. This time he was rewarded
with quick recognition and a wave of his hand to enter.

"Hello Chief, what brings you to my office this morning?"

"I was wondering if you have a moment to speak with me about some
folks you may have treated?"

"Chief, I'm not in the habit of discussing my patient's personal issues
with anyone but those concerned. You understand that of course." The
doctor left no doubt that he was protective of his patient's privacy.

"I understand that. But this doesn't concern private medical things, but
rather some names that I need your help with."

"Maybe you would do better to ask the police."

"No. Let me tell you why. At some point in time, there are very few
people who have not seen you for one thing or another. You know everyone in town. The police don't always see everyone. I've never been arrested
or detained for example, but I have been sick." He hoped that explanation
would be sufficient. He did not want to reveal more about his true intentions.

"Oh, I see. Well in that case, I see no harm in talking about just names. How can I help?" The doctor seemed at ease and the Chief took action to make the most of it.

"I have a list of names that I would like you to take a look at. If you can and without violating any medical ethics, do you think you could tell me a little about each of them?"

"Let me see the list." When he was handed the list he motioned for the Chief to sit down. He didn't want to leave the Chief standing as he collected his thoughts.

Let's take the first name. Lee Rolan. There's only one family by that name in town. Everyone knows Mr. Rolan is confined to a wheelchair as a result of a logging accident about fifteen years ago. His wonderful wife takes care of him. Nice folks."

"Do they have children?"

"Sure. A fine son they are very proud of that teaches at some kind of military school back east and a daughter. She married a preacher from Sandy Point a few months ago."

"What about the other names?" The Chief mentally removed the Rolan Family from the list of suspects. It was not likely that this family was involved in any ill doings.

"Ralston. Let me see, what are their first names? I can't remember but they are dock workers and have their own fishing boat. Some time back I treated the older of the two brothers and you would have thought the younger one was going to die. I had to chuckle when that big man got weak in the knees over a few stitches. It's always the big tough looking ones that faint." The doctor shook his head as he remembered the incident.

"How old would you say they are?"

"Maybe late twenties."

"What else can you tell me?"

"Not much. I've seen them at The Foggy Inn once in a while. I've stopped in myself from time to time. Oh, I just remembered their names, Cole and Flint."

"Are they married?"

"No, I don't think so. But, then it has been a while so they could be."

The Chief made a mental note to check the brothers out with the investigator when he arrived.

"What about the last name on the list?"

"Robison. He lives in a mountain cabin alone. His first name is Lowell but he goes by Robison. He's a loner and if he has any friends it would be Mr. Nash. He hires out in the spring each year for cash only work."

"Are he and Mr. Nash close?"

"I'm not sure. I've heard him speak highly of him. Could be that Robison respects Mr. Nash because he gave him a credit line when others would not. He told me that himself when he paid me. I think he's just misunderstood. He's a classic."

The Chief decided that he warranted checking out also. A man with few friends might just be willing to do anything to help out the only friend he had. The bartender at The Foggy Inn would have more details. The man seemed to know everything about everyone. It could be because once the liquor flowed; people opened their mouths and discussed things they would not normally talk about when sober.

"Thank you doctor. You've been a great help to me."

"Well, if that's all you wanted, it was pretty painless. Believe me when I say that I don't say that often." He grinned at the Chief.

"You do alright."

"Well I certainly try. Let me tell you something that I never thought I'd believe in; Chinese Medicine. I'm sorry to say that I was so pig headed about the whole thing. I've made my peace with Mr. Chang and without a doubt I've learned a lot from him. Ian Fisk is recovering no thanks to me. Your fireman was lucky to have Mr. Chang treat him. I'm glad you sought him out." The doctor looked contrite.

"I think Fisk was lucky to have both types of medical care." The Chief knew that two medical men had to prove better than one.

"I agree with that one hundred percent. That's why I'm writing this article about the treatment of burns used on Ian. I intend to submit it to the Medical Board of New England. They may laugh me out of the state, but I'm going to tell them anyway. It's too important to keep knowledge like this from other physicians." He spoke with such conviction; the Chief didn't think he'd have any problems expressing himself on paper.

"Well, good luck with that article. If it would help, you can use my name as a testimonial to the treatments used and the remarkable progress. Maybe it will help open their eyes."

"Thank you. But one of us being ridiculed may prove sufficient."

"Doc, before I go can you tell me how is Fisk really doing?"

"He's doing great. He's got a way to go of course, but he continues to improve and there is no sign of infection. However, as the tissue has been so damaged, the scars that form after healing will be very disfiguring. The skin will be much tighter than it used to be and in some cases, the scars limit movement of the limbs and face. In Ian's case, his arm will probably heal but the scar might very well limit his ability to move it."

"Is there anything that can be done to prevent that from happening?"

"We're trying to help the skin with bandages as it heals. Mr. Chang is also applying special oils and herbs to the skin several times a day. The burns are being scrubbed on a daily basis—that is like being in the jaws of hell. Thank the Lord that the pipe helps with the pain. Then, we also have a surgical option to help relieve the tension on the skin. That's very risky. We have to take a wait and see attitude for right now. But, on a good note, Ian is young and healthy in every other aspect of his life. He's also very strong mentally so I see no reason to think he won't make it and have a good life."

"I sure hope so. Well, I know you want to get back to your article and I've kept you long enough. Good luck with everything and thanks again for your help." The Chief rose from his chair and started for the door.

"You're welcome Chief." He saw the doctor reach for his pen and when he exited the room, he left the door as he found it; slightly open.

At the home of Mr. Nash, the breakfast table was being cleared and Elsa was in her usual form. She did not notice that her husband had dark circles under his eyes from lack of sleep or the fact that he did not eat well. In fact, he had eaten one slice of dry toast and drank a cup of black coffee.

"The Commerce Ball is such a nice event. I'm glad I was able to order that new dress. The lady at the dress shop says it will be here in only two weeks. Can you believe how beautiful I'm going to look? I've decided to wear my two strands of pearls and my earrings will be the pearl ones that my mother gave me to wear at our wedding." She waited for Rudolph to comment and when he didn't, she raised her voice to get his attention.

"Rudolph, I speaking to you and you aren't listening. Sometimes I swear you just don't care about what I'm saying. It hurts my feelings." She began to pout.

"Elsa, there is something we need to speak about and I want you to remain open minded and calm." He had rehearsed what he would say about selling her jewels and the financial situation they were in.

"Heavens Rudolph, you make it sound like the end of the world." She took another sip of her hot tea.

"It very well could be if you don't come to grips with what I have to say to you. Now, please listen carefully because it's important."

"Alright. I'm listening. Tell me what is so important." She sat straight up in her chair and folded her hands. She placed them on the table and looked straight at him.

"Well, as you know I've always tried very hard to give you all the things you deserve and to make our life as comfortable as possible."

"I love you for that. I am very pleased with all the things I have. I know that I can depend upon you for everything." She fluttered her eyelashes slightly.

"Elsa, please don't interrupt me. It's difficult for me to have to say what I have to say." He didn't want to sound unkind, but he detected a sharp tone in his voice that he wished he had not allowed to happen.

"I'm sorry. I won't interrupt again." She lowered her eyes for a brief moment.

"Now, with that said, you can understand why I purchased a large amount of special spices from the West Indies. I made arrangements with a merchant ship to bring the spices here. I had to pay the Captain his transport fee, the dock workers for loading and unloading the cargo, security men to watch it while the ship was in other ports and a small variety of other costs. Do you understand so far?"

She only nodded her head.

"Elsa, you may speak. Do you have questions so far?"

"Did you intend to sell the spices out of the mercantile?" She sounded mature like the woman he always hoped she would one day be.

"Yes, that's exactly what I hoped to do. But, it was so much more expensive than I anticipated. I had already placed the order with the West Indies Spices Company, and I was obligated to pay for the order. I was forced to borrow money from the bank to pay for the spices."

"How much did you borrow?"

"A small fortune. But, I thought that the resale of the spices would have paid off the loan and still allowed us a good profit."

"Would have? What do you mean would have? What happened?"

"Well, the worst thing imaginable." He blotted his forehead with his handkerchief.

"What?" She was now listening intently.

"The merchant ship from the West Indies left as planned. They moved from port to port as best the West Indies Spice Company could determine, but when they were due at some other port to pick up additional cargo, they never showed up."

"What happened to the merchant ship?" For the first time, she felt a little concerned.

"After some time it was determined that it sunk in a storm. The ship was never found." He felt relief coming over him as he unburdened himself to her. She was being more than he had hoped for. She was listening and being understanding.

"The cargo?" She thought perhaps some may have been saved.

"Completely lost."

"Alright, so it's lost. There can be more things ordered." She thought him over concerned for what had a good recovery.

"No, you failed to understand that I borrowed money to pay for the order in the first place." Now the hard part came.

So, why is that so hard? We have enough to pay them back don't we?"

"No. I borrowed the money and secured the loan with the mercantile and the ice house as security."

"I don't understand Rudolph. What exactly does it all mean?" She still was not grasping what he told her.

"The mercantile burned down so we lost our ability to pay back the loan."

"What about the ice house?"

"It doesn't generate enough money to pay what we owe. I'm afraid that we've lost it to the bank." He loosened his tie and poured out some freshly squeezed orange juice into a small glass. He took a refreshing drink.

"So you are telling me that the bank took the ice house, the mercantile burned down and we still owe more money?" She had a look of dismay on her face.

"Yes, that's almost all of it."

"What! There's more? What could be worse than that?" Now she was concerned.

"We may lose the house as well."

"Rudolph! No! I demand that you work something out. Get another loan, do something else. You do have something else in mind don't you?"

"I do. But let me finish explaining what else is going on."

"Why don't you contact my father? He's very clever about these things. He knows all about finances, stocks, bonds, insurance claims and this sort of business." She thought it a good idea and hoped he would too.

"I don't want to do that at this point." He was trying not to get angry at her for suggesting that the minute she felt some difficulty in their marriage, she would want to run to her father.

"I just thought of something. We had insurance on the mercantile didn't we? I remember seeing some correspondence on the table from some company back east." Her tone had changed and he was grateful for at least that.

"We do have insurance. But the company won't pay in time and the note to the bank is now overdue. We have to raise some money to pay them or we stand to lose the house to foreclosure due to lack of payment."

"Well get yourself to the telegraph office and tell them to wait until our insurance company comes through. It's that simple Rudolph." She almost sounded angry that he didn't think of that by himself.

"Elsa I already tried that."

"And what did they say?"

"They said there was going to be an investigation into the cause of the fire and would not pay anything until it was resolved. They are firm on the matter."

"Do you think someone set our mercantile on fire on purpose?" She looked shocked and a little fearful at the same time.

"I don't know. But it does present us with another thing we have to discuss."

"Oh, I can't believe this! More bad news? I don't think I can take much more of this. I'm beginning to feel sick to my stomach." Elsa could see her comfortable life disappearing before her eyes.

"Get hold of yourself. I have an idea that will buy us some time. It's going to take some courage and a great deal of unselfish sacrifice." He was trying to paint a picture where she saw herself as a great help to their problem.

"What is it?" She was looking at him and he could not read her expression.

"Your jewels."

"My jewels? You aren't thinking of doing something with my jewels are you?"

"Yes. Dearest, we need to sell them to save our house and what we have." He was speaking softly but with determination in his voice.

"Absolutely not! Those jewels are very important to me. They have been in the Wellington family for several generations. My father gave me those pieces and I treasure them. They are part of my family history. No! Think of something else, my jewels are out of the question." She reached for her glass of juice, took a sip and when she placed the glass down, a little bit splashed out of the glass. They were both amazed at how hard she placed it on the table and were taken back by her rude display.

"There is no other solution and I've already made arrangements with a jeweler in Rock Port to look at all the pieces."

"How could you do that?" She was visibly angry.

"I had no choice. Once this is resolved, I can purchase you more jewels. Anyway, they can't be that dear to you or anyone else. I know they came to be in your family by some night time arrangements. They were part of the famous Rip Tide treasure were they not? It's only too bad that your long dead relative the governor from two hundred years ago didn't get more jewels before the chest was placed on the ship that went down. We would have nothing to worry about if that was the case. But, right now, the jewels you have mean we can live another day in the style in which you demand. Why can't you see that?" He was now the one getting angry.

"How dare you? I cannot believe you would bring up past history. Don't ever say anything like that again about my family! Are you saying this is my fault?" She began to raise her voice.

"Not entirely. I should have put my foot down and dismissed some of the help around here. But no, to my shame, I allowed my tender feeling for you cloud my better judgment. Now, there is no choice and tomorrow, I'm leaving for Rock Port with the jewels. I'm also going to give notice to your personal maid. We can't afford her anymore."

"You mean cruel man. I can't believe that you have forced us to live like paupers. Your foolishness will deny me a nice home, money to have for my basic needs and my woman companion. Now, you demand that I give you my personal jewels. This is too much and I'm not going to sit here anymore and continue to be assaulted by your demands on me. I hate all of this and I hate you!" She was now screaming at him.

She rose from her chair and in the process caused it to fall over backwards. She did not turn around to see what happened.

"Elsa please calm down." His words fell on deaf ears. The idea that she would continue to understand and support him was gone. He hated the situation as much as she did, but he could not give into her. He knew what he had to do and he knew that he would do whatever was necessary. He stood up from the table and began to go into his study. He decided to allow her some time to process all that he had said to her. In a short while he would knock on her door and try to comfort her as best he could. He had just entered the study when he heard the bell at the door.

Elsa had already reached the top of the stairs. She heard the bell and stopped to see who might be calling so early. There was no one expected to the best of her knowledge so she watched from the top of the staircase to see who was at their front door so early in the morning.

# Truth and Lies

Karin could not shake the impending feeling of doom that had been with her for a couple of days. She could not shake the odd feeling that had come over her since the storm hit and had no reasonable explanation for it. She decided that she would keep busy and do productive things until he came home. She collected her gardening things and went outside to repair her much loved flower garden. She could not do much clean up before as the earth was too soaked to allow her sure footing. It saddened her to see that the storm had destroyed almost everything.

"Salty can you believe this mess?" She spoke aloud to the kitten as if he could really respond. In a way he did. He rubbed up against her and then jumped up on a little ledge where he stretched, yawned and then curled up to soak up the morning sun.

"Fine, don't help me. I can do it myself." She scratched his ears and then began to clean up.

She lost track of time and before she knew it, it was well past noon. She went inside to clean up and make herself a light lunch. She also poured a little bowl of milk for her faithful furry companion. Taking it outside, she sat down in the sunshine and had a small picnic. The view was beautiful and she could see the how calm the ocean was. It was almost flat and sea birds were visible on the horizon. The day was clear and bright blue with not a cloud in the sky. The trees that gently swayed in the breeze helped complete nature's canvas. Her mind took her to another day, very much like this one almost a year ago. She and Erik had gone to visit his grandparents, and as usual Erik's grandfather told her wonderful stories of his youth and ocean adventures. He had been a sea going man in his youth and she enjoyed him telling her all about his experiences. One such tale made her smile and at the same time like crying whenever she remembered it.

"Oh grandfather, that can't be something you really take seriously." She could not believe anyone would.

"No. It's true. Ask any sea going man. He'll tell you never to whistle on a fishing boat. It brings bad luck."

"Why? You're just teasing me." She laughed.

"Who knows why? I was never one to put it to the test."

"Well I would have. It sounds crazy to me. Whistling can often make the work go faster. I suppose you didn't sing either."

"No, singing is alright. But most men I sailed with had croaking voices."

"I would have sung or whistled anyway." She tried to look defiant.

"No. I don't think you would have. Women aren't allowed on fishing boats. I often remembered the little riddle that goes something like this. A whistling woman and a crowing hen will come to no good in the end. It's been around for a long time and the men believe women bring bad luck on fishing boats."

"Now that really is nuts. The fish don't care what gender catches them. They are just sorry to be caught."

"Nuts or no. It's the way it is."

"I suppose if a woman did sneak on board and things went wrong they would make her walk the plank?" She made her fingers do the walking off the edge of her hand.

"Who can say for sure what they would do."

"Grandfather, that's terrible."

"Yes it is. But this is more terrible. I knew personally of a woman on board a boat once and it met with ill fate. A bad storm came up from the northeast late one evening. It's a bad sign when it comes from that direction, and everyone on board knew the seas would be very rough. Sure enough, it brought high winds, needling rain with lighting and waves so large they crashed into and over the top of the boat. It pounded them for hours and eventually the sea won. She took the lives of all the men on board." He looked at her and she could see that in recalling the story, he felt sorrow for those who drowned.

"Everyone was lost?" The dismay in her voice was apparent.

"No, not everyone. One crewman and the woman survived. I suppose that it helps support the theory of not having a woman on board."

"What happened to them? Did they die of their injuries?"

"No. They lived. The woman married a man from someplace in the south. Rumor had it she wanted to forget all about the ocean and never see it again. As far as I know she's still in that part of the country."

"And the crewman?" She asked.

"The crewman recovered completely but never really went to sea in the same capacity as he had before. Eventually he too married and was blessed with two children. He had a son and daughter."

"Did you ever see him again?"

"Yes. Truth be known, I see him every time I shave." He looked at her and patted her hand at the same time.

"Grandfather; you were the crewman that survived?" She sounded a little surprised but pleased.

"Yes. That was me. I had much to be thankful for and I really felt that if the good Lord had spared me from the watery grave, He had a greater purpose in life for me. I set about trying to find what it was He wanted me to do. I found the answer soon enough and I've never regretted my decision."

"Oh, I'm so glad he spared you. If he hadn't there would be no Erik for me."

"That's true enough. It hasn't been easy to serve the Lord. When my daughter died during childbirth, I was having a difficult time understanding why He would want her to serve in a remote island community where there was no real doctor. After a time, I realized that these decisions were not for me to judge. That is how we came to have Erik in our lives. Esther and I enjoyed every day of his growing up."

"If it's not too painful, can you tell me what happened to his father. He never speaks of him." Karin hoped her questions were not too painful for him.

"He was also a missionary; a very fine man with a generous soul. He died of what the natives called Back Water Fever shortly before Erik was born. He never knew he had a son. Erik looks just like him. When we received word from, The Still Water Mission President, informing us that Erik was orphaned, Esther and I sailed to the island and brought him to live with us."

"I'm so sorry for your loss. At least you had Erik to bring joy into your life."

"He did do that. Now we have you and the joy continues to increase." He gave her a genuine heartwarming smile. She loved this kind and special man.

Her thoughts were interrupted by the sweet voice of Mei Ling. Turning around Karin saw her friend approaching with a sense of urgency.

"Karin, guess what has happened?" She was slightly flushed and a little out of breath.

"I don't know, is your grandfather alright?" Karin didn't know what to think.

"Yes, grandfather is fine. He's here," she spoke softly but raised her voice at the end of the sentence for emphasis.

"Who is here? What are you talking about?"

"The man selected by grandfather to marry me."

"He is? When did he get here?"

"He arrived early this morning. A man from the ship came to our house to announce his arrival. We were expecting him so everything was already prepared."

Have you already had a chance to speak with him?" Karin knew so little about Chinese courting customs that she had to ask.

"Yes, but we were not alone. We were introduced early this morning when he arrived at our home. It was only for about twenty minutes and everyone was present."

"What does he look like? Did you think you will like him?"

"He is young and taller than I thought he would be. I don't think he is very handsome but he has a nice face and kind eyes. He was very polite but confident when he spoke with grandfather. His gifts were very traditional. I think I could like him very much. In time, I'm certain that I will feel love for him."

"I'm glad. I know you have been thinking about this day for a long time."

"I have. I am almost relieved that it is here. But, now I am concerned about other things." She put her hand to her mouth and giggled behind her hand.

"Oh you! Stop worrying about that. I'm sure he will be very considerate of your feelings. After all, he comes from a fine family with an honorable upbringing. I'm sure the men in his family have discussed these private matters with him."

"Do you think so? I have never received any instruction."

"Women are different. Besides, you told me that you were to meet with some lady who is a distant relative of your grandfather. Maybe she will tell you about your role in the marriage ceremony and what to expect later." Karin gave her a knowing smile.

"I hope you are right."

"Of course I'm right. I think you are going to be just fine and your life will be as wonderful with him as mine is with Erik. Marriage is wonderful when you are happy and in love."

"I wish I was in love now. I don't know of anyone who got married and fell in love later."

"I do."

"You do? Can you tell me about it?"

"Sure. It was Erik's grandmother. She married a man she did not love at the time of her marriage. As the days went by she grew to love him dearly. I know that this is true because on the day she died, she told us a little bit about her youth." Karin recalled with some sadness the day that Mrs. Webb had passed away.

"So I guess it is possible to have a happy life even if it isn't starting out with love." Mei Ling felt a sense of comfort and peace and she was glad that she had spoken with Karin about some of her concerns.

"Yes it is. Just be prepared to give it some time and to be kind to one another and the rest will happen. One day, you'll wake up and realize how much he means to you and how special the relationship you have with each other is. You deserve every wonderful thing in the world. I know that your grandfather is so proud of you."

"Thank you. You are such a good friend."

"So what happens next?" She asked smiling.

"Grandfather is preparing a dinner in his honor. More exchanges will be made and final arrangements seen to. It's all pretty involved but I expect that the wedding will take place very soon." Mei Ling looked happy and a little uncertain at the same time.

"What will happen after you are married? Will you depart for China?" Karin felt a sense of complete dread at the thought of her leaving.

"No. I'm told that we will live in this country because he is a doctor and will stay to help the people here. Right now, all I have is my grandfather and he is getting old. I will find out more when we have a chance to speak and he informs me what he plans for us."

"I'm glad you won't be going to China. Will you be able to let me know what's going on now that he's here?"

"I will try. I'm not certain what grandfather has planned in the days ahead."

"Don't worry about anything. I completely understand. Just take care of yourself and honor your family. I know you will and just know that I will always be your friend." Karin felt a certain sense of loss due to the changes occurring in the life of Mei Ling.

"Thank you for understanding. You are a true friend. I think that perhaps I should be leaving now. I don't want to embarrass my grandfather if I should be missed. I hope to see you soon." The two friends hugged each other goodbye.

"Take care of yourself and know that you are also my true friend." Karin would miss her more than she would know.

When she departed Karin was left alone with the memories of the time they had spent together. The changes in the life of one woman meant things would never be the same again for either. She concluded that change could be a good thing and she would not despair over what she felt she lost. She would instead be content to know that her friend was embarking on a new life full of promise and if possible, she would keep in touch with her. She knew enough to know that Mei Ling was no longer going to be her own person, but subject to her husband's desires. She hoped he would be kind to her and love her deeply. Karin went inside her house and walked directly into her bedroom. She took the Bible into her hands and then knelt by her bed. She bowed her head and vocalized her prayer asking the Lord to comfort and bless her friend in the new life she was about to begin. She prayed for Erik, James and Daniel. It was a while before she finished her prayers but when she did she felt renewed. The day was still young so she set about cleaning up her beloved garden once again.

Chief Johnson managed to check out a few things before it was time to have lunch with Ian and Charity Fisk. He made inquiries at various places of business to get a better picture of the people he had set aside as suspects. In his official capacity as Fire Chief and Police Inspector, he was granted access to the private business transactions of the people he had considered suspects. To avoid gossip, he often asked for several folders of prominent persons along with his list of suspects. He was not certain what it was he was searching for, but when he found it, he felt certain he would know it. He checked the fishing logs at the cannery hoping that these logs would give him an idea of the financial status of the men in question. He made note that only two names appeared pretty often on the logs—Rolan and Ralston. He remembered that Doctor Grayson said that Mr. Rolan had been hurt in some kind of logging accident about fifteen years ago. He would probably need money for his care. He learned that the Rolan's had no family in the area and lived very modestly in a small home in the center of town. They attended church on a regular basis and Mrs. Rolan took a job as a seamstress in the only clothing store in the area. Mr. Rolan, although confined to a wheelchair, worked for the cobbler three days a week, and the other two days he went to the cannery where he would shuck oysters. They were well respected and did the best they could under unfortunate circumstances. Chief Johnson had years of experience reading the faces and lives of others. He did not believe that the Rolan's were suspect in anything. He admired their courage and the way that they had raised successful children. The next name he looked closely at was Ralston. These two men had all the indications that perhaps they needed to be watched more closely. The fishing log clearly showed that at one time they were good fisherman but had not been paid much in over ten months. The log also showed that at one time they had pledged any future catch toward a dept owed the cannery for bait and salt. The entry did not reference any payment made, nor did it indicate if the debt still existed. It could be possible that with limited income these men might be capable of almost anything if the price were right. There was also an outstanding large debt to the bank. He learned that they lived on their vessel and stayed pretty much alone. They were not married. He decided that he would look further into the activities of these men. There had been no entry for Robison. The man did not have a banking account, nor did he owe the cannery, ice house or Doctor Grayson. He paid Mr. Nash what little he owed him in cash each year usually at the end of summer. His needs were few and he never visited with anyone for long. His cabin was small but adequate for him and his two dogs. He was an expert hunter and lived alone as he had never married. Chief Johnson did not feel that Mr. Robison was the kind of man who would be willing to change his lifestyle suddenly. He was his own man. He was most certainly misunderstood but in all probability he was not malicious. Chief Johnson dismissed him from the list after a careful look. The man was almost sixty years old.

When Chief Johnson arrived at the hospital he was pleased to learn that Ian had already been bathed and was now in his room. There was the usual routine of cleanliness that had to be observed but once done he gained entry into Ian's room.

"Hello Chief." Ian greeted him warmly.

"Hello. It's good to see you both. How are you doing?"

"Fine. I'm so glad you could join us. I'm getting hungry."

"I'm pleased to be able to join you for lunch. Thank you for inviting me."

"Believe me, it's our pleasure." The voice was that of Charity.

"I've arranged for us to have a little table and two chairs. All we have to do is move them a little closer to Ian's bedside." She smiled at Ian.

"Table and chairs were allowed in here?" Chief Johnson thought perhaps they would use only napkins and stand while eating.

"Yes, but only after I scrubbed them down with lots of hot water and plenty of soap. Mr. Chang insisted upon it. He certainly wants everything clean."

"I think the whole thing is crazy myself." Ian gave a little snort.

"Maybe there's something to it. You haven't had any infection or fever and he assures me that keeping clean is more than half the battle. Doctor Grayson has turned into a true believer."

"How do you know that?" Ian asked.

"I spoke with him this morning and he's very impressed with everything that has been done for you. This is really something considering he was certain that you would be killed by the man." Chief Johnson looked at Ian and was amazed at how well his burns were looking. It was obvious he had a long way to go, but if the present was any indication of the future, he would heal and have a normal a life as possible.

"We owe him a great deal." Charity spoke aloud what the Chief was thinking.

"Who? Doctor Grayson or Mr. Chang?" Ian was being coy.

"Both. You got the benefit of traditional and nontraditional medicine. It's been an eye opener for everyone." Charity smiled at her husband and then turned her attention toward the Chief.

"I completely agree." Chief Johnson was glad that he personally sought help from Mr. Chang.

"Well, what say you both, shall we eat? I'm hungry for my delicious meal. In fact I can hardly wait for my mine." He said this with a little bit of sarcasm in his voice as he knew he would not be enjoying the meal that his wife and the Chief would be.

"I'm looking forward to this myself. Please allow me to move the table and chairs closer to the bed. It's the very least I can do for such a wonderful lunch."

"Thank you. That would be fine." She turned her attention to her basket and pulled out a pretty tablecloth. Once on the table she revealed the contents of the basket. Everything was wrapped in freshly washed white and red checkered cloth.

"Honey, the lunch looks terrific. Thank you for making it for us." Ian really did appreciate her taking time to make everything look nice.

"Well, it's my pleasure. I hope you enjoy everything."

Everyone enjoyed the lunch. Time passed quickly and after about an hour and a half Charity stood up to clear the table and repack the basket.

"If you will excuse me, I'm going to take these dishes to the hospital kitchen and wash them. I'll be back shortly." She placed everything she had into the basket and smiling at Ian, she left the room.

"That was sure a great lunch. I must return the favor when you are better."

"It's a deal. I'm a lucky man to have her."

"True enough. Ian, are you up to answering a few questions I have about the fire?"

"Sure. Is it about the initials I gave you the other day?"

"Yeah. I've investigated and have eliminated all but a couple of names that may provide us a lead. Have you ever heard of anyone named Robison?"

"Yeah, I have. He's the old recluse that lives somewhere in a cabin in the woods. That's about all I know about him."

"Alright, how about anyone named Ralston?"

"That's a name I know. Before I married Charity, I spent a little time at The Foggy Inn with the boys. The Ralston's were always there having meals and drinking ale but I never knew them to work much."

"Weren't they fishermen?"

"There were supposed to be, but they spent more time at The Foggy Inn than on the ocean. It was rumored that they were up to just about anything that would make coin. I never had much to do with them so it could be just talk."

"That pretty much figures with what I had. I didn't gather Mr. Robison would be involved in any underhanded doings—he doesn't fit the mold for lots of reasons."

"What do you suspect?"

"Based upon what you told me right after the fire and the investigation I've already conducted, I strongly suspect as you did. It appears to me that the fire was no accident. As you might already know, this is very sensitive information. I know I can count on you not to share it with anyone—not even Charity."

"I understand completely. What are you going to do next?"

"I'm going to continue to poke around and focus my efforts on the Ralston bunch while I'm waiting for the investigator to arrive."

"When do you expect him?"

"He should be here anytime."

"Great. Do you think I could meet him? I'm thinking of becoming an investigator myself. Right now, I'm told that fighting fires is out of the question but I still need a job. Fire fighting is all I know."

"I'll make it a point to bring him by. It's more than likely he'll want to speak with you anyway about our leads and you finding the pieces of leather that drew us to our own ideas of what caused the fire in the first place."

"Chief, I never thanked you for everything you've done for Charity and me. I owe you my life. I don't know how I'm ever going to repay you for that."

"I'm glad it worked out so well. You can repay me by getting well and back on the job. I can't keep doing your job and mine forever you know."

"I hope I'm not interrupting anything." Doctor Grayson was entering the room.

"Not a thing. The Chief and I were just talking about the wonderful lunch Charity fixed for us."

"I saw her going toward the kitchen. She looked real pretty this morning and I think it might have something to do with how well you are doing." Doctor Grayson was making his afternoon rounds.

"When do you think I'm going to get out of here Doc?"

"Ian, it will be some time yet. In a few weeks I think you can at least sit out on the porch but I have to get with Mr. Chang before anything different happens."

"Maybe I need to excuse myself so you two can speak in private. Please give my best to Charity and thank her for a wonderful lunch and pleasant conversation. Good afternoon Doc." Chief Johnson began to leave.

"Wait a moment. I've thought about this and I wanted to ask you and Ian for permission to use your names in an article I want to submit to a medical school concerning the treatment of burns."

"Is it the same article I saw you working on earlier this morning?" Chief Johnson knew very well it had to be.

"Yes it is."

"I think it would be a good idea," the Chief replied.

"I'm disadvantaged. I have no idea what you two are speaking about." Ian looked at them with questioning eyes.

"Sorry. Let me explain." Doctor Grayson began to inform Ian of his article and the great benefit it could afford other burn victims.

"It sounds like a fine idea to me. What does Mr. Chang say?" Ian asked the question.

"I got his permission yesterday after your treatment. I guess all I have to do is submit it and hope it gets the credit it deserves."

"I'm sure that it will. Well, I guess I'll be going I do have a few things I have to do before the end of the day. I'll stop by again soon." With one last look the Chief departed to place into action another phase of his investigation.

When he arrived at his office, he once again looked at all the information he had gathered. It occurred to him as he placed things in chronological order that there was something a little strange. His records indicated that Cole Ralston had borrowed money from the bank for personal reasons. The debt was still outstanding, actually it was stamped delinquent. He wondered what they had borrowed the money for. The Priscilla was paid for so it was possible that they simply borrowed money to make repairs on her. That was not unusual as several other members of the community had borrowed money for personal reasons. He then noticed that a few of the people who borrowed money were honest enough to say they needed money to pay off Mr. Nash when he called in all his credit markers. Did the Ralston men have the money to pay off Mr. Nash for items purchased like coffee, sugar or tobacco? He doubted they paid in cash since they had not made enough money to adequately live on for at least ten months. Could some kind of an arrangement been made between the two of them? The date on the loan that Cole Ralston signed for was very old. He was sure the credit marker at the mercantile remained because they borrowed the money on the original loan months before the markers were called in, and the original loan was delinquent. Under those circumstances the approval of another loan was not possible. It was no secret that just about everyone in town had credit at the mercantile. Why did Mr. Nash have to call his markers in now? Was he in some sort of financial trouble? A plot began to turn in the Chief's mind and he decided he would go see Mr. Nash and have a little conversation with him. He would take careful notice of his reactions and determine at that time if there was more than a business connection to Mr. Nash and one Cole Ralston. He also remembered the scratched ax head found near the remains of the oil barrels. But, mostly it was the initials on the piece of leather that Ian had provided him that proved the most disturbing. All the initials, L, E, R, L, and N fit the first and last name of only one man in town—Cole Ralston. He looked at the notes he made and after a little more thought he was certain he was correct. The only problem would be in proving a connection. What item would a man leave behind that had his initials on it? He would continue to think about it. He took pen and paper and made a note of his suspicions. He locked it in the safe and gave instructions to his men that the safe contained documents that were only for the eyes of the Fire Inspector, Mr. Gordon. He did this in the unlikely event he was killed by someone quite by accident of course or murdered by the people whom he suspected set the fire. His experiences taught him that desperate people did desperate things. He was the only person who had the combination to the safe so it would have to be opened by someone he trusted. He decided to give the combination to someone above suspicion. He would give it to Leroy.

Elsa Nash was amazed to see such a rough looking man on the front steps of her home. She could not begin to imagine what he might want so she remained out of sight and decided to listen to what he had to say.

"Good morning miss. I would like to speak with Mr. Nash if he is available. It's very important." Cole Ralston stood firmly but removed his hat when the maid answered the door.

"May I inform him who is calling?" She asked politely.

"Yes. I'm Cole Ralston."

"Are you expected this morning?"

"No I am not." He knew that she would announce him anyway so further discussion was not necessary.

"Please come in and wait. I'll inform Mr. Nash that you are here." She motioned him inside and shut the door behind him.

"Thank you." He stepped inside and took notice of all the nice things in the huge house. He concluded that the lavish lifestyle must be costing a fortune—much more than Mr. Nash could afford. His suspicion that he was in financial trouble might have just been realized.

Mr. Nash had just seated himself in a comfortable chair to read his morning paper. He had no idea that someone he never wanted to see again was now inside his home. He heard the bell ring but knowing the maid would answer he gave it little thought.

"Mr. Nash, excuse me, there is a gentleman by the name of Cole Ralston to see you. Will you see him or shall I ask him to return at a later time?"

"He's here now?" He was taken completely by surprise and felt his heart quicken and his mouth was suddenly dry. He wondered what to do and not wanting to spark the maid's curiosity, he quickly decided he would see him and try to keep the meeting short.

"Yes he is." She answered.

"Please show him into the study. I have a few moments before I have to leave." He had no plans to go anywhere, but it left him an opening to escape this uncomfortable situation.

"Shall I prepare coffee?"

"No. Our business will be concluded quickly." He rose from his chair to meet him. He could not believe the nerve of the man.

"Yes sir." She departed to show Mr. Ralston in and when she did, the doors to the study were left open. In only a few seconds they stood face to face.

"Nice house."

"Ralston, what are you doing here?"

"I need my money now. There's a lot of activity in town and I've heard some kind of investigator is coming and Flint and I want out now."

"You know that was not our agreement." He moved to quickly close the doors.

"Things have changed since that agreement."

"Not for me. I don't have that much money on hand right now." He could not believe this was happening.

"Well, how much do you have right now?" Cole was insistent. He did not intend to go home empty handed.

"I can pay you in full by tonight—same arrangement as before. It's the best I can do." He needed time to sell the jewels. From that sale he would make payment.

"Alright. But it better not be later than that. Keep in mind there are a lot of people who would like to know exactly what happened to that building." Cole looked closely at him and felt he really didn't have the money. Placing more pressure on him would not help.

"Are you threatening me?" Mr. Nash felt sick to his stomach because he knew that this wharf rat had him over a barrel.

"No. This is not a threat. I just didn't want you to forget that the Priscilla is ready to sail at any time and if Chief Johnson just happened to find out why the fire started and who was behind it....well, you would still be here along with you lovely little wife." Cole felt very smug having this seemly powerful little man where he wanted him.

"I think you had better leave. I said you would have your money tonight and I meant it. Meet me at the ice house at eight thirty. Don't be late and don't ever come to my home again. I'll have the maid show you out." It was his effort to regain control of the situation.

"Don't bother, I can find my own way out." Cole turned to leave and was glad he had thought to pressure Nash. However, if for some reason he failed to show up at eight thirty, there was not much he could really do about it. He was glad he had thought of another way to get the money they needed. He would not tell Nash that the Priscilla would set sail anyway one way or the other. He would let him worry while he pondered the best way to let Chief Johnson know what happened to the mercantile. Then a new thought came to him. Maybe he should silence Mr. Nash right after he got paid. It would be easy to take all he had and ensure that there was no connecting him to the fire. He needed to think of how best to do away with Nash. He would not tell Flint.

Elsa decided she would go down and speak to Rudolph. She wanted to know what the man at the door wanted. It was not in her husband's character to have people in his circumstances come to the home or do business with. When she entered the study, she found him shaken and pale.

"Who was that man?" Elsa wondered what they could have discussed that had Rudolph looking so badly. He was pale and had beads of perspiration on his forehead.

"It was just business Elsa. Don't concern yourself." He started to walk over to the small table in the corner of the room that held a cut glass bottle full of brandy. He needed a drink.

"Rudolph, you aren't going to pour a drink at this hour of the morning are you?" She was shocked he would even contemplate such a thing.

"Yes, I am. I hope it doesn't offend your sensibilities." With that comment, he poured out the brandy and took a long drink.

"What is going on with you? I won't be married to a drunk! It's bad enough that you lost everything we had. Now you want to forget your poor decisions with brandy. Lord only knows what will be next." She was not being rational.

"Elsa, stop this now! There are things going on of which you know little or nothing at all about. I'm doing the best I can in a very unpleasant situation." He did not want to argue with her.

"Well it isn't good enough is it?"

"What in the world do you want me to do?" He was beginning to feel greatly disappointed in her.

"I want you to fix this mess you got us in. If you can't then I'm not sure I will be able to stay here with you a minute longer." She already knew that she wanted to leave. The situation afforded her the opportunity to leave without feeling like she was the one who failed.

"Are you saying you want to leave me?" He was more than shocked.

"Yes. I suppose I am. It will take only a short while to have my things packed up. I do regret this, but it really is for the best." She felt a sense of excitement at the thought of being free of her unhappy marriage.

"Alright Elsa. If that is what you really want, I won't ask you to stay. May I inquire as to where you plan on going to?" He thought perhaps she would go to her parents. He would speak with her father later and try to settle this misunderstanding.

"I'm not certain. Maybe I will wire you in a few days."

"I understand. Now I hope that you understand that I still need your jewels. You will leave them behind." He had moved very close to her and his tone was not pleasant.

"My jewels? I have not changed my mind about selling them Rudolph. I intend to take them with me." She had moved herself slightly away from him.

"No! The financial situation we are in was created by mutual need. The jewels will help resolve it. You may call it the only good thing you did for our marriage." He turned to leave the room and she knew exactly where he was going.

"Don't you dare enter that room and open the safe to take my jewels! They are mine." She was right behind him in an effort to stop him.

"I am still the head of this family and I'll do what is best for us. Don't try and stop me Elsa. I am determined to take them." He had a look about him that she had never seen before. In a strange way it frightened her. He entered the room and began to unlock the safe. Soon the jewels were in his hands.

"Then take them!" She spat the words at him with great anger.

"I am glad you have come to your senses. In a while things will be alright." He placed the jewels inside his suit vest.

"No they will not. Things will never be alright again. As far as I'm concerned our marriage is over. I will not be back." She gave him a venomous look.

"You know you will. Stop saying crazy things you do not mean." He would reason with her again when she was not so upset. When he returned from the sale of the pieces they could talk more calmly.

"I do mean what I just said. I never wanted to be married to you in the first place. I only agreed because my family was tainted with rumors about the jewels and no reputable family would offer marriage. It was our little family secret, or so we thought. I was forced to accept you. I've hated every minute of our marriage. I never loved you and when you touched me it made my skin crawl. I only pretended to enjoy being with you because you could buy me nice things. Now, you can't even do that. You revolt me!" She was beyond caring what she said.

"You little tart! Get out of my sight before I regret what I may do." He started to brush pass her but she offered him one last barb.

"That's right. I am a tart. In fact I am such a tart that I have a lover and you didn't even know it. I have been with him more times that I have with you. He knows what to do with a woman." She wanted to humiliate him.

"What? That's not true." He was momentarily stunned.

"It is all true. Do you want to know what else is true? When I got pregnant the baby was his, not yours. Now you know why I won't be back." She gave him a smile that was more like a sneer.

"You whore!" He lost his temper and suddenly slapped her across the face. It left a scarlet mark on her lovely cheek. He hated himself the moment he did it. He never thought in a million years he would ever hit a woman, let alone his wife.

"I hope you die!" She ran from the room toward the staircase. In only a few seconds she reached the top and slammed shut her bedroom door.

Rudolph sat down shaken by all that transpired between them. He looked at his hand and deeply regretted his cowardly actions. He was wrong to have struck her and he knew it. She had wounded him deeply with her angry confession. Her check bore evidence where he had struck her. Where she struck him was invisible—in his mind and soul.

James and Daniel were pleased with the progress the Sea Star was making. The ocean was calm and a nice breeze puffed out the ship's sheets allowing her to move at a slow but steady pace. They would be home soon.

"If this weather keeps up, we will be home in a few hours. The tide won't be the best but we can still make it." James was looking at the charts and the horizon.

"That will be nice but it will also feel pretty bad." He was thinking of Erik and telling Karin about his death.

"Thinking of Karin?" James knew exactly how Daniel felt.

"I am. I just wish that we had something to offer her. What were we really doing out here? It seems to me that all we accomplished was getting him killed."

"It was an accident. We did all we could."

"Do you think she has any idea what he was doing out here?" Daniel was thinking that maybe Erik had shared something with her.

"She could have. Erik always said he and Karin shared everything. I guess we could ask her when we get home."

"James, have you gone through any things that he brought with him?"

"No. All he had was his coat and a few pieces of clothing."

"Do you think it disrespectful if I take a look?" Daniel did not want to offend the memory of his friend.

"What does it matter now? Go ahead and look."

Daniel went below and looked carefully at all the clothing Erik had brought with him. There was nothing. He folded everything neatly and went to inform James that he had found nothing. Clearly whatever Erik had been looking to find only he knew what it was. The rest of the trip home was filled with mixed emotions. Glad that they had not lost their lives as well, but deeply saddened over the loss of their friend. They decided that they would make themselves available to Karin to help make repairs to the house or help her relocate to another place if she so desired. No matter what happened in the future, they would remain her friends. They also decided it would be James to tell Karin about Erik. She knew James longer and seemed to have a bond with him that she did not have with Daniel. Daniel did not envy James the terrible task he had ahead of him.

Rue had spent a few hours going through her closets and drawers sorting out things for her trip to Spain. She had purchased a traveling trunk a few years ago and it was now filled almost to the top with things she wanted to keep. She thought it sad that after almost ten years, everything she wanted fit nicely into the five foot by three foot long trunk. She took her ticket out of her jewelry case and looked at it closely for the first time. Plans for the future clearly printed in black and white. It stated there on the ticket that passage for one with various port connections and a final destination in Spain was paid for. The ship was the Mystic Quest. He arranged for them to travel first class. Joaquin had booked them into the same cabin as husband and wife. The cabin offered them privacy and enough space to store their luggage and a bed large enough for the both of them. Next to the bed was a small window to allow for much needed fresh air and light. It would remain open on days the sea was calm. He was assured a table with two stools would also be in the room. On the wall two lamps with oil would provide plenty of light. There would also be a chamber pot for their personal needs. Fresh water would be made available daily in sufficient quantities to ensure they stayed clean. Most importantly a solid wood door with a strong lock secured the cabin. If Rue decided she wanted to rest during the day she could do so safely. If he wanted to join the men for cigars or card playing on deck, he would not have to worry about her. At times when she was away from him everyone would know that she was a married woman traveling with her husband. This would ensure that she would not be the victim of unwanted advances from crew or other male passengers. When Joaquin inquired about the list of passengers, there were no other passengers from the surrounding area traveling with them. Her new life could begin the minute she stepped on board the ship. When she questioned Joaquin about the cost of the ticket and why he had to have first class for them, he told her that any other class would mean poor quality meals, no privacy for her personal needs, very limited fresh water and open sleeping areas on hay. By the end of the week the hay would be soiled and insects would be crawling on their skin. Thieves were everywhere and keeping valuables secure meant keeping them on her person at all times. This alone put her at additional risk from injury sustained in a robbery. It was miserable to travel in another section of the ship other than first class accommodations. He knew it from personal experience. When he left Spain he was forced to live in such conditions as the lowest member of a crew. He vowed never to travel like that again. In their years of being friends, he had never disclosed anything very personal about himself. When she agreed to go to Spain, he felt it necessary to make her aware of what they might encounter. He drew a mental picture that at times touched her deeply and she could only imagine his suffering on the way to America. He spoke quietly of his family and she listened without interrupting him. She learned things about him and it helped her understand more about the man than she ever thought possible. She closed her eyes for a moment and remembered some of the things he said.

On the day he left Spain, his family refused to see him off and give him the family blessing for a safe voyage and good fortune. They thought his ambitions foolish and sure to result in his death. It was only his sweet sister who gave him a hug promising to keep in touch and vowing to keep him in her prayers. She was fifteen at the time and he could still see her crying on the dock as the ship left the harbor. His heart was breaking also at the thought of leaving her. He promised himself that if fortune smiled upon him, he would repay her love and support of him in any way he could. The ship he signed on with was good sized and the crew seasoned. He was an assistant to the cook. The hours were miserable and everyone complained about the food. When he was not doing chores for the cook he was doing the lowest form of work on ship. He was dumping and washing out chamber pots. He spent many hours in the crow's nest during inclement weather and more often than not missed meals because no one offered him relief from his post. On good days, he was allowed to scrub the deck. He considered that a relief from other chores because he was out in the open breathing fresh air. At night it was a different story. He was a handsome young man and found himself the object of attention for some of the men. He was forced to sleep lightly and was always fighting off their unwanted advances. They resented him and made his life on ship harder than it should have been. After a few weeks, he found a safe place to sleep. It was located in the galley. There was a small space between the stove and the wall. It was enclosed in the front and back and one side. He slept with his feet tied to the stove legs with a long length of rope that ran under and behind his body. If anyone should have attempted to pull him out they would have met with resistance. This would allow him time to yell for help and continue kicking his attacker. The only disadvantage was he could not move easily once he lay down and sometimes the heat from the stove would not allow him to sleep. On cold nights it was perfect and he rested completely. This was how he spent the many months at sea until finally reaching the shores of America. He spoke very little English and was forced to work terrible jobs. He made learning to speak English a priority and in no time at all earned the reputation of being a good worker and a dependable hand. He lived in poor conditions to save money. He ate only every other day. Two years later, he had saved enough to rent a small room in a cheap hotel. In time, he moved again and found himself in Valda Bay. It was here that things improved and now he felt he had come full circle. He was on his way home with all his hopes and dreams about to come true.

When he finished telling Rue about his early days, she had a new respect for him. He had suffered to realize a dream. She had suffered also. They had more in common than she ever imagined. It was no wonder that they got along so well—they were two people with a difficult past and a hopeful future. Rue shook herself free of her thoughts and decided that she would let Joaquin know that she was packed and ready to leave whenever he was. She would not miss Valda Bay and was looking forward to a new life with her son and sister in Spain. She decided it was time to tell him about her past and more importantly her son. She closed the trunk and took her hat and wrap from the peg on the wall. She closed the door behind her and walked in the direction of Joaquin's hotel room.

Chief Johnson left his office and was walking toward the home of Mr. Nash. He had already given considerable thought to what he would discuss with him. He knew he had to tread lightly. But there was one stop to make before he went any further. He needed to see Leroy and give him the combination to his safe. He saw Leroy coming out of Mrs. Steele's Sweet Shop. There was a small white box tucked up under his arm. The Chief knew without even asking that she had given him some fresh bread, fruit pastries and coffee. He helped Mrs. Steele by lifting heavy sacks of flour, sugar, oats and various sacks of fruit that she purchased to refill her food bins in the kitchen. He also chopped wood and stacked it neatly for her. She paid him with a small amount of money and baked goods. They had had this arrangement for years. When Leroy saw the Chief, he smiled and walked up to him. The Chief noticed that they were alone and away from prying eyes and listening ears.

"Leroy, I forgot to mention at breakfast that there is one more thing you can do for me if you would."

"Sure, if I can." Leroy said he would help if he could and he meant it.

"I thought of you because I need a person I can trust completely. It concerns something important that is related to the fire at the mercantile. I feel that man is you, but if you don't want to be involved, I understand. Are you interested or would you rather not get involved?" He felt it only fair to inform him to a small degree of what this important matter was about.

"I can help. What is it Chief?" He spoke without stuttering once.

"I'm giving you the combination to my safe. No one else has it except me. I've placed some important papers in it that are to be seen only by Mr. Gordon. He's the fire inspector that will be here anytime now. The envelope is clearly marked and you are to place it in his hands only, no one else. Once you give it to Mr. Gordon, your job is done. Will you do that?" He was looking directly into his eyes and could see that Leroy whom everyone considered stupid was anything but that.

"Yes. I understand completely. You can depend on me." He said it without any hesitation.

"Thank you for helping me. Here is a piece of paper with instructions for the combination. I'd like you to memorize it then burn it at your first opportunity." He gave him the piece of paper and watched Leroy look at it intently.

"Consider it done. Do you have a piece of flint?" He never smoked so he didn't carry any.

"Sure." He reached into his pocket and drew out the box with flint.

"Here goes." Leroy struck the box and when the sparks flew out, he placed the paper close to allow it to catch fire. It began to burn.

"Leroy. I didn't mean burn it now. You have to memorize it." The Chief thought perhaps he had made a mistake.

"I know Chief. I already did." He looked at him and smiled.

"You did? What was the combination—humor me, I'm getting old."

"No problem." Leroy began to recite the instructions exactly as written.

"You are something, you know that?" The Chief smiled and was glad Leroy considered him a friend.

"You too." Leroy smiled back and the two men parted, each to their own way.

As the Chief made his way to the Nash home, he continued to be amazed at how quickly Leroy memorized the instructions. He could remember a time when everyone thought Leroy was mentally deficient. He wondered what they would think if they knew that not only was he not deficient, he could read. That in itself was more than half the people in Valda Bay could do.

The Nash home came into view and when he was not too far from the walkway that led to the front door, he saw a young man leaving the house. They met at the halfway point on the walk and exchanged a pleasant greeting. When the Chief knocked at the front door he was recognized by the woman who had answered the door on his last visit.

"Good morning Chief." The woman was neatly dressed and polite.

"Good morning. I was hoping to see Mr. Nash if he is available."

"Please come in and I'll inform Mr. Nash you are here." She stepped aside and the Chief entered.

"Thank you I appreciate that." He removed his hat and prepared to be announced.

"It's a good thing you arrived when you did. In another moment or two you would have had to wait until Mr. Ralston and Mr. Nash concluded their meeting. He only just departed." She did not realize she had provided a valuable piece of information.

"Mr. Ralston was here but just now left?" He asked.

"Yes sir. I thought you may have seen him leaving the house. Please excuse me." She turned and went toward the study. She knocked and waiting only a few seconds entered the room. She found that Mr. Nash was clearly shaken. She did not know why.

"Mr. Nash?" She did not like the way he looked—pale and sweating. Perhaps it was because of the meeting with Mr. Ralston or worse he actually was sick and needed medical attention. She decided she would not ask about his health. It was not her place.

"Yes?" He did not look up from his chair.

"Will your schedule permit you to see Chief Johnson now? He is waiting in the parlor."

"Chief Johnson?" This was the last thing that he wanted to hear. He wished there was a tactful way to rid himself of the Chief and still not draw undue interest to himself.

"Yes sir." She waited.

"Yes. Send him in after a bit. I need a couple of moments to collect my thoughts after my last meeting. I also need a moment to settle my stomach. Please bring in some tea with crackers after he leaves." He tried to look more collected and calm.

"I'll see to it. Good morning sir." She turned and closed the door to the study behind her. She approached the Chief and began to relay the message from Mr. Nash.

"Chief, Mr. Nash will see you in a few moments. I'll be close by if you should need me." She bowed her head slightly and turned to leave.

Waiting to see Mr. Nash he realized that he had exchanged pleasantries with one of the Ralston men just a few moments ago. There was a definite connection with these two men. All he had to do was ask the correct questions, observe responses and see where it all led. His morning was proving very productive. In a few minutes Mr. Nash opened the doors to his study and invited the Chief in. The Chief noticed that he looked tense and appeared slightly uncomfortable.

"It's good to see you, how can I help you?" He stood before the Chief.

"Well, I have a few questions about the fire I need to ask you. I also need a few things clarified before the arrival of Mr. Gordon. I believe I mentioned that he's the fire inspector that's due to arrive any time now." The Chief noticed that he did not ask him to sit down.

"I see. What is it you need to know?" It was a little too much to the point. This told the Chief that he wanted this over with quickly.

"Mr. Nash, is there anyone you can think of that would have any reasons to do or your family financial harm?" He asked while keeping a keen eye on him.

"No, not off hand. I do have a lot of business associates and after all sometimes business is business. Why do you ask that?"

"In the course of my investigation I've discovered a few things that led me to ask for an expert in building fires. I've found something that warrants his attention."

"Oh you have? Are you at liberty to say what it is?"

"No. Not at this time. But, it's beginning to look as if the fire was not the accident everyone seems to think it is. Please understand that I'm not saying this is a fact or placing blame on anyone." The statement was baiting and meant to draw some kind of attention.

"I understand." He hated not knowing what the Chief had discovered.

"Also, can you tell me if you are acquainted with anyone by the name of Ralston?"

"Ralston? I know who they are." He needed to be careful.

"So have you done any personal or professional business with them at any time?" He detected some reluctance in answering the question.

"I know Cole Ralston much better than I do his brother." He wondered why he was asking this question. Did he already know they were the ones that started the fire and was only playing with him?

"That's fine. But, like I asked, do you or have you had any business dealings of any kind with them?"

"I have done some business with Cole Ralston in the past. I've never done any type of business with his brother."

"That would be Flint Ralston, correct?"

"I believe that is his name."

"Do you suspect them of anything?" He hoped the Chief would reveal more of what he suspected or already had concluded so he tried to bait him.

"Like I said Mr. Nash, I'd rather not say at this time."

"Of course." He wanted this to be over.

"Well, I can think of no other questions I have at this time. However, if you should think of anyone who would be in such a state of affairs as to wish or do you harm, please call me anytime. I assure you that I won't let this rest until I find out who is responsible for you losing your place of business." He was still standing in the same place as when he entered the room. This told the Chief that he was not really welcome and that Mr. Nash did not want to discuss at length anything about the fire. This usually meant that people were hiding something.

"Thank you. I appreciate all you are doing."

"You are more than welcome. I'm sure we will speak again when Mr. Gordon arrives. He will probably want to go over a few things with you in greater detail."

"That will be fine." He found himself breathing a little easier now that the Chief would be going.

"Oh, I'm sorry. One more thing before I go."

"Yes?" He could not believe that the torture would continue.

"Have there been any threats to Mrs. Nash? Perhaps from a gentleman she rejected who may have resented her marriage to you or anything like that?"

"Not to my knowledge."

"I see."

"Will there be anything else?"

"No. You have been most helpful. I appreciate you seeing me this morning especially since I was not expected. Mr. Nash are you feeling alright?" He noticed that he did not look especially well.

"Oh, I'm fine." He lied.

"Well, please give my best to Mrs. Nash. I'll see myself out." He turned and started to leave. Then he thought he would put a little nail into the coffin he was sure that he was hiding in.

"Forgive me. Just one more question. Do you do any type of custom lettering or stamping in your store?" He would look carefully for his reaction.

"No." He wondered where this could be going.

"That's fine. Well, thank you again." The Chief turned to leave.

"Chief, why do you ask that?"

"Well, it's nothing probably. Just a little piece of evidence that I've found that I'm sure Mr. Gordon will figure out. Don't concern yourself. I'll be in touch as soon as there is something to inform you about. It won't take long." He smiled and proceeded out the study. He wished he had eyes in the back of his head. The look on Mr. Nash's face had to be priceless.

As he walked outside, he was certain that Mr. Nash had some terrible secret and connection to the Ralston's. He was not invited to sit down or even offered a cup of coffee. These things coupled with the fact that he didn't provide any additional information no matter how small that may have helped solve the suspected crime. He didn't ask if he could help in any way. He didn't ask for a fire report or progress notes. People who had something to hide already knew the answers, so they would not want what they already had. Things were not going to go well for Mr. Nash.

As soon as the Chief departed, Mr. Nash formulated a plan. He drank his tea and the crackers helped his stomach. After a few minutes, he went outside and spoke with the groom asking that he make ready his horse and buggy. He informed him casually that he would only be gone a few hours. When he was inside the house, he raced up the stairs and closing the door to his bedroom, placed all the jewels inside a handkerchief and began to undress. He would take a few minutes to refresh himself and dress into a suit that was appropriate for a road trip. He needed to sell the jewels quickly to pay off the Ralston brothers and put an end to their threats. He wanted them to leave Valda Bay so that there could be no connection made between the three of them. Once dressed, he began to pack and placed the jewels inside a small trunk. It was almost noon and he knew Elsa would still be home when he returned. There was no evening transport out of town. He thought after he returned he would deal with her and if possible her lover. It was not beyond thinking that perhaps before the Ralston's left, he would have enough money from the sale of the jewels to offer them one last final deal. This time, he would be wiser and have the money to pay them in full. He had come this far, what was one more terrible act? He realized, as he thought about it, that he did not love Elsa at all. He had been attracted to her beauty. That beauty was superficial and cold. She had no beauty within.

# Turn of Events

$\mathcal{E}$lsa was in her room hurt and angry at Rudolph. She despised him and could not believe that he had actually struck her. She had looked at her face in the glass and could see an ugly red mark on her ivory cheek. She had formulated a plan but she needed more information to make it work. She placed some cool cloths over her cheek and carefully put on some face powder to hide the redness. She touched up her lip rouge and brushed her hair and styled it so that it hid a portion of the mark. She would put on a pleasant face and smile when she spoke with the maid. If she kept the maid to her uninjured side, it was possible that she would not notice the mark. She went downstairs and found the maid in the study. When the maid saw her enter, she immediately turned her attention toward her.

"May I be of assistance Mrs. Nash?"

"Perhaps. I saw Mr. Nash depart and wondered if he mentioned to you when he would return? I was lying down because I had one of my nasty headaches and I can't for the life of me remember what he said." She pretended to be concerned.

"Oh, I'm sorry you weren't well. He told me that he would not be back until later this evening. He had some kind of business meeting." She relayed what Mr. Nash had in fact told her.

"Yes. I do recall that now. Goodness, I feel so badly not remembering. Thank you for your help." She smiled at the woman.

"You are most welcome. Will there be anything else?" She needed to return to her work so she would be able to stay on her cleaning schedule.

"Just one thing. I know you are terribly busy, but I was wondering if the gentleman that called this morning was going with him."

"There were two gentlemen callers this morning. Which one are you referring to?"

"The first one. The man looked like one of the brokers we deal with on the dock and I wondered if Mr. Nash left any paperwork for me to sign and later have sent to him." It was a lie but one the maid would have no way of finding out one way or the other.

"That would be Mr. Ralston. As far as I know there was nothing left. Shall I help you look for the paperwork?" She was concerned that perhaps she had misunderstood her orders. She didn't want to be dismissed.

"No. It's not that important. At any rate, Mr. Nash will be home in time for dinner and he and I can discuss any important matters at that time. Please do continue with your work. I will be upstairs resting." She turned and left the study with the knowledge she wanted. She had the name of the man who came to the door.

"I will see to it that you are not disturbed."

"Thank you. I appreciate that." Everything went as she hoped. She had the name she sought—Ralston. After her conversation with the maid, Elsa made up her mind to pack up a trunk with her favorite dresses and accessories. She informed her personal maid that she wanted to lie down and rest. She gave her the afternoon off to ensure that there would be no embarrassing questions to answer. The maid also carried a small sealed envelope; one of several she had delivered in the last few months. There was not much time to waste so she began to pack. She looked into her closet and selected only things that were very flattering, expensive and well made. She packed carefully and was able to accommodate almost everything she wanted into her trunk. It only took a couple of hours and she was pleased with the results. There was nothing holding her back. She was now ready to leave Rudolph and her unhappy marriage. She knew where she would go. She wished it was later in the day but there was no choice. She had to go now while she still felt she could. She put on her hat, gloves and carried a medium sized purse. She threw a small wrap around her shoulders. She opened her bedroom door and didn't see anyone. She could hear noise downstairs and knew she could go out by way of the back door. She made her way downstairs and without anyone knowing, she left the house.

Rue had reached the cheap hotel in which Joaquin rented a room. It was located on the second floor next to a stairway that was used as a discreet way for gentlemen of quality to leave rooms they had been entertained in by the house ladies. She entered and knocked on Joaquin's door. She hoped he was in.

"Rue this is a nice surprise. Please come in." Joaquin was also in the process of packing his belongings.

"I hope you have a moment to speak with me."

"For you I always have time."

"Thank you. I have already packed myself, but there is something I must tell you before we make the trip."

"You still want to go don't you?"

"Yes. I still want to go, but like I said, there is something important that you must know about me if we are to really do this together." She looked at him and in a way was sorry that she had not confided in him earlier.

"Alright Rue. You have my complete attention." He sat down in a chair next to her and gave her his complete attention.

"It's not easy for me so let me finish before you say anything." She took a deep breath and began to tell him about her early life and the son that she had. After about ten minutes, she was finished and was looking at him for his reaction.

"Is that it? You have a son who will no doubt come to Spain in a few months?" He thought she was going to say something terrible, like she was dying or something.

"Well yes. I think that is pretty significant don't you?" She was surprised by his reaction.

"I do because having a son is a wonderful thing. He will be welcome as will your sister. They matter to you and you matter to me. I can only say that I'm sorry I'll have to wait so long to meet them." He smiled at her and walked over and touched her cheek with the back of his fingers.

"Joaquin, I can honestly say that very few people surprise me. You just did. Thank you for your understanding. I should have known that it would be alright."

"Yeah, you should have. But, I forgive you. Does your family know about me?" He wasn't sure why he asked that.

"Yes. I wrote to them a few days ago. I mentioned our plans and that I would write when I could." She felt relieved and was glad things were now out in the open.

"Good. I think we are finally set. We leave on the tide tomorrow. Would you like a small glass of wine to celebrate?" He stood up and went to the table to get the glasses and bottle of wine.

"Yes. But only a little bit. I have a few things I still have to do." She smiled at him. He was standing close to her and he could smell the faint aroma of her perfume. She had the unique ability to arouse him without even trying. He looked over to the bed and then to her.

"No. Don't even think it." She reached out and placed her palm on his chest in an attempt to keep him at bay.

"I won't. Can I hold you close for a moment before you go?"

"For only a moment." She wished he was not so handsome and that she did not know the great pleasure he gave her.

"For only a moment." He repeated softly and reached for her. He moved her against him and placed his hands on her neck and slowly ran them down the length of her back. He found her neck and gently planted warm deliberate kisses where his memory told him she liked to be kissed. He was amazed at how he reacted to her even after all these years. They moved well together almost as if they were patterned for each other. More often than not, they reached their pleasure together.

"Rue, let's get into my bed." His voice had turned slightly husky.

"Joaquin, I don't have my things here." She needed to be the voice of reason.

"I'm here." He reached for her hand and held it tightly while continuing to kiss her neck and now her face. He brushed her lips with his and then kissed her deeply. His mouth was expert and they both tasted slightly of wine. He knew where to touch her.

"You know what I mean. Please stop this before I don't want you to." She used her firm tone with him. She was feeling desire flow in her veins and in only a short time, she would be in his bed. She would hate herself later for having taken a foolish chance at getting pregnant. If she had her things with her it would be a different story.

"Rue, if it were any other woman but you ..." He gently released her and moved away.

"Joaquin, what in the world happens to us whenever we are alone? I didn't come here to ask that we not be together. You know why I came." She felt terrible that she could not be with him as he wanted.

"I don't know what happens. You are so damn beautiful and we pleasure each other so well. You must think that's all I think about." He felt a little ashamed of himself for his actions especially when she came to inform him about something important—her son.

"I know better than that." She handed him the glass of wine, and took a drink from her own glass.

"Thank you, I need that." He smiled at her and drank the wine in his glass in just a couple of swallows. He was trying to get his body relaxed again.

"Me too." She laughed lightly.

"Yeah? Nice to know I wasn't alone. Well, getting back to this packing business, I think that everything is just about ready. I have only a few things left to put into my trunk. Now, let me tell you something that you will find....well, I don't know."

"What?" She could not imagine what it might be.

"Of course you remember Elsa Nash?"

"Yes."

"Well, she sent a note to me earlier this afternoon and wants to see me about some urgent matter."

"Oh Joaquin, she's not pregnant again is she?"

"Not by me. I haven't touched her since you helped me out of that mess."

"Well, that's good. Do you have any idea what it could be?"

"None. I was hoping to leave Valda Bay and never see her again. The note she sent says she will be here this afternoon."

"You mean here in your room?" Rue was more than surprised to learn that.

"Yeah."

"It must be important. I should be going. I wish you would have said something sooner. I don't want to be here when ..." Rue was interrupted by a knock at the door. There was little doubt it was Elsa Nash.

"I bet that's her now." Joaquin did not want her to know of his travel plans or of Rue.

"It's alright. I'll leave quickly without too much being said. Go and answer the door." She quickly collected her things while Joaquin waited a moment to open the door.

"Elsa, it's nice to see you again. Please come in." He greeted her with forced zeal and motioned her inside. He closed the door behind him quickly. He was not sure what to expect of her. He decided to make introductions and hope that Rue would be able to depart quickly.

When she entered she immediately saw Rue and despite appearing civil and composed, she was angry that she was in his room. Why was she here?

"Ladies, may I make introductions? Rue this is Elsa, Elsa this is Rue."

"How do you do?" Elsa spoke first.

"It's a pleasure to meet you. I regret that I cannot stay; I was just leaving when you knocked, if you will excuse me, I must be on my way." With that she moved toward the door.

"Thank you for coming." Joaquin opened the door and she left without incident. He breathed a huge sigh of relief as he closed the door.

"Joaquin, who was that woman?" Elsa was looking upset.

"She is just a friend." He tried to sound causal.

"What was she doing here?" She knew it was none of her business but she couldn't help herself.

"Never mind that, what are you doing here? You said it was urgent." He had just realized that he had not asked her to be seated. "Please have a seat and tell me."

"I have finally done it. I feel no regret and in a way, I feel better than I have in months. We can have a life now." She was looking at him with an adoring look that made him feel trapped.

"What have you done?" He knew that he would probably not like it at all.

"I've told Rudolph our marriage is over and that I would not suffer his horrible attentions again. I also said that I never loved him." She smiled hoping for his approval.

"You did what?" He was shocked.

"Yes. It had to happen sometime my love. We had a terrible quarrel and before I knew it, I was telling him that I had a lover. In fact, it was so terrible that I even told him about getting pregnant with your baby. He called me a terrible name and struck me across the face." She was turning her head so he might see the bruise.

"Elsa, did you tell him who I was?" He could have cared less about all the details of the argument as long as her husband did not know who he was. Rudolph Nash was still a rich and powerful man. He did not want to have any exchanges with him or have the law seek him out. He cursed himself and the day he first gave in to his lust for her.

"No, of course not. He left this morning before we spoke again. Does my cheek look terrible? I hope it won't leave a permanent mark. You would not want to have an ugly wife would you?" She stood up and moved closer to him and put her arms around his neck.

"Elsa, I never said we would be together. We had a good time but I thought you knew that I wanted you to stay with your husband." He reached up and removed her arms from his neck.

"What do you mean we had a good time?" She had an odd look on her face.

"Just that. We enjoyed each other in bed and even that met with disaster when you got pregnant. I never told you I loved you. Why did you think that we would be getting married?" He did not want to sound cruel, but he was speaking the truth.

"All the times you made love to me. I felt your love then." She did not understand this conversation.

"I've made love to a lot of women. It does not mean that I'm in love with them. I just enjoyed the pleasures their body offered me." He hated this.

"So you are saying that you never loved me, only used my body for your own pleasure?" She had finally grasped what he was saying.

"That sounds badly. I think we were good friends, more perhaps, but not lovers in the true sense of the word." He thought that sounded better than the truth.

"It comes down to the fact that you used me for nothing more than a tumble." She was getting angry.

"Elsa, I don't want this to end badly. But, it does have to end here and now. I do not want a life with you now or at any time. You are a very pretty woman and I feel that if you wanted to, it would not be too late to make amends with your husband."

"If that is not the statement of a cad, I do not know what is." Her color was high and she was angry.

"Now listen here. I did not lift your skirts without your approval and encouragement. I never promised you anything. I think it best you leave now before you are seen and everything is lost." He knew that this day would arrive, but he hoped when it did she would just realize he had gone. He hoped she would not know what happened to him.

"I will leave since I can see by that packed trunk that you are planning on leaving soon and obviously without me. Perhaps you will not be able to depart before I give Rudolph your name."

"Do what you must. If you feel that you have to drag that decent man down with us, I can do nothing to stop you." He was getting angry now.

"At least he is decent man. Much more that you will ever be. You can go to hell." She retorted.

"Ladies first. I know I have to account for a lot but so do you. The only decent thing you were capable of doing you killed while it was still in your belly. May God forgive both of us for what we did and the terrible people we are." He had thought about that day countless of times. If he had it to live over again, he would have done things very differently. He regretted not calling out her name when she walked away from him that afternoon even if it meant they were discovered and he would have to give up his own dreams.

"I cannot believe you just said that to me." She said it barely above a whisper.

"Elsa, we have hurt each other enough. I never meant to but I did. Please forgive me for not being all you wanted and needed and for saying the hurtful things I just said. It accomplishes nothing, what is done is done." He looked at her and saw that there was hurt and disbelief in her lovely eyes. She had tears on the rim that threatened to spill over.

"I do forgive you. Can you forgive me for the baby and everything I did?" She felt him reach for her hand and allowed him to hold her close for a moment.

"There is nothing to forgive. Let us part friends and remember the pleasant days we shared." He released her but placed her hand over his heart while continuing to hold it securely.

"I agree. I must leave now. Take care of yourself and be happy in whatever you decide to do and wherever your travels may take you. I promise I will not tell anyone about you." She meant it.

"Take good care of yourself." He lifted her hand from over his heart placing a small kiss on the back of her hand. His lips formed a faint smile and he released her hand gently. She turned away and knew his memory would remain safely locked away in her heart. When the door to his room closed behind her, she knew beyond a shadow of any doubt that she had been a fool. He had never loved her. Squaring her shoulders, she knew there was still time to make at least one thing right. She would put her alternative plan in motion.

Cole and Flint had been deep in conversation for the better half of the morning. Things had not gone as well as expected with Mr. Nash. He didn't get any money so they could depart. Now, with few options, they were thinking of something that was more daring and required considerably more planning than the mercantile.

"I wish there was another way of getting money other than this idea." Flint did not like the idea proposed to him from the start.

"Well if you can think of one I am sitting here ready to hear it." He gave his brother a hard glare.

"I didn't say I had a better idea Cole. But you have to admit, this is a first for us. I wish we could catch a break for once in our damn lives."

"I know. That is why I've decided that I'm going to walk up by the lighthouse and from there I can see the house clearly. It will allow me to look around without anyone suspecting anything."

"What if someone comes by and sees you checking out the house?"

"Good point. Let me get the almanac. If I'm not mistaken, it's a low tide around six thirty this evening." He got up and found the information he needed. He was correct about the tide.

"That's only about three hours from now." Flint was thinking they would not have time to do what they wanted.

I have time to get up there and take a look around. I'll be sure to take a bucket with me."

"Why are you taking a bucket?" Flint had no idea.

"To pretend I'm clamming and not checking out the house. You were the one that said someone might come by." Cole wished his brother would help him think.

"I could be a lookout for you." Flint was sure he would be going along.

"No. When you see me coming down the road from the point, cast-off all the ropes from the boat except for one. Make sure everything is ready to go. We will probably have to move fast."

"Will the tide be right for us to get out?"

"Yeah. I'll do what needs doing so the tide is with us. We will be going at night so make sure the lantern is ready. Do you have any questions before I go?"

"I was just thinking that...." Flint never finished the sentence. They heard a woman's voice calling and that drew their attention away from their conversation.


The woman was Elsa Nash and she was looking directly at them. She made known through gestures that she wanted to speak with them. Cole was the first to recognize her as Rudolph's wife. He asked Flint to wait on the boat. He stepped off the Priscilla and wondered what she could possibly want.

"Hello Mrs. Nash. May I help you?" Cole had no idea why a lady of her social status would be coming to the dock.

"Good afternoon. I was wondering if you had a moment to speak with me. I have some business that I believe you may be able to assist me with." She looked like a woman with a purpose and not the flirtatious one he remembered behind the counter.

"I have time. What kind of business are we talking about?" It was not often that he was blindsided.

"Do you think it possible for me to get on your boat? I was hoping we would be able to speak in private." She had come this far and now felt she had no choice but to put herself at the mercy of these rough men.

"Of course. Allow me to help you onboard." They walked toward the side of the Priscilla and he called out to Flint. She saw the man approach and a look of uncertainly came across her face.

"Flint is my brother and shipmate. We have no secrets from each other. I hope that won't be a problem."

"No. I'm sure it will not be." She braced herself to be helped onboard and extended her right hand to Flint. Cole took hold of her other hand while standing on the dock and in only seconds, she was standing on the deck of the Priscilla.

They made their way to the small galley and offered her the best place to sit. She had never been on a boat of this nature and was amazed at how everything seemed to be in place. She noticed the small stove and pots and pans that seemed to be nailed to the wall. The room smelled of rum, cigar smoke and coffee. It was not unpleasant, just different. She decided to state the reason for her visit.

"Mr. Ralston I hope that what we speak about will remain with the three of us. I need to get to San Francisco and I was hoping you could take me."

"I don't take passengers. This is a fishing boat and we have few accommodations for us and even less for a lady." That was not a lie.

"Perhaps you would make an exception. I have only one trunk and I could pay you very well. I promise I would not be underfoot or interfere with the operation of the boat. I simply must leave as soon as possible." She remained calm and business like.

"I see. Will you excuse us for just a moment Mrs. Nash?" Cole needed to have a small conference with Flint. After several moments, they returned and agreed that they would take her to San Francisco if the price was right. There were a few more questions he needed to ask.

"Mrs. Nash if we do agree to this trip you will have to pay us in full prior to departure." Her husband had cheated them already; they would not add her to the list.

"I can do that. How soon can we sail?"

"In a few hours if you want to. Can you be ready?" He suspected she was already packed.

"I can. But, I must tell you that your payment will not be in currency. I have set aside some valuable jewels that you could sell at your convenience." She debated on whether or not to show them what was in her purse. She decided she would as she had no other option. These were not all she had set aside, but it would be enough to bait them.

"Jewels?" Flint spoke for the first time.

"Yes. If you will permit me to show you, I brought a few with me so that you could see their quality. I know they will command top dollar." She dumped out her purse and four unique and very beautiful pieces spilled out onto the table. Even in the poor light, they sparkled brightly. There were rubies, emeralds and diamonds in several of the pieces. All of them were set in solid gold.

"My compliments on your taste in jewels Mrs. Nash." Cole was impressed with the collection. He looked at Flint and received a positive nod. "Flint, check the upper deck and make sure that Mrs. Nash wasn't followed and the coast is clear for her to leave. I think we are all in agreement."

"We are and I'll let you know if I see anything." Flint departed quickly.

"Thank you for thinking of my safety. Now, let me tell you about these pieces. They are custom made with the highest quality of jewels so there are no two alike. They are worth a considerable amount of money."

"Flint and I would be pleased to have you as our guest. I trust these pieces are only a partial payment for your passage?" Cole knew if she was willing to part with them so easily perhaps she had a few more she was not disclosing. It was the break that Flint said he wished they could get.

"They are. Now I have something else I wish to speak to you about." Elsa went on with questions about what sort of things she should expect while at sea.

She was a little fearful that they would simply take the jewels she had shown them and refuse to give her passage. But when Cole reached up and placed them inside the bag, and returned them to her she felt he might have some honor in him. It was also possible that he wanted to get his hands on the remaining jewels she had promised. It didn't matter to her, she had nothing to lose.

"Don't forget Mrs. Nash, we sail at nine o'clock tonight. The tide will be with us and it might be better for you to travel at night."

"I understand. My trunk is available now but I need help to get it to the boat. Will you be able to help me? Remember I am willing to pay well."

"It's better if I send someone I know and can trust. I can have him there by six tonight. You must have things ready by then."

"That will be fine."

"I think that about covers it. We'll see you tonight."

"Thank you Mr. Ralston. I appreciate your help and discretion." She got up and made her way to the deck. The men helped her get off the boat and watched her walk away for a brief moment.

"Flint, you know that statement you made about us getting a break? I think we just got one." He slapped his brother lightly on the back.

"I'm glad you don't have to go by way of the lighthouse."

"Me too. But, this changes nothing. We still need to be ready to go with the tide. I have an errand to run so I'll be back as soon as I can. You get the Priscilla ready and find a place for her trunk."

"Where are you going?" Flint asked.

"I need to make arrangements to get someone to pick up her trunk. I have Leroy Grazer in mind. I'll be at The Foggy Inn. I won't be long." Cole gave him a reassuring look and departed. Flint set about doing what his brother asked.

At The Foggy Inn things were pretty much normal. In the corner in his usual seat sat Leroy Grazer enjoying a hot meal. He could always be found at The Foggy Inn or the Chinese Dragon around this time and Cole knew it. He was lucky to have found him on his first attempt. He approached him and hoped that this would go well. They were not friends or even good acquaintances, but he knew that Leroy always accepted work if there was nothing illegal in it.

"Leroy, if you have a few minutes I'd like to talk with you about a lady who needs a man to help carry a trunk. She is willing to pay for the help and I thought of you." Cole tried to sound casual but not condescending.

"Oh yeah." He looked at Cole but he could not read the expression on his face.

"I would do it myself, but it happens that the lady needs the trunk delivered to my boat and I'll be getting the Priscilla ready to sail. Flint will be taking care of the usual odds and ends. So, what do you think?"

"Tell me about it." He motioned for Cole to sit down and so he did.

"The trunk needs to be on my boat no later than six tonight. Will that work for you?" Offering a little respect but certainly not groveling.

"It could. Does it belong to anyone I know?" He didn't want to deliver stolen goods or break the law.

"I think you know the lady. The trunk belongs to Mrs. Nash. It will probably be a good sized one, but she will pay you well for your trouble. She told me that personally."

"Well if it belongs to Mrs. Nash I will do it. What time does she want the trunk picked up and from where?" He knew the Nash's to be respectable and if she needed a trunk to be taken by ship somewhere, he saw no problem with that.

"At her home. But, you have to be there no later than six this evening. She will be expecting a man to come by and pick it up. I didn't tell her it was you because I wasn't sure if you could." Cole thought this was going better and easier than he thought.

"I'll finish this soup and be on my way."

"Great. Thanks for helping me out. I'll see you later on the boat when you deliver the trunk. Sorry to have disturbed your meal." He stood up and began to leave.

"It's alright. See you later." As Leroy sat eating his lunch, he was glad to have the work. He thought it a little odd that Ralston would think of him. They had known of each other for years and this was the first time that he had really spoken with him; let alone offer an employment opportunity. He decided not to look a gift horse in the mouth and just be glad he would make a little coin.

As Elsa walked back to her home for the first time in her life she did not care what anyone thought of her. If she had been seen with Mr. Ralston and people began to gossip she would not be in Valda Bay to hear it. She entered her home through the back door and closing it quietly behind her she stopped once inside and listened for anything out of the ordinary. There was nothing. She made her way toward the kitchen and saw the cook busy with kitchen duties. Since she had not spoken to her at all this day, she decided that she would see if anything had happened in her absence.

"Mrs. Nash, how are you feeling? I was told you were resting so everyone tried to be as quiet as possible. I hope we did not awaken you." She was wiping her hands on her crisp white apron.

"I am feeling a little better. I came down for a glass of cool milk and sweet bread. Please do not tell Mr. Nash. He hates me eating sweets." She put her finger to her lips to indicate silence, and then gave her a little laugh.

"I understand. Sometime men just do not understand that a woman might like something sweet once in awhile. Your secret is safe with me." She smiled and poured out a glass of milk and placed the sweet bread onto a plate and offered it to her.

"Thank you. I will enjoy this treat in my room. Oh, later this evening, a man will call and ask for a trunk. Please give it to him quickly along with this envelope. The trunk is filled with things for charity. I know I can count on your discretion. Rudolph hates publicity when it's for charity.

Will you help bring it down in about ten minutes?" She hoped that Rudolph would not arrive in the next fifteen minutes.

"I'll be glad to. I'll also be sure he gets the trunk and no one takes notice." The cook smiled back.

Once in the room she realized she was hungry and quickly ate the sweet bread and drank the milk. Knowing she had not been missed was a stroke of good luck and in only a few minutes her trunk was completely packed. There were only a few things left to do. She had to burn the notes from Joaquin that were hidden in the floor under the dressing table. She had spent several hours working the floor boards loose so she could hide notes, money and jewels there. It was all part of her plan for the time that she would leave with Joaquin. It had not taken her long to learn that Rudolph did not keep track of every piece of jewelry she owned. Taking money out of the store till in small quantities proved easy. The money was not missed by him because she often never entered the sale into the log. She did this over many months with customers who were not regular buyers at the store. It had proved profitable and now there was a tidy sum. She allowed herself the luxury of crying over the loss of Joaquin for a few minutes. Loving him meant never hurting him on purpose so the notes were thrown into the fireplace. The bucket containing hot coals served its purpose well, and soon the notes were in flames. As they burned she said goodbye to him. She took the money and all the jewels from the safety of the floor. She placed the money into a handkerchief and sewed the handkerchief into the hem of a dress. The jewels she would give the Ralston's she put into her purse. Now all she had to do was wait for the man to come and get her trunk. She hoped it would be soon. It was already five-thirty.

Karin had finished her dinner and after cleaning the kitchen decided she would sit outside for a while. The early evening was beautiful and her thoughts turned to Erik. Salty was in her arms purring. She noticed that the sea gulls were flying low to the water and that usually meant they were feeding. Her eyes went to the water and that's when she noticed a boat off in the distance. It was too far away to make out at first. After ten minutes had passed she knew it was the Sea Star. Erik was on his way home. She jumped to her feet and ran into the house. Going into the bedroom she quickly took off her dress and filling a basin with water gave herself a quick bath. She put on a fresh dress and brushed her hair. She took a pretty ribbon she saved for special occasions and tied back her long hair. She took her prized fragrance and put a little on her neck. She looked into her glass and was pleased with how she looked. She went into the kitchen and found the drawer that contained a few precious spices. She removed a clove and popped it into her mouth for its freshening power. She reached for a wrap and locked the door behind her. She decided to walk to the dock and meet them. It was all she could do to keep from running.

After a short time she was standing at the dock watching the Sea Star come into the port. She saw James and Daniel moving about the deck securing the boat with several ropes. She did not see Erik and when James approached her with a sullen look she felt a knot form in the pit of her stomach.

"James where is Erik?" She looked at him and then quickly back to the boat.

"Karin there was a terrible storm and Erik was hurt very badly." He hoped he would be able to tell her without showing too much emotion. She would need him to be strong.

"Well where is he?" She was starting to move toward the boat.

"Karin, Erik died a few days ago. There was nothing we could do. I am so sorry." He was looking at her and for a few seconds she just stared at him.

"Erik is dead?" She managed to whisper.

"Yes. Daniel and I said a prayer then we let him go into the ocean he loved. He did not suffer at all." He reached to gently touch her arm when she swayed slightly. She allowed it and fell against him.

"Tell me what happened." She was leaning against him and he had his arm around her waist. She felt that if he let go her knees would buckle and she would fall down.

"A storm hit us hard and the mast broke. When Daniel and Erik tried to repair it a huge wave hit the boat and the mast hit Erik on the head. He was knocked unconscious and never woke up. We were at his side when the Lord took him." This was hard beyond belief.

"Thank you for telling me." She looked up at him and the pain in his face was evident. His eyes were sad and she noticed he was trying to keep his emotions under control. Seeing this was too much for her. She turned her face into his shirt and started to cry. They did not speak for several minutes and after a while, she thought to ask about Daniel. "Is Daniel alright?" She managed to ask.

"Yes he is. He is on the boat because he just couldn't bring himself to tell you about Erik. He feels so badly since he was the one with Erik. I think he feels guilty over the accident."

"I'd like to go home now." She wanted to leave the dock and be any-where but where she was.

"I'll walk back with you." He started to move but she didn't.

"Will you get Daniel?" They were her friends and despite her pain, she wanted to ease Daniel's.

"He's on the boat. Let me call out to him." He moved away from her and called out to Daniel. When he appeared she held out her arm to him. Seeing this he jumped from the boat and took her hand.

"Karin, I'm so sorry about Erik." His voice was filled with sadness.

"I know. Let's go to the house. I feel so very cold now." She pulled the wrap tightly around her and walked slowly back to the home she had shared with Erik. She felt such terrible pain that even breathing was an effort. Halfway to the house, she began to cry from the depths of her being. James and Daniel each took an arm and guided her home.

It did not take long for the town people to learn of the tragedy that befell the Sea Star. Erik was one of the better known people in town and most could not believe that he had died. There was speculation about why he went to sea so late in the season. Some said he was making a last ditch effort to catch fish and supplement his income. Others disagreed and thought he was seeking an employment opportunity elsewhere. There was of course the age old rumor that he was after the treasure his grandmother had knowledge of. The people would continue to talk for several days, but not one of the fine Christian people of Valda Bay offered Karin their condolences or even offered to be a help to her in any way. There was one person from town whom despite family obligations and tradition did—Mei Ling. She came to Karin's home with a large basket filled with all kinds of meats, cheese, fruit and breads. She cried with Karin and yet offered her words of solace. She was of great comfort to her friend and would help see her through the terrible dark days ahead.

In his room Joaquin was thinking about Elsa and the way they parted. It had been bittersweet. He finished packing his trunk and took one long last look at the room he had lived in for several years. He was leaving it exactly as he had found it. He said goodbye to it and closed the door behind him for the last time. Joaquin carrying his trunk went down the back stairs and headed toward The Foggy Inn. He planned on spending the night with Rue and in the afternoon they would board the Mystic Quest. When he reached her room he knocked and she answered. For a moment he was taken aback by her appearance. Her long hair was completely pinned up into a loose bun. She was wearing a dark navy suit and a crisp white blouse with small pearl like buttons. There was a little lace around the collar and on the cuffs of her sleeves. Her shoes were ankle high black boots that were tightly laced. She wore no jewelry and he detected no fragrance. She still looked beautiful. He had never seen her with her hair up or dressed in such a fashion. She did not look like a lady of pleasure but rather a respectable business partner. She would be an asset to them both.

"Don't you like my traveling clothes?" She asked when she saw his face.

"I do. I just didn't expect to see you looking like a missionary that's all."

"Do I look that bad?" Her face screwed up into a frown.

"May I come in?" He was still at the door holding the trunk.

"Yes of course. Sorry, I didn't mean to leave you standing in the hallway." She moved so he could put down the trunk.

"You don't really look like a missionary. I'd say more like a business man's wife or sister. You're still very beautiful no matter what you wear." He smiled at her and sat down on the edge of the bed.

"I want to look like what I could be, not what I am. We must have a good start in our business and first impressions are everything. I'm not apologizing for me please understand, I'm just explaining what I'm doing with this suit." She sounded prepared for anything. He understood what she meant.

"I think you will be a wonderful business partner. Let me have a better look at the new you." He stood up and walked around her to have a better look.

"Very nice and very businesslike."

"What will we say when people ask how we met?" They had never discussed this before.

"I'll say you are a wine expert and wanted to purchase your own vineyard. I made an offer to you for your expertise in exchange for a portion of my vineyard. Thus, we own it together." He made it sound easy.

"Joaquin, I know nothing about vineyards. Think of something else." She almost laughed at his suggestion.

"You're right. We can think on it." He knew that they would need some kind of a cover story. The voyage was long and by the time they were on the shore of Spain, he would know what to say.

"Do you want to discuss what Mrs. Nash wanted or shall I not ask?" She began to undress. She neatly folded her clothes and placed them on top of her trunk. When she unlaced her boots, she quickly kicked them off. They would be the hardest thing to get used to. She reached for her old clothes and unpinned her hair. Her auburn locks fell with ease to her waist.

"Elsa wanted more than what I could give her." He stated it simply and hoped that Rue would not press the issue.

"I see. She thought you would take her away on a white horse." She was guessing but was pretty sure she was right.

"Yeah, I suppose she did." She was still her perceptive self but didn't ask more than he wanted to reveal. He loved that quality in her.

"Are you getting hungry? I am. With all the packing I've managed to miss lunch and look at the time. It's almost six, no wonder I'm starving." She changed the subject not only for him but because it was true.

"I could eat. Let's order something nice to be brought up to the room. We have never done that. It's always been wine and cheese." He thought it would be a nice way to say goodbye to the room and honor the good times.

"Don't forget the bread," she added.

"What do you mean?" He didn't get what she said.

"We've always had wine, cheese and lots of bad bread." She laughed a little at the memory.

"You're right of course. How could I forget the bread?" He gave a short laugh.

"I'll order us something nice along with a bottle of the house wine."

"House wine, why not the good stuff?" He was hoping for a change.

"To mark the time we had when we had to settle for bad wine. After this if we drink bad wine it will be because we are waiting for our own good wine." She hugged him.

The meal arrived and it was delicious. The wine was cheap but the conversation good. By the time it was over, they were relaxing on her bed and he was rubbing her feet.

"I've got your new identify for Spain." He said it with no doubt this time.

"You do? What am I?" Her eyes were full of curiosity.

"You my dear, are a bottle and label designer for fine wines." He liked it.

"I am?"

"Yes. So you had better start thinking about our label. A bottle is a bottle. But our label is who we will be forever. Are you up to it?" He had lost the lightness in his voice.

"I like that idea and more importantly, I know that I can do it." She felt a surge of joy. He was making sure she would be a partner in their new business.

"Good. It's settled then. Let's go to bed early. I want to make love and hold you close to me for a while. Is that alright with you?"

"It's more than alright." She reached for his hand.

They had never been in bed this early. After a time, they were feeling content and were listening to the sounds of the inn and the street below. It would be the last night spent in Valda Bay.

Leroy was just about at the front door of the Nash home. He wasn't sure which entrance to use so he decided that since his actions were honorable, he would knock on the front door. He did and waited for an answer.

"May I help you?" The maid inquired. She had been informed by the cook that a man would come by to pick up the trunk. She was given instructions and an envelope containing his payment.

"Yes. I'm here to pick up a trunk for Mrs. Nash." He had stuttered only once.

"You were expected. The trunk is just inside the door. Please come in."

"Thank you." He entered and found everything as he expected—perhaps more. The interior was lovely and spacious. Any concerns he may have had about picking up a trunk and delivering it to the Priscilla faded. The maid didn't act as if anything was wrong.

"May I be of any assistance?" She knew the trunk was heavy. She and the cook had dragged it downstairs earlier; luckily it slid down most of the stairs. Elsa only watched their efforts.

"No. I think I can manage it." It was a good thing that Leroy was a well built man because it was heavy.

"It's a fine thing you are doing helping Mrs. Nash. She's a lovely woman and so generous." She smiled at the thought of her mistress being so kind to others.

"Yes she is. I'm pleased to help out." He was checking to make sure the straps were secure. The trunk was not locked.

"Are you donating to the charity drive as well?" She thought he must be a participant because he knew about the trunk full of things Mrs. Nash was donating.

"I'm only here to pick up. I'm not part of the charity drive." He was ready to lift it and depart the home.

"Mrs. Nash left this envelope for you. She asked me to express her sincere appreciation to you." She handed over the envelope and he knew it contained the fee he was promised.

"Please thank Mrs. Nash for me." He placed the envelope into his shirt.

"Well, on behalf of the Nash family I thank you for your help in this matter." She opened the door a little more to accommodate the trunk which Leroy had lifted and now rested on his shoulders and back. He hung on to it by the side straps.

"Good evening." He began to walk away.

"Good evening." The door closed behind him and he quickened his pace to have the trunk on the Priscilla by the agreed upon time. This was some of the easiest money he had made in a long time. He was glad that he earned it doing work for charity. He would have never thought it of Mrs. Nash. He figured that the trunk would be going to another port where the recent storm had done so much damage.

It was almost six o'clock when Leroy approached the Priscilla. He set the heavy trunk down carefully. He called out to the boat and hearing his call Cole soon appeared. He was glad that he was on time. He had a schedule to keep.

"What do you want me to do with Mrs. Nash's trunk?" He was speaking to Cole as Flint was nowhere in sight.

"Nothing. Flint and I will get it in a moment. Sure am glad you could deliver it." Cole wanted to get rid of him quickly.

"Have a safe trip. See you when you get back." He put up his hand and waved bye.

"You bet. Take care." He waved back and watched him turn and leave the dock. Cole smiled to himself. This was going better than he hoped.

Leroy was walking working out the stiffness that had settled into his shoulders and upper arms. He pulled out the envelope that contained his delivery fee and when it was opened there was a generous payment. He was amazed at the amount. Cole had been correct when he said Mrs. Nash would pay well.

On the Priscilla Cole went into the bunk area where Flint had been waiting at his request.

"Flint, help me get the trunk on board. I want to get it in place and secure before our fine lady gets here."

"Where is it now?"

"On the dock. Let's be real careful with it. I'll hand it to you and then you and I can take it below."

When the trunk was below Cole asked Flint to get some rope to secure it. When he returned Cole roped it shut and anchored it to a stationary post. When Elsa arrived at nine o'clock they could be underway. He thought about how quickly things changed. Only this morning he had no prospects for money. Then he planned to rob Karin and Erik only to learn that it would not have happened because the Sea Star had come home and there were people at her home. A short time later his prospects changed again with Elsa Nash willing to pay him well to leave Valda Bay. Then of course, there was Mr. Nash who would also pay him for services rendered at the mercantile. In less than a day, fortune had smiled on them. The money would make possible a fresh start someplace else. The Priscilla was now ready to sail. Flint had done a good job getting everything ready. Cole looked at his watch. He had time to rest on his bunk and think about the best heading to take for the trip to San Francisco. There was still a little time until he would have to leave to meet Mr. Nash at the ice house. He was certain he would be there because unlike Cole and Flint, Mr. Nash had never had any trouble with the law and wanted to keep it that way. Cole wondered what he would think when he discovered Elsa gone. The escape of Mrs. Nash was risky for everyone. If he had any regrets it was the fact that he had to seek the help of a third party to take care of his business. He didn't like using Leroy but concluded he was the best choice of all the people he knew. To have picked up the trunk himself would be to invite suspicion. The housekeeper had already seen him there with Mr. Nash. That visit was more than enough to allow her to make a connection between the two men. One so called business visit was enough. That left only Leroy. Everyone knew that he was not too bright, had no family in the area or any close friends.

# The Trunk

Rudolph Nash was running late. He sold all the jewels and received what he considered a fair price. There was enough money to pay Cole Ralston and have enough left to make a payment at the bank. He had sent a wire to his father-in-law explaining that Elsa would be visiting soon as she was distraught over a failed business opportunity that he had pursued. He informed him that she was upset because she did not understand the business complexities but assured him that things were fine. He was certain she was going home to be with her parents and he did not want to suffer embarrassment by sending such a wire from Valda Bay. What he did not mention was that once she was there he had no intention of asking her to return. In truth he had spoken to his solicitor about dissolving the marriage. She had made a fool out of him and he would never forgive her. It was not possible to forget her terrible words to him. Urging his horse on to a quicker pace he began to think about something new. Suppose she decided not to go home and went someplace else making a fool of him? That possibility had not entered his mind when he sent the wire. He was angry with himself for sending it. After pondering the situation he thought maybe things could work out better than he hoped. If she did not show up at the home of her parents he could say as far as he knew that was where she was going. There would be no undo attention drawn to him because the wire was sent prior to her departure. A guilty man would not even make mention of a potential departure much less admit that his wife was upset with him. Anything could happen to a pretty woman traveling alone. She could be robbed or fall ill. She could be kidnapped or killed. Did he have the nerve to hire someone to kill her? The answer was yes. He needed to rid himself of a woman he no longer cared for and was proving the financial ruin of him. He decided to stop and rest the horses for about ten minutes. In that time, he took out his purse and counted his money.

There was more than enough to entice Cole Ralston to kill her. He would give him a little extra to depart by early morning. The details of the killing he would leave to him. He would have to dismiss Elsa's personal maid and the housekeeper because he could not afford them. The cook he would keep because he needed her. He would make do with the food goods already purchased. Once the insurance money arrived he could get back on his feet. As far as anyone was concerned Mrs. Nash went to see her parents. He would say that her return was questionable because she fell ill and the salt air and dampness would not be good for her. It was common knowledge that ladies of high society and fashion always seemed to be so frail. The only thing to take care of was his solicitor. A quick trip and a lunch appointment would allow him to set that conversation straight.

Once he was on the road again he decided he would tempt the greed of Cole Ralston. There would be no witness to that conversation. When he arrived in Valda Bay he would not even go inside his home. He would inform the groom he wanted to stretch his legs and go for a walk. The groom was a married man and he would casually mention to him that Mrs. Nash hated these business trips and she always seemed to be unhappy when he made them. He would say he needed a little time alone before going into the house and facing an unhappy wife. The man would understand that. He would still have time to meet Cole at the arranged time and place. It was perfect and soon he would be free of Elsa.

Leroy walked away from the Priscilla with the distinct feeling that all was not as it seemed. He knew of various charity drives and collections that took place in the area from time to time. These drives were done mostly by religious groups and all had one thing in common; they were well publicized. The success of the drive depended on the generosity of the contributors. He also knew in all the time he was in Valda Bay Mr. Nash and his wife had never given anything to those drives. They were of the opinion that everyone should help themselves. Now, they were generous to the point of filling a huge trunk with donated goods as well as pay for its transportation to places unknown. The whole charity donation story seemed just like that—a story. He could not remember hearing anything about such an activity. Also out of the normal way of things was the involvement of the Ralston brothers. They never did anything for anyone without some kind of payment or trade for services. He also wondered why Cole did not pick up the trunk himself—it seemed like a poor excuse to say he was making the boat ready to sail. It wouldn't take too long when a man has an experienced seaman in his brother to help him. Leroy took less than thirty minutes to run the errand. Did thirty minutes really make that much difference? He found it odd but could not put his finger on what was really going on. He decided to walk around for a while and think about it. In a short while he found himself at The Foggy Inn where he would order a bit of warm rum. Maybe he was wrong. He decided not to make issue of it. There was nothing illegal in what he had done so it was best not to frown upon his good fortune.

The cook was doing everything she knew to keep the food she prepared for dinner from being ruined. She finally decided to throw it out and make something different. Mrs. Nash had already had dinner in her room deciding not to wait for Mr. Nash. Since he was long overdue from his business meeting she decided to ask her mistress what she should do. Her day began very early and she was hoping that she would be told to retire for the rest of the night. All the help in the house had already retired. Knocking on the bedroom door she hoped to find her in an agreeable mood. There were times that Elsa Nash had made her feel angry and abused.

"Yes? Who is it?" Elsa hoped it was not Rudolph.

"Mrs. Ivy. May I come in for just a moment?"

"Enter."

"Forgive my intrusion. It has gotten so late and I was wondering if I may be permitted to retire?" She noticed that Mrs. Nash was already in her night dress.

"Has Mr. Nash arrived from his business meeting?"

"No, he has not arrived yet. I prepared a sandwich for him and I left it covered on the kitchen table along with a glass of buttermilk in the ice bucket. I know how much he enjoys a cool glass." She hoped that would meet with her approval.

"That is very thoughtful of you. Is everyone else retired?" Elsa knew the whereabouts of her personal maid but not of everyone else.

"Yes they have." She tried to sound final.

"Well, I see no reason why you cannot join them." She was glad to have the cook out of the way. It would be easier to leave undetected.

"Do you require anything before I retire?"

"No. I will retire now myself. Mr. Nash and I will see you in the morning. Good night."

"Good night mistress." She smiled and did a quick curtsy before closing the door behind her.

Elsa sat in her chair rocking back and forth. It was done in an attempt to try and settle herself down. It was still too early to depart for the boat. Mr. Ralston had put great emphasis on the fact that they would sail at nine o'clock. She did not want to begin the trip by creating problems before they even departed. Some part of her was worried that this was not a good idea. She did not know these men or what they were capable of. She would be alone with them at sea. There was not a soul who knew that she was going with them. For just a moment she contemplated not going at all. The only thing she would lose would be a trunk full of lovely dresses and some expensive accessories. What were they when she compared them to her life? Thoughts of indecision raced back and forth until she felt drained. She had already been brave enough to go to the docks and do what she had done. Thoughts of Joaquin flooded her mind. How she loved him and wished that she was going away with him instead. This was not the time to think about what might have been but rather what was. It was too late to change things now. Any life she may have had with Rudolph was ruined. In some distant part of her being she regretted telling him about her affair. The plan she put into motion was already underway. No matter the risks she had made her choice. Now all she needed to do was live out her life as best she could and start over. She was nice looking, had money, youth and most importantly she had no children. There was nothing to stop her. Her thoughts were interrupted by the wall clock striking on the half hour. It was time for her to go. Rudolph was not home to complicate her departure and everyone in the house was now in bed. She quickly got up from her rocking chair and redressed herself. She was glad that she had dressed for bed as part of her normal routine and more importantly, that the cook had seen her that way. She took one last look around the room and double checked everything to ensure that she had left no clue as to her intentions. Satisfied that everything was in order she set about leaving. The house was quiet when she left her bedroom and made her way out the backdoor. She had less than thirty minutes to walk to the boat.

The Foggy Inn was busy with the usual crowd. Cole could hear them inside as he walked past the building. The night had turned crisp and he noticed that there was a good wind that would help with his departure. He was going to meet Rudolph Nash at the ice house and was thinking of what he would do if for some reason he was not there. As he approached the back of the ice house he saw that someone was approaching from the other direction. He stopped walking and took a few minutes to look around. When he was sure that no one was around he proceeded with caution. There was only a small sliver of a moon and he was grateful for that. He stood in the shadows of the building across from the ice house until he saw movement along the side of the building. He had no doubt it was Mr. Nash. A few moments later he was standing in the shadows talking with him.

"I'm glad you showed up on time," Cole spoke first.

"I said I would be here. I have your money as promised. You can count it if you want to." He would be careful because he needed this unscrupulous man one more time.

"I'm sure everything is as we agreed, because if for some reason it isn't we both know what that could mean." Cole standing so close to Rudolph made him appear much shorter than he really was.

"Let us set that aside. I have another offer you may want to consider."

"Well I don't have much time. What kind of offer?"

"It has recently come to my attention that my wife has been unfaithful to me. I know it's someone in Valda Bay."

"That's none of my business so what does that have to do with me? I'm not her lover."

"I have a great deal of money that I will pay you tonight to make sure that Mrs. Nash does not ever come home again. And, if possible, I want her lover to meet the same end."

"Let me see—you're offering me more money to make sure Mrs. Nash permanently disappears and if she is with her lover, him too."

"That is correct. And hopefully you can do it as soon as possible. Perhaps even tonight then you could depart on the next tide quickly."

"Before anything happens, I want to see the money."

"It's right here." Nash reached into his coat pocket and pulled out a leather pouch. It was filled with gold coins and he withdrew a few of them to show Cole.

"Well, I really appreciate the offer. However, I already have a job for tonight."

"Can you get out of it or can it be changed? I'll make it worth your while." Mr. Nash was certain he would want to since his offer might prove more financially beneficial.

"I don't think it can be changed. You see Mrs. Nash has already paid me a great deal of money to make sure that you never come home again."

"What are you saying?" He sputtered. Cole could see that he went pale despite the poor light offered by the moon. He took several steps backwards. Cole reached out and grabbed him by the front of his shirt holding him in place.

"I can't let you leave Nash—but it has been a pleasure doing business with you." Cole reached into his jacket pocket and pulled out a knife with a long blade. He held it up to Mr. Nash and with one quick motion, sliced open his throat.

In the time it took to die, he could not believe that she had gotten the better of him. She had managed to make him miserable everyday with her demands, ruin him financially, make a fool of him with another man, and now she had arranged his death. She was truly a black widow. With his last thought, he cursed her and hoped that Chief Johnson would discover the truth.

Cole watched as he made a choking noise and then fell limp to the ground. Looking at the limp portly body he wondered how many people in the small town had wished this little greedy man dead. He felt as if he had done a service for all those he had threatened, cheated or remained indifferent toward. He deserved what he got. The leather pouch was still clutched in his hand. Cole quickly removed the pouch from his hand and placed it inside his jacket. He reached for the piece of fabric that he had ripped away from a dress belonging to Mrs. Nash. He opened Nash's hand and placed the piece of fabric in it. He thought to take the fabric from her trunk when Flint left the cabin to get rope to secure it. It would make Mrs. Nash the murder suspect, not him. He would not feel sorry for her if she were to be hanged for a murder she did not commit. She considered him and others like him inferior in every aspect of life. He knew her to be spoiled, self centered and extravagant. She drove her husband to desperate acts. He did not consider her a real lady. On the way back to the Priscilla, he wondered if he should tell Flint about the coins in his jacket. He decided it would be best to be underway and later they could have a conversation in private. Flint had no idea of any plans to murder anyone and Cole needed it that way because he was not certain if Flint could hold up to intense questioning or pressure by authorities. If he knew nothing, he could tell nothing. He now had the money that they needed. Reflecting on the night's events he concluded that it had not been as difficult as he thought it would be.

Flint had done all he could and was now just waiting for Cole to arrive. He had taken Mrs. Nash below and instructed her to stay there. When he saw Cole approach he went to the wheel knowing that Cole would release the lines holding the boat in place. Cole approached the boat and called out to Flint.

"Is the cargo on board?"

"Everything is here and we are ready to go."

"Good. I'll release the lines and let's get underway now."

After he released the lines he quickly boarded and made sure the boat was free of the dock. He looked around and saw that all was quiet.

"Cole, you're late. Did Nash give you trouble?"

"No. Everything was fine and we got paid in full. Where is Mrs. Nash?"

"She's below. I told her to wait there and we would let her know when she could come on deck."

"We have a fair wind right now so I will give her a bit of canvas to get out of here quickly. You stay at the wheel and keep your eye open."

In just a few moments Cole had the boat configured to catch as much wind as possible. They would continue in this manner until they reached the open water, then it would be all sheets to the wind. He needed to speak with Flint so he returned to the wheelhouse.

"As soon as we clear the bay we need to set a course of south by southwest."

"So we really are going to San Francisco?"

"Well, let's head this way for a while." Cole was looking out to sea.

"What do you mean for a while?" Flint asked.

"Well there's no hurry and after all, Mrs. Nash or should we just say Elsa, goes where we go. We'll be at sea for quite a while. We need to be friendly to each other. It could be a long lonely trip. Who knows, maybe Elsa possess a few talents we don't know about. Who knows, she might even cook. Flint, you ever wondered what it would be like to have a pretty senorita in your bed?" He looked at him with a little glee in his eye.

"Senorita? Like one from Mexico?"

"Yeah, maybe even two senoritas. Just set and keep on that course my brother. I need to go below and speak with Elsa. I'll be back in a while."

Flint did as Cole instructed and in just a short while they were in open water. The weather looked good and a steady wind helped them move at a good pace. Flint wondered what the future would hold for them and for just an instant he looked back over his shoulder. He could see the familiar lighthouse and the dark shadow of the shoreline that was Valda Bay fading from view.

Cole went down into the berth and found Elsa sitting on the end of his bunk.

"May I come in?" Cole asked out of respect.

"Of course. Where is your brother?" She wanted to speak with him in private about the arrangements they had made.

"He's at the wheel. I see you are dressed for the sea."

"Yes, I thought I would be more comfortable this way. I do not understand why I must stay in this small room. Am I to be in here the entire trip?" She hoped not because closed in small places always bothered her.

"No. I asked Flint to tell you to stay below until we cleared the harbor and bay to ensure your safety and privacy. You said you wanted to be discreet in your departure and we can't risk you being seen. When we get further away from the bay and into deeper waters, I'll let you know."

"Then I may leave this room to walk on deck?" She asked.

"That's right. In fact we wanted to know if you would help out with some duties on the boat. We have to eat and we aren't the best cooks and our shirts could stand the use of a needle and thread."

"I would be pleased to repair your shirts. I am not a good cook, but I am grateful for whatever is prepared. I could help wash some dishes." She was amazed at how low she had sunk. She hated the thought of doing dishes because she did not want to ruin the appearance of her hands. She thought of the compliments she often received concerning their soft and delicate appearance.

"That would be just fine." Cole turned to leave the berth.

"Mr. Ralston?"

"Yes?" Cole turned around to face her.

"I trust that everything went well this night and you took care of Mr. Nash as I asked?" She was hoping that he would bring up the subject.

"Everything went as you paid for. He will not be bothering you or anyone else ever again. You paid me well to do a job and I did it." He sounded almost as if they were talking about making repairs to something.

"Let us now hope that our journey is a pleasant one." She looked indifferent as she spoke of her now dead husband.

"I'm sure it will be. I'll probably be back in about one hour if we see no other boats. Do you need anything now?"

"No thank you. I will be fine." She gave Cole a small smile and sat down on the bunk. She positioned herself until she was resting her back against the wall. She would wait for his return.

Cole left the berth and decided it would be a good time to talk to Flint. He climbed up the stairs and stood behind him unobserved. He watched his brother at the wheel of the boat for a few moments before deciding that he would tell him everything. It was going to be several days before they were in San Francisco. Cole would have time to reassure Flint things would be alright because he had taken care to ensure that they would. If he had questions or doubt about what transpired, Cole would have time to put any concerns to rest. It was better that he knew the truth; they had never lied to each other. He made his presence known and Flint turned around.

"Is she alright down there?" Flint asked.

"She's fine. When we get a little further out I'll go down and tell her she can come out on deck. The cabin is a bit small."

"Have you figured out where we are going to sleep?"

"We can bed down in the storage room. When we moved out all the rope, lanterns and netting to the forward hole it left plenty of room for us to sleep. I can take the bedding from one of the bunks in the berth and we can light the small stove for heat. We have to leave the porthole open but it should be alright."

"That will work. Did you ask her if she could cook or were you busy being friendly?" Flint looked at him with a playful look on his face.

"She says she can't cook and no I didn't get friendly with her. In fact, that is something we need to talk about. She won't be up on deck until I go and get her so we can speak freely."

"What about?" Flint always recognized that tone and it usually meant something that he didn't understand or didn't approve of. He was certain that this was going to be one of those times.

"About what happened before we left Valda Bay." Cole was looking around for any lanterns in the distance. It could only mean that a boat was in the area. He saw nothing.

"I'm listening."

"Remember I was a little late getting back from something I said I had to do before we sailed?" He looked at Flint and when he nodded, he continued. "Well, Mrs. Nash wanted us, or really I should say me, to do something for her right before we sailed. She paid very well for what she wanted. We now have quite a bit more money than we did before all this started." Cole wanted to present the positive before he did the negative.

"What did she want you to do that paid so well?" Flint was not looking at Cole. He was not certain that he wanted to know what his brother had done.

"She paid us very well and in advance—to get rid of Nash."

"Get rid of Nash? You mean you killed him?" Flint looked at Cole with dismay on his face.

"Yeah, I did. It was over real quick and now we have extra money for everything we ever wanted."

"But I never wanted anything so much that I would have blood on my hands." Flint was a horrified at hearing his brother's confession.

"Oh yeah, you're a real saint aren't you? Let me tell you something that might shed a little light on the subject. Before I slit his throat, Nash offered me money to kill her. They were two of a kind. They had no use for each other, were filled with hate and they each wanted the other dead. If I hadn't done the job someone else would have." Cole felt like he was being judged by Flint. He didn't like the feeling.

"I'm not saying I'm a damn saint. I just wish you would have talked to me about it before it happened. Don't you trust me?"

"I trust you completely. I just didn't want you involved in case it went badly. That's the reason I didn't want you to go to Nash's house for the trunk. I didn't want there to be any connection to you. Leroy Grazer was perfect. He needed the money and everyone knows he's an idiot. Who better to go to the house than him? It was me just taking care of our business that's all." Cole hoped he would understand and let the matter rest.

"As usual, you're on top of things." Flint had turned contrite.

"Thanks for the vote of confidence. Now, here is something that will ensure we are in the clear in case things go bad." Cole looked around to ensure that Elsa had not gotten impatient and came up on deck; she had not. They were alone.

"What are you looking around for?" Flint asked.

"Just making sure we are alone. Now, like I was saying, I took steps to make sure that no matter what happened we won't be blamed for anything. Remember when Leroy dropped off the trunk and we took it below and I sent you to get some rope?"

"Yeah, I remember."

"Well, when you were gone I opened her trunk. I ripped a piece of fabric from the bottom of one of her dresses. After I killed Nash, I put the fabric in his hand and then I hurried to get on the boat so we could leave." Cole was looking at Flint and could see his face dimly lit by the light given off by the lantern.

"So by doing that it looks like she killed him and not us?" Flint now understood the strategy.

"That's it. There is no connection between us and Nash. When he's found dead, the police find the fabric and she's blamed for his murder. It's perfect."

"Yeah, I guess it is. You did alright for us Cole." Flint had turned into the supportive brother he had always been.

"That's not all. I have something that the police won't find. I think you'll be a happy man. Take a look at this." Looking around again, he reached into his shirt and pulled out the bag of gold coins. He shook the bank bag a little in front of him.

"How much is there Cole?"

"Ten thousand dollars cold cash." He laughed quietly.

"Shit, we're rich! That doesn't include what Elsa paid us either. How much do you think we have all together?" He had already forgotten how the money was acquired.

"I'm not sure. I don't know that much about jewels. But when we get to the right port I can have them turned into cash. We can live pretty well for a long time."

"What about her?" Flint knew his brother would have a good answer.

"Well, we can all be real friendly for a while. She's a pretty woman and she can't go anywhere. What do think about that?"

"I don't know. Let's think about this for a minute."

"What's there to think about?" Cole didn't understand his reaction.

"What if we don't get friendly and instead take her directly to San Francisco?"

"Now why would we do that?"

"She doesn't know that she is wanted for murder. She would act normal and we could use her to unload the jewels for cash. She knows their value and how to sell them. We would then leave port quickly for the open waters heading for those senoritas you mentioned. She would be arrested and the search for the murderer of Nash would be over. But, if we treat her badly, then we have to dump her in the ocean and there is no one to be found and put into jail." He didn't finish all his thoughts before Cole understood what he was trying to say.

"And the law keeps looking because they don't have anyone in custody." Cole added.

"That's right. Remember we all left Valda Bay at the same time." Flint looked at Cole.

"Flint, I'm impressed. You're right in every account. Let's play it your way and head for San Francisco." Cole gave his brother a playful punch to the stomach and Flint returned the gesture. They were as they had always been—two men thinking as one.

# The Search Begins

*L*eroy was celebrating his good fortune at The Foggy Inn and enjoying his rum. He ordered bread and cheese and as usual he looked around to see if he could see Rue. She was not working the night but the fireplace was nice and he had no money worries for now. There was no reason to hurry home. It wasn't long before a tavern waitress approached him.

"Leroy, how are you? It isn't often we see you in the tavern for the evening meal." She was polite but distant.

"I'm fine. I just came in to celebrate my good fortune."

"Good fortune? Did you find a treasure off the beach or got left a large inheritance from some distant relative you never knew you had?" She teased him lightly.

"Well, almost as good. I just delivered a trunk for the charity drive and made a good coin off of it."

"What charity drive is that?" She asked.

"The one in some other port I guess. Haven't you heard about it?"

"No. As far as I know, we haven't even got one going in Valda Bay yet. And, I don't mind telling you that there are plenty of people in need here."

"That's true. Maybe it's just the start of one, but anyway I got paid well and I'm here to celebrate." He smiled at her and took a drink.

"Well good for you. Let me ask the bartender if he has heard of anything going on for charity in the nearby ports. I'll be back in a moment." She turned to leave and Leroy noticed that she wasn't really a pretty woman, but she had a nice cleavage.

He stretched and placed his feet on a nearby bench. The evening was crisp but not unpleasant and he thought perhaps in a little while he would go out for a walk and sit by the lighthouse. It was quiet up there and he had a lovely view of the bay. The lit lanterns in the homes emitted a golden hue and the waves lapping on the shore made it look and sound beautiful. After a short time the waitress returned.

"Well, I asked the bartender and he knew of no charity drive or collections currently going on. Are you sure you heard right that it was a trunk for charity?" She asked the question in a benevolent manner. She did not want to break his good mood.

"Yeah. That's what I was told."

"Well, anyway it's a nice thought. I'd better get back to work before I lose my job and need charity. Do you want more rum?"

"No. It's almost nine. I have to get up very early."

"I'll say goodnight then. See you later."

"Goodnight."

Leroy drained his cup and left the tavern. He walked toward the lighthouse and noticed some activity behind the ice house. He worked at the ice house for a long time and knew that there was no business conducted there at this time of night. With the recent fire at the mercantile he thought to watch for a few minutes and see what was going on. He hid in the shadows with a view of the building but could not make out any clear details. He listened intently and thought he heard voices. It didn't take too long and he saw a figure move away from behind the ice house. It moved away quickly. He listened but heard nothing. After what seemed like a long time, but in reality was not more than fifteen minutes he moved quietly toward the ice house. Even before approaching completely, he could see something was lying on the ground. Getting closer he discovered that it appeared to be a person. He could not tell if it was a man or a woman. Leroy started to feel anxiety and sank into the shadows of the building. He remained still for several more minutes. Nothing moved. He gathered his courage and decided he needed to investigate. As he moved in closer he could see that it was a body and immediately identified it as Mr. Rudolph Nash. His throat was sliced open and blood was everywhere. He backed away quickly and felt sick to his stomach. He fought down the nausea. Several thoughts ran through his mind at once. Would he be blamed for the murder ... he had been at his house ... he had coin he never had before … he told the waitress about how he earned the money and no one else knew of any charity drive … this was not good. He paced around for a few minutes. Despite being in a panic he had the good sense to think about the only person who might be able to help. He ran to the home of Chief Johnson.

Chief Johnson had just gotten into bed when he heard a knock at his front door. He quickly got out of bed and put on his pants. His nightshirt hung to his knees. Taking the lantern he went to answer the door. The knocking had become more almost constant and he could now hear his name being called. He recognized the voice as that of Leroy Grazer. When he open the door he found that he was correct.

"Chief, I have to speak with you now!" He stepped passed the Chief and into the house. He did not wait to be invited in. He was breathing fast and he looked pale.

"Alright Leroy. Calm down and tell me what happened." The Chief closed the door and set the lantern on a table.

"It's terrible! I just found him honest. I didn't do anything to Mr. Nash." Leroy was speaking fast and his stuttering was inhibiting his ability to be understood.

"Leroy I'm trying to understand but you have to slow down so I can help you." He placed his hand on his shoulder. "Start over and tell me what happened."

"Mr. Nash has been murdered." He took a deep breath and wiped his brow.

"Murdered? How do you know this?"

"I saw him."

"Where?" Chief Johnson could hardly believe what Leroy had said.

"He's lying on the ground behind the ice house."

"And you are sure he's dead and not just unconscious or drunk?" He needed more information, but he knew that he would go and investigate this for himself.

"He's dead. I know he is because his throat is slit wide open and there's blood all over the place." He placed his hand over his stomach.

"When did you see this happen?"

"I saw him maybe twenty to thirty minutes ago. I came here as soon as I realized what happened."

"You did the right thing. Did you tell anyone else?" He hoped that Leroy had not.

"No. I'm sorry I got so scared. I didn't want anyone to think I killed him." He had calmed down considerably and his color was getting better.

"I need to get dressed. I'll be just a moment." He got up and went into his bedroom but left the door open so they could continue to talk. "What makes you think that people would accuse you of doing something to Mr. Nash?"

"I went to his house." He shook his head.

"Why were you at his house and when did you go?" That statement got the Chief's attention.

"Today. I went to his house at six o'clock."

"Morning or evening?"

"Evening. Is that important?" Leroy had no training in crime solving so getting details eluded him.

"It could be. What were you there for?"

"I had to pick up a trunk that Mrs. Nash was giving to charity."

"Charity? What did you do with the trunk?" He knew of no charity drives or collections being conducted in Valda Bay.

"I took it to the Priscilla and left it for the Ralston's to put on board." He could not remember which one of the men actually took it off his hands.

"How did you know the trunk would go to the Ralston's boat?" He found that interesting.

"Cole Ralston told me to pick up a trunk at the Nash home and take it to the Priscilla by six o'clock. So, I did." He was glad that the Chief was good at figuring things out because he had no idea why a trunk would be important when Mr. Nash was laying dead.

"I'm dressed. We need to go to the ice house. I know that this is unpleasant for you, but I do need you to come with me. You don't have to see the body again, just show me where it is." He opened the door and both men began to walk quickly to the ice house.

"Chief, you do believe me when I said I didn't kill him?" He knew perhaps that was a stupid question but knowing the town people and the way they thought of him he had reason to be concerned.

"I believe you. Now, tell me about this trunk business. Were you paid by the Ralston's to pick it up?"

"No. Ralston said Mrs. Nash would pay me well when I picked up the trunk."

"And did she?"

"You bet. I never made such easy money in my life. I had a bit of rum at The Foggy Inn and was going to the lighthouse afterward and that's when I saw some movement behind the ice house." He felt a chill go through him when he remembered what transpired.

"How much rum?"

"Chief, I'm not drunk. I know what I saw." Leroy countered.

"Alright. I can see that you aren't drunk. Now, tell about what you saw behind the ice house." This fact did not elude the Chief.

"I know someone left and no one else came by. I was in the shadows of the building across the way so I couldn't see real clear but I know that much. I wondered why anyone would be there at that time of night." He wished he had gotten a better view.

"Could you make out anything at all?"

"No. I just saw two people and then only one leaving." Leroy did not want to see that horrible scene again so when they reached the body, he stayed back and just watched from a distance away as the Chief looked over the body. It was Mr. Nash.

It was as Leroy said. Mr. Nash had been murdered. He took his time looking at everything he could with the limited light of his lantern. He also noticed that his hand held a piece of fabric. He placed the fabric into his pocket and quickly ran his hands over the person of Mr. Nash. No purse was evident. Perhaps he had struggled with his assailant or assailants and robbery was the motive. When he resisted, they slit his throat. After about twenty minutes Chief Johnson sent Leroy to get Doctor Grayson. He knew that he would have to inform Mrs. Nash. That was always the hardest part of his job and he hated it.

When Leroy arrived at Doctor Grayson's home he was composed. He knocked and saw that the doctor had also been in bed as he had on his night clothes.

"Leroy are you sick?" He had never known him to come to his office for anything medical much less his home.

"No, I'm alright. Chief Johnson sent me to get you because something really bad happened and he needs your help."

"Have a seat and I'll only be a minute." The doctor hurried dressing and in only a few minutes had everything he needed.

"We have to go to the ice house." Leroy was carrying the lantern.

"What happened at the ice house? Who's hurt?"

"No one is hurt, but there is someone dead."

"Dead. Do you know who?"

"It's Mr. Nash."

"Mr. Nash? Does the Chief know what happened?" He could hardly believe it.

"He didn't say anything to me. I guess he needs your help because he made sure to tell me he wanted only you."

"Do you know if Mrs. Nash has been informed?" The doctor had no idea when all this happened.

"I don't think so. I think that is part of the reason that the Chief asked me to get you. I'm pretty sure he will want you to go with him to the Nash home."

"I can't imagine how that lovely Mrs. Nash is going to take this. I'm glad I have some sedatives in my bag." He felt certain that she would get hysterical.

"She's so young and pretty. It's a shame that's for sure."

"Perhaps that's an advantage," Doctor Grayson said.

"How's that?"

"With the passing of time, she can begin her life anew. Her family will no doubt offer her support and understanding. It's very possible she may find love again and even have a family, not right away of course." The doctor had seen that happen many times before.

"The night is getting chilly isn't it?" Leroy was glad that they were walking fast because it helped keep him warm.

"Yes. I'm glad we are almost there."

A few minutes later they were approaching the ice house. They were met by Chief Johnson who had written several notes concerning the scene and all that he observed. He was glad that the doctor arrived quickly and even more grateful that his friend Mr. Gordon was expected in Valda Bay anytime. He would share all the information he had with him and together he was certain that the murder and fire could be solved. He couldn't help but wonder if the two were connected. When the Chief saw them, he put away his notepad.

"He's over here doctor. Did Leroy fill you in on anything?"

"A little. I know it's Mr. Nash and that he's been murdered. Not much more. Let me have a look and maybe I can shed more light. That is why I'm here isn't it?"

"You go ahead and look. I'll give you light." He held up his lantern and the doctor began to look at the body. He examined him briefly but confirmed that he had died as a result of hemorrhage. He was not dead prior to the neck wound. He had not been placed there, but rather died on the spot. It didn't appear as if he gave much of a struggle.

"Doctor, I know I don't have to say this but since I do have to conduct an investigation I need to ask that you not discuss anything about this case with anyone. That would of course include Mrs. Nash." He officially had to say that.

"I understand. I've done all I can do here. Let's move him to the hospital where we can clean him up and get him ready for whatever Mrs. Nash decides to do with his remains."

It was not long before people in The Foggy Inn noticed the lanterns by the ice house. Chief Johnson asked for help in taking Mr. Nash to the hospital morgue. Several men volunteered to take him and the doctor rushed to clean him up. He did not want Mrs. Nash to see her husband in a terrible state. In less than one hour, he was ready to be seen by Elsa Nash. Waiting for him to finish his preparations was Chief Johnson. They were now ready to go to the Nash home and break the news to Elsa Nash. Leroy asked if he could go home. He did not want to be involved anymore than he had to be. Once home despite being drained mentally and physically he did not go to bed. In the quiet darkness of his room he drank a cup of warm rum hoping that when he closed his eyes he would not see Mr. Nash lying in a pool of blood.

Doctor Grayson had asked that his horse and buggy be brought to the hospital so that they could ride to the Nash home. In only moments the two men stepped out of the buggy and walked to the front door of the Nash home. Chief Johnson took a deep breath and rang the bell. A gentleman answered the door. He immediately recognized them.

"Gentlemen, how may I be of assistance?" He was no doubt the butler.

"We deeply regret the hour, but we are here on a matter of great importance. Would you please inform Mrs. Nash that we are here and need to speak with her?" The man recognized Chief Johnson.

"Please come into the library and I'll have one of the ladies wake Mrs. Nash." He quickly left and the men went to wait in the library.

"This is some house isn't it Chief?" Doctor Grayson had never been inside the library. When it had been necessary to treat someone, it had been in the servant's part of the house or in the bedroom of Mr. or Mrs. Nash.

"Yes it is. I'm sure Mr. Nash was very proud of it. This library is pretty well stocked with expensive books. Makes me wish I had more time to read." He looked around admiring all the nice things.

"I know what you mean. I love to read but it seems like I never have enough time. It's all can do to keep up with my patients and read the little bit of medical news that is mailed to me on a monthly basis. Then of course there was the article I submitted recently. I hope those closed minded fools really open their eyes and put into practice what I learned from Mr. Chang." Both men looked at each other and they chuckled slightly. They were remembering Doctor Grayson's own closed mind not that long ago. They heard the study doors open and turned to see the butler and the cook.

"Chief, Mrs. Nash is not in her room or the obvious places, so I've asked the staff to help locate her." He looked as if he were apologizing for something when it was not his fault.

"I'm sure she is in another part of the house." Doctor Grayson thought perhaps she was in the kitchen or dining room.

"We are all looking at the moment and I've sent my son to look in the stable. He will return in only a minute or two. While we are waiting may I offer you a hot cup of cocoa or perhaps a little brandy?" He moved toward the table where Mr. Nash kept a lovely crystal decanter and the matching glasses.

"No thank you. I appreciate the offer." Doctor Grayson wanted a clear head in the event he should have to administer any medication to Mrs. Nash.

"It's kind of you to offer, but I think not." Chief Johnson walked around the room a little looking for anything that might help him in his investigation. He noticed a few pieces of paper in the waste can by the desk, but other than that, there was nothing out of the ordinary.

"Excuse me sir." A young man was at the door of the library.

"Yes, come in. Did you find Mrs. Nash?" The butler asked.

"No sir." He entered and stood before the butler who was also his father. "We looked everywhere and she is not to be found. I checked the greenhouse and the back gardens. I even spoke with the horse trainer, Mr. Smith. He knows everything." It was a complete report and correct to the best of his knowledge. But, he wished he had not said anything about Mr. Smith.

"Thank you for looking. Chief, if there is nothing else I think it best he retire for the night. He is my son and has early duties." He really wanted him out of what he knew could turn into a messy situation.

"I understand. But, I do have a few questions for him. Will you please excuse us? I'd like to speak with him alone." If the boy knew anything of importance he did not want him to feel he could not reveal it because it might not meet with his father's approval. The Chief did not miss the look of immediate regret when he made mention of Mr. Smith.

"Of course. I'll be near if you need me." He departed quickly but gave his son a look that said to be honest, polite and to remember his place.

"Are you employed by the Nash Family?" The Chief now turned his attention to the young man.

"Yes I am. I work with Mr. Smith. He's in charge of the stable and the horses." He was very polite and the Chief liked him.

"I see. Did you speak with Mr. Smith about Mrs. Nash's whereabouts?"

"I did. He told me he did not know where she was."

"Did he say anything else to you?"

"Only that he was sorry to hear of Mr. Nash's death." He looked at the floor.

"Did you already know that?"

"No sir. I didn't know it myself until he mentioned it. I was only told to look for Mrs. Nash. Mr. Smith had already learned of it. I was sorry to learn of it myself."

"Did he say how he heard of it?" The Chief was taking notes.

"He was at The Foggy Inn. It was his day off and he went into town for a pint after he cleaned the buggy and rubbed down the horse." He hated to reveal that his friend often frequented The Foggy Inn. Employment was often terminated for what was perceived as excessive drinking.

"Do you know for certain if Mr. Nash made a trip this morning, or I should say more correctly yesterday morning?"

"Yes sir. I was in the stables when he said that he would be going on a business trip but I don't know where because he didn't say. He came home late but he said that he would go for a walk because Mrs. Nash always hated his business trips. I remember it well because Mr. Smith teased me about how it would be when I got married. Forgive me, I didn't mean to make light of the situation. That's the last time we saw him. Mr. Smith and I were just discussing how you can see a person only a few hours before and then you'll never see them alive again." He took a deep breath and the Chief realized that he had been standing at what could be almost military attention during the entire questioning period.

"You may go young man. Thank you for your help. I will speak with Mr. Smith later." The Chief knew it would probably not be necessary because of his father's position and the fact that the young man had no reason to lie. He left quickly hoping that what he said would not end in Mr. Smith losing his job. He did not have a chance to say anything to anyone because the Chief immediately called for Mr. and Mrs. Ivy.

"Is it possible that Mrs. Nash had another engagement this evening?" Chief Johnson hoped she had.

"I would have to say no. I went to her room to ask if she needed anything prior to retiring for the night. She was already in bed and she made no mention of having an appointment or needing to go anywhere. She said she and Mr. Nash would see me in the morning." The cook looked at the men with concern written on her face.

"Do you remember what time that was?" Chief took out his notepad.

"Yes. It was about eight o'clock."

"Was Mr. Nash home?"

"No sir he wasn't. He had gone to a business meeting and he was expected late but he was so late I just left him a sandwich …" She stopped talking and looked at Doctor Grayson. "Oh, please say that Mr. Nash is alright." She had suddenly realized that they were not asking for him but rather for the lady of the house.

"Is Mr. Nash alright?" Mr. Ivy moved closer to his wife.

"There has been an incident and that is why we need to speak with Mrs. Nash." Chief Johnson did not wish to go into details at this exact moment. He decided to get their attention elsewhere. "Would it be alright if we went to look in her room once more?"

"Yes, of course. I'll have to accompany you out of respect for Mrs. Nash." He appreciated the opportunity to look in her room for any clues concerning her sudden disappearance.

When he entered her room it was neat and very feminine. There was nothing out of the ordinary. Then he opened her closet. It was almost empty.

"Mrs. Ivy, I find it odd that Mrs. Nash has so few dresses. Is this the extent of her wardrobe?" He could hardly believe it.

"Goodness! There is nothing in this closet. Mrs. Nash has several beautiful dresses and accessories to match. I can't imagine what happened to them." She was shocked.

"Does she keep her accessories anyplace else?" Every lady of society had several hats, shoes, jewelry and the like. He looked around and saw none of those things. He opened a drawer in a tall chest and noticed it contained very few accessories. There were no jewels of any kind. Most women kept at least one small pair of pearl earrings or a nice hat pin for everyday wear.

"No. But, I assure she has lovely accessories. Mrs. Nash is a very elegant lady."

"Try and think for a minute. Have you ever seen her wear a light lilac dress or anything made of lilac that would be worn as an outer garment?"

"Lilac?" She was thinking. "Oh yes, I remember now. Last year for the annual Commerce Ball she had a dress of that color made. She adored it because of the cut and style." Her curiosity was peaked but she knew it was not her place to ask questions.

Does she own a trunk?" He remembered what Leroy told him.

"Yes. Well, I really should say she did. This evening a young man came and collected it. She said it was filled with things for charity. I helped her take it downstairs." She was not certain what to think.

"What time did the man come for the trunk?"

"It was about six o'clock." She answered.

"Did you see her pay the man and do you know where the trunk was going?" He was confirming what Leroy had told him.

"Mrs. Nash didn't pay the man personally, her maid did and said everything went as I had instructed. Mrs. Nash asked that he be given the envelope. It was sealed so I don't know what was inside. I thought it contained money, but I can't say for certain." She hated these questions and was wondering if she should continue to answer. She did not want to cause trouble for her employers.

"I see. Well, I think we are concluded here. May I take another look around the library, if that's alright?" He suspected Mrs. Nash never gave that trunk to charity especially when she had kept dresses considered plain by comparison to what he had seen her wear in the past.

"That would be fine." They left the bedroom and in only a minute were back in the library.

Doctor Grayson had already scanned the room for clues on her where-abouts. When the Chief returned to the library, he gave him the papers he pulled out of the waste basket. Both men realized they were looking at a list that contained estimated values for pieces of jewelry. He would check the list to determine if the jewels were being insured for greater replace-ment value if lost or stolen, or if they were being sold for cash money. He had a lot of questions, and not too many answers. He hoped that Mr. Gor-don would arrive soon. He had the best mind for solving things of anyone that the Chief knew. Before he could think further, he was interrupted by the butler.

"Sir, can you tell me if something has happened to Mr. Nash?" The room fell quiet and he decided that it would do no harm if he told them of Mr. Nash's death since their son already knew.

"I'm very sorry to inform you that Mr. Nash is dead. It happened only a few hours ago as best we can determine."

"How did it happen?" Mr. Ivy asked.

"I'm sorry. I must speak with Mrs. Nash before I can disclose the details."

"We understand." Mr. Ivy put his arm around his wife who was visibly upset.

Chief Johnson spared them the details of his death. They were both saddened and shocked enough. Mrs. Ivy quickly composed herself. She would need to be strong for Mrs. Nash. In only a few hours, everyone in town would be aware of what happened. He felt it only fair to inform them of their employer's death. Now he had to concentrate on finding Mrs. Nash to inform her of her loss ... that is if she didn't already know.

Early the next morning the town was talking about the murder of Mr. Nash. He was buried in the town cemetery with only a few people in attendance. Chief Johnson was one of those present. Looking at the mourners he did not feel that the murderer was among them. He noticed that everyone in the small church were established businessmen and members of the household staff. Mrs. Nash could not be located. The undertaker waited as long as possible but after several hours it soon became necessary to place Mr. Nash to rest. After the burial Chief Johnson went to his office and looked at his notes and all the evidence he had collected.

In a room at The Foggy Inn, Joaquin and Rue were packing the last of the things to be placed inside their trunks. They were aware of the murder and Rue noticed that Joaquin was nervous and checking his pocket watch frequently. He also went to the window several times.

"Joaquin, what on earth has gotten into you? You are as nervous as a virgin bride." She had never seen him like this.

"Nash is dead! Someone murdered him." He was looking at her as if she were unaware of the fact.

"I know. What does that have to do with you? You didn't kill him." She knew that for a fact because they had spent the night together.

"Have you forgotten that I was spending time between the sheets with his wife? She was pretty upset when she left my room. I have no way of knowing what she did. It's possible she even left a note or sent a message to the authorities that I killed that poor bastard." He looked out the window again.

"In less than one hour the ship leaves the harbor. I'm finished placing all my things in the trunk. If you help me close it we can be on our way. You are done packing aren't you?" She looked around and saw his trunk locked.

"Yeah. I guess the only thing to do is lock your trunk and get on that ship." He went to the trunk and locked it. With the final strap in place they were ready to leave. Joaquin went downstairs and brought back a man he hired earlier to help carry one of the trunks to the ship. He would carry the other one. When they left the room no one looked back. In twenty minutes they were standing on the deck of the Mystic Quest and were looking out over the bay. The crew was busy making the ship ready for departure.

"I can't believe it. Just think, after all this time we are on our way. In a few months we will be in Spain. I was thinking that maybe tomorrow we can begin my first Spanish lesson if that's alright with you." She smiled at him.

"It's more than alright. Something I've been thinking about is the name of our vineyard. What do you think of RuCutta Vineyards as the name of our vineyard and the name we put on our labels? It's a combination of both our names."

"I like it." She really did. "Thank you for making this possible for me." Rue hugged Joaquin.

"We made it possible for each other. Let's go below and get everything settled in so we can enjoy our departure and not worry about things down there." He took her arm and they went to their cabin. Once inside he placed the trunks out of the way and opened the port hole. The cabin was as promised so the voyage home would be very pleasant. Soon he would have the things he always hoped for and could begin life with the woman he loved. Rue could make a home with her son. When he remembered all he had gone through to get to this moment he remembered another such voyage. This accommodation was a far cry from the galleon that had brought him to the shores of America. Rue noticed his faraway look and knew he was remembering something that was of a hurtful nature. After ten minutes everything was properly placed and secured. She suggested that they go out to the main deck to watch the ship leave port. Fifteen minutes later the ship pulled out of the harbor. They stood still for some time and said nothing as Valda Bay began to disappear from their sight. Rue leaned against Joaquin and allowed herself the pleasure of feeling the light wind on her face. She could smell the salt in the air. The gulls appeared to be escorting the ship from the harbor and the sails puffed out in wonderful display. Ship departures were a familiar occurrence to him but he always took pleasure in it. He noticed that she was completely captured by the scene before her. He could not remember when she looked more happy and beautiful.

Mr. Gordon stepped off the transport about the time that the Mystic Quest pulled out of the bay. He was a middle aged man of average height. He wore a nice suit and his full moustache and keen brown eyes gave him the appearance of a distinguished gentleman. He looked around for his friend and in only a moment saw him driving up in a two horse drawn buggy.

"Johnson, old friend it's good to see you." He gave his friend a hug and stood back to look at him.

"Good to see you too. You look well; sporting a moustache now I see." He reached down and picked up a piece of his luggage.

"Yes. I think it makes me look more intelligent. The women love it." He looked at Johnson and laughed. He also picked up a small bag and placed it into the back of the buggy.

"How was your trip?"

"Long and longer. I swear that coach hit every bump in the road. I also had the misfortune to be seated next to a lady that just would not be quiet for one moment." He shook his head at the memory.

"Almost as bad as a baby that won't stop crying."

"True enough, but at least you can understand that. I swear another day and I think I would have rung her neck." He moved his hands in front of him and made the motion of choking a person.

"Well, speaking of neck and choking, there has been a horrible occurrence since I've sent you the telegram about the fire. It's bad business. But, let's not talk of that now. You need a chance to rest and get a hot meal." He hated to burden him so early so he decided that he would wait a while and let his friend at least rest before going to work.

"It's alright. I'd like to hear what's going on. I'm actually feeling refreshed since getting away from that parrot of a woman. I am hungry so if you want to, we could get a bite and you could fill me in. What do you think?"

"Sure. Let's go to my house and leave the luggage just inside the door and then we can go to Mrs. Steele's Sweet Shop. She makes a delicious sandwich, has great pies and her coffee is the best in town." He wanted to offer his friend a nice place to eat away from inquisitive eyes and ears. Most of the local people favored The Foggy Inn because of the relaxed atmosphere and lower prices.

After the men were seated and their order taken, they began to talk about all the events that made Chief Johnson request his presence in Valda Bay.

"So what do you think?" Chief Johnson asked.

"I think you've done well. When we finish here, I'd like to speak with Ian Fisk if he's up to it and hopefully by then, you will have an answer to your wire from Rock Port. Also, let's stop at the bank on the way to the hospital. I'd like to take a look at the bank records of Mr. Nash. I trust you gave orders to have them closed?" He looked at him hoping to hear that he had.

"I did. I've also drafted a missing person notice on Mrs. Nash. If you approve the notice it will go out to all the major ports and cities within a thousand mile radius. I thought that would be far enough. I used the United States Notification System to assist us since we have no idea what happened to her." He knew that the system he spoke of was very efficient and used by law enforcement officials. It was used to track escaped convicts and to seek help from other towns in the event of natural disasters.

"Good idea. Let's also confirm whether or not there was a charity drive anywhere in the area." He drained his coffee cup and appeared he was ready to leave.

"I'm ready to go to work." Chief Johnson and Mr. Gordon stood up at the same time and when Chief Johnson paid the bill, Mr. Gordon protested.

"You really should not have paid for my lunch. I do however appreciate it." He smiled at his friend.

"It was my pleasure. Besides, I'm going to abuse you enough in this investigation. Buying you lunch will help ease my conscience." He chuckled a little but knew that there was truth in what he said. The two would no doubt research everything and spend countless hours piecing together what caused the fire at the mercantile, who murdered Mr. Nash and the whereabouts of his wife.

Karin was sitting in a chair that Daniel and James had made for her. They had proved wonderful friends and she was grateful for their constant support and friendship. Her heart was still breaking over the loss of Erik but she now felt she had a new reason to be happy. She was now certain that she was going to have the baby that she and Erik had so longed for. Fate had crushed her with one hand and blessed her with the other. She had not mentioned her condition to anyone because she was debating something terribly important. She was trying to decide if she wanted to tell her friends the reason that Erik had asked them to go sea with him. She thought she had all the clues necessary to find the lost treasure. This time of year the seas could be rough. She had looked at the charts and knew that with steady wind they could be north of Valda Bay and near the Cascades in only a couple of weeks. The Sea Star was still in dry dock being repaired. She had no idea how to go about getting another boat or plotting courses. She would not concern herself with that. That was what James and Daniel were for. They were Erik's most trusted and dearest friends. He trusted and loved them like brothers, so would she. The decision was made. She got up from her chair and went to where the two of them were replacing the shutters that the storm had torn off. They had repaired the cracked window, cleaned up the yard, helped her replant her garden, made her a new chair, chopped fire wood and hauled away or burned a great deal of trash that had been blown around the house. Seeing her approach they gave her acknowledgement but continued working.

"I need to speak with you for a moment." She looked at the both of them.

"Of course." James answered and stepped toward her.

"I mean both of you." Daniel didn't say anything but moved off the ladder and was soon standing by her.

"Not outside. We need to go into the house. Will you be much longer with the shutter?"

"I need about five more minutes. Daniel has a few nails he needs to pound and then he will be finished." He looked at Daniel and he nodded.

"That's good. I will have time to put on a fresh pot of coffee." She turned and walked inside the house.

"Now what do you suppose that's all about?" James asked.

"Who knows?" Daniel went back up the ladder and finished repairing the shutter. They picked up the tools and took the ladder to the work shed where they brushed off their clothes so they would not make a mess in her house. When they knocked on the door, the fresh smell of coffee filled their nostrils.

"Come in. I'm just getting a few things. Please have a seat at the table and close the door." She was still gathering Erik's nautical charts, notes and maps.

"Did she say to close the door?" James asked.

"She did." Daniel pushed the door closed.

In a moment she appeared with her arms full of what looked like nautical charts. She placed them on the table and motioned for them to sit down.

"Relax. Nothing is wrong. You are so dear to me and I can't begin to thank you for all you have done." She was feeling emotional so she stopped speaking for a moment.

"I'll get our coffee cups if that's alright." James stood and went to the cupboard where he knew the cups were always hanging. It was done in an attempt to allow her time to regain her composure.

"Thank you, but I don't think the coffee is ready just yet." She was now feeling better. James was always so thoughtful and she appreciated that quality so much.

"I'll just place them on the table until the coffee is ready." He did so and then sat back down. He waited for her to begin as did Daniel.

"I know that you must have been wondering why Erik wanted you to go out to sea with him." The men nodded their heads but remained quiet so she could continue. "Erik was given a Bible and a poem by his grandmother before she died. It seems that there was a secret message contained in them but his grandmother could never understand what it was." She took the Bible and showed it to them.

"Nice Bible." James spoke.

"Yes it is. It was given to her by a sea captain who died young. It was rumored that he found the treasure of the Rip Tide. Since he and Mrs. Webb had been in love, it was thought that he told her about the treasure. In reality he died before he could tell her anything." She turned her head to look at the coffee pot. It still needed a few minutes.

"Did anyone else have the Bible before that?" Daniel asked.

"No. She got it directly from the Captain. That is why she was so certain it contained an important message in the poem he wrote for her. And Erik spent countless hours trying to figure out the poem and the point of the circles on each of the verses in the book of Esther."

"So what was the message in the poem and the point of the circle on each verse?" James picked up the Bible and opened the Bible to the Book of Esther. He saw the circles on certain verses. He handed the Bible to Daniel who also looked at them.

"I think our coffee is ready." She got up but continued to talk. "Well aside from the fact that Esther was Mrs. Webb's first name, Erik learned that they mark what he said was longitude and latitude. Pull out the chart and see where Erik marked." She poured out the coffee and knowing that Daniel liked milk and sugar she placed that on the table as well. By now James and Daniel were looking at the chart.

"This is amazing." James was looking at the plotted course. It was the same one they were on when the storm struck them down.

"Yes it is. It's even more amazing that Erik figured out the poem. Look at the back of the map. It marks a place in the Cascades does it not?" She looked at James while he looked at the coordinates.

"Yes it does. But, if I'm reading this correctly once you drop anchor off shore, you have to walk to reach the place it's buried. You'll have to use a compass." He smiled at her.

"That's exactly what we both thought. The compass will help us find it. The poem told us what the treasure consisted of. If we are right the lost treasure of the Rip Tide consisted of many diamonds and solid gold pieces of eight." She took a sip from her coffee cup and watched them staring at all the information in what could be considered a state of mild disbelief coupled with utter amazement. She said nothing but allowed them to enjoy and process what she had told them.

"Karin, you must be careful with this information. There are people who would do anything to get their hands on this." James was thinking of her safety.

"I know. Erik said that also. That is why we three are going to get it first." She made sure to mention all three so that there would be no doubt she considered them equal partners in retrieving the treasure.

"All three of us?" James said

"Yes."

"I don't know what to say." James was at a loss for words for once in his life.

"Say yes. All you have to do is get us a boat. Erik and I have some money put aside for emergencies and I think this is one. I know it won't be enough to buy a boat by myself. But, if we all went in together we could purchase one if you're willing to try again." She hoped they could because if they couldn't they would have to wait until next spring so the repairs to the Sea Star could be finished. She would not be able to travel and did not want to stay behind.

"I can help considerably. I have about half of what we need to buy a boat." James was offering all he had.

"I have the other half. Karin your share can buy the provisions and supplies we will need for about a month." Daniel offered. He was glad he had done without some things he only wanted but did not really need.

"That sounds fine. What if people get suspicious of us going out again so soon after you just got back? Everyone knows that the Sea Star is still in dry dock—what would make you want to leave again in a hurry?" Karin had a good point.

"You." Daniel piped up.

"Me? What are you talking about?" Karin did not understand what he meant.

"You asked us to take you to your family. It's not uncommon for women to go to their family when they lose their husband." His voice trailed off as he thought he sounded insensitive to her loss and his. "I'm sorry, that was awful of me."

"No it wasn't. It's a good idea. I understand what you meant. When do you think we can be ready?" She hoped soon.

"In a day. I've already got a boat in mind. The boat for sale is the one we looked at about a month ago James. It's a little bigger than the Sea Star so she has more canvas but quick and fast can be good. Mr. Ludwigsen is looking for a quick sale. It's only a little after noon. We could use this day to ready ourselves."

"I think we could depart on the tide tomorrow. What do you think?" Daniel asked.

"I can do it if you two can. We could buy food provisions in the next port to save time. I'll clean out my pantry of all the canned goods. There is enough food for about two weeks." She was glad she had home canned all kinds of fruit and vegetables.

"That will see us to Port Herron with no problem. So do we try or what?" Daniel asked the question.

"Let's do it." They all looked at each other and in five minutes there was a swirl of activity in the kitchen. She set about collecting food items. Then men secured the charts and maps. They went outside and prepared the home for an extended absence. Daniel stayed behind to help Karin with final preparations while James went to purchase the boat. He would have to stop at the Ludwigsen home first and negotiate a price. Once he did that he would return for Karin and Daniel. They would go to the bank and James would pay Mr. Ludwigsen. Daniel and Karin would return to the house where he would help carry the goods to the boat. James would make the boat ready to sail. When the tide proved favorable they would depart. Karin had mentioned to the men that she would not leave Salty behind. They had no problem with the little cat coming with them. If things went as planned and on the first favorable tide, three people and a small cat would sail into what they hoped would be a safe and very profitable trip. After a couple of hours of negotiation and finally agreeing upon the purchase price the two men shook hands. James hurried to the bank and made appointments for Karin and Daniel. He also was forced to make conversation with the bank president.

"I was sorry to hear of your friend's passing. Mr. Johansson was a fine man." The bank president had done business with Erik in the past and found him to be honest and a pleasure to talk to.

"Thank you. I'm going to miss him and Mrs. Johansson as well. She has asked that my partner James and I take her to be with her family. It's the least we could do." He had just laid the ground work explaining their absence.

"I see. When do you anticipate leaving?"

"If all goes well, we will depart tomorrow. That is why I've made appointments for my partner to come to the bank as well as Mrs. Johansson. We, of course, will be returning because I still have the Sea Star in dry dock but I can't speak for her." He thought that was enough information.

"I think that is a kind and generous thing you are doing. I hope you have fair winds and a good trip. The North Star is a good boat as I recall." He extended his hand and the men shook hands in parting. By the time he reached the house he could see that Daniel and Karin were ready to go. They had packed everything and the only one protesting what was going on was Salty. He didn't like the box Karin had placed him in and he was meowing loudly. James and Daniel loaded the ship while Karin walked to the bank. Her appointment was first. She had already been briefed by Daniel concerning his conversation with the bank president.

"Please accept my condolences on the passing of your husband. I understand your need to be with your family and hope the days ahead will be easier for you. Take care and I hope you have a pleasant trip." He smiled faintly and when she extended her hand, he took it lightly in his and shook it gently. He was a well educated and refined man.

"Thank you for processing my account so quickly. I appreciate your kind words and wish you the best also. Good day." She turned and quickly walked out of the bank and toward the waiting boat. When Daniel saw her approaching, he went into action. He concluded his business in record time and when he returned to the ship there was good news waiting. The ship was equipped with a small row boat that was big enough for four people. They would use it to go ashore once they reached the Cascades. When checking the galley and various compartments Karin discovered all manner of supplies from extra rope to a small barrel of oil for the lamps. They had planned on buying supplies at the Port of Seattle; this discovery would save a little money. The berth of the North Star was larger than the Sea Star and could afford Karin a little privacy by placing a blanket suspended with a rope above her bunk that could serve as a curtain. The same arrangement was not possible for the men but it didn't matter to either one of them. Salty would have the run of the boat. He would pay for his fare by keeping the rodents and other unwanted little creatures away. Karin would cook, clean and wash their clothes. James would navigate the ship as he was better at the wheel and plotting a course than anyone else. Daniel would ensure things were in good repair and stayed secure. He would help James at the wheel. Everyone would serve as a lookout. It was decided that the departure time would be the next day in the late afternoon. The tide would be perfect and the wind good. James and Daniel were also glad that they would not be departing on a Friday. Every seaman knew that you just didn't start anything new on a Friday. Karin just smiled at their superstitious ways.

# *Paths Cross*

hings on the Priscilla were good. The wind was steady and the seas calm. For most of the night Elsa had laid awake thinking that perhaps she had made a mistake in requesting that she be taken to San Francisco. Everyone knew she had often spoke of the wonderful social life and culture that she had been privileged to be a part of. The hub of society on the west coast was in San Francisco and that fact in itself put her in danger of being discovered. She needed a new plan. After many hours and contemplating the advantages and disadvantages of making a change to her plans she decided a change was necessary. She would mention this to the Ralston's in the morning.

"Good morning Mrs. Nash. I hope you slept well." Cole had already started breakfast. The coffee was freshly made and the smell of bacon cooking filled the galley.

"Good morning. It smells wonderful in here." She noticed he was very capable and that impressed her.

"Pour yourself a cup of coffee. Breakfast will be just a moment." He pointed to where the cups were hanging.

"Mr. Ralston, I was wondering if it would be possible to change our course?" She took a cup from the hook and handed it to him. She did not think for one minute that she would pour it herself.

"Just put the cup on the table. I wouldn't want to burn you pouring it out." He was a little annoyed at her lady on the hill attitude but he let it pass.

"Oh, I did not think of that." She did as she was told and soon was enjoying the hot brew. She wondered if he had heard her inquire about the course change. She did not have long to wait.

"Now, what's all this about changing course?" He had his back to her and continued cooking.

"I'd like to go to Seattle instead of San Francisco." She wished she could read his face.

"Seattle?" He could do it easily enough. It would mean that they would have to make changes to the plotted course, something that happened all the time.

"Yes. Can it be done?" She asked.

"It can. But, I have to chart a new course, and we will lose a day or two because we have to sail back from where we've just been. Seattle is north of us from this location." He turned around and placed the plate of bacon on the table.

"Will it take very long to plot the course?"

"No. I can do it while you eat breakfast. How do you want your eggs?" He had the eggs in his hand waiting for her to decide.

"Scrambled would be nice thank you." She watched as he cooked her eggs. They were cooked well and she enjoyed them. He did as promised and by the time she was finished with breakfast, he had already plotted the course and went to tell Flint.

"Now you say she wants to go to Seattle? Is she crazy or what?" Flint knew that a woman on a fishing boat was bad business. As far as he was concerned women were good only for one thing—relieving sexual frustration.

"Take it easy. I've plotted the new course and all it means is that we've lost a day or two." He laid the charts back on the table and Flint turned the wheel and soon they were on a new heading.

"Why do you suppose she wants to go there instead of San Francisco? I was looking forward to spending time there with a woman. I guess Seattle is just as good." Flint pressed his lips together.

"I have no clue. Frankly, I don't care and neither should you. Let's just get her there and be done with all this. You want more coffee?" Cole reached for Flint's empty cup.

"Yeah that would be great. When you get back, do you think you should take a look around with the glass?"

"Good idea. I'll be back in a minute." When he was pouring the coffee he noticed her plate and fork in the little dish bucket. She had not even bothered to rinse her plate. Despite her statement about helping with the dishes, she had yet to wash a single dish. He hoped she would at least wash her own dishes if not theirs. The woman was totally useless. He went back up on deck.

"Here you go." He handed Flint the cup and reached for the glass. He carefully scanned the horizon. There was not a ship in sight. The clear sky indicated there was no threat of inclement weather coming. He would speak with Flint for a while.

"There's not a thing out there we need to concern ourselves about. I'm going to wash some dishes." He turned to leave and Flint caught him by the arm.

"What should I do if we run into another boat?" He was a little concerned because of who was sailing with them.

"Sail away from them and make sure you don't acknowledge their signal. I'll take a look from the port hole below and try and identify the boat. If it's no one we recognize, they don't know us either. If it's a boat we know we can probably stay far enough away to keep well ahead of them. Besides, we may not all be going to the exact same place either." He noticed that Flint had that worried look on his face.

"Stop being a worry bird. It'll be fine." He went below to clean up the galley.

Elsa was glad that things went smoothly concerning the course change. She could have kicked herself for not thinking of Seattle in the first place. She looked around the room and found it small. She hated small places so she went to the galley where Cole was washing dishes. She did not offer to help.

"Excuse me. Would it be alright if I were to go on deck for a few minutes?"

"Sure. Just be careful and make sure you hang on to something. I'd also wear a hat. The sun off the water could burn your face." He went back to washing dishes.

"I guess I'd better get my hat." She turned to leave.

"Wait a moment. Take the one off that rack. Your lacey brimmed hat won't do the job. The wind will tear it up and you will still get burned." He was looking toward the cup rack.

"Alright." She reached for it and placed it on her head. It fit her to large so she piled her hair underneath it. It fit better and Cole seemed pleased that she had decided to wear it. "How do I look?" She turned her head to the right and then the left. She was obviously playing with him.

"Like the prettiest woman I've ever seen wearing a man's hat." He laughed and went back to doing the dishes. Then a thought came to him that would prove advantageous to all of them. She had to agree and that was the hard part. "Mrs. Nash, I know that what I'm going to suggest will at first seem odd to a lady such as yourself, but I think it would be safer if you changed your clothes."

"Changed my clothes? Why would I do that and what would I wear?"

"There are all kinds of sailing vessels in these waters. I don't think we will come across any, but I'd like them to think we are all men. It would be safer for you." What he said was not completely untrue.

"I don't have any male clothing with me."

"I thought as much. There are some clean clothes in my trunk. You can use a bit of rope for a belt and tuck in the shirt. Put all your hair under that hat and you could pass for a man from the distance."

"I see. It is distasteful to me but if you think it's safer, I'll do it. Where is your trunk?" She thought he was telling her that sailors at sea could ravish her despite efforts to protect her. She appreciated his concern for her.

"It's under your bunk. I'll go on deck until you are dressed. Just give a yell and then I'll come down and finish the dishes." He was glad she had been agreeable. He was not at all concerned for her safety. He did not want to be questioned about why she was with them or have to engage in some form of fighting to be able to flee. He was good with weapons, but Flint was not. He did not want them to be hurt or killed for this selfish, spoiled woman. He went up the ladder and waited for her to dress. In a few minutes she was dressed like a male crew member.

"Oh my goodness! If my friends could see me now I'm not sure what they would think." She went up the ladder and was soon on deck.

Cole breathed a sigh a relief. He did not want her going through her trunk just yet for a different hat or anything else for a while. The dress he tore the piece of fabric from was on the bottom of the trunk so chances were good that she would not wear that dress for some time. He learned a long time ago that women packed the things they were going to need soon on top. It was hoped that the authorities would apprehend her with the torn dress in her possession. They planned to inform the authorities anonymously that she was in Seattle, then depart for the warm waters of Mexico. While in Seattle they would get cash for the jewels, buy supplies and pay a couple of whores for an hour of their time. Cole would rather they wait for Mexico to sexually enjoy themselves but Flint mentioned he wanted a woman when they got to Seattle. Once all that was accomplished they could set sail. Getting supplied in Seattle meant being able to pass Valda Bay without having to replenish anything. It was a good plan.

In Valda Bay a wonderful celebration was taking place in China Town. Two young people had exchanged marriage vows in a traditional Chinese wedding. The stores had all closed early to participate in the wedding dinner. Lovely red decorations hung from high places and musicians played beautiful songs on special hand crafted musical instruments. Food was plentiful and everyone brought lovely gifts for the happy couple. Mei Ling wore a traditional grown and despite its great weight and several layers she seemed to walk as if on air. She looked radiant. The groom was also dressed in an honorable traditional fashion. He looked happy and pleased with the activities around him and of course with his bride.

Two days before the marriage of Mr. Yong Tao Sung to Mei Ling Lee, the couple spoke about his plans for their future. She knew that what he decided for them would be final. She had little or nothing to say at all in these matters. But he did something that was not an ordinary occurrence in their culture or for that matter, in most marriages. He asked her opinion about staying in Valda Bay. He was a trained medical doctor in his native China and there was a need for a doctor in China Town. He would work with Mr. Chang and Doctor Grayson. When Doctor Grayson learned he was actually a medical doctor, he was very pleased. He hoped to introduce Doctor Sung to some of his patients who were more opened minded and in a few years, perhaps he could retire leaving his practice in good hands. It would take time, perhaps more than the good Lord would allow Doctor Grayson, but he wanted to try. When Mei Lei heard this she was very happy. She didn't want to leave Valda Bay. So, the decision was made. They would make their life in America and raise their family with the traditional values of China and the opportunities of a new land.

Ian Fisk was eating breakfast when he heard knocking at the door of his hospital room. He answered gladly to his name being called when he recognized the voice of Chief Johnson.

"Come in Chief." He saw two men enter both wearing clean sheets over their street clothes. They had removed their shoes and smelled of soap. No doubt they had been told to scrub their hands and faces.

"How are you doing Ian?" He noticed that he looked well and seemed to be improving greatly. His legs were under a sheet that had been propped up with four little poles to keep the fabric off his legs.

"I'm doing great. How are you?"

"Doing well myself. I see Mr. Chang has placed you under a new contraption." He said pointing to the sheet that was covering his legs.

"He has. It allows the air to move and keep the fabric from sticking to me. It works. Mr. Chang is really something." He said it with admiration in his voice.

"Yes he is. I'd also like to introduce you to Mr. Frederick Gordon. He's the Fire Investigator I spoke with you about a few days ago."

"Yes sir. I remember it well. It's real nice to meet you." He wished he could have shaken his hand but that was strictly against medical advice.

"My pleasure. I'm told you are coming along fine."

"I am. I guess being hurt is just a hazard of the job we all accept." He wasn't sure what else he could say.

"Chief Johnson tells me that once you are recovered you have expressed a desire to investigate fires. Are you still interested in that line of work?" He could tell that this young man had a quiet strength about him. He discovered that he did not complain and did exactly as he was instructed. He liked him and he was usually right about first impressions.

"I sure am. I know that I can't be a on a hose anymore, but I can't see myself doing any other kind of work." He looked down at his burns.

"There's more than one way to fight a fire Mr. Fisk. In fact that's part of why I'm here. Are you up to answering a few questions about the night of the fire?" It was his experience that after a trauma such as the one that Mr. Fisk sustained he needed to be careful. He would go slow and then determine if he should continue with the questions.

"Sure. I already told the Chief all I know." He didn't want the Chief to think that he would tell Mr. Gordon something that he did not already know.

"Yes, I'm sure you did. Chief Johnson did tell me that you had informed him of some things that you saw, but I'd like you to tell me in your own words about that night. Take your time and know that I may write down things as you speak but don't think I'm not listening." He took a pen and a little notepad from his pocket. Ian Fisk began to recount the events of the fire.

"Well, as I recall the night was dark and cool. When we got notice that there was a fire in town we responded quickly. When we arrived we saw the mercantile was engulfed in flames and the inside was going fast. After a short time we felt it was going to be a loss. I was inside the building with Mr. Wheeler." He stopped a moment and reached for a glass of water. He was remembering that Mr. Wheeler died when the roof collapsed. Mr. Wheeler had been his best friend.

"Was he the fireman that died when the roof collapsed?" There was no other way to ask except to be direct.

"Yes. There were also a few others slightly hurt. I guess we were just the unlucky ones." He took a drink of water and the men allowed him time to collect his thoughts.

"Was it foggy that night?" Mr. Gordon was trying to refocus his attention from the death of Mr. Wheeler and back to the details he observed.

"It was. In fact, I remember feeling the soot sticking to me a little more than normal because of the damp air and the way the glow of the shooting flames looked through the fog." The strategy worked because he was now refocused on the fire itself.

"What else can you tell me?" He was writing down a few notes.

"Well, I believe the fire started in the center of the building. The flames had burned the side walls and on top of the ceiling. The back of the store had not been fire damaged yet but there was a lot of smoke everywhere. As I fought the fire, I was looking around and I saw something that seemed out of place. I know the store well because I've purchased things there on a regular basis for years. Anyway, I saw an ax head that looked new on the edge except that it had some deep scratches on it. The head was lying far from the new ones. Also, there was a piece of leather with some initials on it not far from the place I saw the ax head. I picked up the piece of leather, but the ax head was too hot to handle. I gave the piece of leather to the Chief. I guess that's about it. Funny, now that I tell it again it all seems so insignificant." He thought perhaps now that it sounded silly and alarmist in nature.

"It doesn't. You did the right thing. If it's of any comfort to you, I think you are right. There are also a few things that I'm not at liberty to discuss right now that are very suspect. You just concentrate on getting better. I'll be in touch and when you are on your feet again I'll expect a wire to inform me when you can start school." He smiled at Ian for his keen eye and courage.

"I'll do that. Thank you for coming to see me." He was excited at the thought of learning a new skill.

"No problem. Take care. Chief, if you don't have anything else for Mr. Fisk, I'd like to get started on a few things if that's alright with you." He had already thought where he would go next.

"That's fine with me. We'll talk later and when you see Charity please give her my best. Do you need anything before we go?"

"No. Just find who killed Mr. Wheeler. He deserves that." He gave his Chief a look that spoke more than words could have.

"Right." The Chief and Mr. Gordon left his room. Ian could not wait to tell Charity about the school he would attend to become an official fire inspector. He knew she would be pleased for him.

When they were about ten yards away from Fisk's room Mr. Gordon began to speak about the piece of leather that Fisk had given him. He asked to see it. The Chief handed it to him. For just a moment he stopped and looked at the piece of leather. He handed it back to Chief Johnson and they continued walking toward the hospital front doors. When they were outside and away from the hospital they could speak freely.

"He's one of your best firemen isn't he?" Mr. Gordon asked.

"He is. I think he will enjoy that school you spoke of and will be a credit to the department. I'm glad he's willing especially after such a horrible injury."

"It looks like he's getting good care. I have to admit I've never worn a sheet to see a burned person before." Mr. Gordon was remembering all the injured people who were burned much less severely than Fisk. They died of infection. Perhaps there was something to this germ business.

"It is a different kind of treatment. But it seems to work."

"What do you think about us going to the cobbler shop?" Mr. Gordon had an idea.

"Let's go. The shop isn't far from here."

In a few minutes they were inside the shop and speaking to the man who was the best leather worker that Mr. Gordon had ever seen. All his leather goods were unique and his shop was filled with all kinds of money pouches, belts, saddles and the like.

"I was wondering if we might have you look at this piece of leather and tell me a little about it." Mr. Gordon handed the little piece to the owner.

"It looks like it came off something I made." He fingered the leather and looked quickly at the piece.

"What makes you say that?" Chief Johnson asked.

"The quality of the leather and the way the letters were made and branded into the leather. They were made with my initial branding irons." He handed the piece back.

"What kind of thing do you generally personalize?" Mr. Gordon asked this question.

"Usually it's a wallet, a pair of gloves or a belt. Once I did a saddle with three shells on it for a high society lady. I can't remember exactly when I did that one, but it sure was pretty." He was proud of that job because it brought him a great deal of work.

"Do you have a log or receipt book that shows what people had custom made or personalized?" He was hoping there would be.

"Sure. I guess it would be alright seeing how this is official police business. There are some people who don't like folks poking into their affairs. I'll only be a minute." He left and when he returned there were two large books in his arms.

"I brought both my books. The green one is for ordering leathers, thread, needles that sort of thing. The second one shows payment for a job done and what the job was."

He was confident that his records were in order. He took pride in keeping the logs straight because often he had repeat customers from different places. If they wanted another of what was ordered previously he would have a record of it. It was just good business practice.

"Do you think you might be able to tell what this piece came off of and for whom you made it?" Chief Johnson looked at the man and he could tell that he was pleased to have been asked to help. It would allow him to show off his business and the large demand he had for his products from as far away as Boston.

"Let me look at that piece again." This time when Mr. Gordon handed it to him he looked more closely. "It's a leather of excellent quality that I use only for making gloves." He was certain of it.

"What about the initials?" Mr. Gordon had already begun to scan the book entries.

"What about them?" He didn't understand the question.

"Are you certain that the iron is yours?"

"Oh, I see what you mean. The brand is definitely mine. I evenly space each letter in a name. Then I space differently between the first and last name. It makes it look crisp and clean and easy to read. I have the irons if you want to see them. I fashioned them myself so the letters would be unique to my work. The letters curl down on the top and flare out to the left slightly at the ends indicating that was an iron I used five months ago. I change the irons every month."

"Can you tell just by looking whose gloves this piece may have belonged to?" It was a stretch but Mr. Gordon learned that if he didn't ask the hard questions, he never got the hard answers.

"Probably. Let me look at my log. Seems to me I only had one order for gloves that month. Belts were popular, but not gloves." He scanned it for about three minutes and came across the name that was not new to either one of the investigators. "Here it is—Cole Ralston. I made a pair of gloves for him about five months ago. I only made one pair that month so this has to be a piece from one of his gloves." He smiled at the men because he felt like he had made a big contribution. In truth, he had.

"You have been a great help. I appreciate your help and your discretion. Have a nice day and thank you so much for your time." They shook hands with the old gentleman and left his shop.

"Well that proved worthwhile. What do you want to do next?" Chief Johnson was looking at his friend.

"Do you know Mr. Ralston?"

"I've seen him and his brother around town and said hello from time to time but nothing more. They visit The Foggy Inn on a pretty regular basis and live on their ship the Priscilla. Why do you ask?"

"We should talk with them after we check out the bank. Let's stop at the telegraph office to see if there is any word on Mrs. Nash. Sound alright with you?"

"You're the boss whatever you say is fine with me. I'll show you his boat on the way to the bank."

The two continued to discuss the case until they came to the dock. Chief Johnson scanned the harbor but did not see the Priscilla. He thought perhaps they had gone fishing despite being so late in the season. Mr. Gordon offered another conclusion—they were gone never to return. This development helped reinforce his suspicious nature that they were involved in some way in everything that had happened in Valda Bay recently. The proof was adding up against them. By the time they reached the telegraph they discussed their next move and knew which records they would ask to see at the bank. When they reached the telegraph office they were informed there was still no reply to any of their inquiries. They stood outside talking and planning about what they would do next.

"Well, that takes care of that, not a word on her whereabouts. I don't like it. Could we be barking up the wrong tree?"

"What do you mean?" Chief Johnson wasn't following his thought pattern.

"She's the wife of a rich man. Could she have been kidnapped and they murdered him when he came to her aid? Could Mrs. Ivy be wrong about the time frame?" He looked at Chief Johnson for his thoughts.

"Maybe, but I don't think so. What kidnapper takes the clothes of the person they kidnap? Remember her closet was empty." He had never heard of that happening.

"Indeed. No, more than likely she is someplace that we just don't know about. Let's keep on the path we are on and see where it leads. If we don't have any better idea soon we can always expand the search for her. Let's go to the bank and see what Mr. Nash was up to financially."

The men left the telegraph office with a request that if a wire should arrive in reference to Mrs. Nash that they be informed as soon as possible. Mr. Gordon informed the clerk that they would be at the bank. They began to walk toward the bank and passed the burnt remains of the mercantile. Looking at the burnt remains it was decided that it was no longer needed as part of the investigation. The rubble needed to be removed. Mr. Gordon and the Chief had already taken a couple of days to examine the burnt material of what was once the mercantile. Careful examination by Mr. Gordon led to the discovery of a large area that was oil stained. This residue proved that something had been spilled to serve as an accelerant. According to Mr. Fisk he also found the ax head in the oil soaked area which helped Mr. Gordon conclude that someone had smashed a large container holding the oil. This left little doubt that the fire was started on purpose and in that spot. Mr. Fisk had provided all information required to officially declare that the fire was a result of arson. When they reached the bank and entered they were made welcome and received no delay in acquiring what they requested. Soon they were seated at a large table with an assistant assigned to them should they require anything.

"This looks pretty complicated to me." Chief Johnson was amazed at all the transactions that Mr. Nash had been involved with.

"He was involved in a number of things wasn't he?"

"Yes, he was. Take a look at this." He handed the paper that described all the details of the spice negotiations to Mr. Gordon.

"It looks like he borrowed quite a bit to see that business transaction complete. But I just saw a paper that shows he signed a note promising the house as security. He also pledged the ice house and made a large withdrawal from his bank account." Chief Johnson continued to look at all the official papers.

"Here's one letter where he wrote the spice company for time to get some money together. You know this looks like he was in deep financial trouble." Mr. Gordon had seen this situation before.

"I received a notice a short time ago where he asked I pay off my account at the mercantile. I didn't owe much, about five dollars. I usually pay at the end of the month, but the notice emphasized that I needed to clear my account within two days of receipt."

He looked to see if there was a master copy of the notice he and no doubt others had received. He searched the stack of papers and found it and gave it to Mr. Gordon for his review. "Here's the master of that notice I was speaking of. I think he sent one to everyone who had an active account at the mercantile."

"Does it say anywhere if Cole Ralston got one?"

"Let me look." The Chief went down the list and found the name. "He did get the notice."

"Did he pay in full like everyone else and if he did how much did he owe?"

"It doesn't say that he paid. The debt was large compared to others, but I don't see any credit mark by their name. There's only the debt." Chief Johnson was starting to think like his friend.

"Is anyone else entered like that?" Mr. Gordon asked.

"No. There is only one entry and that one is for Mr. Cole Ralston. What do you suppose it means?"

"I think he got credit for his outstanding debt. A trade situation if you will."

"Let's say you are right. What does Mr. Ralston have that Mr. Nash would want?"

"Nothing in the traditional sense I'd say. There might be one thing to shed a little light. Do you remember that list of itemized assets that you said was in the wastebasket in the library?"

"Yes. I still have it." Chief Johnson pulled it out of a pocket in his vest. He saw the reaction of Mr. Gordon who laughed out loud.

"What are you laughing at?" The Chief looked at him but had no idea why he was laughing.

"I swear you are the only person I know who carries every bit of evidence in his coat pockets. I bet you forget just how much stuff you have in them." He stopped laughing and went back to looking at all the paper in front of him.

"I have to admit it is a bad habit I have. Sometimes I find things that I forgot to throw out and left in there. It's not that often mind you." He straightened out his tie while trying to suppress a laugh.

"Let me think about this list for just a moment." Mr. Gordon studied it for a moment and then he put it down among the other papers.

"What are you thinking?" The Chief was amazed at what he was seeing.

"I think that Mr. Nash was in deep financial trouble and needed money fast. He tried everything he knew to get it honestly and then was forced to do something desperate. The papers here indicate that he owed heavily. A great deal of money was going out for his domestic life. Look at all these purchases that Mrs. Nash made. Fine clothes, several pieces of art, new everything for the house from ceiling lamps to rugs. She was an expensive woman to keep." He took a deep breath.

"That explains his bank account and why the notices were sent out."

"In part. But that still didn't generate enough money. So he signed papers on the house to be the security for the spices he was purchasing from abroad. Here, look at this." Mr. Gordon handed him a piece of paper showing where the mercantile and his home would serve as collateral for the money borrowed to acquire the spices.

"So if his home and the mercantile were the collateral and the spices didn't prove profitable, he would lose both. Let's not forget he also needed to make payroll for his employees and his savings account was void of funds."

"That's right. The only thing I can't figure with one hundred percent certainty is the order in which these things occurred. I suspect she was demanding and to keep up with her, he took a chance on the spices. That failed and needing money fast he sent notices demanding payment from people with credit at the mercantile. That still didn't help him enough so he took additional steps." He was thinking that the pieces fit together well. He also determined that the life of Rudolph Nash since marrying Elsa Wellington Nash must have been a nightmare.

"Enter Mr. Cole Ralston." He could now see clearly what Mr. Gordon was talking about.

"Correct. Let's find the policy on the mercantile and see who he had it insured with." Both men searched the pile of papers and after a few moments found it.

"Got it."

"Who was the Insurance Company?"

"Frederick & Lawrence Insurance Company."

"I know them well. They have a wonderful reputation for paying out a partial payment only. They have an in-house policy that states every fire will be investigated if the claim is over a certain money amount. They will also grant loans to certain customers. In the case of Mr. Nash he claimed his mercantile as a total loss. They put into effect the policy guideline that ensures such cases are automatically investigated. Most people who borrow money or insure with them don't know that. I bet Mr. Nash was one of them. I work for that bunch so I know their methods of doing business. I'm still on their payroll." He looked at the papers before him and things were making more and more sense to him.

"So I guess we are going to send a wire to the insurance company to see where Mr. Nash and his claim stand?" Chief Johnson already knew the answer.

"You got it. Let's get this all cleaned up and send a wire. In the mean time, let's plan on going to Rock Port in the morning." Mr. Gordon began folding up the papers and placing them into the bank box.

"Why are we going to Rock Port?"

"That's where the closest custom jeweler is located. Look at the assets list again. It shows several pieces of valuable jewelry along with the estimated value. Do you see any sales receipts here or find any jewels at the house?"

"No." He had looked briefly at all the papers and saw nothing like that.

"Exactly. But, he took the time to list them so he was considering doing something with them. The answer is in Rock Port." He continued to fold papers but was looking one more time at every piece of paper that Chief Johnson was putting in the box. The Chief noticed.

"Why are you double checking every piece of paper I'm putting in the box?"

"Sorry. I'm looking for the name of Mr. Nash's solicitor. Every successful business man has one."

"I'll help you look." Again they scanned every piece of paper. They found nothing. Then it occurred to Mr. Gordon to look into Mr. Nash's wallet. Perhaps there would be a business card. They would have to go to the Nash home as all his personal things had been sent to his home. "We are wasting time here looking for the solicitor's name. Let's go to his house and check there." He placed all the remaining papers in the box and closed the lid.

Where does Cole Ralston fit in all this?" As far as Chief Johnson was concerned, they had no real proof of any wrong doing on his part.

"I'm not certain yet. But, I know he's in this somewhere. Let's try and prove it." With that said the men got up and turned in the box to the bank president. They told the man who was their assistant that they could be reached at the home of Mr. Nash.

Before going to the Nash home they made a stop at the telegraph office. There were two ladies inside speaking to the woman who operated the telegraph. The men looked at each other and decided to send the wire when they returned from Nash's home. They did not want to engage in any type of conversation with the women. One woman in particular was the town gossip. It was now well past three in the afternoon. They had lost track of time and as a result had not eaten lunch. They decided to dine early. It would serve their purpose well as they needed to get an early start in the morning. The walk to the Nash home helped settle their meal. Arriving they learned that there had been no word from Mrs. Nash. Asking permission they were given access to the library and study once again. This time they asked to be alone since an official investigation was now being conducted. They looked into the desk and found what they were looking for; a business card with the solicitor's name. There was also a locked drawer on the side of the desk. They looked around for the key.

"Damn, where do you suppose he put it?" Chief Johnson had looked inside the center drawer and opened all the others. He had no luck.

"Let's think. You sit in the chair and pretend to be Mr. Nash. You want to open the drawer would you get up out of your chair or not?" Mr. Gordon was observing from a distance.

"No. I'd probably stay seated."

"Me too. So, let me pick up the lamp and you look underneath for a key." He lifted it and there was nothing.

"Nothing there."

"Alright. Run you hands under the desk on the sides and in front of you." Chief Johnson took his time and felt around the desk. "I don't feel a thing."

"Look under and over and inside that plant on the corner." He did and found only dirt and a water stain on the top of the desk where the plant had been sitting for some time.

"Turn around and tell me what you see." Mr. Gordon was deep in thought.

"I see a large painting on a wall, a little table with some things on it that can't hide anything, a wall lamp and good sized bookcase with nice books in it and some things that are nice to look at on top. There's a ship in a bottle that looks nice. That's about it."

"Can you reach any of them without getting up?" Mr. Gordon was studying the situation.

"Yes. I can reach the bookcase if I roll out my chair a little bit."

"Can you reach the ship in the bottle?"

"Let me see." He rolled only a little bit and found that he could. "Yes. I can reach it."

"Pick up the bottle with care and place it on the desk." Mr. Gordon walked behind the Chief and put his theory to the test. The bottle was placed on the desk.

"Remove the cork and gently tip the bottle like you were trying to pour something out of it." Mr. Gordon watched with great interest.

"Here goes." He tipped the bottle and a small key slide out and onto his hand.

"I'd say that key will fit the locked drawer." Mr. Gordon raised his eyebrows while motioning with his head up and down and looking at the locked drawer.

"How did you know?" Chief Johnson was amazed and impressed that his friend could analyze so quickly.

"It was small and it could blend in with the brown colored bottom of the boat. It's not a very likely place either. Actually, I'm impressed with his decision to hide it there. Now, let's see if it opens that drawer." Mr. Gordon watched while the Chief placed the key into the lock. They both heard the little bolt slip and the drawer opened slightly. He pulled it all the way out.

"It only has a few papers in it." The Chief reached in and pulled them all out placing them on the desk so that they could both see them.

"They look like telegrams from the insurance company of Frederick and Lawrence as well as some company called G.T.K. Investors. If I'm reading this correctly, it appears like they were the ones that would take the house if he didn't pay off the loan for the spices. Here, you take a look." He handed it over.

"Let's me see what this is about." He took just a quick minute. "You're right. He couldn't pay them off until the insurance company paid him for the loss of the mercantile. Sadly for Mr. Nash he didn't realize that his insurance company would not pay off until the fire was investigated. He was caught in a very bad situation." Mr. Gordon almost felt sorry for Mr. Nash. There would be no need to send additional wires to any companies. They had the answers before them.

"I think we may have just figured out why and how the mercantile caught fire." Chief Johnson knew that Ian Fisk had been right. This was a case of arson.

"I think that Mr. Nash hired Cole Ralston to set that fire for the purpose of collecting the insurance money." Mr. Gordon was pretty sure that was what happened.

"Let's say you are correct. That leaves the jewels doesn't it? He must have paid him off with the jewels."

"Unless he sold them at Rock Port for cash which I think makes more sense. Money leaves no trail, but jewels can be traced."

"The jewels look like they were custom made and...." Their conversation was interrupted by a knock at the door of the library.

"Please excuse my interruption but there is a young man from the telegraph office here to see you Mr. Gordon. He's waiting by the front door." Mrs. Ivy stepped aside allowing him to pass.

"Thank you Mrs. Ivy." He saw a young boy standing by the door with the telegram in his hand. When he saw him approach, he politely handed it over.

"The gentleman at the bank said you would be here. I did hurry and was told to wait for a reply if you wanted to send one." This was the same young boy that had made several trips to this house over the past month. It allowed him to make more money than he had in over a year.

Mr. Gordon read the message. He thanked the boy, gave him a couple of pennies and put the telegram into his pocket. He went back to the library. Mrs. Ivy went back to the kitchen.

"Is everything alright?" Chief Johnson wondered if it concerned their investigation.

"Yes. It appears that there was no charity drive in the area. Mrs. Nash lied about the trunk going for the storm victims in the neighboring ports." Mr. Gordon had that far away look in his eye.

"I'll be damned." He would have never guessed that such a refined lady would be of questionable integrity.

"No. But she may be. I bet you whatever you want that she isn't missing at all. She left Valda Bay for good as part of a plan that she made."

"I do believe you are right. That would explain why Leroy took the trunk to the Priscilla. She was planning a trip and needed her things because she wasn't coming back. She sailed away with someone. Maybe it was Cole Ralston." The Chief was almost stunned at the recent development.

The wind was blowing in her face and she loved it. Karin was thinking about Erik and the times he told her of the sea. He spoke of the tranquility he felt from the vast expanse that seemed to go on forever. On a still night he looked at the stars and knew with certainty that something or someone much greater than himself created all he could see. It gave him a feeling of being a small part of something wonderful and filled him with knowledge that he was created as an important part of it all. There was a role he had to play in all of it. He counted himself among the lucky ones for the things in his life. He was happy and that gift alone was more than a lot of people had.

"Karin, are you hungry? Daniel is fixing some sandwiches." James stood beside her and looked at the sea before them.

"I should have made them. I wish you would have said something earlier." She came down from where she was perched and went down into the galley area with Daniel.

"I'm almost finished. Coffee is ready if someone will pour." He continued making the last sandwich.

"I'll do it. Do you think we could eat on deck? The day is so beautiful." She was pouring out the last cup when she thought to ask.

"Let's do it." Each of them took their sandwich and cup of coffee and found a place to sit on deck. "This is a good sandwich Daniel, thank you."

She was glad that she thought to bring the ham from her smokehouse. Daniel nodded his head in acknowledgement.

"How long before we reach Seattle?" She asked.

"Well, we've made very good time so far. If the winds continue to favor us and the weather holds, we'll be there in probably five or six days at the most. What do you think?" He directed his gaze toward James.

"That's about it." He looked out over her shoulder and then looked again. Something caught his attention. Daniel noticed his attention was drawn away from them.

"What are you looking at?" He had turned his head in the direction his friend was looking.

"I think that's a ship out there. Where is the glass?" He put his sandwich down and handed his coffee to Karin.

"It's by the wheel. I'll get it." Daniel went to get the glass and in the process spilled a little coffee on his pants. He looked at the spill and disregarded it just as quickly. His pants were that of a fisherman and one small stain seemed insignificant. He handed the glass to James.

"Yeah, I was right. It looks like the Priscilla. Here, you take a look." He handed the glass to Daniel.

"It is the Priscilla. I can see Flint at the wheel and Cole on the deck standing next to some other man." He squinted his eyes a bit to get a better look.

"Anyone we know?"

"I can't see his face yet. He needs to turn around." Daniel continued to look.

"I wonder what brings them out this far?"

"Maybe they are catching fish." Karin offered.

"Maybe. But I don't see any nets or poles out. They seem to be sailing rather than fishing. Here, you take a look." He handed the glass to James.

"Let me see." He looked through the glass and it was as Daniel said. Then suddenly he took the glass away rubbed his eye against his shirt. He put the glass quickly to the eye again.

"What?" Daniel knew he was trying to clear his vision to get a better look.

"If I'm seeing right, I'm looking at Mrs. Nash on that boat." He continued to look for a moment. "Yeah. I'm right, it is her." James was now positive.

"No shit? Oh, excuse me Karin." He did not mean to swear in front of her.

"Really, you take a look." He gave the glass back.

"You're right. It is her but she's dressed like a man." If he were not seeing it with his own eyes, he would have thought it a tavern tale.

"What could she be doing out here with them dressed like that?" Karin knew that statement was not appropriate since she was also on a ship with two men and neither of them was her husband. She realized that perhaps there was some danger and she should be dressed the same as well.

"There is no real need for a woman to be dressed like that, at least none that I can think of." Daniel offered. "There is a very slim chance of having trouble with other sailors at sea, but I don't think it warrants dressing like that."

"Not unless she is trying to hide or she was taken by force and the villains don't want anyone to recognize her." They all looked at each other.

"Oh no! Mr. Nash was murdered and she could not be found. Remember Chief Johnson was looking everywhere for her. This is so terrible. The poor lady must be frightened out of her mind. What do we do?" Karin was almost in a panic when she thought of Mrs. Nash being abducted and forced to do whatever these men wanted of her. It was too horrible to think about. She looked at James and Daniel.

"I don't think we have a choice. She's in trouble and we have to help." James spoke with strong conviction.

"I agree. We have enough provisions to last a few days so that doesn't concern me. We can always drop our nets and fish. It's the fresh water that concerns me. We have to be careful. From now on we don't wash our clothes, and we freshen up only every other day. No washing of our hair or shaving, and only one pot of coffee a day. Are you still willing to do this Karin? It could be very uncomfortable for you."

"I am. Her life may be at stake." It seemed a small price to pay for helping another human being.

"I know that Cole and Flint Ralston have a reputation for some shady dealings. Personally, I don't like them, but this seems a bit much even for them. I say we continue to watch and see where it leads."

"I'll make an entry into the log book of our plans. We can follow behind keeping our distance. If they pass close to any port we can inform the authorities there. However, I think we should consider the fact that we may not be able to help. If they keep sailing for more than two weeks, we will have no water no matter how careful we are. We can't continue the pursuit or we risk our lives. Do we all agree?" Daniel made sense and they all nodded in agreement.

"What do we do if they recognize us?" Karin was not familiar with protocol on the high sea.

"I don't think they will. We can keep our hats on low and remember they associate us with the Sea Star not this boat. As a precaution, we can drop a line on the side that is closest to them. They will see it and think we are fishing. It's also possible they will think someone just bought the North Star. They knew it was for sale. Karin, you must keep your back to them at all times. James and I will let you know where to be on the deck. If they recognize you, it's all over. There is of course the fact that we don't have to do this." He offered one last chance for anyone to change their mind. No one did.

"Do you think we can still talk about the poem? I would welcome something else to think about beside Mrs. Nash. I hope that doesn't sound like I don't care what is happening to her." She looked at them hoping that they didn't think the worst of her.

"It's a good idea and we know exactly what you mean. Isn't that right Daniel?" James was quick to offer her assurance that she was not perceived as selfish or uncaring.

"That's right. Let's continue with our journey. If we can help Mrs. Nash we will. I think talking about the poem will be good for us in many ways."

"Thank you. Erik was very thoughtful to have left me with such good friends."

About that time Salty came around to see if there was a little bit of sandwich left that he might be able to nibble. He found that James had left his sandwich unguarded by the railing when he went to get the glass. He quickly claimed the ham as his own and went running down the length of the ship with the piece of ham. It was too big for him and he looked funny running sideways with the piece of ham dangling from his mouth. Then, the unthinkable happened; to his complete horror, he dropped it. He looked around and saw that the three humans were watching him. Thinking they might want it back, he quickly picked it back up and dragged the piece of ham into a small space where they could not easily reach. Daniel, James and Karin burst out laughing. Salty didn't care; he was enjoying a special treat.

The trip to Rock Port was pleasant. The day broke clear and sunny and two men traveling on horseback had much to talk about making the trip seem short. They had contemplated taking the buggy, but wanted to be back on the same day and the buggy was a slower mode of transportation. When Chief Johnson and Mr. Gordon arrived in Rock Port they had no difficulty finding Mr. Nash's solicitor. His office was located on the corner of a busy street. The men entered his office and were greeted by a gentleman who was some type of assistant or perhaps a secretary.

"Good morning gentlemen, how may I help you?" He was neatly dressed and had a professional appearance to him.

"I'm Inspector Gordon and this is Chief Johnson. We would like to speak with Mr. Dency."

"Do you have an appointment?" It was the standard question for these types of office professionals.

"No, we do not. We are not here on personal business but rather a professional one. If you would inform Mr. Dency of that fact, I'm sure he will be able to accommodate us." His tone was that of no nonsense.

"I see. Will you have a seat and I'll return in only a moment." He motioned to a chair and at the same time stood up and began to walk toward Mr. Dency's office. He knocked on the door lightly, waited a moment and then entered. He was gone for only a moment and then returned to the waiting area.

"Gentlemen, Mr. Dency will see you now." He walked in front and opened the door to his office. He shut the door behind him.

"Good morning. I'm Mr. Dency." He stood up and extended his hand in greeting. "How may I be of service this morning?"

"Good morning. This is Chief Johnson and I'm Inspector Gordon. It's nice to meet you." All three shook hands.

"Please, be seated." He sat down in his chair and waited for them to begin.

"We rode in from Valda Bay this morning and we are here as part of an official investigation. We understand that you have done business in the past with a gentleman by the name of Mr. Rudolph Nash." He paused a moment to see what reaction he would get from Mr. Dency. The one he got was expected.

"I'm afraid that I can't be of any help. I never discuss my clients with anyone unless I'm ordered to by court order. You understand of course." He sounded final.

"Then it is possible that you don't know that Mr. Nash has passed away?"

"Passed away? When did this happen?" He had not been informed.

"He was murdered just a couple of days ago." Mr. Gordon watched for his reaction. He appeared to be stunned.

"Murdered? You did say murdered?" He was not sure he had heard correctly.

"Yes. We are here as part of that investigation. That is why your help is important." Mr. Gordon pulled out his notepad and pen.

"What do you need to know?" He had known Rudolph Nash for many years, even before he married Elsa.

"Did Mr. Nash have a will or make any changes to one recently?" Chief Johnson sat quietly looking at his friend in action.

"He did. But it's been almost a year and he made no changes to any part of it. I have it in a file cabinet if you would like to see it." He looked toward the cabinet.

"I don't believe that will be necessary." If the will had not been changed for that long in all probability it was some other motive.

"Did he discuss any other business transactions with you or mention anything else that might be important for us to know?" Mr. Gordon wanted to know if he knew about the spice business.

"Not really." He did not know if what he was thinking was important enough for them to know about. He had taken no action on what was discussed.

"Did he speak of his marriage to you at all?" He noticed that Mr. Dency seemed uncertain what to say. "Did he mention it as a friend but not in an official capacity?"

"That he did do. He mentioned his unhappy marriage, but he took no action to dissolve the union." Mr. Dency wondered if perhaps Mrs. Nash had murdered him.

"Did he say anything else?" Chief Johnson spoke for the first time.

"In parting he said that he had to go to the jewelry store to discuss something about some custom pieces."

"Did he mention the name of the jewelry store or who he was meeting?" This statement sparked the interest of both men who knew that the jewels were very much a part of the investigation.

"I'm certain he said he had an appointment at King's Jewelers." Mr. Dency was wondering about a lot of things, but he did not ask.

"Can you tell us how to get there?" Chief Johnson asked.

"Sure. Turn left from my office go two blocks, turn right and it's the first store on your right. It's a nice building with bold lettering out front. You can't miss it." He wondered where else this questioning would go. He had a few questions of his own. "How is Mrs. Nash? Is she well considering the circumstances of her husbands' death?"

"I wish we could say. At present, we have not been able to locate her. However, we are searching even as we speak. If you should receive any word on her whereabouts, please wire us at Valda Bay." Mr. Gordon put away his notepad and pen. "Thank you for your time." Almost as if on cue, both men stood up and extended their hand in appreciation for the assistance they received from him.

"Good day gentlemen." All shook hands and Mr. Gordon and Chief Johnson left feeling they had a good lead to follow.

They would go to King's Jewelers and see what Mr. Nash had done or discussed with them. The day was young and it was proving better than they thought. They left Mr. Dency's office and followed his instructions to the jewelry store. It was not difficult to find and when they walked inside there were several people in the store. They were politely acknowledged by a gentleman assisting an elderly couple of obvious means. They nodded their heads indicating they understood they would have to wait. It afforded them the opportunity to look around. They were impressed with all the beautiful things in the store. The chairs were all beautifully made with detailed carvings on the legs and back. Tall plants were everywhere adding a touch of quiet elegance. The men behind the counter were dressed in black suits and white shirts with appropriate neck wear. Behind the counter they observed several doors that no doubt lead to rooms where private negotiations could take place. The safe was not visible from the front entrance but Mr. Gordon was certain it was located somewhere in the back of the store. They had just about decided to sit down when a gentleman approached them.

"Welcome to King's Custom Jewelry Designs. May I show you anything in particular?" He motioned them to his area at the jewelry counter.

"No thank you. We would like to speak with the individual who is authorized to purchase previously owned jewelry or exchange custom made pieces." Mr. Gordon had never been in a store like this. He had never had the need to do so in his career. Chief Johnson had not either.

"That would be Mr. Edwards. He is with a client right now but I assure you I am very experienced in these matters." He spoke quietly but was easily understood. He was thinking that money would be a concern for them.

"Actually, we are not here to purchase or exchange any items. We are here as part of an official investigation. We need to speak with Mr. Edwards in private as soon as possible." He noticed that the jeweler did not change the expression on his face.

"I understand. Please be seated and I will inform Mr. Edwards that you are waiting." He waited until they were seated and then backed away from them a few steps before turning his back on them.

"He's a peacock if I've ever seen one." Chief Johnson said in a whisper to Mr. Gordon. They both laughed with some restraint.

It took a few minutes for an older gentleman wearing spectacles and an elegant pocket watch to approach them. Both men stood up to greet him.

"Hello. I'm Mr. Edwards." The man extended his hand in customary greeting.

"It's nice to meet you. I'm Inspector Gordon and this is Inspector Johnson."

"I was told you wish to speak to me in private. Please come into my office." He led them into his office that was beautifully decorated and modern. Everything in it was expensive.

"Please be seated. May I offer you a cup of coffee or some other refreshment?" He waited for them to be seated and then he sat down.

"We're fine thank you. I appreciate you taking time this morning to speak with us. I can see that you are a busy man so I'll come to the point of our visit." Mr. Gordon pulled out his notepad and pen.

"I like the direct approach myself. How can I help you?" He made himself comfortable in his big chair.

"Mr. Edwards it's our understanding that you were the designer for some expensive pieces of jewelry that were purchased by Mr. Rudolph Nash. Is that correct?"

"Gentlemen, I'm afraid that I'm not at liberty to discuss my client's personal purchasing habits. Perhaps you should contact Mr. Nash directly." He smiled politely but made it clear that he would not provide any information about Mr. Nash.

"I regret to inform you that it is impossible to speak with Mr. Nash because he has been murdered. Chief Johnson and I are investigating his death. Any help you can give us would be greatly appreciated." Mr. Gordon could see that the older gentleman was stunned. He had not heard of Mr. Nash's death.

"I'm sorry to hear it. What is it you wish to know?"

"Did you design some jewelry for Mr. Nash?" Chief Johnson carefully observed the exchange between the two men.

"Yes. We did several nice pieces for his wife."

"Is there a log or something that records the pieces you make, what they look like that sort of thing?"

"Oh yes. Our records are impeccable so I have a complete record on Mr. Nash. Would you like to see it?" He expected the answer would be a positive one so he was already up and getting the file from his cabinet.

"That would prove most helpful. When was the last time you saw Mr. Nash?" Mr. Gordon asked.

"He was in my office only a few days ago. Here is the file you asked for." Mr. Edwards placed it on the table.

"Was he alone?" Chief Johnson spoke this time.

"He was."

"Did he seem upset or nervous to you?"

"He was a bit unsettled. I thought it was because he wanted to sell some jewels quickly." Mr. Edwards shook his head at the thought of that sale.

"Had he ever sold jewels before?" Mr. Gordon asked.

"Not in my store. I told him I could sell the jewels quickly but they probably would not command as good a price as they should have because he gave me no time to negotiate for him." He shook his head at the poor business decision made by Mr. Nash.

"So what happened?" Mr. Gordon was taking notes.

"I sold the jewels for a good price to a fine lady who told me that if he ever wanted to sell she would buy the pieces. I contacted her and she purchased every piece. I gave the money to Mr. Nash, minus the cost of my services."

"Was the money in cash?" Mr. Gordon looked at Chief Johnson quickly then back to Mr. Edwards.

"It was. I offered to wire the money to his bank directly but he insisted in cash. I gave him currency against my better judgment. It was a lot of money to be certain. I've entered the amount in the log." He pointed to where it was entered.

"I'm looking at this file and I need a little help in understanding what it all means. Will you tell us what some of these annotations mean? I think you should look at this also. I may need your memory later." The Chief agreed and moved his chair closer to allow him to see the book better.

"Certainly. Every one of our clients is given an account number. This number is never used again. When we custom design a piece of jewelry, the client's number stays with the piece. It is then drawn in color with great detail and a complete history is written up describing the stones, weight, cut, clarity and other pertinent facts. After that there is an alphabetical letter that will appear on the history log of the piece if there has been any work or repair to the item once it has been made. The alphabetical code will appear on the back of each folder as a reminder to our clients what they mean. After the work has been completed the craftsmen will enter the date and time the work was completed along with his name. This allows us to know what was done to each piece, when it occurred and who had the piece to work on it. The last thing before it is placed under the clients name in the vault is to have it inspected one more time. The description must match exactly to ensure that stones have not been exchanged or others placed in the design by mistake. The purpose of this inspection keeps everyone honest and should there be a problem, we can resolve it internally quickly. Then when the inspector signs off on the completed piece, I personally log it in under the client's number and it placed into our vault until it is picked up or I place it into our private security boxes here in the store." Mr. Edwards was very proud of his control system.

"Does anyone else have the combination to the vault?" Chief Johnson inquired.

"Only I and one other person have the combination. He is he my security partner for just that purpose. It's part of our security system but if it's absolutely necessary I can disclose his name. In all the years we have been in business that has never been necessary. Is it necessary now?"

"No. I must say that your system is very efficient. I guess you have never had any jewels stolen or misplaced then?"

"We most certainly have not! Never have we even come close to such an incident. Our check and recheck system has worked without fail since the day we opened these doors almost forty years ago." He stiffened his shoulders and looked directly at them in an almost challenging manner.

"We thought not. But, we had to ask because the next question is very important to our investigation. You understand that we must be as thorough as you are. So I was hoping that you would be able to tell us if there were any pieces that Mr. Nash did take home with him." Mr. Gordon hoped that would sooth his perceived attack on his accountability and security system. It had the result he hoped for.

"If my memory serves me correct, he picked up everything. Let me double check the log." He flipped through the log and in a few moments he confirmed what he said. "I have no more pieces in my possession. Mr. Nash has everything."

"Do you have drawings of every piece that Mr. Nash has ever ordered or placed in your vault?" Mr. Gordon was thinking that Mr. Nash may not have had all the jewels with him. In fact he knew that he didn't because Mrs. Nash had left no jewels behind in her room. She had them with her or she sold them.

"Yes. The folder is divided into several sections. If you will permit me I'll show you all the drawings." He reached for the file folder and flipped it to a section that had nothing but drawings and the original history of the piece on the back. There were several drawings.

"I would like you to separate which ones he sold to you. Also, can you determine which are in the store now, in the vault, or in the display case and which to the best of your knowledge are in his possession?" He was trying to determine which pieces if any Mrs. Nash may have with her.

"I can do that. Do you need me to bring in a small table so you may write down your notes easier?" Mr. Edwards noticed that writing in the small pad wasn't the easiest thing to do.

"That won't be necessary. I appreciate your offer but I'm ready to begin whenever you are." He began to look at the sketches and then the log. Chief Johnson and Mr. Gordon remained in the room while he worked. They kept conversation to a minimum so Mr. Edwards would not be distracted. In about thirty five minutes he had three piles of drawings.

"All the pieces are accounted for and are divided into these stacks of paper. Gentlemen, I regret to say you must excuse me. I need to take a personal moment. I'll return shortly. Are you certain you won't have a cup of coffee or other refreshment?" He stood up and standing at the door waited for their answer.

"I'm fine, thank you." Mr. Gordon replied.

"I'm alright. I appreciate the offer."

"Very well. I'll be just a moment." He closed the door and left them alone in the room.

"So, what do you think?" Chief Johnson asked.

"Very efficient." He answered.

"Yes, but aside from that. What are you thinking?"

"I'm thinking that Mrs. Nash may have some valuable pieces with her." He answered.

"We already knew that."

"True. But, we didn't know which pieces, their worth or more importantly what she is going to do with them. It occurs to me that perhaps she has or had plans for the jewels. Maybe she plans on selling them elsewhere or perhaps she paid someone with the jewels to take care of her husband." He looked at the stack of drawings and picked one up to look at it. Each was most certainly a one of a kind. He turned to his friend as another thought entered his mind. Chief Johnson noticed his reactions and waited for him to continue speaking.

"What do you think of this idea? Suppose she has the jewels with her but plans to sell them elsewhere. It would have to be at a store similar to this one to get a good price. Smaller jewelers just couldn't afford to engage in this kind of transaction. I think we should send a wire to all the large jewelers on both coasts. There can't be that many but he would know more about that than we would." He rubbed his forehead almost like his head hurt from thinking too hard.

"Agreed. I'm sure he would know and have the information at hand." The two sat back and were looking at the drawings when Mr. Edwards returned.

"Thank you for waiting patiently. Gentlemen, one day you will be my age." He chuckled lightly. They joined him.

"Now, let me get back to the task at hand. As you can see there are three stacks of drawings. The first drawings are the pieces I made and the one I recently purchased. I have sold all of those to the lady I spoke of earlier. The second grouping shows the pieces that Mr. Nash has in his possession now and the third shows the pieces that were going to be made in the future." He waited for their reaction.

"So by your accurate records they tell you that he has some jewels in his possession?" Mr. Gordon now knew that he would have to send a wire.

"That's correct." He was looking at the log.

"How many pieces are we talking about it?" Chief Johnson asked the question Mr. Gordon was thinking.

"There are seven pieces. There is one bracelet, two rings, a necklace with ear bobs to match and a broach." He showed them the drawings so they might see what he was speaking of.

"Just one more thing. Do you have a list of associates that would handle this quality of jewels? We are particularly interested in the Pacific coast."

"I do. Mr. Wellington's Custom Design is the only place that could offer any services for jewels of this caliber. I admit I was surprised that Mr. Nash didn't contact him first since these pieces are part of his father-in-law's collection. I'll have my secretary give you a list with the information you require." He reached for his papers and began to place them neatly in the folder.

"Mr. Edwards, who exactly is Mr. Wellington?" Chief Johnson did not recall hearing his name before.

"Forgive me. Mr. Wellington is Mrs. Nash's father. All the jewels we have been speaking of have been in her family for generations. Legally they belong to Mr. Nash through marriage but morally they belong to Mrs. Nash."

"Her father. Then Mr. Wellington is a jeweler." Mr. Gordon offered.

"No. Not to my knowledge. I understand that he inherited the jewels. In finer circles it is said that the Wellington jewels were part of a lost treasure. It adds mysterious appeal to the jewels. I have no way of knowing if all that is true or not. Mr. Wellington will not say one way or the other although he has never denied their origin because it enhances their value. It's good business and personally, I think I would do the same. Well, enough of that. Let me get started getting you what you requested."

"Mr. Edwards, you have been so helpful and very informative. We appreciate your time especially since we had no appointment." The men stood up to leave and exchanged handshakes prior to their departure.

"It's been my pleasure to be of assistance. I'm sorry to hear of Mr. Nash's passing, please give my condolences to his wife." They walked toward his office door.

He opened it allowing them to exit first. He went to a man who was no doubt the secretary.

"Please be seated and Mr. Smith will provide you the list you requested." He motioned them to a seat and then departed.

In a moment Mr. Smith approached them and handed each of them an envelope. The contents were the same but he had provided each a copy as a professional courtesy. The men appreciated his thoughtfulness.

"Will there be anything else?" He asked politely.

"No thank you. We appreciate everything." The man nodded at the reply offered by Chief Johnson and like the man before him, he looked quickly before he took a step backwards and then turned his back to them.

"A smart peacock." Mr. Gordon offered.

The men left the jewelry store but Mr. Gordon stopped along the way and leaned on a wooden beam. He was not in the way of people walking by but he had a look on his face that said he was thinking of something important. He took a cigar out of his vest and lit his cigar. Chief Johnson said nothing. He knew he was thinking or just needed a quiet moment. After a few minutes, Mr. Gordon spoke.

"Mr. Edwards said that Mr. Nash had a great deal of money on his person right? So, where's the money? Did you find any on his person and put it inside that deep coat pocket of yours?" He teased him a little on that last statement.

"No to both questions. Are you thinking he was killed by an unknown robber and we shouldn't be looking to Cole Ralston?" Chief Johnson asked.

"I was just thinking of that. You didn't find any money pouch from the jeweler did you?"

"No."

"But, it was gone when you arrived. No one knew he was slain to the best of your knowledge until Grazer came and got you. The robber had to have taken it."

"I'd say that would be a good guess."

"But that isn't totally right either. Was Mr. Nash wearing any valuables like a pocket watch or rings?"

"Yes. He had both on him when he died. As a matter of fact he had his wallet with him." Chief Johnson remembers securing those things and taking them to the Nash home.

"So, if you were going to rob someone, why would you leave that behind? You probably wouldn't know that he had a little bag of cash from some big sale. You would hope like hell he just had a decent pocket watch and some money in his wallet." Mr. Gordon continued to look ahead and flipped the ashes off of his cigar.

"True enough. Does this mean we are still looking for Cole Ralston?"

"It does. Let's keep on this path like my daddy's old hound. I think I'm right."

"So you think it's possible that Ralston knew he had that kind of money on him?"

"Let's talk about it. Ralston would have no way of knowing how Mr. Nash would get the money. But he would know if Mrs. Nash told him. Since robbery wasn't the real first motive, he didn't think to make it look like a robbery he wanted to make it look like only a murder. So he didn't think to take something to make it look like robbery. He intended to kill Mr. Nash all along and make it look like someone else did it." He put the cigar in his mouth and drew a long puff.

"But what if she didn't know about the money?"

"She knew. Do you think for one minute a married man could be gone all day and into the night and not tell his wife where he was going? I wouldn't do it and I'm the brave sort. I'd rather face a rabid animal than have to listen to the constant badgering that would go on for days when I returned home. Keep in mind Mrs. Nash was demanding and probably a most unreasonable woman. No, my guess is she knew."

"That would explain why he wasn't hit over the head, face or shoulders like a common thief would do." Chief Johnson offered.

"Correct. I'd say that Mr. Nash was talking with his murderer face to face. Murder was the motive. She had her husband killed. I'm pretty sure of it now."

"Why?"

"We can ask her that when we see her." He rubbed out the end of his cigar and wrapped it in his handkerchief. He would enjoy the remainder on the way home.

"So where do we go from here?"

"The telegraph office." Both men resumed walking.

The wire was sent as planned and all they had to do now was wait to see if it would prove successful. Everything that was hoped for had been accomplished and in some respects exceeded their expectations. Before leaving Rock Port they had something to eat and then left for Valda Bay. It was very late by the time they reached home.

# Destinations Unknown

The next few days at sea continued to be nice. For the small crew of the North Star the days were filled with normal boat duties and talking about their pursuit of the lost treasure of the Rip Tide.

"After looking over the notes we already have, I agree that we are on the right course. I think we should discuss what the rest of the poem means." James said. Daniel was holding the wheel while James sat next to him and Karin was on a small stool just out of sight.

"I have the poem memorized." Karin's comment was a welcome bit of news.

"Good. I guess the best way to do this is to take one line at a time. What do you think?" Daniel wasn't addressing anyone in particular just offering a suggestion.

"That will work." James offered.

"It's the way Erik and I came to figure out the first few lines. We put ideas out and thought about them until something made sense." She recalled that happy time and felt tears form in her eyes. She missed him so very much. She bowed her head and blinked them away. One escaped and ran down her face which she quickly brushed away. If either of them noticed it, they said nothing.

"Alright. What is the next line we need to figure out?" Daniel took a drink from his one and only cup of coffee for the day.

*In stream end and standing straight*

"Let's look at the first half of that line." James spoke for the first time.
"I have no idea." Karin said.

"It's not the easiest thing to figure is it? Let's think a moment. Let's take the stream part. What thing or item or place is a stream?" Daniel was trying all angles.

"It could be like several things in a row that is very long. It's usually slang for something like that." Karin suggested.

"I know what you mean. Like a steady stream of people in line or something like that?" James gave her comment some thought.

"Could it be that he was talking about a place where people go in and out of a lot like a hotel, or tavern?" Daniel said.

"Maybe. Let's think of something else. A public place hardly sounds like the place you would find clues to a valuable treasure. Remember the year he was hiding this. Nice hotels were few and far between." James looked at Karin and just shrugged his shoulders.

"What else is a stream? Wait ... we are so funny we forgot that it is also like a little river isn't it?" Karin remembered that there was a small stream of water that flowed behind her grandfather's home in Norway.

"Yes it is. Maybe it's nothing more than that. It makes perfect sense because the line before it speaks of a cascade. We already determined that the cascade was in the mountains. Maybe what we seek is a stream in the Cascade Mountains." Daniel felt they were getting someplace.

"That's nice. There are only a million small streams up there." James felt certain that the stream he mentioned was in fact a stream. The only problem was there were so many streams, lakes, and rivers. How would they find the one he was referring to? They needed more information.

"So it's a stream. What else do we know?" Daniel asked hoping that one of them might have a new idea.

"He says the word in. Could he need to get in a stream?" Karin wondered how foolish this sounded.

"It could be. What was the rest of that poem Karin?" James felt he was on to something. "Didn't he say something about standing straight?"

"Yes."

"Then how does this sound? He or something would have to stand straight, or up, if you will while standing in a stream of water."

"I think that's it." Daniel agreed.

"Now, we have to find which stream of water among so many." She said that with a little bit of despair as she had just heard that there were lots of streams of water in the Cascade Mountains.

"Not so many when you stop and think that a cascade can also mean a waterfall as well as the mountains." James looked at them to see if they were thinking as he was. Daniel was immediately but she was a little slower to understand.

"Tell me." She said.

"We go to the Cascade Mountains. Find a waterfall that is falling into or forming a stream and at the end of that stream of water, we stand up in it." James and Daniel looked pleased.

"How do we find the right waterfall?" She looked at them hoping they had already figured it out.

"Well, it's hard to know for certain, but I bet it was the first one he came to. It would be inland a little bit no doubt. What would you do James?"

"The same thing you suggest."

"So we are looking for the first waterfall after we come on shore based upon the stars and compass and all the other readings we already figured out?" The men looked at her with smiles on their faces. She smiled back. That part of the poem was now solved.

"That's done. Let's go on to the next line." Daniel was ready for more.

*There we can see where Eagles mate*

"I think it means that when you are actually standing in the stream, you look up high to see if you can see where an Eagle might be. I know that they usually pick a high place and it's usually on a very tall tree or the edge of a tall mountain or cliff." James made the suggestion.

"I do believe you are correct. We have to look around for that spot even if we have to turn around like a top on a pulled string."

They all laughed at the thought expressed by James.

"Do you want to continue or shall we take a break?" James was thinking of her.

"I'm fine. Do either of you need a break?" She heard them say they did not.

"Let's continue. Karin tell us the next line of the poem if you please." Daniel gestured as if she were being introduced to a crowd of adoring fans. She chuckled but then turned more serious as she spoke the words.

*From Love's lofty edge where they do fly*

"That line supports our previous one by saying that eagles always nest or perch themselves up on a high place." Daniel was thinking they would have to look for a cliff or a ledge where they could see the eagles.

"Yeah it does. So, at this point we need to be standing in a stream looking straight ahead toward a place that would be where eagles nest or perch themselves. We'll have to get a land map before we start off on this mountain adventure." James felt he wasn't as capable on land as he was on the sea and he was not looking forward to any camping they might have to do.

"I imagine the scenery will be beautiful. But, I agree that we need to get a map and prepare ourselves for bad weather. It will probably be raining and cold."

"It could also be windy. The higher we have to climb the cooler it will get. Being properly outfitted will be important. We'll need to make a list of the things we need so we don't forget anything." Daniel hoped they would not have to camp out for long. If they were lucky it could be possible to find everything they needed to in only a couple of days.

"Wait a second. I just thought of something in that line. He wrote about an edge didn't he?" He looked at her for confirmation. She nodded her head in the affirmative. "Well that means the edge of a cliff or mountain. Not a tree or some nest in a tree, but an actual ledge. That means we could very easily have to climb a mountain in order to get to the next clue. What do you think?" He turned to look at Daniel and Karin.

"Oh my goodness." Karin realized he could be right.

"Say that you're right. There is a mountain or a cliff that we have to go up. I don't know, let's keep it in perspective and think like he would. If you were a pirate carrying a treasure, more than likely it's in a box of some sort. It would be heavy and bulky. You don't have a lot of time or equipment with you. Would you climb to a high place?" He looked at them for ideas.

"You would go someplace close to where you came ashore. You would want to bury it or hide it quickly." James was thinking what he would do.

"I bet he thought the same thing. I don't think I'd want to climb the highest mountain in the area carrying a heavy box, with no equipment and little time. No, this is not that high a place. It's more like a cliff or a high ledge." He rubbed his faced briskly.

"One you could walk up to but still high enough that the eagles would want to make a nest there. The edge could be another word for ledge." Daniel agreed.

"When we get that land map, we will know for sure." Karin looked at her friends and knew just how special they were. They were taking a trip with an uncertain outcome and were optimistic to the point of being almost unbelievable.

"I think we have done a lot so far. Is there more to the poem that we need to discuss or is it self-explanatory?" James looked at his companions.

"There are three more lines. Do you want me to say them now because I'm not sure if they are easy to understand or not?"

"I don't see why not. Let's finish the poem and when we get to shore, we can see how good or bad we've done." Daniel stretched his arms toward the air and then placed them on his lower back. This action told James that he needed a rest from the wheel.

"Let me have the wheel for a while. I might think better on my feet." He left his seat and switched places with Daniel.

"Thank you. I guess I had been there for a while." He was glad for the relief and moved about a little before sitting down. He reached for the glass to see what the Priscilla was doing. Everything was the same as it had been.

"Alright. Are we ready to figure out the next part?" She looked at them and James gave her a thumb up.

> *Walk away and watch the sky*
> *When the sun is halfway to the crashing sea*
> *Old shadows will fall for my love and me*

"I understand that to mean that once you are on the ledge, you have to walk back a bit." Karin suggested the idea.

"Yeah. But walk to where? Off the ledge? No, that's crazy. You wouldn't walk up just to walk off. What's that about the sky again?" Daniel was feeling a little tired and hungry. If they couldn't figure it out in the next half hour, he would suggest another day.

"Watch the sky."

"If I'm watching something, it's happening now or will soon be happening."

"Maybe once you are on the ledge you have to wait for something to happen."

"Karin, you just said that the sea would be half way down or something like that didn't you?"

"I did. Maybe he is waiting for the sun to go down from the ledge?" She felt a little excitement that perhaps she had contributed a vital piece of information.

"It could very well be. In fact, I think that's perfect. He's on the ledge watching for the sun to set from the sky and when it's half down something happens."

"Half way down on the ledge?" Now she was lost.

"No. I think half way down means when the sun is setting and if we are standing on the ledge, we could see it go down." James looked at Daniel thinking the same thing.

"That's got to be it. When we are on the ledge, we wait for the sun to start to set and when its half way down we need to watch for the next clue because we have to then leave the ledge and go someplace else. What's the last line again?"

*Old shadows will fall for my love and me*

"The sun will be setting and what happens when the sun sets?" Daniel asked Karin.

"It gets cold and dark." She could offer nothing else at the time.

"Yes it does. But before it gets dark, shadows are created by the angle of the light. When that old sun goes down it casts shadows."

"Old shadows will fall. That's got to mean that when the sun is setting a shadow is cast on something we need to find." James was certain he was on to the last clue. "But, everything there will give off a shadow. Maybe that was nothing." Now he felt uncertain again.

"Yeah, but not just any shadow—an old shadow. He wrote that old shadows will fall for my love and me. I take that to mean that something old will be in the shadows."

"How's this instead? Something old will be casting a shadow." James thought that he would suggest it because the word old was the first word in the sentence. "What could be old that we could see from a ledge?"

"Everything is old. The sea, the beach, the trees, the mountains." She had given only a few names to the countless items that fit the criteria.

"It has to be something that would stand the test of time. Maybe it's a big rock or a big boulder or some kind of pinnacle." Daniel was more thinking out loud than talking to his companions.

"Daniel, what does pinnacle mean?" She had not heard the word before.

"It's something tall that comes to a point like a tower or a steeple." He smiled at her and was glad that she felt comfortable enough with them to ask a question when she didn't understand.

"Maybe we have to wait to get there to see what fits the criteria mentioned. We have an idea of what we are going to be looking at and that will certainly help. What do you think?" James thought that best because what was referenced in the poem they had to look for when the shadows were falling. Then they would see something old that was visible from a ledge but only when the sun was half way down on the ocean.

"I think we have done all that we can. We could guess all day and still be wrong. Let us wait to get to the spot on the ledge and see what happens. We may find that we are wrong in everything and all this is for nothing. But, no matter what happens, one thing is for sure. We haven't wasted our time for nothing. We can still help Mrs. Nash. That boat is moving at a steady pace and it looks like it's going to Seattle." Daniel was pretty sure that the Priscilla was going to Seattle because of the direct course it was on. The ship had not altered its course once.

On the Mystic Quest, Rue was busy putting the finishing touches on the wine label she had designed. It had kept her busy for several days but now she was ready to show it to Joaquin. He had picked the name of the vineyard on the day they departed Valda Bay. He left the design up to her. She held it up and then leaned it against a small bottle of fragrance that she had brought with her. It looked beautiful and she knew that she would not change one thing in its design. When Joaquin returned from his morning smoke on the deck with the men, she would show it to him. While she waited she brushed her long hair and washed her hands and face. She poured water into the basin and enjoyed a sponge bath which made her feel nice. She tried to use the water to every advantage as she knew how precious the fresh water was. She had just finished her bath when Joaquin entered the room. He noticed immediately how nice she looked.

"You look beautiful this morning." He was amazed that she had gotten more beautiful since beginning the trip. He thought it was because she was getting more rest and did not have the aggravation of male attention or having to help the baker in the hot kitchen. Whatever was making her look more beautiful everyday was a welcome occurrence.

"Thank you. Did you enjoy your walk?" She asked as he went to the basin and washed his hands and face. He rinsed his mouth and ran his fingers through his hair. He sat down on the edge of the bed and watched her for a moment. She was holding something behind her back.

"What are you up to?" He reached out but she playfully moved away from him. "I have a surprise for you that I hope will make you happy." She smiled and her full lips revealed a tongue that danced along the edge of her teeth. She was sensual without even trying.

"Do you want me to guess?" He asked playfully.

"No. This is a serious surprise. So, I want you to think about the vineyard and our label. I finished it last night and now I want to show it to you." She held up the piece of paper that showed the design she had given so much thought to.

"Rue, I don't know what to say. It's perfect and more than I hoped for. How did you come up with the design?" He was impressed.

"I thought about our lives, how we came to be in this country and stuff like that. Do you want me to tell you what it means to me and why I drew what I did?" She looked at the label and then at him. She gently touched his face.

"Tell me." He resisted kissing her because he knew it would be his undoing.

"The gold edge of the label represents the money we hope to make but also our friendship which is much more valuable than gold itself. I made the letters of our vineyard name black to show our strength and determination while we work the land. The ship traveling on the rough sea represents the way we both traveled to different countries to realize a dream. The oval shape is for the shapes of the wine barrels. I know it may sound a little crazy but with all that said, what do you think?" She looked at him with loving eyes hoping that he would like the label.

"I think it's perfect. You put a lot into this and I really like it. Don't change a thing." He stood up and turned his back to her for a quick minute. He was deeply touched and he wanted to wipe his eyes without her seeing him do that. He never wanted to appear weak in front of her. He had never shown emotion like this in front of anyone.

"Joaquin, please turn around and look at me." She came up behind him and hugged his waist as she placed her cheek on his upper shoulder.

"Yeah, just give me a second." He took a deep breath.

"I'm glad that you like the label. It meant a lot to me when you entrusted me with it. I never felt I did anything worth much in my life. I love my son very much but he was raised by my sister. But, this label is a legacy, a dream realized. It's our lifetime in a three by four inch piece of paper. I put my heart into it. Thank you for letting me know it touched yours." She dropped her arms from his waist and came around the front to face him. She hugged him again.

"Rue." He looked at her. His eyes were moist and for a moment something more than friendship passed between them. He didn't understand exactly what it was, but he felt a deep and urgent need to hold her close and feel her warmth. He kissed her and she responded to him immediately. It was always this way with them. He moved them slowly to the bunk and with practiced skill they made love to each other as never before. This time they felt the love and not just the act of loving.

Mrs. Ivy was walking at a brisk pace. She wanted to speak with Chief Johnson before he left his office. She held a telegram in her hand that was addressed to Mrs. Nash. As she approached she could see through the office window that both men were inside. She opened the door and saw the men enjoying a cup of coffee and a pastry. When the men saw her enter they immediately stood up.

"Good morning Mrs. Ivy. How are you this morning?" Chief Johnson quickly wiped his fingers on his napkin and greeted her properly. Mr. Gordon did the same.

"Good morning. I'm well thank you. Please excuse my interruption of your breakfast I normally would not do so, but I have something that I think needs your attention. I don't know what to do. It's addressed to Mrs. Nash." She reached into her purse and handed him the telegram.

"When was this delivered to you Mrs. Ivy?" He asked.

"Last evening." You had to have returned from Rock Port late so I was reluctant to bring it over at that hour. I hope I did the right thing." She put her hand to her neck in a nervous gesture.

"You did." Chief Johnson placed the telegram on his desk.

"I have a great deal to do this morning. If you don't need me for anything I shall be on my way." She had spent most of her life in service to wealthy families. She had learned long ago that most things were none of her business. She did not expect to be informed of the contents of the telegram.

"I believe that Mr. Gordon and I can handle things from here. Have a nice morning Mrs. Ivy and thank you again." He went ahead of her and opened the office door for her. She smiled at them both and then left.

"Well, what do you suppose this is all about?" Chief Johnson asked as he picked up the telegram.

"There is only one way to find out that I know of." Mr. Gordon looked at him and picked up his coffee cup. He walked over to the coffee pot and poured out a fresh cup.

"Right you are. Let's see what this is all about." He took a pair of scissors from his desk and snipped off the top of the envelope. He resisted tearing it open as it may be used as evidence in the future and he did not want to appear as unprofessional.

**Dear Elsa**

**The telegram we received from Rudolph explained your marital difficulties. We will arrange transportation and accommodations for you and a lady companion. Please keep us informed on your planned departure date from Valda Bay.**

**Always**
**Father and Mother**

"They don't know that she is missing do they?" Mr. Gordon scratched his chin.

"I'd say no. But they did offer something to our investigation. She's not with them so they aren't a party to what is going on. The Nash's were having some kind of problem in their marriage and he was planning on sending her packing home to her mother." The Chief was now looking into his coffee cup thinking.

"We already knew that because Mr. Dency said that Mr. Nash mentioned something about a divorce from Elsa." Mr. Gordon offered.

"That's right. But suppose this. Nash wanted to get rid of Elsa—he just couldn't afford her anymore. But, it would cost him dearly to do that. So, he arranges to have her leave but not in the sense that everyone thinks. He sends the telegram as a way to cover his tracks." The Chief took out papers that he had made notes on.

"Cover his tracks? What are you thinking?"

"If you wanted to kill someone, it would not make sense to send a telegram saying your wife was upset with you. It makes better sense to say nothing. Nash sent the telegram hoping that it would throw us off track. He wanted us to believe that he put her on the stage and she left. He would then be totally surprised that she never arrived at her destination." He was continuing to flip through his notes. Chief Johnson had made a small mess of his papers.

"What are you looking for in those papers?" Mr. Gordon had to ask.

"Remember I told you that I spoke with Mr. Nash at his house a few days before his murder and prior to your arrival?"

"I do."

"I asked Mr. Nash a variety of questions that led me to believe he was lying then about the fire and his relationship with Cole Ralston. Now I think I know why. Here it is in my notes." Chief Johnson quickly scanned them to refresh his memory.

"Tell me. I'm not sure I follow."

"I called upon Mr. Nash very early and I had no appointment. I thought for sure I would be the first one of the day. But, Ralston was already leaving when I was just arriving. The maid confirmed it was Ralston who left right before me. When I did see Mr. Nash, he looked pretty bad. It was pretty obvious to me that he wished I were not there. Yet, I was the person who was supposed to be bringing him news about his store. If he had been sick in the morning before Ralston arrived, I think he would have cancelled seeing him. But, he didn't. Instead he saw him sick and all and that tells me that they had something pretty important to discuss. He couldn't very well refuse to see me when he had just met with Ralston."

"So you suspect that maybe Ralston had the nerve to go to his home when under normal circumstances that would never have been socially acceptable." Mr. Gordon was very familiar with the social order of things.

"That's right. But, Ralston felt he could take that liberty because he had something to gain or possibly had Mr. Nash over a barrel."

"Like a little arson perhaps?" Mr. Gordon offered.

"That would be my guess. Maybe he paid him for other things as well—like getting rid of his wife." The Chief vocalized his thoughts on the subject for the first time.

"But she was one step ahead and hired Ralston to kill him instead." Mr. Gordon's mind was working fast.

"We are pretty sure she left with Cole Ralston and his brother as evidenced by the fact that her trunk was delivered by Leroy Grazer to the Priscilla."

"That's true. Maybe they were lovers after all." Chief Johnson looked at Mr. Gordon to see if what he said was making sense to him. It was.

"In my notes I was looking at something I had not thought of because I hadn't put it all together yet. But, when Doctor Grayson and I went to the Nash home on the night he was murdered, I spoke at length with the stable boy. Young Ivy told me that Mr. Nash returned from a business trip after dark. He went someplace from there and he never came home." Chief Johnson was looking for his notes on the subject at hand.

"So it stands to reason he was meeting someone, probably Ralston to pay him off for the mercantile job and things didn't go the way he hoped. He was murdered by the person he met in all probability."

"That's right. I wrote down here that the murderer cut Mr. Nash's throat pretty deep and wide open. Doctor Grayson said he died on the spot. I think we can rule out Mrs. Nash as the killer. She is too short to reach his neck for that kind of effect. The killer had to be someone taller than Rudolph Nash." Chief Johnson showed his notes to Mr. Gordon. After looking for a few minutes, he reached the same conclusion.

"Mr. Nash isn't very tall, but Leroy said the person he saw was tall. How tall do you suppose Ralston is?" Mr. Gordon leaned back in his chair as the question was asked.

"He's at least six feet tall. He would be strong enough to easily overpower Mr. Nash in a struggle. Wait just a moment! I know there was some kind of a struggle because he had a piece of fabric in his hand. I have that piece of fabric in my coat. I'm losing my mind old friend. I should have shown it to you a long time ago." Chief Johnson got up quickly and pulled out the piece of fabric from his jacket pocket. He handed it over to Mr. Gordon.

"It's a fine piece of silky lilac material." He looked at it closely. "How many men do you know especially around here who would wear something in a silky lilac?"

"None."

"But Mrs. Nash had a dress out of that material. Mrs. Ivy told me so. Now I'm beginning to think they weren't lovers at all. It was only business. I bet you a fine cigar that Ralston intends to rob her and then he would have gained everything. I bet she doesn't know that piece of fabric was left in her husband's hand."

"Does it seem to you like it came off the top or bottom of a piece of clothing?" Mr. Gordon gave the piece back to the Chief.

"I'm not sure. I'm no tailor. What are you thinking?" He looked at Mr. Gordon who appeared lost in thought.

"I'm thinking about going to the tailor shop. Let's find out what we can about that piece shall we? It may tell us if she knows about the piece or not depending upon where it was torn from. Who knows, she may even have the dress or whatever it came off of with her." With an approving nod from the Chief, both men left the office and went down the street to the only tailor shop in town. On the way they continued to talk about the case.

"How many pieces of jewelry did Mr. Edwards say were not accounted for?" Mr. Gordon wanted to confirm the number.

"Seven pieces."

"Let's say for now that Mrs. Nash paid Ralston to kill her husband. She would leave with him on the Priscilla. She could have paid him off with the jewels."

"If they were payment what would be your first step after getting them?" Chief Johnson asked.

"If I were Cole Ralston, I would want cash."

"So would I. And if I were Mrs. Nash I would get as far away as I could. I would tell Ralston to take me to a major port where I could get the best price for all the jewelry and pay him the cash he no doubt wants." Mr. Gordon liked what the Chief was saying. It made good sense to him.

"I agree. So, it looks like there is only one thing to do next."

"What's that?"

Send a telegram through the United States Notification System that we want Elsa Nash, Cole and Flint Ralston detained."

"What do we charge them with?"

"Arson and murder. We want them detained for additional questioning." Mr. Gordon looked as if he did not have a doubt in his mind. When they were in custody he would get the truth.

The men reached the tailor shop and were forced to wait for about fifteen minutes until they could speak with the person they needed.

"Thank you for waiting. How can I help you this morning?"

"This is Mr. Gordon." The Chief turned his head in the direction of his friend.

"Nice to meet you."

"Mr. Gordon and I wanted you to take a look at a piece of material and tell us what you can about it." He handed over the piece of material.

"I'll do what I can." He looked at the fabric for a moment then spoke. "Well, it's a quality silk blend with evenly distributed color. It's off of something very expensive because I can see a few seed pearls. The stitching is neat and tight indicating a professionally made product." He handed the piece back.

"Is there any way to know if it was removed from the middle, top or bottom of something?" Mr. Gordon inquired.

"Well, it would only be a guess. But if you look at the stitches, they are most commonly used as a hem on a garment. May I show you?" He extended his hand and the Chief placed the fabric in it.

"Yes. The material is folded over about one inch in a section. That is a standard hem and considering the color, texture and material of the fabric I would say it came off of an expensive ladies dress. It could also be a bustle or perhaps a sleeve."

"Is it likely that it came off of something on the front of the dress and above the waist?"

"I would say that is very unlikely. The hem indicates it's the bottom of something. Any dressmaker worth his salt would never fold and stitch fabric like this piece to the front of a dress. It would add unwanted bulk in places ladies don't want bulk." He snorted in disgust at the very thought of it and handed the piece back to Chief Johnson.

"You have been very helpful and we appreciate your time. Good morning." The men left his shop and found a nice place to sit outside. The day was beautiful.

"So it looks to me like the dress piece was a plant to put the blame on someone else other than the killer." Mr. Gordon was looking out across the bay. The water was blue and several ducks were swimming in the water near the shore.

"I agree. The fabric was meant to cast suspicion on someone else. I think that someone was Mrs. Nash. Mrs. Ivy told me that she remembered a lilac dress worn by Mrs. Nash for some kind of a ball. It wasn't in her closet. I think she would have taken it with her because according to Mrs. Ivy, she really liked it. Someone wanted to frame her for murder. Sadly for whoever it was, it didn't work. They didn't count on you." The Chief was watching the ducks and he found it to be very relaxing. He liked animals and enjoyed watching them swim and chase each other in the cold waters of the bay.

Mr. Gordon and the Chief knew this break would be short lived. They still had to send the telegram they had spoken about earlier. For now, they would take a moment and each would enjoy a cigar and just talk like the friends they were. After about one half of an hour they went to the telegraph office.

"I'm afraid that I won't be able to send this wire all the way to Seattle Chief." The lady behind the desk had a disappointed look on her face. She did not know how he would react to bad news.

"Why is that? I've received a wire just this morning with no problem."

"The storm knocked down some poles further up the coast and they were threatening to break the line. So, before that could happen I received a telegram about two hours ago saying the service would be down for a few days to make repairs. I have no capability to send anything out. I am so sorry I can't help you." She looked at him for understanding.

"I understand completely. I'll check with you again soon." He turned around and left the woman to her work. He still had another way of getting the arrest notices out. It would take longer to get there, but at least it was something.

"Let's go to my office and prepare some arrest notices. We can put them on the afternoon transport with instructions that if the telegraph is working at their location to wire the arrest notices." Both men thought the idea was good and set about doing just that.

Elsa Nash considered Cole and Flint Ralston to be the most uncouth men she had ever had the misfortune to be associated with. She found their lack of refinement terribly upsetting and especially hated when they would spit out tobacco juice in her presence. They laughed when one of them passed gas often teasing the other about the foul smell for at least a couple of minutes. They would not shave for several days at a time and she noticed that they never seemed to properly wash out their coffee cups before adding more coffee. She stopped drinking coffee because the pot was black and she wondered what else might be in it. Burping loudly after meals and hitting oneself on the chest was a perfectly normal thing to do. They did not seem to notice that they offended her feminine sensibilities and if they had she was certain that they would not have changed. If their manners were poor, their treatment of her was not. They did their best to treat her well. On a sunny morning near the end of the journey it was particularly unpleasant.

"Flint, what the hell have you been eating?" The terrible odor assaulted Cole's nostrils while he was still eating breakfast.

"That mud you call coffee tears up my guts. This is your damn fault." He quickly responded.

"That weren't a coffee fart—that was pickled herring. Go on deck and air out your pants before Mrs. Nash and I die." He waved his hand about to move the air in an attempt to disperse the odor.

"I need to go on deck anyway. I'll be at the wheel because one of us has to work." He took a piece of toast with him and left them alone in the galley.

"This trip has been a little hard on all of us. I bet you will be happy to reach Seattle." Cole took a bite of his sausage that he had pierced with a fork and was holding in front of him rather than have it sit on the plate and eat it one slice at a time.

"It will be nice to reach Seattle. I am looking forward to a nice hot bath and putting on my clothes again." She looked down at her attire and knew she was a far cry from the lady that first boarded the Priscilla.

"You'll have time to freshen up before we arrive. There's plenty of water because we have used it sparingly until now. Flint and I will allow you the cabin for a couple of hours so you can dress properly." He finished his breakfast and pushed the plate away from him.

"Oh, that would be so wonderful. What about you?" She was hoping that he would want to clean up because she did not want to be seen in his company looking like he did. His hair was dirty and his shirt soiled. He needed a shave. Both men looked dirty.

"We will have time. When we arrive Flint and I will be staying at the same hotel you will be staying at. I thought we could get cleaned up nice and proper like, and then we could all go and sell the jewels. You are more experienced and if you negotiate for us all, I think we could get a better price. Don't you think that's a good idea?" He looked at her like prey.

"I think that would be fine. We can get two rooms and after a couple of hours we can go to a jewelry store I know of with a wonderful reputation for honest dealings in precious stones." She felt she had no choice so she agreed to help. The sooner she could get rid of them the better off she would be. She was glad he said they would clean up.

"Good. It's settled. I'd better go on deck and see what Flint is up to." He got up and started to go up toward the deck.

"Wait a moment please. Can you tell me when we will reach Seattle?" She had never asked the question before because she promised she would not be nuisance.

"We arrive on the high tide tomorrow." He smiled at her knowing the news would be welcome.

"Tomorrow?" She almost wanted to jump up and down for joy.

"Yes. Well, if you will excuse me I have to go now." He smiled at her and then went up to join Flint on deck.

"Before you go, would it be possible for you to remove the ropes that hold my trunk secure? I'd like to get some personal things out of it. I only need a moment of your time." Cole had untied the ropes before and he always watched her as a precaution. He did not want her to discover what he had done just yet.

"Sure. I'd be glad to do it." That was a lie. He would stay near to see what she was pulling out. He hoped she would not want to wear the lilac dress. He did not really think so because it appeared to be much finer than the others. They both walked to the trunk and he untied the ropes for her.

"Thank you so much. Everything I need is right on top. I packed that way to make it easy for me." In a few moments, she had taken everything out of the trunk. Cole pretended to look away when she pulled out her delicate underclothing. She did not take notice of the lilac dress.

"I'm finished so you can secure the ropes again."

"It was my pleasure. I'll make sure that we stay on deck until you let us know when we can come down again." He turned and left her to wash her hair or whatever it was women like her did.

Elsa went to her bunk and planned how she would style her hair. She also organized her small area and then began to remove the hairpins in her hair. She would brush it out and then shampoo it until the offending smells of the boat were gone. Later she would take a sponge bath with more water than she had been using ensuring that she was clean from head to toe. The trip had been hard in many ways but it was worth it. She was free of Rudolph and would start her life anew in a new city. Elsa had no idea her parents were concerned for her. She did not know that Rudolph had sent a telegram to her parents informing them that she would be coming home. She did not think to contact them to make them aware of the recent changes in her life.

When Cole was on deck he walked over to where Flint was standing. His big hands were on the wheel and his eyes on the horizon. It was a beautiful day.

"Flint, we have to talk."

"What are we going to talk about—how well I fart?" He was more than annoyed that he had insulted and embarrassed him in front of Elsa.

"Alright, maybe that was a bit too much. But there are some important things we need to talk about now that she is busy." He looked at the door he had closed that separated the deck from the rest of the ship.

"Start talking." Flint was listening but not looking at his brother.

"When you see that door open we have to change the subject quickly. We are almost to Seattle and when we get there we need to make sure that we are clean and presentable. I have our clean shirts under my bunk and since there is plenty of water now that we are close to land I want us to both shave, wash our hair and sponge down." Cole was looking at the door and talking fast.

"What's up?" Now Flint turned and looked at his brother.

"We will all go into a nice hotel where she will get a room. You and I will share a room. We watch her room closely and after a while we all go and sell the jewels that she gave us. Do you have a question because if you do, now is the time to ask." Cole was still watching the door.

"Why does she need to go with us?" Flint didn't think he liked the idea.

"We need her experience and expertise. She has the ability to get the best price for the jewels. Once we have the money we get out of Seattle."

"Are we still going to go to Mexico and get us a pretty senorita?" Flint would leave the details of the jewels to his brother. Right now all he was interested in was the planned trip to Mexico.

"Damn right we're going. But not before we turn Elsa over to the police for the murder of her husband and we take her money."

"How do we do that?" Flint was glad that Cole was good at figuring things like this out.

"I'll take care of that. You just do what I said and we will be rich men." He placed his hand on Flint's shoulder and gave him a light pat. It was their way of saying that they would always be close and that nothing would come between them.

In the cabin Elsa had finished washing her hair. She ran a comb through it and pulled it back with a ribbon. She was in the process of preparing her bath and while she did that she tried to recall the name of the most reputable jeweler in Seattle. The Ralston's had been good to her in the fact that they did not hurt her physically in any way. They were coarse men but they had done her a service and she felt they had earned their money. She would do her best to get them the best price she could for the pieces she had given them. She kept three of the seven custom made pieces for herself. She could not bear to part with the necklace or the earrings. They were the most expensive pieces but she needed them to complete the look she wanted when she would be out in high society.

James noticed that Karin looked a little pale and had not touched her breakfast. She nibbled at a piece of toast but that was all she did. He followed her as she left the galley and found her sitting down on the port side of the boat. She was facing the wind and taking deep breaths when he sat down next to her.

"Karin, are you feeling alright?" He looked at her with scrutiny.

"I'm fine. I'm just a little tired I guess and I'm concerned over poor Mrs. Nash." She did not want to be deceitful but did not yet want to discuss her pregnancy with him.

"I think we will all be glad to get back on land. I hope that boat goes to Seattle because we aren't prepared to follow much longer." Actually, he and Daniel were in their element. They loved the sea and when the ocean was nice like it had been for these several days there was no place they would rather be. They felt they had sea water in their veins instead of blood.

"I know. I was thinking of that just yesterday. What are we going to do if they don't stop in Seattle?" She was holding her hair down with one hand so it would not whip around.

"I'll inform the port authorities and let them handle it from there. We can't do much more than that. They have a way of taking care of these things. Try not to worry it does no good." He took her hand in his and gave it a little squeeze. It felt cool to the touch despite the warm day.

"You're right. Are they still several hours ahead of us?" She had not seen the ship since the first day it was seen by the men. She kept out of sight as instructed.

"It's still there. Do you want me to bring you any crackers or anything?"

"No. This is nothing really. I'll be fine but thank you for the offer." She smiled at him and then felt Salty come up next to her and rub his face and side on her arm.

"Hey, Salty ol' boy. Come to say hello to your mom?" James reached over and ran his hand down the back of the cat and up to the point of his tail.

"He's done so well on the trip. He's a good boy." She petted his little head.

"Did you tell him that he's not going to be the only baby in the house?" He said it so matter of fact that she almost didn't react.

"Now what makes you say that to Salty?" She wondered how he knew. She had never been sick before and nothing was noticeable on her physical appearance yet.

"Something in the way you look. It's an inner beauty that some women have when they get pregnant. You have that look. Am I wrong? If I am I apologize for such a personal statement." He looked out to sea and saw some porpoises a short distance away and just slightly off the starboard side of the boat. "Quick, look over there." He pointed out the porpoises and for a minute they watched them swimming and playing.

"What are they?" She was thrilled to have seen something so beautiful and graceful.

"There're porpoises. They travel in family groups called Pods." He was glad that she had seen the animals. They had not seen any sea life other than birds since leaving Valda Bay.

"James, you're right." She took her eyes off the animals and faced him. "I am going to have a baby. I just didn't want to say anything because I wanted to come with you on the trip. I didn't know if you would take me along if you knew. I feel good and this is the first time I had a little stomach upset. It's almost gone now." She turned her head to watch the playful antics of the creatures she now knew were called porpoises.

"Well, I'm not sure what I would have done if I'd known earlier. Did Erik know about the baby?"

"No. I wasn't sure of anything when he left." Her eyes filled with tears.

"Well, he knows now. I do believe he's walking around up there crowing like a rooster. I feel like crowing myself and I'm not even the responsible party. Hell, I'm going to do it anyway." He stood up and made a big crowing sound. He did feel happy for her and wanted to break her saddened mood. It worked. She laughed out loud and yanked at his pant leg to sit back down.

"Don't worry. No one can hear us. Well maybe the porpoises, but they don't care." He looked down at her and smiled big. Hearing all the noise Daniel left the wheel and came running over to see what had happened. He heard a noise and wasn't sure if it was supposed to be a rooster crowing or a yell of pain. Either way, it wasn't a normal thing to do.

"What the hell was that noise?" The look on his face was that of concern.

"I just crowed like a rooster."

"Why?"

"Karin?" James looked at her. It was not his place to share her news.

"I just told James that I'm going to have a baby." She smiled.

"Really?" He nudged his way next to James and then he too began to crow like a rooster. They all laughed. Salty became frightened and his hair stood on end. He decided that they lost their minds and quickly went down into the galley where it was much more quiet and safe.

# Broken Trust

The harbor in Seattle came into clear view. It was a busy place with all manner of activity easily observed from the deck of the Priscilla. Elsa Nash had already packed her things the night before and was wearing a pretty dress and matching hat. She was glad to be rid of the male attire and now all she had to do was wait for the Ralston's to dock the ship and then they could be on the way to a nice hotel. After about one hour the ship was in port.

"Mrs. Nash, we are secured to the dock but I have to leave for just a moment to speak to the harbor master and pay for the moorage. Flint will stay with you and I ask that you not come out on the deck yet."

"Why is that?" She was disappointed to be asked to stay in the room.

"Because this is a busy harbor and there are many sailors here. They come from all parts of the world and some don't respect women or our customs. I would not want you to suffer the rude language or be insulted by them. You are an attractive woman and we don't want to draw attention to ourselves."

"I see. Thank you Mr. Ralston, I'll wait below. Do you think you will be very long?" She was anxious to get off the ship.

"No. I should be about half an hour or less. I can see the Harbor Master's office from here." He was aware of her desire to leave the ship. It had been a long trip for all of them. He appreciated her understanding.

While he was gone, Elsa could hear Flint on deck. She had no idea what he could be doing but she suspected that it had to do with ship duties. In less than forty five minutes Elsa heard voices on deck. She leaned into the door and placed her ear to the door. The voices were that of Cole and Flint speaking. A few moments later she heard a knock at the door and was relieved to see that Cole had returned.

"We are all set. Flint and I will get your trunk because there is a coach waiting outside. I told the driver to take us to The Majestic Palace. That was the hotel you said you wanted to stay in."

"That will be fine." She proceeded to go up the ladder.

He stepped aside to allow her to exit the berth. Flint was waiting top-side and immediately went to assist Cole with her trunk. Cole checked to ensure the straps were secure. Once Flint had her trunk and was loading it on the coach, Cole took a couple of minutes to look around the cabin once again. He was satisfied that everything was in order. In a few moments they all boarded the coach. The men sat on one side while Elsa sat on the other. She appeared different to them than she did just a few hours ago. She was poised and had an arrogant look about her. She was in her element. They were not.

When they arrived at the hotel a doorman met the coach and when he opened the door he surveyed the occupants. His years of experience told him that the lady was a woman of elegance and substance. The men on the other hand he could not begin to guess the purpose for their visit. He would not expect any consideration from either of them. He quickly proceeded to assist the lady by offering his arm as support while she stepped down from the coach. She accepted his arm without an acknowledgement. Flint and Cole trailed behind. At the desk a very slender man with soft hands greeted her.

"Good day ma'am. Welcome to the Majestic Palace. How may I help you?" He politely asked.

"I'd like a room with a nice view."

"Of course. How long will you be our guest?"

"I expect to conclude my business in a couple of days."

"I understand. We have a nice room overlooking the bay on the second floor. Shall I send a lady to assist you?"

"That would be appreciated. I would also like to have a hot bath. Can you arrange that?"

"Yes. The lady will see to your needs." He pulled out his guest book so that she might register. He saw her write her name down and then turned the book to face him.

"Thank you Miss Wellington. You will be in room 24, here is your key. I hope you will enjoy you stay with us." He turned and called for someone to take her trunk. "Boy! Take Miss Wellington's trunk to room 24."

A young man immediately appeared. "Yes sir." He picked up her trunk and began to go toward her room.

"Please follow the young man Miss Wellington. Enjoy your stay." He then began to thumb through the guest book. He did this for a couple of minutes. The Ralston's were still waiting by the desk.

Cole grew somewhat impatient and spoke up. "Mister, after you are finished fooling with that book we also want a room."

"I see. How long are you planning to stay?"

"Just one night." Cole didn't like this mousy man.

"Will that be one room or two?" He was a bit curt.

"One will do us fine. But we need two beds."

"I have one room available. It's on the first floor near the back door."

"We don't care about that. Does it have two beds?"

"It does."

"Fine. We'll take it."

"Alright. That will be four U.S. dollars in advance." He held out his hand.

Cole paid the man and was given the key to room 19. He started to leave and go to the room but thought to ask directions. "Where is this room located?"

"Go through the glass doors and go all the way to the end of the hallway. It's the last door on your left. I don't suppose you men require a valet?"

"No, I don't suppose we do." He answered.

Walking down the hallway Flint had a question. "Cole, was that man funning us?"

"He thought we weren't peacock enough to stay in this hotel." He looked at Flint and shook his head.

"Maybe when we leave I ought to show him just how peacock we are by beating his ass."

"I know what you mean."

"This place sure is fancy. Did you notice the silver and gold fixtures and the rugs?"

"I did. Tell you what I didn't see and that was one good spittoon." They had arrived at room 19. They unlocked the door and went inside. There was a small lamp near the door along with some matches and Cole lit the lamp.

"Damn look at this room." Flint reached down and grabbed himself by the groin. "This is much nicer than the Crabs' Inn where we've stayed before." Cole laughed at the comment. "It ought to be. It cost us four damn dollars."

Flint walked over to the bed and pulled back the blankets. "Look at this—the sheets are clean. Maybe that's why it cost us so much."

"Could be. I need to think a minute. We have to find a way to watch Elsa. We can't let her get away from us so we have to be on our guard. Let's go out the back door and up the fire escape and to her room. Let's remind her that she said we would go to the jewelry store today."

"Let's go."

The men did as they discussed and were soon knocking on Elsa's door. When she answered she was a little surprised to find it was them. She had not had a chance to have her bath. She was a little angry at their intrusion.

"What are you doing here?" She asked.

"We've come to take you to the jewelry store. No time like the present."

"I can't do it now. I've just arranged for my bath. I told you I needed a couple of hours to make myself presentable. Aside from that, the jewelry store won't be open until eleven o'clock. It simply isn't fashionable to go earlier. We have time." She would have said more, but about that time two ladies approached her room. They were both carrying two buckets of hot water. They realized she had spoken the truth.

"Enjoy your bath. Flint and I will be back in a couple of hours." Cole and Flint left and walked down the hallway of the second floor.

"Now what do we do?" Flint asked.

"We go down to where that peacock is and get a newspaper."

"Why are we going to do that? You can't read and neither can I. All we learned how to do was sign our name." Flint thought the idea dumb.

"We have to keep watch and we can't do it from our room." Cole was tired of telling him that.

"You're going to pretend to read but keep an eye open for her coming down the stairs so she can't get away from us. Cole, you're always thinking aren't you?"

"I try." Now, let's go down to that fancy lobby and wait for her majesty."

Cole sat down in a big overstuffed chair in the lobby. He picked up a newspaper and was faced with a new problem. He wasn't sure which way to hold the newspaper because he didn't know how to read. He held it in his lap for some time while Flint smoked a cigar outside. When an older gentleman sat down not too far from him, he pulled out his newspaper and began to read. Cole turned his paper to match the gentlemen's. He copied his moves a minute or two after they were made. The gentleman never became aware that he was being a teacher to the illiterate. If Cole had not been illiterate he would have read all about the murder of Mr. Rudolph Nash and the search for his wife Elsa.

On the North Star, James, Daniel and Karin watched as the Priscilla disappeared from view. The only conclusion they reached was that she had pulled into the harbor area in Seattle.

"I wonder if we will be able to see the ship when we pull into the harbor?" Karin had no idea how big the harbor was. On the trip she learned that the port was a large one and very busy.

"We might but I doubt it. It's a huge harbor. I think our best bet is to inform the authorities." James knew that they were trained to handle these situations better than they were.

"What will you tell them?" She asked.

"I'll tell them that Mr. Nash was murdered and that his wife Elsa could not be found. We know that she is with the Ralston's and we think she might be held against her will or be in great danger."

"That's a good idea." Daniel agreed.

"We are at least two hours out of Seattle so let's check our lists to make sure we make the most of our time. After that we need to prepare the ship for docking." Daniel was thinking ahead.

"Good idea. But, there is one thing we need to talk about right now before we get busy. Seattle Harbor is infested with sharks." James looked at her and was quite serious.

"Sharks? What kind of sharks?" Her eyes opened a littler wider.

"The most dangerous type of shark there is—the kind that walk on two legs. So when we get to the harbor please stay below until we call for you. The place is not Valda Bay and we will all leave the ship together. Stay close to us. If there is anything that you especially need we can get it together. Don't worry, we are used to places like this and everything will be fine as long as we all stick together." James offered her a reassuring smile.

"I understand. Just let me know when you want me to stay below. In the meantime I'll get Salty and lock him in the berth and get the galley in order." She did not want to be in the way of deck duties or create undue burden for them. She went to the galley and they secured items on deck.

A few hours later they were pulling into the harbor. They did not see the Priscilla and the North Star was docked without incident. James spoke with the harbor master and paid moorage for one night. He thought to ask the man about the Ralston's ship.

"As I was entering the harbor I thought I saw a ship from my home port. Is the Priscilla moored here?"

"Yes. She's in the west harbor." He replied.

"Do you have any idea where the crew might be staying?" James hoped he might have overheard something or been told by one of them.

"I'm not sure but I did see a nice coach pull up and pick up some folks from that side of the dock. The coach was from The Majestic Palace."

"The Majestic Palace? That's an expensive hotel if my memory serves me correct."

"Your memory is correct." The older man shook his head.

"Well, it's nice someone can afford it. Thanks a lot I appreciate it."
James left the office. He now knew where the Priscilla was moored and
where they were probably staying. He could now provide the authorities
with information that would help them find the Ralston's and rescue Mrs.
Nash.

In less than one hour they were all standing in the constable's office and
finished relaying their concerns about Mrs. Nash. The constable was aware
of the murder of Mr. Nash because he read about it again in the morning
newspaper.

"Are you certain that it is the Ralston's from Valda Bay?" The constable
and his men were interested in making an arrest. However, they did not
want to be accused of arresting the wrong individuals and facing public
embarrassment.

"Yes. We make our home in Valda Bay just like they do. It's them."
James did most of the talking but Daniel and Karin indicated their support of what he was saying.

"Well, that's good enough for me. I'll arrange to get the warrants issued
for their arrest. My men and I will follow up on your suggestion that they
may be at The Majestic Palace." The constable sent one of his men to
acquire the arrest warrant and the other four deputies prepared to take the
men in custody.

"There is something else that will be essential to our arrest. We don't
know what they look like, you do. One of you or all of you will have to
come with me and my men to identify Cole and Flint Ralston. All I have is
a physical description and I know at least two other men that could fit that
description. So, what's it going to be? Who is going with me?" He looked
at the men thinking that the lady would not want to be involved in such
unpleasant business.

"I think I should be the one to go with you." Daniel spoke before anyone else could. "James, you need to stay with Karin and away from the
hotel. There is no need to have her involved in identifying them. I could
meet you somewhere afterwards."

"That would be good. We'll wait for you somewhere near the hotel. Is
there a place where we can safely wait?" James addressed the constable.

"Yes. Across the street there is a tea and coffee house with a large window that will allow you to see the hotel from across the street. I'll have one of my men ensure that you have a seat near the window. After the men have been identified and arrested, you can walk into the shop and join them for a cup of coffee. The Ralston's will never know it was you that identified them. Do you have any questions before we get started?" The constable had done this sort of thing before and found it worked best for everyone concerned.

"No. I'm ready to do this." He was willing to help Mrs. Nash but the sooner it was behind him the better.

"Good." He motioned to a deputy to escort James and Karin to the tea and coffee shop. "My deputy will escort you both to the shop. Do either of you have any questions?" He looked at them and waited for the answer.

"No sir, I don't. Do you Karin?" James asked.

"No. I'm ready to get started." She felt a little unsettled.

"Then let's go." With those final words everyone did as instructed.

After only ten minutes, James and Karin were in place at the shop. They had ordered a cup of coffee but neither of them were drinking it. They had their eyes and mind on the events across the street.

Cole was still seated in the lobby with the newspaper in his hands. Flint had entered the hotel again after having enjoyed his cigar and sat next to his brother. They had been waiting for Elsa for two and one half hours. They were getting impatient. Cole decided that enough was enough and he made a decision to go and get the woman. Flint stayed in the lobby. About the time that Daniel and the constable arrived at the hotel Cole was already with Elsa. She was dressed in high fashion.

"Do you see the Ralston's?" The constable asked Daniel.

"I see only one of them. Flint Ralston is the man wearing the blue shirt that is seated in the overstuffed chair. He's the younger of the two brothers." He looked around the lobby and then noticed that Cole was escorting Elsa down the staircase. He had her elbow in his hand as they walked. "Wait. I see Cole Ralston with Mrs. Nash. They are coming down the staircase right now. He's the tall man with the lady wearing the green and white dress." He looked at the constable who nodded that he had seen the man and lady he spoke of. Once the identification had been made the constable informed his deputies who were standing near him. "Thank you Mr. Batley. You've done well. I suggest you go to your friends across the street. My men and I will take care of this from here." The constable waited only a moment after his departure to make his move.

Daniel walked quickly out of the hotel but not in a fashion that would draw attention. He crossed the street quickly and made his way to the coffee shop. As planned, he joined James and Karin. They were to wait until the men were in custody and taken to the jailhouse. Then, they would leave the shop and go about their business. The Ralston's would never see them. The plan was working and Daniel was relieved that now they could get on with the real reason they were in Seattle; to find the treasure of the Rip Tide.

Back at The Majestic Palace Hotel things were proceeding as planned.

"Are you Cole Ralston?" The constable asked.

"Who wants to know?"

"I'm Constable Jones. Are you Cole Ralston?"

"Yeah. I'm Ralston."

"Is that man on the couch your brother Flint?" He looked over at the chair where Flint was seated.

"He is." Cole had no idea what these men were asking these questions for.

"Excuse me Ma'am, are you Mrs. Nash?"

"I am." She said it in a weak voice.

"What's going on Constable Jones?" Cole was beginning to get uncomfortable.

"You are under arrest Mr. Ralston for arson, kidnapping and the murder of Mr. Rudolph Nash." The constable reached for his arms and placed handcuffs on his wrists. The deputy was ready to assist if needed.

"What's going on? What are you talking about? I didn't do anything." Cole was caught by complete surprise. He had no idea how they knew about the events that took place in Valda Bay.

"Mrs. Nash, would you please go with the deputy. A lady escort will be here in just a moment to serve as a chaperone. Please remain in the lobby. The deputy will be with you at all times. You have nothing to fear."

"Oh thank Heaven you've arrived! I've been so frightened. I didn't know what to do. I thought they would kill me." She began to appear faint and she trembled when the deputy led her away. She managed to force tears into her eyes.

"What are you saying?" Cole directed his comment to her. "Don't believe her. She arranged everything. She's lying." He realized that somehow she had managed to get to the authorities without his knowledge. Had Elsa informed the authorities while he was waiting for her to come down stairs? Why would she do that?

"Please don't let him near me! They forced me to go with them." She began sobbing and began to act a little hysterical. She was a tremendous actress.

"You lying bitch!" He yelled out as she was led away in the protective care of the deputy.

"That's enough of that Ralston. Keep your damn mouth shut. You'll have a chance to have your say later." Constable Jones led him out of the lobby and into a horse drawn prison wagon. When he entered the wagon Flint was already being escorted inside.

"Cole, what is going on?" He knew they were in trouble but the magnitude of the situation did not really sink in yet.

"Elsa played us Flint. She turned us over to the law pretending to be the innocent victim in this whole thing. She's blamed us for the murder of her husband, kidnapping her and setting fire to the mercantile. I underestimated her." Cole could not believe how they were in this situation when he had taken great care not to be.

"You mean the cops don't know that she was in on it with us?" He was beginning to understand a little more of what was going on.

"That's right. She's playing a good part and is the respectable lady of a wealthy old man who they say I murdered. Flint, unless something happens in our favor pretty quick, we're going to come to a bad end. So, you have to listen to me very carefully. Let me do the talking. No matter what they say to you or say that I said, you just remember one thing. I'm your brother and I would never hurt or turn against you. I wouldn't save my skin and sacrifice yours." He needed Flint to understand that they needed to stick together and not turn against each other. It was their only hope.

"I understand. I won't say anything unless you are in the room. If you can't be then I just keep my mouth shut. Is that it?" He was used to this role. It would come easy to him to continue to let Cole be in charge.

"That's right. Don't say anything. Don't let them provoke you into signing anything either. Right now, things look real bad for us. But, I'll think of something. You just do what I say alright?" He tried to sound confident that he could get them out of the mess they were in. If the truth be known, he felt that within a week, they would be hung for the murder of Rudolph Nash. He also felt certain that she would get away with everything; including murder. In the five minutes it took to reach the jail, they had agreed upon what Cole suggested. Once at the jail, they were taken into separate rooms and questioned.

"Mr. Ralston, You are wanted for murder and arson in Valda Bay. I intend to turn you over to the authorities there. My concern right now is in getting to the truth." The constable had been questioning Cole for several hours and was now convinced he was guilty. Flint had said little or nothing as directed.

"Constable Jones, she is lying to you. I did not kidnap her or take her by force. She gave me the jewels to bring her to Seattle at the request of her husband. I owed him money and he would settle with me if I did this for him. I didn't do anything else." Cole would not admit to murder or arson but only to transporting Elsa Nash to Seattle for payment.

"Mrs. Nash tells me that you stole the jewels from her and that is how you came to have them in your possession."

"We were going to the jewelry store to exchange them for cash. It was part of our agreement." Cole knew he was not believed.

After several hours of discussion and interrogation Constable Jones was ready to speak at length with Elsa Nash. She insisted that the jewels were in her possession and that they had been stolen from her.

"I know that this must be terribly painful for you so I'll try and be as brief as possible. You are officially saying that Mr. Ralston murdered your husband while you and he were returning from a trip to your jewelers in Rock Port. You also say there was a struggle between your husband and Mr. Ralston as he tried to protect you from his attack. This resulted in his death and you're kidnapping. Ralston took the money from your husband and forced you to go with him to Seattle. Is that correct?" He had ordered notes be taken of her account of what had happened.

"Yes. It was terrible. He came at my darling Rudolph out of the dark. It was so sudden I couldn't even move I was so frightened. Forgive me; may I have a glass of water?" She started to cry and used her handkerchief to dab at her eyes and add to the effect, but in reality was irritating them with the cloth.

"Get Mrs. Nash some water immediately." A deputy left the room and brought her back a glass of water.

"Thank you. Forgive me, I didn't mean to fall apart. Recalling all this is very hard. But, like I was trying to say, my husband fought back. He isn't a very big man; not like that beast Cole Ralston. He knew that he had to take me with him because I was a witness to the murder." She took a sip of water but forced her hands to shake while doing so.

"Why do you suppose he didn't kill you on the spot Mrs. Nash?" The constable was looking at her closely.

"At first I had no idea. I thought I might be ravished. Then, it occurred to me while I was a prisoner in the cabin of that ship that he needed me to exchange my jewels for cash. I had on some nice pieces but the rest I packed in my trunk. He has absolutely no refinement and he felt that he would draw attention trying to sell them. If I sold them, it would appear as normal. My husband gave me those jewels because we loved each other so much. Please, please tell me he will pay for this." More tears.

"I don't mean to sound harsh, but can you tell me how it was you happened to have all your clothes with you. Mr. Ralston tells me that you packed them from home to be placed on his ship. How did the clothes get to his ship?"

"I had gone to Rock Port with my husband for a few days. We had not had very much time alone lately so my husband invited me to go with him so we could have a small vacation after his business trip. I needed my nicer things with me. I always liked to look nice for my Rudolph. He was such a wonderful and gentle man." She was glad he was so accepting of her answers. But then why wouldn't he be? She was a refined lady.

"I see. So you believe that your trunk was taken by Mr. Ralston? To what end Mrs. Nash?"

"They took the trunk because they are greedy and mean and thought it might have more valuables in it. I know because I overheard them talking about it one night. I just want to go home to my parents. I want the safety of my father's home again. If I can't be with Rudolph then I need my father....I want to go home!" She looked at him with sad eyes and a pathetic look and began to cry a little harder so that her body shook with little spasms. He looked at her with sympathy and understanding. Everything she said made sense to him. He would make arrangements for her immediately to catch the next transport out of Seattle as he was satisfied with the answers she provided.

"Mrs. Nash. Calm yourself. Do you need a physician?" He was concerned for her state of mind.

"No. I'll be alright. I am still Mrs. Rudolph Nash and I can be strong if I have to. I think the best thing would be for me to just be on my way as soon as possible. My trunk is in my room and if you send word to the hotel, I'm sure they can quickly pack up my things so I can be on the next transport."

"That can be arranged but I have a few more questions. If we should need to contact you, where will you be?"

"I'll be at the home of my parents, Mr. and Mrs. Wellington. They live in Philadelphia. The address is Twenty Four Liberty Avenue." She was now in the clear. All she had to do was remain in character just a little longer and leave Seattle quickly.

"There is just one more thing we need to discuss." Mr. Jones pulled out the small bag of coins that had been on the person of Cole Ralston.

"Yes?" She noticed the bag but was not concerned. She had already practiced what to say.

"These coins were in the possession of Mr. Ralston when he was arrested. He says you gave them to him. I'm certain there is an explanation for that. I'd like to hear it from you." He fingered the small bag while looking at her for anything that might help Mr. Ralston. He wanted to be fair.

"That bag contains money from the sale of some jewels that I no longer wanted. I never really cared for the style or settings so I mentioned to Rudolph that we should sell them. He did and that money was from the sale of the jewels. We were going to use the money to decorate a nursery. We both wanted a family so much. Now, it's all gone. I'll never have a baby now." She placed her hands over her face and slumped deeply into her chair. Her sobs could be heard through her hands. She got the effect she wanted.

"Easy now. I know it seems bleak now. Once you are with your family things will get better for you. I see no reason why you can't take the money and save it for future plans. These things have a way of working out. I'm very satisfied with all the answers to the questions I had. I need you to sign for the money and it will be returned to you." He noticed that she did not ask for the money but rather seemed distraught over the incident that led to her husband's murder. He called for the secretary and instructed him to bring all the necessary paperwork and make arrangements with the hotel to have her bags packed. He would see to it personally that she was on the next transport to the Philadelphia. He excused himself from her and left to make arrangements. After twenty minutes he returned. She stayed in the room quietly sobbing in case she was being watched.

Within the hour she was at the harbor ready to board a ship that would take her to her father's home.

"Mrs. Nash, you are booked onto a ship that will take you directly to the east coast. I wish to express my sympathy over the loss of your husband. I hope your trip home will be pleasant under these trying circumstances." He could not imagine how she must have felt having to travel alone. A lady of her social standing should have a woman traveling companion.

"Thank you Constable Jones. You have been so kind and helpful. I appreciate you recovering my jewels, the money taken in the robbery and having my trunk delivered to me on the ship. I don't know what I would have done without you." She extended her hand and he kissed the top of it. She blushed slightly and turned to board the ship. He departed thinking her a lovely lady.

When the constable was out of sight, she went into action. She asked a deck worker if there were any other ships leaving with the tide that would be going to Europe. The answer was yes. There were two ships leaving on the tide. Of the two ships, the Sea Maiden would depart sooner and was destined for England and then France. She thanked him for the information and left the ship to purchase passage on the Sea Maiden. The young man was paid to take her trunk to the other ship and soon she was settled inside her cabin. Within thirty minutes, the ship departed.

Elsa safe in the confines of her cabin burst out laughing at the stupidity of Constable Jones, the Ralston's and Rudolph. She was thinking of the fortunate turn of events that allowed her to formulate a good cover story. She had been standing looking out of her hotel window when she had seen three people she recognized from Valda Bay. She quickly removed the dress she had on and changed into the green dress that contained the money she had sewn into the hem. Cash would facilitate her escape. Elsa suspected that the three persons from Valda Bay had seen her and the Ralston's earlier in the day. She concluded that Cole and Flint would be arrested. She looked over to the newspaper on the bed that she had read while soaking in the hot tub. The newspaper made no mention of wanting her for questioning. She had time to formulate a good story because she was aware of everything that transpired since her departure from Valda

Bay. It had served her well because unlike Cole and Flint Ralston—Elsa Nash could read.

"That has got to be the most beautiful dress I've ever seen. You look wonderful." A young woman was admiring her friend's new dress.

"I still can't believe she gave it to me." She was looking at herself in a full length closet glass.

"I can't either. What happened that made her not want it anymore?"

"Well, after I prepared her bath water she told me to open her trunk and refresh all her clothes. I laid them out on her bed and went to get an iron, cloths and the board. When I returned I started to iron the dresses and that's when I noticed that this lilac dress was torn on the bottom. I told her about it right away and she got this odd look on her face." She turned around to look at herself from a different angle.

"Can you blame her? I would have been sick if the dress were mine." She let out a small sigh.

"Anyway, she asked me to help her out of the tub and get her dressed. She selected a nice one and I helped her put it on. I brushed her hair and styled it nice and left her to clean up the bath area. I noticed that she went to the window and then asked me to help her change into a different gown. She put on a green one that I didn't think was as pretty but she insisted that I hurry up. After she was in the green dress, she looked at me and asked if I would like to have the lilac one." She turned back around and looked at her friend.

"Then what?"

"I was so surprised that I didn't answer right away. She smiled at me and actually apologized for offering me a dress that was slightly damaged on the bottom. She told me it was one of her favorite dresses but she didn't have the time to get it repaired and she didn't want to travel with it because she felt the fine fabric would only continue to rip. I told her that I understood completely and I would be pleased to have it. I know it was wrong, but I lied and told her I was pretty good with a needle and thread and I could make a repair that would not even be noticeable. She told me to make the repair but to keep the dress anyway." She giggled a little at that last comment.

"That was terrible. You know you can't sew a stitch."

"I know that. But, you can. Will you fix it for me? It's so pretty I just couldn't think of it in the rubbish pile." She looked at her friend like a child who had been discovered with candy after having been told they couldn't have any.

"I'll fix it for you. Let me take a look at it and I'll get started tomorrow after you buy some thread to match." She walked over to her friend and lifted the hem of the dress. She then walked to her sewing basket and began to pin where the repair needed to begin and where it would end. She made a few folds and then knew what she would do.

"Thank you for fixing it for me."

"You're welcome. It is beautiful and you are my best friend." She smiled at her and began to help her friend out of the dress.

With the dress in the hands of two women known only to Elsa—it was doubtful that its whereabouts would ever be discovered by anyone.

Three days later Cole and Flint Ralston were still sitting in jail. They overheard a deputy announce in the front office that the telegraph had been repaired and it was now possible to contact Valda Bay. Constable Jones planned to inform the authorities there that the Ralston's were in custody in Seattle. This news brought mixed feelings. In the three days since Elsa departed for what everyone thought was home, Cole had carefully planned his defense.

"Cole did you hear that?" Flint looked tired and he wished he knew what his brother was thinking.

"I did. That's good news. Don't worry, I've got a plan and we'll be alright. Just keep doing what you're doing. I'll take care of us. Are you doing alright? You haven't signed anything have you?" Cole was nervous because it didn't take the deputy long to realize that Flint was not the sharpest pencil in the pencil box. He had spent time alone with Flint and that always was a cause for concern.

"I haven't said or signed anything. I'm doing just what you said. Can't you tell me anything?" He needed to be reassured. The deputy had told him about going to the gallows and how he had seen grown men cry and beg not to be hung. He told him about how his eyes and tongue would bug out of his body. But mostly he told him about how long it took to die.

"I can tell you not to listen to that damn deputy. He's just trying to scare you into confessing something that you didn't do. Don't listen to him. If a telegram is sent to Valda Bay it means that we can get a proper trial there. Those people know us and Chief Johnson may not be my favorite person but he's not stupid and easily taken in by a woman's tears and act." He tried to sound as if going to Valda Bay was the best thing that could happen to them.

"So you think we have a chance there?"

"Sure I do. Mr. Nash is dead, Elsa is gone; what can they possibly have on us? You're doing fine. Just continue like you are and I bet in no time at all we are going to be told we are going home."

"What about the Priscilla?"

"We can come back for her and sail to Mexico like we planned." He knew that this conversation was doing Flint a world of good.

"With what money? Elsa took all we had." He waited for an answer but didn't have the chance to hear it. The deputy opened the door to the cell area and entered.

"Well boys, I've got some news for you. We sent a wire to Valda Bay a couple of hours ago and guess what?" He stuck his hand into his vest and stood up on his toes.

"We can't begin to guess. Why don't you just tell us?" Cole said this with a bit of sarcasm in his voice.

"It looks like Chief Johnson is on his way to see you up close and personal like. Isn't that nice?" He grinned wide.

"Yeah, real nice. Thanks for letting us know." Cole turned his back on the deputy and Flint went to sit on his bunk. In reality, things were going exactly as Cole hoped they would. Now all they had to do was wait for his arrival.

Chief Johnson and Inspector Gordon were on their way to Seattle. After receiving the telegram from Constable Jones they quickly gathered their notebooks and prepared the proper documents to legally transport Cole and Flint Ralston.

"I still can't believe that Mr. Jones allowed Elsa Nash to leave Seattle. If only the damn wire had been working we would now have all of them in custody." Chief Johnson was disappointed to learn that Elsa had been allowed to depart on a ship to the east coast. There were lots of questions at this point and not too many answers.

"It's a tough break. But in fairness to Mr. Jones he had no idea we wanted Mrs. Nash for questioning because she was a murder suspect. As far as he was concerned she was the victim. The newspapers failed to mention her possible involvement and he had no way of knowing any different." The logic offered by Mr. Gordon did little to comfort the Chief.

"I know that you're right. I guess I'm getting too old for this nonsense. I think after this case is over, I'm going to retire and spend my time chasing fish instead of criminals. I've been saving up a little money to buy me a place not too far from where I now live. The view is great and the fishing has always been good. When I'm out there on the water I don't think about the ills of the world." He smiled to himself when he thought of the little cabin by the water.

"It sounds real nice. I'm a city boy myself and I always wondered what you fishing types did with so many fish. Do you really eat that many?" Mr. Gordon looked at the Chief and when he saw him laughing he wondered what he said that was so funny.

"No. I like fish alright but I can't eat as many as I catch. Mostly I release them but have a good time letting them play on the line."

"I see. Well, I hate to change this most pleasant conversation but we are almost to the station. Do you want to get a hotel room near the jail or one downtown?" It didn't matter to Mr. Gordon which location his friend would pick.

"I guess by the jail. It's why we are here in the first place. I'd like to drop off our luggage, freshen up a bit and then go see Mr. Jones if that's alright with you."

"Sounds fine. But, I'd like to add getting a sandwich to that list. Once we begin to question the Ralston men there's no way to know how long we will be detained." Mr. Gordon hated to stop questioning a suspect once he was on a hard path.

"That's a good point. Let's plan on that." Chief Johnson looked out the window of the coach and saw the station come into sight. "I see the station now. I believe we have just arrived in Seattle." He turned to see that Mr. Gordon was already collecting his things. He did the same.

Two hours later the men entered the jail and were greeted by Mr. Jones. The men exchanged pleasantries and were given a briefing on the events that led to the arrest of the men. It was decided to interrogate them separately and begin immediately. A room was set up and in only a few minutes, Cole Ralston was brought in to speak with Mr. Gordon and Chief Johnson. Mr. Jones was not in the room with them.

"Mr. Ralston, it's important that you know that everything you say will be written down by Chief Johnson. We will begin if you are ready." Mr. Gordon sat down facing the man across the table with keen eyes.

"Yes sir. I'm more than ready. Can you tell me where my brother is?" Cole had no idea if Flint had been taken someplace else to be interrogated or left in his cell.

"At the present time he is in his cell. Are you concerned because he is not well or were you just curious as to his whereabouts?" If the man needed a doctor one would be called for him.

"I was just wondering. He's not stupid but he is a little slow. I've always looked out for him."

"So we may conclude that he follows your lead?" The process had begun.

"Look, I'm older and we've been together all our lives." It was the truth and everyone knew it. There was no danger there.

"Tell me why you left Valda Bay?"

"The fishing was bad and we had been talking about moving on." Cole decided he would go slow and think carefully before answering questions.

"So you couldn't make a good living there anymore. Is that correct?"

322    Point of the Circle

"Pretty much. We weren't the only ones that had it tough—all the fishermen did and some are still struggling."

"So what happened that forced your hand and sent you to Seattle?"

"The notice that I received from Mr. Nash."

"What notice might that be?"

"The one that informed me that all I owed at the mercantile had to be paid in full." It was a good response to a carefully thought out question.

"The notice that you reacted to badly?"

"I didn't say that. But sure, I was worried about it. I owed money and I didn't have it. I think that would worry most people."

"I agree. But you took it a step further didn't you? You were angry at the situation so you decided to do something. Like try to get back at Mr. Nash."

"Damn right I was angry. I mean the way I figured it, he had everything and it wasn't enough. So I was forced to do something that ripped my guts out I'm very sorry to say." Cole shifted position. For the first time he noticed that the chair was not comfortable. Perhaps it was by design.

"Like set fire to the mercantile?"

"What? No. I didn't do that." Cole looked at them squarely in the eye with a rock solid look.

"Then what did you do?"

"I went crawling on my belly to ask for an extension. I ain't ever done anything like that in my life." The self loathing in his voice was evident.

"And what happened?"

"He told me that an extension was not possible. He needed me to pay in full."

"Then what?"

"Then nothing. I started to leave thinking I might go to the bank. I knew I'd probably be turned down because I still owed them money from repairs I made to the Priscilla."

"So did you go to the bank?"

"No. I guess he could tell how desperate I was because he called me back and told me he had a proposition for me." So far the line of questioning had not taken him in any direction he had not thought of.

"What kind of a proposition?"

"He wanted me to take Mrs. Nash to Seattle."

"Why Seattle?"

"I didn't ask. It wasn't any of my business. I figured a fancy lady like her probably needed more than she could get in Valda Bay. This is a busy town with a lot of fancy ladies like her."

"Tell me about the proposition."

"He said that if I took her quietly on the Priscilla, he would forget all about my debt at the mercantile. I told him that I needed more money than that because my debt was small compared to what it would cost to take her to Seattle. You know, I sure would like a smoke if you have one on you. The constable here didn't allow us much." Cole was grateful when Chief Johnson reached into his pocket and offered him one of his cigars.

"Thank you Chief." He lit it and sat back in his chair to enjoy the effect.

"So did Mr. Nash pay you more money or did he refuse?"

"He agreed and said he would mark my account cleared once I returned to Valda Bay and informed him that Mrs. Nash was safe in Seattle."

"How much did he give you?"

"He gave me fifty dollars in cash. He put it in that little bag that Mr. Jones so willingly gave to that little bitch Mrs. Nash." He took a long puff off the cigar and looked at them in the way one man looks at another to make them understand that she was something else.

"Let's put that aside for just a moment. Tell me what you did to get ready for the trip."

"The usual. What do you mean?"

"Did you do anything out of the ordinary to prepare the Priscilla for a lady passenger?"

"No."

"Where did she put her things?"

"I don't know. I made a little curtain for her bunk so she could have a little privacy. I guess she kept them in her trunk."

"Did she bring the trunk on board?"

"Yeah. She only had one trunk."

"So a lady, very petite carried a large trunk all by herself. Is that what you want me to believe?"

"No. I said she had a trunk. I never said she carried it. I can tell you exactly how the trunk came to be on the Pricilla. I was busy getting supplies and Flint was making preparations to get underway. I didn't have time to go get the trunk for her because I wanted to be able to depart on the tide. I asked Leroy Grazer to get it for her and bring it to the boat." Cole knew he had to be very careful because he wasn't dealing with the likes of Constable Jones.

"Did he?"

"He did."

"The supplies you purchased—did you pay in cash or was it part of the deal?"

"It was part of the deal."

"What did you purchase?"

"Food items mostly. I got a can of coffee, some sugar, flour, eggs, bacon, lamp oil, and a pair of new gloves."

"What happened to the old ones?"

"I threw them out." Cole had already thought about the gloves he used to split open the barrel of oil. In the unlikely event they did not burn up, he had created a good cover story. Mr. Nash was dead so he couldn't say otherwise.

"Do you remember where?"

"At the mercantile. Why?"

"Was that after you set it on fire?"

"I didn't do that. I have no reason to want to burn down the store."

"Let's talk about Mrs. Nash for a moment. Were you two having an affair that just didn't work out?"

"No! I only provided that woman transportation to Seattle."

"What about her claims that you made her wear men's clothing to hide her presence on the boat?"

"That's true. I did ask her to wear men's clothing—for her protection of all stupid things. There are a lot of boats on that ocean out there. I didn't have the men or weapons to protect her in case of a confrontation from men wanting a woman. I didn't want to see her raped on the high sea. Did she say I made her dress that way to degrade her? Is that what she said?" Cole was pretending to be angry.

"How long did she wear the men's clothing?"

"The whole trip. Look, I'm getting tired of all this. When can I go?"

"Just a few more questions. When was the last time you saw Rudolph Nash?"

"The day we left for Seattle."

"Was it night or day?"

"Night."

"Was he alone?"

"He was saying goodbye to Mrs. Nash at the harbor. I think they were having some kind of an argument."

"What did they say?"

"Who the hell knows? I'm no snoop. I just wanted to get paid and be gone."

"So you're saying that when you pulled out of the harbor he was alive and had just had an argument with his wife."

"That's right."

"Mr. Ralston, when did you first learn of Mr. Nash's death?"

"When Constable Jones arrested me at the hotel in front of the damn world."

"You didn't know before that?"

"No."

"Why didn't you know since you were seen reading the paper and the story was all over the cover page?"

"I can't read," it was not said too loudly.

"What was that?"

"I said I can't read," he said it more loudly.

"According to Constable Jones you didn't seem too surprised that Mr. Nash was dead. Why is that? Could it be because you killed him?"

"I was worried about myself at the moment. Is that a crime?"

"No. But slitting open someone's throat is."

"Is that how he died?"

"Stop playing games with me. You know that you killed him, robbed him and hoped to leave Seattle before you were discovered. Now, tell us the truth about what really happened. It will go easier for you."

"I didn't do it. Now I have a question. How is it that you knew I was reading the newspaper? Were you there or are you getting all this second hand so to speak?"

"You were seen by the hotel clerk."

"Oh, you mean that skinny peacock behind the desk?"

"Tell me again, why you killed Mr. Nash—there was a witness."

"Impossible. I didn't kill Mr. Nash, burn his store or anything else. Maybe your so called witness did it and is trying to blame me. Ever think about that? Who is this witness anyway?"

"That's not important right now. What is important is that you were seen running away from the murder scene."

"And this witness saw me kill Mr. Nash? He said it was me without a doubt, not someone like me, but rather me without a doubt?" Cole was worried for the first time since the beginning of the interrogation.

"Now you're getting it."

"That's wrong. I'd like to speak with him."

"How do you know it's a man?"

"Who else would be out at that hour of the night walking around like they were on a Sunday stroll? It had to be a man who wasn't afraid to be out after dark. He could even look like me and therefore blamed me. Who found the body Chief Johnson?" Cole could sense that he was planting doubt in the minds of the two men questioning him.

"It's not your place to ask questions. That's my job."

"I have a right to know who plans on stretching my neck wouldn't you say? Isn't the law that I know my accuser?"

"Leroy Grazer found the body."

"Leroy Grazer?"

"That's right."

"Well how do you know that he didn't kill Mr. Nash? He found the body, he's about my height and build and everyone knows he's an idiot. He has an ax to grind with Mr. Nash not me. If I remember correctly, at one time Mr. Nash fired him for some difficulty in the store. Maybe he never forgot it. No one else would hire him in Valda Bay because of that incident. I can't believe this." He was acting like a professional on stage.

With those final words, Mr. Gordon and Chief Johnson looked at each other but did it in a manner that Cole could not see their faces. It was time to take a break. They needed to talk to each other in private.

"Mr. Ralston we are going to take five minutes. We'll be right back. Do you need anything before we go?"

"How about my freedom because I didn't do anything wrong? Can you tell my brother I'm alright? He'll be worried about me because I've been in here a long time."

"Sure." With that final word they left the room not as certain of things as they had been only one hour before.

"Could we be wrong about Ralston? His answers were believable and I've got to confess I'm not as certain as I was only one hour ago. What do you think?" Chief Johnson was expressing what he hoped they were both thinking.

"Well, he certainly has a reasonable response. It makes sense to me. But before we make any wrong conclusion, I suggest we talk to Flint." Mr. Gordon was also having some doubt. He hoped that Flint could shed some light on the situation.

"Good. I'll go and see to it now." Chief Johnson left and spoke with Constable Jones. In only a few minutes they were both talking to Flint.

"Mr. Ralston, we have a few questions we would like to ask." Chief Johnson did the questioning this time.

"I don't know anything." Flint remembered what his brother had told him.

"I haven't asked anything yet. But, I want you to know that you will be helping Cole a great deal by just telling us a few things. That won't be too bad now will it?"

"I don't know."

"Believe me when I tell you that Cole won't mind. We've already spoken with him. He knows we are speaking with you."

"He does?"

"Yes."

"Well alright."

"Let's go back to the night you left Valda Bay. Tell me what happened."

"Well, it was night and Cole wanted to leave with the tide. He went to buy stuff for us to eat and he told me to stay on the Priscilla and get ready to leave."

"Were you alone?"

"Yeah."

"The whole time he was gone?"

"No, not the whole time. Leroy Grazer brought over a trunk that belonged to Mrs. Nash."

"I see. Did you and he put the trunk on the Priscilla?"

"No. Cole and I did that. He was back pretty quick."

"Where did Cole go?"

"To buy stuff like I told you."

"Did he have anything with him when he returned?"

"Just the coffee, sugar, bacon and some other stuff. I don't know. When can I see Cole? Is he alright?"

"Cole is fine. Now, did you see Mr. Nash at all that night?"

"Yeah."

"When was that?"

"When he said goodbye to Mrs. Nash before we left."

"What were they doing? Did he kiss her goodbye or give her a small present?"

"No. I think they had a fight. They were talking kind of loud."

"Then what?"

"Nothing. Cole and I finished doing what we had to and then we sailed away."

"I see. Well, I think we are done here. I'll tell Cole you said hello and are fine."

"When can we go home? How long will we be here?"

"We'll let you know as soon as we can."

"I hope it's soon."

When Flint was returned to his cell, there wasn't a doubt in his mind that he had done exactly as Cole instructed him to do over the past several days. He had said only what he had been told to say and not one thing more. He would tell Cole everything that transpired and more importantly about the police attempt to play them against each other.

Chief Johnson and Mr. Gordon were now convinced they could prove nothing. They had been on the right trail but all they had was circumstantial evidence. The Ralston's had explained everything in complete detail and had no hesitation in doing so. They both knew that the other guilty person had probably sailed away earlier and had made them all look like a pair of amateurs. They returned to the room where Cole Ralston was waiting. He was tired and wondered what had kept the Inspectors. He felt nervous inside but hid it well.

"Mr. Ralston, I'm pleased to inform you that you are free to go." Inspector Gordon broke the news.

"I am? What about Flint?" He could not believe his ears.

"He's free to go as well. I regret you were detained for so long."

"Well, I'm just glad you came from Valda Bay and got things straightened out. I assure you we are leaving as soon as possible. I never want to see Seattle again." He stood up and offered his hand in appreciation for their hard work. He left the room and had to resist giving out a yell. He went to the front desk and was given his personal effects and was joined by Flint. The men hugged each other briefly and walked out of the police station free men. One hour later they were on the Priscilla laughing and preparing to leave. If all went well in less than two hours they would be underway with the high tide.

At the police station no one was laughing.

"You know my friend; my stomach feels as if I've eaten too many pickles," Inspector Gordon said.

"I feel the same way. I know that they are guilty but we had no choice but to let them go."

"You're right. Knowing someone is guilty and proving it are two different things."

"Well, we are in the big city for a short while. We might as well enjoy ourselves before we go home. I know of a place that has some terrific calms and good cold beer."

"What are we standing here for?"

When the Priscilla was a few hours at sea, the men on board had much to celebrate.

"Cole you said we would be alright and we are."

"Flint, we have a bottle of rum in the storage compartment. Let's celebrate our good turn of events."

"I'll drink to that." Flint started to get up from his seat but sat back down when he noticed that Cole had begun to speak.

"Let me tell you something that will make you enjoy that drink even more. Remember when we first arrived in Seattle and we were all busy preparing the boat to stay in the harbor for a while?"

"I remember."

"Well, I'm here to tell you that we aren't as broke as you think. I took most of the money out of my pouch that the stupid constable gave back to Elsa. We have all the money that was on Nash, most of what she paid us to take her to Seattle and all of the jewels except for two of the smaller pieces. I only took those with me because I needed to have something to sell to keep her from being suspicious. I considered that Elsa might be tempted to pull something like this on us and for our trouble I didn't want us to come out of this mess broke. I admit she did surprise me especially since things were going so well, but I know women like Elsa. That's why I didn't take all our money with us when we left the ship. Elsa had no idea how much money Nash had on him or she would have mentioned it. My guess is that he got it without her approval or knowledge. If she appeared not to care about the money, it made her story more believable. Either way we ended up with the goods. Come on, let's get our money now." Cole stood up and they began walking toward the stairs that led to the galley and the berth.

"Where is it? You said there wasn't a safe place on ship for that kind of money."

"That's true. So I nailed the pouch to the wall of the only safe place on ship—the head. I nailed it high enough that it's not under the sea water but still not visible if someone were crazy enough to look down the smelly hole. All they would see would be ocean. Believe me no one will be sticking their hand or head in the hole to look for money. We are rich men." Cole removed his shirt.

"I can hardly believe this, it's just too good." Flint had always trusted in Cole. His trust had just been rewarded again. "Do you need help?"

"No. I know exactly where it's at. Take off your hat and use it to catch the money and jewels. Then hand me a towel and that bar of soap. I'm going to drop the bag down the hole and then quickly go wash my arms and hands."

Flint did as instructed and was looking at a lot of money and jewels that even in the dim light of the cabin sparkled brightly. When Cole returned they poured out the rum and spoke of the future.

"Where are we going now?" Flint was not certain of the next move.

"Well, let's talk about it. We can pursue Elsa and get even with her for what she did to us or we can forget her for now and go to Mexico. What do you want to do?" Cole knew what he would say.

"Let's go to Mexico. I sure want to bed a pretty senorita." He grinned.

"Mexico it is."

# The Homecoming

*A*fter a couple of days of shopping for food and supplies James, Karin and Daniel were sitting in the galley of the North Star. They had been discussing the events of the past few days and were now ready to get on with their quest; to find the Rip Tide's treasure.

"I'm glad all this unpleasant business is over with. I'm ready to get back to the sea and start looking for the Rip Tide's treasure." Daniel didn't like the sights and sounds of the city.

"I think we all are. I've made some final calculations I'd like to discuss with you. If everyone agrees there is no reason why we can't sail at the first opportunity." James was reaching into his jacket pocket and pulled out some papers.

"What do you have there?" Daniel asked.

"The plotted course and what I believe to be the place that Mrs. Webb's sea captain buried the treasure."

"How do you know for sure?" Understanding sea charts was not one of her talents.

"I know that from the notes that Erik left us. He figured out that the whole point of making a circle on certain verses was to mark coordinates. Mrs. Webb's sea captain used the bible verses as numbers indicating the latitude and longitude of where he buried the treasure."

"But there were so many verses circled. How do you know in what order to put them?" The sea charts all seemed to look the same.

"Latitude is always figured before longitude. Knowing that, I took the verses in order as they appeared on the various chapters. They figured out to be 48 degrees and 13 minutes north. The next circled verses calculated to be 124 degrees and 7 minutes west. After I had the information I plotted them on the chart." James took his finger and showed her on the chart where he plotted the course.

"I'm still a little confused but keep going." She didn't want James to lose his train of thought. Daniel had probably been informed because he was not showing any response to the information. She concluded the explanation was only out of consideration for her.

"The coordinates on the nautical chart mark a place called Pillars Point. It's a rocky shore, isolated and the perfect place to go ashore and hide something quickly. It's our belief that the treasure is located there. I've already figured we can depart on the late tide tonight and make it to Port Angeles by tomorrow evening, maybe sooner. I don't think we need to travel at break neck speed and draw attention to our ship."

"That would allow us to reach Pillars Point with plenty of daylight left to look for some of the clues." Daniel offered.

"Exactly. On the way there we can make some final preparations for going ashore. I don't think we will have to walk very far once we are on the beach."

"Why is that?" She asked.

"Like we all discussed earlier, the treasure chest would be heavy especially if it's filled with gold coins. It's probably in some kind of a heavy wooden box with some metal and thick straps to reinforce it." James suggested.

"For that reason I think that the good captain would not go too far inland with it. He would want a safe place to hide or bury it not too far from the beach but most certainly out of the water." Daniel was looking at the maps.

"That's right." James agreed.

"I was thinking I might get some rest so I can take her out tonight. Will you wake me about one hour prior to setting sail?"

"Sure. In the mean time Karin and I can prepare for the trip as much as we can."

"See you both in a few hours." Daniel left them to go to his bunk.

"I hope I can sleep. I find myself so excited about tomorrow I can hardly stand it." Karin continued to look at the map. She trusted James and Daniel as she was sure Erik must have.

"I know what you mean. Just don't do too much and make yourself sick. I'll be on deck if you need me." He folded the charts and placed them in a safe place. In only a moment, he made his way to the deck. They were only a day or two away from what he hoped would be the lost treasure of the Rip Tide.

As Mr. Gordon and the Chief traveled to Valda Bay they resigned themselves to looking elsewhere for undisputable evidence of guilt as far as the Ralston brothers were concerned. The case would remain open and if by some investigative procedure evidence found that they were involved again—they had a place to begin anew.

"Well, in just a few days I'll be on my way home. I regret we didn't have a more successful conclusion to this case." Mr. Gordon felt certain that the guilty parties had escaped.

"We certainly did our best. But, there was a positive thing or two that came out of this. We can always work the case if anything new develops. Ian Fisk has a new life taking shape with a new job as a fire and insurance investigator, thanks to you. Mr. Chang opened new medical ideas and practices for everyone who is willing to let him help. That alone has tremendous value for everyone. But on the other hand, the town won't have a new mercantile and it was for absolutely nothing because it was a case of confirmed arson. That is what your report will say won't it?" Chief Johnson knew how disappointed his friend was with the outcome of the investigation.

"Everything you say is true. I sent the report before leaving Seattle to the insurance company and there will be no money paid out. It's all too bad. But, I'll be very glad to get Fisk into that school. It's a tough one but he seems up to the challenge. It's nice to know that Valda Bay is a nice town under normal circumstances. Maybe next year I can return and we can do some of that fishing, or maybe I should say releasing, that you told me about. Of course that will depend on that place you want to purchase being all fixed up for company."

"I'm sure it will be. I think I'll have it ready because one of the first things I'm going to do when I get home is to purchase it. You know you are welcome anytime. I also plan on looking in on Fisk until he's on his way to you. Will you let me know from time to time how he is doing?" Chief Johnson would miss Ian Fisk on the hose. He was a good man in many ways.

"Sure. We'll keep in touch; we've been friend too long not to." Mr. Gordon looked at his friend and even though no more words were spoken, much was said.

When the stage arrived in Valda Bay and departed a few days later, the men said goodbye in the same location they had first said hello. Chief Johnson felt a sense of loss with Mr. Gordon's departure but knew he would busy himself with his personal life which he had much neglected over the past several weeks. He wrote down all his notes about the case into a log book that he would keep to refresh his memory in the future should the need arise. He submitted his retirement papers and in only a few days would become a private citizen. He fixed up a small boat that he named Nora, in honor of his deceased wife, and planned on spending the lazy days of summer on the lake relaxing and fishing.

On another boat, it was anything but relaxing. There was much excitement on the day that Pillar Point came into view. Karin was amazed at the rugged beauty of the coastline and the rocky beach that loomed ahead. She wondered how they were going to get ashore so she decided to ask Daniel who was at the wheel.

"Daniel, how do you plan to get us ashore?"

"Do you see the point?"

"What point?"

"The rocks that are jetting out are called Pillar Point. To the east of Pillar Point is a small cove. We will approach from the west and anchor with the bow to the wind."

"Won't the water be too deep to walk in?"

"Yeah it will but we will take the dingy ashore with all our gear. It's big enough to hold all we need." He turned from her and called out to James.

"James, we're about ten minutes out and we need to prepare to anchor. I plan to approach from the west and we'll anchor in the cove with the bow to the wind."

"I'll take care of it." James moved to the bow while Karin stayed with Daniel. After a few minutes passed the boat had reached the cove.

"Go ahead and drop it and let me know when you feel it's hooked." He waited to hear from James.

"She's down and hooked solid. Are you ready to drop canvas?" James called out.

"Yes. I'll take the aft and you take the mainsail." Daniel moved into action. In a few additional minutes, the North Star was secure at anchor in the cove. It was not to long before the three partners were standing on the beach. They had brought everything they needed to spend a few days on shore and took a few minutes to look around at everything from where they were standing.

"So, where do we begin?" She asked.

"Let's move a little inland. Remember we are looking for a high point and a waterfall." James did not want to set up camp so close to the water.

"I noticed as we were coming ashore, there was a small creek to the west. Maybe the creek will lead us to a waterfall." Daniel had the advantage of looking at the shoreline from being at the wheel longer.

"It sounds as good as an idea as any. We might be able to hear the waterfall once we get away from the noise of the beach." They all agreed and began to walk in the direction of the creek. They followed the creek for about twenty minutes and then stopped.

"I wonder if the good captain would have gone this far inland to bury something so heavy." Daniel was thinking they were on the wrong trail.

"Wait a minute. I hear water. Do you hear that?" Karin looked at them. They waited and listened.

"I don't hear anything. Do you Daniel?" James looked at him with hope.

"Not a thing. Are you sure Karin?" James asked.

"I'm sure. Let's go in a little further." They followed where her ears led them. In a few minutes there before them was a lovely waterfall gently falling over smooth rocks and into a small pond that overflowed and became the small creek they had been following.

"I told you I heard water," she said with excitement in her voice.

"You sure did and there it is." The men stood at the front of the waterfall and remembered what the clue said to do.

"So, which one of you is going to stand in the pond?" She inquired.

"James, you stand in the pond and I'll climb something high to help you see the lofty ledge. Or you can climb and I'll go wading. Which do you prefer?"

"I think I'll go stand in the pond." James rolled up his pants and removed his socks and shoes and waded into the very cold water.

"Damn, its freezing!" He called out.

"Forget that you're freezing. What do you see?" Daniel yelled back. Karin continued to watch his progress.

"Nothing." He called back. He looked around for several more minutes.

"Turn around again slowly." Karin suggested.

"I see something that looks like a high ledge. That could be it but I don't see any birds of any kind. It's the only high thing around. It's to the south east from where I'm looking. Do you see it from up there? I've got to get out of this cold water." James waded back and sat down on a rock to brush away the sand and rub his feet to get them warm again. They waited to hear from Daniel.

"Do you see anything yet?" James called out again to Daniel who had now reached the top of a large fallen tree.

"I see the high ledge and it looks like some kind of nest may have been there at one time or another. That's got to be it." He climbed back down and joined James and Karin.

"Do we head for the ledge now?" Karin asked.

"We head to the ledge." James had just finished putting on his socks and shoes.

"How far do you think it is?" She was not feeling sick or tired but she was curious since she had not seen what the two men had seen.

"It might be a stretch. Are you doing alright?" He was thinking of the baby.

"I'm doing well." She smiled at him for his concern.

"Actually it's closer than you think. From the top of the tree I could see a trail of sorts that led across the waterfall. If we climb up there and then walk toward the ledge we can save a lot of time." Daniel didn't think the climb too difficult.

They began to climb helping each other along the way and after about an hour of walking they reached the lofty ledge spoken of in the poem. It was as Daniel observed and there was evidence that at one time eagles had nested there. There were several feathers that came from the majestic birds still stuck in the material of the nest. The three looked around a bit more and saw no other nesting sites or lofty ledges.

"The poem says we have to walk away. Walk away to where?" Daniel was looking but could not see where they were to walk.

"It doesn't say walk away very far. Maybe we just have to take a few steps backwards." She didn't see that making much sense either.

"Don't forget the part about the sky. We have to look to the sky."

"That's right. Let's look up." They all looked up as James suggested.

"I don't see anything but a blue sky and a few clouds."

"Me too."

"What is it about the sky he wrote exactly?" Daniel inquired.

"He wrote that we walk away and watch the sky," Karin said

"So let's watch the sky." They watched the sky for a few minutes and like before nothing happened.

"This is crazy, we're missing it," Daniel said.

"I know why this isn't working—the next line of the poem tells us why we are watching the sky. It says when the sun is halfway to the sea or something like that."

"So you're thinking the real clue is not the sky but rather the sun in the sky. Something must happen with the sun." James looked up toward the sun to see where it was at this time of day. It was almost overhead.

"It has to be half way to the sea. That means almost sunset to me. What do you think?"

"No. I don't think it means sunset but rather early afternoon. That would make the sun about half way to going down. The line specifically says half way. So what time of the day is halfway between the sky and the sea?"

"I would guess from noon until about one o'clock in the afternoon." He took out his pocket watch.

"Well, it's about eleven o'clock. The sun is at the wrong position. We have a small wait and I think we should refresh ourselves. Let's get something to eat and in about an hour we can see if anything happens." James suggested the lunch break for Karin whom he was certain would appreciate it.

"We can make some sandwiches. I brought bread, cheese and fruit. While we wait we can position ourselves so that each of us is facing a different direction. We can each keep an eye out for anything unusual that might give us a clue. Remember he said something about shadows that may fall."

Everyone thought it was a good idea so they sat down and had lunch. After they finished eating they patiently waited for something to happen knowing that they had no idea at all of what it could be. They didn't speak much but enjoyed the quiet beauty that was all around them. When James noticed the sun was casting a shadow on the beach, they all stood up quickly and began to take in the scene before them.

"Quick, look at the beach. There are some shadows being cast by the sun right now." James was pointing toward the beach.

"The last clue says that old shadows will fall for his love or something like that. I don't see anything like old shadows. They all look the same." Daniel was looking down on the beach where several shadows were now visible and more were appearing at a fast rate.

"I don't see anything either," James offered.

"I do," Karin said

"Where?" James asked.

"It's not far from where we came ashore. Look at the boat and then look up and to the right. Do you see two rock formations that are casting two shadows? Let's watch for another few minutes to see what happens." Karin was certain she was right.

"We might as well." Daniel looked at his watch and marked the time. After only four minutes passed, the rocks began to form only one shadow when the larger rock overshadowed the smaller. Both men focused their attention to where she had suggested.

"They are separate until the sun hits the rocks and changes their individual shadows. It makes them appear as one for a short time. When the larger shadow covers the smaller one it's like a marriage and he is protecting her. I bet that's the old shadow he was talking about. Those rocks have been there for longer than anyone knows. That's got to be the spot." She turned to them to see if they could see what she was looking at.

"I can see it now. Could that really be it?" Daniel asked.

"I've marked the spot well in case it is." James wanted to benefit the most from the sun in the event there was another possible location, so he turned his attention to other shadowed areas as well. Everything else was blended in a tangle of mixed shadows that seemed very ordinary to him, while others did not change much at all.

"I think that is the spot. It's high enough for the treasure not to be washed away in the tide and permanent enough not to be changed with time. Let's get down there. I think we've done it." The excitement was evident in Daniel's voice.

Just short of an hour later, they stood by the rock and prepared to dig. They started to dig at the exact spot where the shadows first came together. The only question that remained was whether or not they would find the treasure. After digging for about ten minutes, the sound of metal hitting upon something solid caused them to pause.

"Did you hear that?" Daniel asked.

"I did and I don't think you hit a rock." James stopped digging with his shovel and fell to his knees. He began to feel around with his hands and in less than half a minute looked up and gave them a big smile.

"What is it?" It had been a long time since she felt so excited and nervous. In fact the last time she felt like she did now was the day she married Erik. It was a good feeling.

"Daniel, give me a hand. I'm feeling a container of some kind and it's heavy." He moved over so Daniel could help him lift it out. Both men were now attempting to lift it. It didn't move.

"Damn. It's too heavy. We have to dig more to be able to get the head of the shovel underneath it." They stood up and began digging with a sense of urgency.

"What can I do to help?" Karin asked.

"Nothing. We just about have it." Daniel lifted the chest with his shovel and James used his strength to place it along the side of the hole. As predicated the chest was made of metal and wood. It was locked or rusted closed from all the years it had been buried. There were visible signs of damage from the ravages of time and moisture.

"I see it but I can't believe I'm looking at it." Karin had fallen to her knees and was now looking at the box and touching it.

"I think we should take it to the North Star right away. If we open it here, there's no telling what might spill out. It's not in the best of shape. We can open it on deck. Let's fill in the hole and get out of here." James being an old sailor didn't want to push their luck. Buried pirate treasure was a real prize and it was sought after by sailors for longer than he could remember. His eyes scanned the area.

"You're right. Karin, do you think you could shove the sand back into the hole?" We will take the chest to the dingy and come back for the other stuff.

"I can." She stood up and began shoving the sand with her hands and by the time the men returned—all evidence of the hole was gone.

It seemed to take forever to row back to the boat. Karin could not wait to open the chest. As the men rowed, she thought of Erik. How she wished he could have been here with his friends as they made the discovery. She found some comfort in the fact that he had been right. Even if the treasure chest was empty—they had found something and all his efforts had given them a wonderful adventure and a stronger friendship.

On the North Star, James, Daniel and Karin were looking at the treasure chest. James had gotten some tools and was working to open it while Daniel held it firmly in place. When the lock finally yielded they resisted the urge to open it. They slowly moved away from the chest looking at what they hoped would be a discovery of a lifetime.

"Karin, no matter what is or what isn't in this chest, Daniel and I want to say that we're glad you allowed us to share this moment with you. I know it belonged to you and Erik and if not for his grandmother this would not even be happening for us. Thank you for including us in this." He motioned for her to open the chest and he stepped aside to stand by Daniel.

"Thank you for saying that. Let's open it," she said it with great emotion in her voice.

Karin took a deep breath and lifted the lid. Her hands flew to her mouth and she looked up at them wide eyed and totally amazed.

"Look at it!" She dropped her hands and placed them inside the chest and grabbed fists full of jewels.

"We did it!" Daniel was beside himself with excitement, something that rarely if ever happened. He reached into the chest and picked up several of the gold coins.

"It's filled with gold coins, diamonds and emeralds. It's a great fortune." She was almost speechless and began to cry.

"I can't believe it. Look at the size of these diamonds and emeralds. This diamond alone is about the size of a small peach pit." James had also reached in and was admiring a large diamond that he held up to the sun which created bright colors that sparkled from within the stone.

"There must be a several hundred gold pieces of eight." Daniel saw countless coins in the chest and was admiring the ones in his hands up close.

"Look at the inside of the box. It's from a ship called the Rip Tide." Karin noticed the name on the lid of the box.

"Rip Tide? Then it was all true about what they said about Erik's grandmother and the pirate that loved her. I had heard the rumors and talk in the taverns, but I never gave it any thought. This is incredible." James remembered all the stories he had heard of the famous treasure and the rogue pirate who dared to love a lady missionary.

"It is but evidently it was true. Imagine after all these years. It was meant for Erik's grandmother. Now, her great grandchild will have it. That's something isn't it?" James said.

"It is. I can't thank you enough for making this possible for me. I'm glad you are my friends." Karin had smudges on her face from where she had wiped away tears with dirty hands from covering the hole on the beach.

"How much is this treasure worth?" Karin was standing up and went to hug them both.

"It's a fortune beyond measure. It has to be worth countless thousands, maybe millions." James was touching several pieces at once.

"I don't want to be a spoiler, but we need to get this treasure picked up and set sail. I'll feel better when we are underway. Right now, we could be sitting ducks for any other boat that happens by." Daniel had calmed down enough to think of the danger they were in.

"You're right of course. Let's get this down below and then we can clean it up and admire it later." James knew that what Daniel said made good sense.

In the few days it took to sail home, they cleaned each piece of jewelry as well as the gold coins. It was decided to keep the chest as proof that they had found the lost treasure of the Rip Tide. The chest coupled with the rumors of Erik's grandmother would ensure that they were in the clear of any accusations of theft or gain by misfortune. Satisfied that they had thought of everything necessary to protect the treasure and themselves they celebrated their good fortune.

"Karin, we were thinking that before we reach Valda Bay, you should pick the jewels you want. The treasure was yours and Erik's first and it would make us feel better if you did." They were all seated in the galley when they spoke of this to her.

"That's very kind of you. I would like to have just one stone in particular. It's the only ruby in the box and it reminds me of something Erik once said to me." She smiled at them.

"It's yours. Take it and place it someplace safe. When the world wants to see the treasure, we won't mention the ruby." James spoke and Daniel nodded his head.

That night Karin was in her bunk with Salty at her feet. She remembered Erik and clutched the ruby to her heart. She remembered how happy and nervous she was the first time she was alone with Erik after becoming his wife. She was not certain what to expect and didn't want to disappoint Erik with her lack of experience in intimate matters. He comforted her with how a ruby and a woman's virtue were both very special. She never forgot what he said. He was gone but the memory of his love would stay with her forever.

After several days at sea, the North Star and her crew reached Valda Bay.

"Karin, are you sure that you won't have me go with you?" James did not like the idea of her walking alone to the bank. There would be rumor and speculation about her return since she departed under the pretense of being taken to her family. He did not want her detained by those who might be bold enough to approach her.

"I will be just fine. I will walk calmly and directly to the bank. It's not far and it's the middle of the day." She offered him a reassuring smile and left him and Daniel to secure the ship and watch the treasure. Her walk was uneventful and when she reached the bank and went inside she let out a small sigh of relief. She approached a man who was behind the counter. He did not appear interested in helping her and after standing by the counter for several minutes, she finally spoke up.

"Excuse me. I'd like to see the bank president if he is available." She looked for any reaction. The man looked up briefly then returned to his paperwork.

"He's busy. Can anyone else help you?" It was spoken with complete indifference.

"Will you please inform him that I'm here on a matter of some importance? I'll be pleased to wait a few moments." She used her most official sounding tone.

"Be seated and I'll tell him." He looked over to some chairs by a large window where she could wait. After another few minutes passed he left to inform the president of her request to see him. Karin did not like the man's attitude toward her and no doubt thought that women had little or no business conducting important banking matters. When he returned from the president's office, he spoke in a rather curt manner.

"It appears the president has a pressing appointment in a few minutes. You'll have to come back tomorrow." He turned to leave.

"Please wait. Did you tell him it was very important?"

"I informed him you would like to see him. I can only tell you what I was told. Now, if you will excuse me." He walked back behind the counter leaving Karin still seated in the waiting area. He had dismissed her. She sat for only a few moments and was contemplating her next move when she saw the president walk past her going toward the door. She took the opportunity to speak with him despite it being considered rude.

"Excuse me. I'm Karin Johansson." She looked at him hoping he would recognize her from the one encounter they had only a few weeks ago. He did.

"Mrs. Johansson, I must say I'm a little surprised to see you. I thought you had departed to be with your family." He looked at his watch.

"I did leave for a time. But, now it's most important I speak with you now." She looked at him and could see he was debating between giving her a few minutes and being late for what she thought must have been an important meeting.

"I have a business luncheon to attend. I'll return in a couple of hours, we can speak then." He expected her to say that it would be acceptable.

"No. This is much more important that any business luncheon. I believe you will agree with me once you know the nature of my visit."

"I see. Well, in that case perhaps I can give you five minutes. Let's go into my office." He motioned for her to walk in front of him and when they walked inside, she turned and faced him. She shut the door behind her and he was shocked at this most bold move. They had no chaperone.

"Mrs. Johansson, this is highly irregular. I must insist that you open the door. Our reputations are subject to soiling. My wife would not appreciate the gossip." He started to move past her but she remained standing by the door and blocking it closed.

"What I have to say requires privacy. Are you ready to listen for only a minute?" She braced herself against the door.

"Yes, yes! Quickly get on with it!" He took a handkerchief out of his vest and wiped his mouth. He was regretting his decision to give her five minutes.

"Sir, my friends and I have found the lost treasure of the Rip Tide. It's in our possession now and I need your help in bringing it to the bank for safety. It's a large fortune and it will need protection. I trust you can help us?" She was relieved to have finally said it.

"What? You found the treasure from the Rip Tide?" He was more than shocked.

"Yes. Can you help us protect it in your bank safe until we decide what to do with it?"

"Are you sure it's from the Rip Tide? It's said to be worth millions."

"I'm certain. Here is a sample of what we discovered." She reached into her purse and retrieved two gold coins, a large emerald and diamond ring and a pair of pearl earrings. She handed them over to him.

Walking over to the light he admired the pieces and looked at her. "I'm stunned to say the least. Let me think a moment." He sat down at his desk and she gave him a moment to gather his thoughts. When he didn't speak, she did.

"Chief Johnson may be able to help us. Perhaps you could send for him." Erik always spoke highly of Chief Johnson and she knew him to be a person of honor and integrity.

"The business luncheon! It's in his honor. The local business men are meeting to give him a small gift in appreciation for all he's done for our town. I'll send word that he's to come here immediately. In fact, I'll send for all of them to come. That way, we all see the treasure at once and there is safety in numbers."

"That's a great idea."

"Let me get someone to run to Mrs. Steele's and bring everyone here." He looked at her and then spoke again as he rose from his desk. "Congratulations on your discovery. I'll be anxious to hear how it all came about." He walked toward her and handed back the things she had given him. Opening the door he called out to the man at the counter and gave him instructions. The man left immediately wondering what in the world could have been so important. He had never known the president to close the doors and be alone with a lady before.

"You never did say where the treasure is now. Can you tell me?" He looked at her hoping she would reveal its whereabouts. He wanted to break the news but knew it was not his place.

"When everyone arrives you can make the announcement of its discovery. I'll disclose the information at that time. I have to consider my partners."

"Partners?"

"Yes. You'll be told everything in only a few more minutes. Thank you for giving me the five minutes. I think I took a little longer than that." She gave a little laugh, and he joined her.

The president posted a closed sign out front. It was not long before only the president, Karin and two bank employees were in the bank. When the small crowd arrived there was much anticipation. Among the group was Chief Johnson. He hoped this development would not affect his retirement plans as everyone stood still waiting for what would come. The president began to speak and a tense hush fell over the room.

"Gentlemen, I have a wonderful bit of news. It appears a discovery of great wealth and historical significance has come to my attention. I'm pleased to announce that the lost treasure of the Rip Tide has been discovered and in only a few moments ..." He was interrupted by gasps and disclaimers of his statement.

"Gentlemen, please I know how you feel. I felt that way myself only a few minutes ago. But, I assure you it's true. I have seen proof of the treasure and in only a moment, we will all see it. The bank will remain closed until further notice. I will send word to the telegraph office that additional security will be required. Until then, Chief Johnson, may we depend upon your experience in safeguarding the treasure?"

"You can depend upon me. I'll need someone to go to the telegraph and inform the authorities that we need some security specialist here as soon as possible. I can draft a note if someone will take it." He knew the job was too big for him alone.

"I have a man standing ready. Prepare your note." He went to the counter and drafted a note with his request. He did not elaborate on specific details only that the request was urgent and he needed at least four men come as soon as possible. He instructed the courier to wait for a response. The courier made haste.

"Gentlemen, I'd like to introduce the person who made this wonderful discovery. I give you Mrs. Erik Johansson." From inside his office, Karin made her presence known. The room fell silent.

"Mrs. Johansson, if you please." The president turned his platform over to her.

"Thank you. It is true. The treasure from the Rip Tide is now in my possession. It's currently with my partners until such time I'm advised by Chief Johnson to disclose its location. Chief Johnson when may I do that?"

"That depends on only one thing. Is the bank prepared to safeguard such a fortune until the security men come from Rock Port? I anticipate it will be only a few hours until they arrive."

"We are. I'll close the bank and post two security men here as well as you and I and any others who wish to work as guards. I'll pay well for that service and provide meals and any weapons required." He was glad that he had required his employees to all have training in bank security. That had been accomplished at the request of Chief Johnson years before.

"I see no reason why its location can't be disclosed. We could go in a group for safety and honesty." About the time that Chief Johnson finished speaking, the courier arrived with the response from Rock Port. Everyone in the room waited for him to read it before speaking. "Gentlemen it appears that three security specialists will arrive by early evening. This is most welcome news. I think we should go and get the treasure together and place it in the safe. I think if Mrs. Johansson would disclose the location of the treasure, we can all go and safeguard it here."

"Gentlemen, if you will follow me, I shall take you to the treasure." Karin moved toward the door and the small group of men followed.

It was not long before James and Daniel saw the group approaching. They were relieved that Karin had been successful and it appeared everything went as they had planned. The treasure was removed from the North Star and taken to the bank. Once inside, all precautions were taken. The treasure was inventoried, signed for and secured. Several men stayed behind to serve as guards because they wanted to be a part of this historical moment. An artist was sent for to begin drawing the most valuable pieces. Everyone in town was talking about the treasure. Most were happy for the three, but a few resented Karin and her good fortune. The women in town who were often unkind to her were uncertain of what to do in her presence. Once considered socially unacceptable to them, she was now rich beyond belief. The women in town were not certain what to do when they encountered her. Karin did what she did best … she took little notice of them.

"Karin, what will you do with your share of the treasure?" The three friends had never discussed personal plans before.

"I'll give some pieces to a museum. I'd like the public to see the beautiful and historic pieces. Some I'll sell for the obvious reasons. But, I think what I really want to do is help Doctor Grayson expand the hospital. The rest, I'm not sure of yet. I never gave much thought to being so rich. I think I'll buy a house by the ocean and plant a big flower garden. What about you?" She looked at James.

"I don't know. I'd like to modernize the Sea Star. Maybe travel a while and then come back to Valda Bay and open a fine mercantile. Make it a grand store with the prospects to expand to other cities and towns. Then, I'd like to live right here and be close to my true friends."

"Daniel, what will you do?" Karin asked.

"Well, I think the town will continue to grow. In one respect I hate that but we can't stop progress. So, I think I'll open up a lumber mill. I'm tired of seeing fisherman go hungry when the season is bad. The mill will provide a good living because I think it's going to be a big industry. Lumber will be needed for all the construction that will no doubt come our way. Then I plan on living right here and in just a short while I'm going to get married."

"Married? To whom?" Karin couldn't help asking the question.

"I never said anything because I couldn't afford to get married anyway, but now … well things are a bit different." He smiled.

"Who Daniel?" James asked.

"Laurel, she works at The Foggy Inn." Daniel replied

"The Foggy Inn?" Karin tried to hide the disbelief and disappointment in her voice.

"She's the baker at The Foggy Inn," James said with joy in his voice.

"That's her. She took your place when you married Erik. I've been seeing her for about a year and a half. She's a good person but because she works at the Inn, well you know how that goes. She's never been in the back room business. In fact, she's a lot like you, bakes well except for the bread." He grinned.

"I'm happy for you. Let us know what she says." Karin reached out and hugged him.

"Congratulations." James said as he reached out to shake his hand. He was happy for Daniel but some part of him was sad at the same time. He knew about Laurel but never thought the relationship was very serious. No one spoke as the three of them realized things had changed and would never be the same again.

# *Epilogue*

*A*s the months and years unfolded, each went about their lives. Daniel started his lumber company and soon had several other companies in various towns. The town grew as he predicted and he always found work for the fishermen when the season proved bad. He married Laurel and they had a daughter and two sons.

James traveled for a couple of years but always kept in touch with Karin. He returned to Valda Bay and built a prosperous and honestly run mercantile. He soon had plans for several others in the neighboring states. He employed several people in town.

Mei Ling Sung and her husband remained in Valda Bay. They had three daughters and a son. Karin purchased a large piece of land that she presented to them as a wedding gift. It would have been considered rude not to accept it especially when Karin presented it quietly and without any publicity. She knew that Dr. Sung wanted to build a good modern hospital for people in China Town who did not yet trust in Dr. Grayson. It was built and served the community well. Dr. Grayson and Dr. Sung often worked together on cases.

Dr. Grayson was asked to speak in a conference of his peers concerning the care of burns. Attitudes changed and new treatments were implemented. Many lives were saved as a result.

Chief Johnson retired, bought the cabin on the lake and fixed it up. He was often visited by Mr. Gordon who did learn to appreciate the art of releasing fish. Mr. Gordon also retired and he and his wife traveled abroad often.

Salty grew up and became quite irresistible to the ladies. White kittens were often seen running and playing in Karin's garden.

Valda Bay became a fine place to live. One summer day a little boy and his great grandfather were sitting on some rocks enjoying a day of fishing.

"Grandfather, what is your name?" A little boy of five years asked.

"My Christian name is Quinton. Why do you ask?" Mr. Webb looked at his great grandson with love.

"I was wondering about my name. Mama says she named me Erik after my daddy." He was looking out to sea more than looking at his fishing pole.

"That's right, she did." He smiled at the boy who looked so much like his grandson Erik; one would have thought the elder reborn.

"Did he like to fish and be on the water too?" He looked at his pole then out to sea.

"Oh yes. In fact your great grandmother Esther used to have to scold him sometimes because that boy just wanted to spend every waking minute on the water. Sometimes because he didn't want to study his lessons ... and you know how your mama gets when that happens. Well, your great grandmother got the same way." He chuckled a little under his breath.

"I want to be a sailor like my daddy. I don't want to help in my father's mercantile. And, I don't think I want to work with Mr. Batley as a land server in his lumber company." He had a bit of a sour face when he mentioned either one of those things.

"It called a surveyor son, not a server." He corrected.

"Oh, well, anyway I don't want to be that either." He countered.

"Erik, there is nothing wrong with wanting to be a sailor. Working at the mercantile with your father can be very good. James is a fine man and he loves you very much."

"I love him too. Mama says that he picked us from all the families he could have had. I can't wait until I'm big so I can get a boat and go out on the ocean. I know, maybe my baby brother James will help him in the store." He looked at his great grandfather as if the problem had just been solved.

"Maybe. Tell you what, don't say anything about this until you are a little older and if you still feel the same, I bet he'll understand. What do you think?"

"I think that's a good idea." He reached out to check his pole and noticed that the bait was gone. "Grandfather, the fish ate my bait and I didn't even know it!" He had a look of despair on his face.

"It happens if you don't pay attention." He reached for more bait to put on the boy's line but before he could put more on, he heard James approaching from behind them.

"Son, your mother is waiting for you to eat some lunch. You better not keep her waiting."

"She is? I'm hungry. Are you coming too Grandfather?" He picked up his pole and secured the hook like he had been shown.

"Not just yet. You go ahead," he replied. Erik was off running toward the house in only a moment.

"He's getting big and looks so much like Erik it's amazing." James sat down next to Quinton Webb. The men liked each other and agreed upon most things. Ever since James married Karin they had become very close.

"I hope Erik didn't make you crazy with a million questions," James said.

"No. He was just asking me about his namesake."

"He was? I've told him often that his daddy was a good man and an even better friend. I still miss him. I'm sure that Karin does. I know that this sounds awful, but there are times that I think I see her remembering him at our special moments and I'm not sure what to make of it or what to do or say." For a moment he wondered if he should have said anything at all since he was Erik's grandfather.

"Say nothing James. I had the same experience with my Esther over another Erik. I lived with it and so can you. Just love her and one day you'll find it just doesn't matter. You have each other and that's more than a lot of people have." He looked at him with an understanding that went beyond words.

"You knew about Captain Erik all this time?" He was surprised.

"Sure. But I also knew that I was loved. That was enough. You can't fight a memory or a past. Don't try. Make your own memories with Karin and live life fully. Enjoy your sons. Believe that she loves you and that she will love you more with the passing of the years. That's all a man needs—because in the end that's all that matters.

# RuCutta Vineyards

# *Threatened*

Rue looked concerned. "Can we save them Joaquin?" She asked.
He looked at her and then back at the grape vine. "I don't know. This calls for an expert because it's beyond me." The despair was evident in his voice and face.

"I can't believe this is happening. What will we do?"

"Get a full assessment of the situation and then do what we must, even if it means we lose everything we worked for." Joaquin looked at her through troubled eyes.

"Eleven years down the drain. At least we have enough in reserve to see us through the next year. That will allow this epidemic to pass won't it?"

"Maybe, if it passes quickly. But that won't be enough to keep the workers and us going. We'll have to let them go."

"Lord, what else could possibly happen?"

"Never challenge that." Joaquin was looking over their beautiful and prosperous vineyard, now being threatened by a grape mildew that had already ruined the vineyards in France.

"It's been a lot of hard work. Our wines are famous all over Europe and the Americas. Remember when we were in Valda Bay and you first told me about your dream?" Rue placed her hand on his shoulder and closed her eyes briefly at the memory.

"I do." He looked at her and smiled.

"Senior! You have a telegram." The voice was that of his housekeeper who departed quickly after giving him the message.

"What is it? You look funny." Rue said.

"It's from Elsa Nash. She's here in Spain and wants to see me. She says it's important."

"You were right. I shouldn't have challenged worse."

"I don't have to see her."

356

"That's true. But, what if she came here? Can you see what kind of a conversation she and Brisa would have?"

"I don't even want to think about it."

"Think how I feel? She could destroy my life here Joaquin. She has us over a barrel; you better go find out what she wants and then get rid of her fast."

"I guess I'll go."

"I'll be here."

"I'll let you know." He walked away thinking the worst.

He had no idea that things were going to get worse than he ever imagined. When he walked into the hotel lobby he saw her immediately. She was lovely but more mature and refined.

"Hello Elsa."

"Joaquin." She extended her hand.

"You look lovely. What brings you to Spain?"

"Well, thank you. I suppose there's nothing like coming right to the point. Let's have a seat shall we?" She moved over to a small bench and they sat down.

"Well?"

"I need your help."

"How so?"

"It's difficult to say." She took off one of her gloves and played with it for a moment

"Try."

"Cole Ralston is trying to kill me."

Sitting in the comfort of his home Chief Johnson was reading the morning paper. An article caught his eye and made him retrieve his notebook containing information about the murder of Rudolph Nash. For years he had thought about the case. He went to his desk and decided to write a letter to his old friend Mr. Gordon. They made a good team in the past, they just might again. Perhaps things would be different this time around; now that he was armed with new and more incriminating evidence.

Printed in the United States
212722BV00002B/4/P